D0485334

CLASSIC VICTORIAN &
EDWARDIAN GHOST STORIES

CLASSIC VICTORIAN & EDWARDIAN GHOST STORIES

Selected by
REX COLLINGS

WORDSWORTH CLASSICS

This edition published 1996 by
Wordsworth Editions Limited
Cumberland House, Crib Street
Ware, Hertfordshire SG12 9ET

ISBN 1 85326 186 6

© Wordsworth Editions Limited 1996

Wordsworth® is a registered trademark of
Wordsworth Editions Limited

All rights reserved. This publication may not be
reproduced, stored in a retrieval system, or
transmitted, in any form or by any means, electronic,
mechanical, photocopying, recording or otherwise,
without the prior permission of the publishers.

Typeset by Antony Gray
Printed and bound in Great Britain by
Mackays of Chatham plc, Chatham Kent

INTRODUCTION

Macbeth has murdered sleep. Haunted by the ghost of his victim the murderer is denied sleep; the ghost or the spirit seeks revenge; but also the ghost, imprisoned on Time's wheel, can be the spirit of the perpetrator endlessly waiting to be released from the perpetual punishment of forever re-enacting the crime.

> At the eleventh hour of the thirteenth day of the second month the spirit of the wicked Sir Ranulph appears in the great hall and the flagstone marking the place where he struck down his brother grows dark again with his brother's blood.

It is to be observed that the ghost, aided by some supernatural news agency, has been alerted about the loss of the eleven days and has accordingly adjusted his calendar.

In Cornwall our ancestors used to pray: 'From ghoulies and ghosties and long-legged beasties and things that go bump in the night, Good Lord deliver us.'

'Do you believe in ghosts?'

How many times has one been asked this question and how many times has one hedged one's bets and answered: 'Well actually I haven't seen a ghost but . . . ' or, being literary, have murmured: 'Well, "There are more things in heaven and earth, Horatio, than are dreamt of in your philosophy." '

'Well,' one begins, and using 'well' usually means that one is going to dissemble and refuse to offer a straight answer.

What is a ghost? One dictionary definition gives:

> *n*. a spirit: the soul of a man (or woman): a spirit appearing after death.

It is with the latter definition that the ghost story is concerned. Usually but not always it is the unquiet soul or spirit of the dead person seeking peace that does the haunting; for example, in one of the most famous unexplained factual ghost stories, the Versailles sighting, the ghosts are apparently completely unaware of those who see them. It is as though a video had been slotted in and the gardens of the Petit Trianon had become an immense screen. The two bluestockinged, eminently respectable ladies, Miss Moberly, daughter of a bishop, and Miss Jourdain, a vicar's daughter, on 10th August 1901, witnessed what they afterwards believed was a scene from the days of Marie Antionette. Other visitors to the gardens in the years that followed also claimed to have witnessed strange sights in the same place. No satisfactory explanation of the event has ever been found.

'Real' ghosts, like that of the immured nun of Borley Rectory, whose existence was investigated in great depth in the thirties by the late Harry Price, or those seen at the Tower by Edmund Swifte, the governor, in the last century (his account is included in this collection in an appendix), are very different from those ghosts of the other stories in this book which are fictional characters; a 'real' ghost cannot touch, cannot inflict actual bodily as distinct from mental harm. This is one reason why in the Gospel reports of the Resurrection the writers are so resolute in recording the fact that the Risen Christ ate with His disciples and that Thomas put his hand into the wound in Christ's side; it is the solidity, the 'realness' that is of so much importance – that there was present at these events a whole physical person, neither a disembodied spirit nor an eidolon. Ghosts cannot eat nor can they make love, for they are immaterial, without substance: one can never touch nor indeed be touched by a ghost.

The ghost stories in this collection are taken largely from the works of Victorian writers and reflect the culture of those years and the background of their creators, middle or upper class – when was there a really interesting working-class ghost? Except of course in Dickens; Dickens is always the exception, but even the ghosts in the two Dickens stories lack the substance of 'Mrs 'arris'.

Underlying many of the stories is a foundation of considerable erudition. M. R. James, for example, published his stories under the title *Ghost Stories of an Antiquary* and Sir Walter Scott's considerable historical knowledge is manifested in *The Tapestried Chamber*. Many of these stories appeared first in weekly and monthly journals, such as *All the Year Round* and *Household Words* – the latter of which Dickens, according to the title page, 'conducted' rather than edited.

Hamlet may not be the most famous ghost story but it could be argued that the play contains the most famous ghost – and that without the ghost there would have been no *Hamlet*. Unfortunately I could not include *Hamlet* in this collection, nor the most famous and most popular ghost story of all – *A Christmas Carol*. The easy unlaboured mastery of Dickens is so overwhelming that one ought not to attempt comparisons. In this collection, however, I have tried to mix the well-known with the lesser known works of some of the writers. The delightful story by Oscar Wilde, 'The Canterville Ghost', although undoubtedly a story about a ghost, is often regarded as a children's story, while E. Nesbit in 'Man-size in Marble' demonstrates an unfamiliar side of the creative ability of the author of the *Railway Children*. Saki's interest in the supernatural – manifested in the stories about the cat Tobermory and Gabriel-Ernest the wolf-boy – is here represented by 'Laura'.

Ghost stories are normally connected with place: it seems sometimes as though the ghost is chained to a particular spot; the ghost of Brooke's Rural Dean does not turn up to disrupt the Diocesan Synod nor do the spirits of the little princes and Anne Boleyn haunt the corridors of Buckingham Palace. In fiction the ghost can pursue its victim across countries and continents but in fact this can only happen if some actual physical object is involved.

There is a difference between the horror story and the ghost story although sometimes the exact line that separates them is difficult to define. I have eschewed horror. A ghost story can be a horror story and make the reader's or listener's blood 'run cold', but it should not perhaps inhibit sleep or terrify; the successful ghost story is one that, like *A Christmas Carol*, is read out loud to the whole family, in a darkened room in front of a blazing fire.

I hope the reader will enjoy this collection in which I have included two stories set firmly in far distant lands. 'Fisher's Ghost', set in Australia in the early part of the nineteenth century, is by an Australian lawyer whose date of birth is uncertain but who after qualifying in England spent most of the rest of his life in practice in India, where it is reported he perished through too great a fondness for champagne. The other overseas offering is an allegedly true report from an un-named clergyman which was published in *Murray's Magazine* in 1860.

'No,' said the elderly man with the stained moustache sitting opposite me in the train, 'I don't believe in ghosts, lot of nonsense.' Having said that he vanished.

REX COLLINGS

CONTENTS

AN APPENDIX OF THREE TRUE GHOST STORIES

The Tapestried Chamber

SIR WALTER SCOTT 1771–1832

ABOUT THE END of the American war, when the officers of Lord Cornwallis's army, which surrendered at Yorktown, and others, who had been made prisoners during the impolitic and ill-fated controversy, were returning to their own country to relate their adventures and repose themselves after their fatigues, there was amongst them a general officer, of the name of Browne – an officer of merit, as well as a gentleman of high consideration for family and attainments.

Some business had carried General Browne upon a tour through the western counties, when, in the conclusion of a morning stage, he found himself in the vicinity of a small country town, which presented a scene of uncommon beauty and of a character peculiarly English.

The little town, with its stately old church, whose tower bore testimony to the devotion of ages long past, lay amidst pastures and cornfields of small extent, but bounded and divided with hedgerow timber of great age and size. There were few marks of modern improvement. The environs of the place intimated neither the solitude of decay nor the bustle of novelty; the houses were old, but in good repair; and the beautiful little river murmured freely on its way to the left of the town, neither restrained by a dam nor bordered by a towing-path.

Upon a gentle eminence, nearly a mile to the southward of the town, were seen, amongst many venerable oaks and tangled thickets, the turrets of a castle as old as the wars of York and Lancaster, but which seemed to have received important alterations during the age of Elizabeth and her successor. It had not been a place of great size; but whatever accommodation it formerly afforded was, it must be supposed, still to be obtained within its walls; at least, such was the inference which General Browne drew from observing the smoke arise merrily from several of the ancient wreathed and carved chimney-stalks. The wall of the park ran alongside of the highway for two or three hundred yards; and through the different points by which the eye found glimpses into the woodland scenery it seemed to be well stocked. Other points of view opened in succession – now a full one of the front of the old castle, and now a side glimpse at its particular towers, the former rich in all the bizarrerie of the Elizabethan school, while the simple and solid strength of other parts of the building seemed to show that they had been raised more for defence than ostentation.

Delighted with the partial glimpses which he obtained of the castle through the woods and glades by which this ancient feudal fortress was surrounded, our military traveller was determined to enquire whether it might not deserve a nearer view and whether it contained family pictures or other objects of curiosity worthy of a stranger's visit, when, leaving the vicinity of the park, he rolled through a clean and well-paved street and stopped at the door of a well-frequented inn.

Before ordering horses to proceed on his journey, General Browne made enquiries concerning the proprietor of the château which had so attracted his admiration and was equally surprised and pleased at hearing in reply a nobleman named whom we shall call Lord Woodville. How fortunate! Much of Browne's early recollections, both at school and at college, had been connected with young Woodville, whom, by a few questions, he now ascertained to be the same with the owner of this fair domain. He had been raised to the peerage by the decease of his father a few months before and, as the General learned from the landlord, the term of mourning being ended, was now taking possession of his paternal estate, in the jovial season of merry autumn, accompanied by a select party of friends, to enjoy the sports of a country famous for game.

This was delightful news to our traveller. Frank Woodville had been Browne's fag at Eton, and his chosen intimate at Christ Church; their pleasures and their tasks had been the same; and the honest soldier's heart warmed to find his early friend in possession of so delightful a residence, and of an estate, as the landlord assured him with a nod and a wink, fully adequate to maintain and add to his dignity. Nothing was more natural than that the traveller should suspend a journey which there was nothing to render hurried to pay a visit to an old friend under such agreeable circumstances.

The fresh horses, therefore, had only the brief task of conveying the General's travelling-carriage to Woodville Castle. A porter admitted them at a modern Gothic lodge, built in that style, to correspond with the castle itself, and at the same time rang a bell to give warning of the approach of visitors. Apparently the sound of the bell had suspended the separation of the company, bent on the various amusements of the morning, for, on entering the court of the château, several young men were lounging about in their sporting-dresses, looking at and criticising the dogs, which the keepers held in readiness to attend their pastime. As General Browne alighted, the young lord came to the gate of the hall, and for an instant gazed as at a stranger upon the countenance of his friend, on which war, with its fatigues and its wounds, had made a great alteration. But the uncertainty lasted no longer than till the visitor had spoken, and the hearty greeting which followed was such as can only be exchanged betwixt those who have passed together the merry days of careless boyhood or early youth.

'If I could have formed a wish, my dear Browne,' said Lord Woodville, 'it would have been to have you here, of all men, upon this occasion, which my friends are good enough to hold as a sort of holiday. Do not think you have been unwatched during the years you have been absent from us. I have traced you through your dangers, your triumphs, your misfortunes, and was delighted to see that, whether in victory or defeat, the name of my old friend was always distinguished with applause.'

The General made a suitable reply, and congratulated his friend on his new dignities, and the possession of a place and domain so beautiful.

'Nay, you have seen nothing of it as yet,' said Lord Woodville, 'and I trust you do not mean to leave us till you are better acquainted with it. It is true, I confess, that my present party is pretty large, and the old house, like other places of the kind, does not possess so much accommodation as the extent of the outward walls appears to promise. But we can give you a comfortable old-fashioned room, and I venture to suppose that your campaigns have taught you to be glad of worse quarters.'

The General shrugged his shoulders and laughed. 'I presume,' he said, 'the worst apartment in your château is considerably superior to the old tobacco-cask in which I was fain to take up my night's lodging when I was in the bush, as the Virginians call it, with the light corps. There I lay, like Diogenes himself, so delighted with my covering from the elements that I made a vain attempt to have it rolled into my next quarters; but my commander for the time would give way to no such luxurious provision, and I took farewell of my beloved cask with tears in my eyes.'

'Well, then, since you do not fear your quarters,' said Lord Woodville, 'you will stay with me a week at least. Of guns, dogs, fishing-rods, flies, and means of sport by sea and land, we have enough and to spare; you cannot pitch on an amusement, but we will find the means of pursuing it. But if you prefer the gun and pointers, I will go with you myself, and see whether you have mended your shooting since you have been amongst the Indians of the back settlements.'

The General gladly accepted his friendly host's proposal in all its points. After a morning of manly exercise, the company met at dinner, where it was the delight of Lord Woodville to conduce to the display of the high properties of his recovered friend, so as to recommend him to his guests, most of whom were persons of distinction. He led General Browne to speak of the scenes he had witnessed; and as every word marked alike the brave officer and the sensible man, who retained possession of his cool judgment under the most imminent dangers, the company, looked upon the soldier with general respect, as on one who had proved himself possessed of an uncommon portion of personal courage – that attribute, of all others, of which everybody desires to be thought possessed.

The day at Woodville Castle ended as usual in such mansions. The hospitality stopped within the limits of good order; music, in which the young lord was a proficient, succeeded to the circulation of the bottle; cards and billiards, for those who preferred such amusements, were in readiness; but the exercise of the morning required early hours, and not long after eleven o'clock the guests began to retire to their several apartments.

The young lord himself conducted his friend, General Browne, to the chamber destined for him, which answered the description he had given of it, being comfortable, but old-fashioned. The bed was of the massive form used in the end of the seventeenth century, and the curtains of faded silk, heavily trimmed with tarnished gold. But then the sheets, pillows and blankets looked delightful to the campaigner, when he thought of his 'mansion, the cask'. There was an air of gloom in the tapestry hangings which, with their worn-out graces, curtained the walls of the little chamber, and gently undulated as the autumnal breeze found its way through the ancient lattice-window, which pattered and whistled as the air gained entrance. The toilet, too, with its mirror, turbaned, after the manner of the beginning of the century, with a coiffure of murrey-coloured silk, and its hundred strange-shaped boxes, providing for arrangements which had been obsolete for more than fifty years, had an antique, and in so far a melancholy aspect. But nothing could blaze more brightly and cheerfully than the two large wax candles; or if aught could rival them, it was the flaming, bickering faggots in the chimney, that sent at once their gleam and their warmth through the snug apartment, which, notwithstanding the general antiquity of its appearance, was not wanting in the least convenience that modern habits rendered either necessary or desirable.

'This is an old-fashioned sleeping-apartment, General,' said the young lord, 'but I hope you find nothing that makes you envy your old tobacco-cask.'

'I am not particular respecting my lodgings,' replied the General; 'yet were I to make any choice, I would prefer this chamber by many degrees to the gayer and more modern rooms of your family mansion. Believe me, that when I unite its modern air of comfort with its venerable antiquity, and recollect that it is your lordship's property, I shall feel in better quarters here than if I were in the best hotel London could afford.'

'I trust – I have no doubt – that you will find yourself as comfortable as I wish you, my dear General,' said the young nobleman; and once more bidding his guest good-night, he shook him by the hand and withdrew.

The General once more looked round him, and internally congratulating himself on his return to peaceful life, the comforts of which were endeared by the recollection of the hardships and dangers he had lately sustained, undressed himself, and prepared for a luxurious night's rest.

Here, contrary to the custom of this species of tale, we leave the General in possession of his apartment until the next morning.

The company assembled for breakfast at an early hour, but without the appearance of General Browne, who seemed the guest that Lord Woodville was desirous of honouring above all whom his hospitality had assembled around him. He more than once expressed surprise at the General's absence, and at length sent a servant to make enquiry after him. The man brought back information that General Browne had been walking abroad since an early hour of the morning, in defiance of the weather, which was misty and ungenial.

'The custom of a solder,' said the young nobleman to his friends; 'many of them acquire habitual vigilance, and cannot sleep after the early hour at which their duty usually commands them to be alert.'

Yet the explanation which Lord Woodville thus offered to the company seemed hardly satisfactory to his own mind, and it was in a fit of silence and abstraction that he awaited the return of the General. It took place near an hour after the breakfast bell had rung. He looked fatigued and feverish. His hair, the powdering and arrangement of which was at this time one of the most important occupations of a man's whole day, and marked his fashion as much as, in the present time, the tying of a cravat, or the want of one, was dishevelled, uncurled, void of powder, and dank with dew. His clothes were huddled on with a careless negligence remarkable in a military man, whose real or supposed duties are usually held to include some attention to the toilet; and his looks were haggard and ghastly in a peculiar degree.

'So you have stolen a march upon us this morning, my dear General,' said Lord Woodville; 'or you have not found your bed so much to your mind as I had hoped and you seemed to expect. How did you rest last night?'

'Oh, excellently well – remarkably well – never better in my life!' said General Browne rapidly, and yet with an air of embarrassment which was obvious to his friend. He then hastily swallowed a cup of tea and, neglecting or refusing whatever else he was offered, seemed to fall into a fit of abstraction.

'You will take the gun today, General?' said his friend and host, but had to repeat the question twice ere he received the abrupt answer, 'No, my Lord; I am sorry I cannot have the honour of spending another day with your lordship; my post-horses are ordered and will be here directly.'

All who were present showed surprise, and Lord Woodville immediately replied, 'Post-horses, my good friend! What can you possibly want with them, when you promised to stay with me quietly for at least a week?'

'I believe,' said the General, obviously much embarrassed, 'that I might, in the pleasure of my first meeting with your lordship, have said something about stopping here a few days; but I have since found it altogether impossible.'

'That is very extraordinary,' answered the young nobleman. 'You seemed quite disengaged yesterday, and you cannot have had a summons today, for our post has not come up from town, and therefore you cannot have received any letters.'

General Browne, without giving any further explanation, muttered something of indispensable business, and insisted on the absolute necessity of his departure in a manner which silenced all opposition on the part of his host, who saw that his resolution was taken, and forbore all further importunity.

'At least, however,' he said, 'permit me, my dear Browne, since go you will or must, to show you the view from the terrace, which the mist, that is now rising, will soon display.'

He threw open a sash-window and stepped down upon the terrace as he spoke. The General followed him mechanically, but seemed little to attend to what his host was saying, as, looking across an extended and rich prospect, he pointed out the different objects worthy of observation. Thus they moved on till Lord Woodville had attained his purpose of drawing his guest entirely apart from the rest of the company, when, turning round upon him with an air of great solemnity, he addressed him thus:

'Richard Browne, my old and very dear friend, we are now alone. Let me conjure you to answer me upon the word of a friend and the honour of a soldier. How did you in reality rest during the night?'

'Most wretchedly indeed, my lord,' answered the General, in the same tone of solemnity; 'so miserably, that I would not run the risk of such a second night, not only for all the lands belonging to this castle, but for all the country which I see from this elevated point of view.'

'This is most extraordinary,' said the young lord, as if speaking to himself; 'then there must be something in the reports concerning that apartment.' Again turning to the General, he said, 'For God's sake, my dear friend, be candid with me and let me know the disagreeable particulars which have befallen you under a roof where, with consent of the owner, you should have met nothing save comfort.'

The General seemed distressed by this appeal and paused a moment before he replied. 'My dear lord,' he at length said, 'what happened to me last night is of a nature so peculiar and so unpleasant, that I could hardly bring myself to detail it even to your lordship, were it not that, independent of my wish to gratify any request of yours, I think that sincerity on my part may lead to some explanation about a circumstance equally painful and mysterious. To others, the communication I am about to make might place me in the light of a weak-minded, superstitious fool, who suffered his own imagination to delude and bewilder him; but you have known me in childhood and youth and will not suspect me of having adopted in manhood the feelings and frailties from which my early years were free.'

Here he paused, and his friend replied: 'Do not doubt my perfect confidence in the truth of your communication, however strange it may be. I know your firmness of disposition too well to suspect you could be made the object of imposition, and am aware that your honour and your friendship will equally deter you from exaggerating whatever you may have witnessed.'

'Well, then,' said the General, 'I will proceed with my story as well as I can, relying upon your candour, and yet distinctly feeling that I would rather face a battery than recall to my mind the odious recollections of last night.'

He paused a second time, and then perceiving that Lord Woodville remained silent and in an attitude of attention, he commenced, though not without obvious reluctance, the history of his night adventures in the Tapestried Chamber.

'I undressed and went to bed, so soon as your lordship left me yesterday evening; but the wood in the chimney, which nearly fronted my bed, blazed brightly and cheerfully and, aided by a hundred recollections of my childhood and youth, which had been recalled by the unexpected pleasure of meeting your lordship, prevented me from falling immediately asleep. I ought, however, to say that these reflections were all of a pleasant and agreeable kind, grounded on a sense of having for a time exchanged the labour, fatigues and dangers of my profession for the enjoyments of a peaceful life, and the reunion of those friendly and affectionate ties which I had torn asunder at the rude summons of war.

'While such pleasing reflections were stealing over my mind, and gradually lulling me to slumber, I was suddenly aroused by a sound like that of the rustling of a silken gown and the tapping of a pair of high-heeled shoes, as if a woman were walking in the apartment. Ere I could draw the curtain to see what the matter was, the figure of a little woman passed between the bed and the fire. The back of this form was turned to me, and I could observe, from the shoulders and neck, it was that of an old woman, whose dress was an old-fashioned gown, which, I think, ladies call a sacque – that is, a sort of robe completely loose in the body, but gathered into broad plaits upon the neck and shoulders, which fall down to the ground, and terminate in a species of train.

'I thought the intrusion singular enough, but never harboured for a moment the idea that what I saw was anything more than the mortal form of some old woman about the establishment, who had a fancy to dress like her grandmother, and who, having perhaps, as your lordship mentioned that you were rather straitened for room, been dislodged from her chamber for my accommodation, had forgotten the circumstances and returned by twelve to her old haunt. Under this persuasion I moved myself in bed and coughed a little, to make the intruder sensible of my being in possession of the premises. She turned slowly round, but, gracious heaven! my lord, what a countenance did she display to me! There was no longer any question what she was, or any thought of her being a living being. Upon a face which wore the fixed features of a corpse were imprinted the traces of the vilest and most hideous passions which had animated her while she lived. The body of some atrocious criminal seemed to have been given up from the grave, and the soul restored from the penal fire, in order to form, for a space, a union with the ancient accomplice of its guilt. I started up in bed, and sat upright, supporting myself on my palms, as I gazed on this horrible spectre. The hag made, as it seemed, a single and swift stride to the bed where I lay, and squatted herself down upon it, in precisely the same attitude which I had assumed in the extremity of horror, advancing her diabolical countenance within half a yard of mine, with a grin which seemed to intimate the malice and the derision of an incarnate fiend.'

Here General Browne stopped, and wiped from his brow the cold perspiration with which the recollection of his horrible vision had covered it.

'My lord,' he said, 'I am no coward. I have been in all the mortal dangers incidental to my profession, and I may truly boast that no man ever knew Richard Browne dishonour the sword he wears; but in these horrible circumstances, under the eyes, and, as it seemed, almost in the grasp, of an incarnation of an evil spirit, all firmness forsook me, all manhood melted from me like wax in the furnace, and I felt my hair individually bristle. The current of my life-blood ceased to flow, and I sank back in a swoon, as very a victim to panic terror as ever was a village girl or a child of ten years old. How long I lay in this condition I cannot pretend to guess.

'But I was roused by the castle clock striking one, so loud that it seemed as if it were in the very room. It was some time before I dared open my eyes, lest they should again encounter the horrible spectacle. When, however, I summoned courage to look up, she was no longer visible. My first idea was to pull my bell, wake the servants, and remove to a garret or a hay-loft, to be ensured against a second visitation. Nay, I will confess the truth, that my resolution was altered, not by the shame of exposing myself, but by the fear that, as the bell-cord hung by the chimney, I might, in making my way to it, be again crossed by the fiendish hag, who, I figured to myself, might be still lurking about some corner of the apartment.

'I will not pretend to describe what hot and cold fever-fits tormented me for the rest of the night, through broken sleep, weary vigils, and that dubious state which forms the neutral ground between them. An hundred terrible objects appeared to haunt me; but there was the great difference betwixt the vision which I have described and those which followed, that I knew the last to be deceptions of my own fancy and over-excited nerves.

'Day at last appeared, and I rose from my bed ill in health and humiliated in mind. I was ashamed of myself as a man and a soldier, and still more so at feeling my own extreme desire to escape from the haunted apartment, which, however, conquered all other considerations; so that, huddling on my clothes with the most careless haste, I made my escape from your lordship's mansion, to seek in the open air some relief to my nervous system, shaken as it was by this horrible encounter with a visitant, for such I must believe her, from the other world. Your lordship has now heard the cause of my discomposure, and of my sudden desire to leave your hospitable castle. In other places I trust we may often meet; but God protect me from ever spending a second night under that roof!'

Strange as the General's tale was, he spoke with such a deep air of conviction, that it cut short all the usual commentaries which are made on such stories. Lord Woodville never once asked him if he was sure he did not dream of the apparition, or suggested any of the possibilities by which it is fashionable to explain supernatural appearances, as wild vagaries of the fancy or deceptions of the optic nerves. On the contrary, he seemed deeply impressed with the truth and reality of what he had heard; and, after a considerable pause, regretted, with much appearance of sincerity, that his early friend should in his house have suffered so severely.

'I am the more sorry for your pain, my dear Browne,' he continued, 'that it is the unhappy, though most unexpected, result of an experiment of my own. You must know that, for my father and grandfather's time, at least, the apartment which was assigned to you last night had been shut on account of reports that it was disturbed by supernatural sights and noises. When I came, a few weeks since, into possession of the estate, I thought the accommodation which the castle afforded for my friends was not extensive enough to permit the inhabitants of the invisible world to retain possession of a comfortable sleeping-apartment. I therefore caused the Tapestried Chamber, as we call it, to be opened and, without destroying its air of antiquity, I had such new articles of furniture placed in it as became the modern times. Yet, as the opinion that the room was haunted very strongly prevailed among the domestics and was also known in the neighbourhood and to many of my friends, I feared some prejudice might be entertained by the first occupant of the Tapestried Chamber, which might tend to revive the evil report which it had laboured under, and so disappoint my purpose of rendering it a useful part of the house. I must confess, my dear Browne, that your arrival yesterday, agreeable to me for a thousand reasons besides, seemed the most favourable opportunity of removing the unpleasant rumours which attached to the room, since your courage was indubitable, and your mind free of any preoccupation on the subject. I could not, therefore, have chosen a more fitting subject for my experiment.'

'Upon my life,' said General Browne, somewhat hastily, 'I am infinitely obliged to your lordship – very particularly indebted indeed. I am likely to remember for some time the consequences of the experiment, as your lordship is pleased to call it.'

'Nay, now you are unjust, my dear friend,' said Lord Woodville. 'You have only to reflect for a single moment, in order to be convinced that I could not augur the possibility of the pain to which you have been so unhappily exposed. I was yesterday morning a complete sceptic on the subject of supernatural appearances. Nay, I am sure that, had I told you what was said about that room, those very reports would have induced you, by your own choice, to select it for your accommodation. It was my misfortune, perhaps my error, but really cannot be termed my fault, that you have been afflicted so strangely.'

'Strangely indeed!' said the General, resuming his good temper; 'and I acknowledge that I have no right to be offended with your lordship for treating me like what I used to think myself, a man of some firmness and courage. But I see my post-horses are arrived, and I must not detain your lordship from your amusement.'

'Nay, my old friend,' said Lord Woodville, 'since you cannot stay with us another day, which, indeed, I can no longer urge, give me at least half an hour more. You used to love pictures, and I have a gallery of portraits, some of them by Vandyke, representing ancestry to whom this property and castle formerly belonged. I think that several of them will strike you as possessing merit.'

General Browne accepted the invitation, though somewhat unwillingly. It was evident he was not to breathe freely or at ease till he left Woodville Castle far behind him. He could not refuse his friend's invitation, however; and the less so, that he was a little ashamed of the peevishness which he had displayed towards his well-meaning entertainer.

The General, therefore, followed Lord Woodville through several rooms, into a long gallery hung with pictures, which the latter pointed out to his guest, telling the names, and giving some account of the personages whose portraits presented themselves in progression. General Browne was but little interested in the details which these accounts conveyed to him. They were, indeed, of the kind which are usually found in an old family gallery. Here was a cavalier who had ruined the estate in the royal cause; there was a fine lady who had reinstated it by contracting a match with a wealthy Roundhead. There hung a gallant who had been in danger for corresponding with the exiled court at St Germain's; here one who had taken arms for William at the Revolution; and there a third that had thrown his weight alternately into the scale of Whig and Tory.

While Lord Woodville was cramming these words into his guest's hear, 'against the stomach of his sense', they gained the middle of the gallery, when he beheld General Browne suddenly start, and assume an attitude of the utmost surprise, not unmixed with fear, as his eyes were caught and suddenly riveted by a portrait of an old lady in a sacque, the fashionable dress of the end of the seventeenth century.

'There she is!' he exclaimed – 'there she is, in form and features, though inferior in demoniac expression to the accursed hag who visited me last night.'

'If that be the case,' said the young nobleman, 'there can remain no longer any doubt of the horrible reality of your apparition. That is the picture of a wretched ancestress of mine, of whose crimes a black and fearful catalogue is recorded in a family history in my charter-chest. The recital of them would be too horrible; it is enough to say that in yon fatal apartment incest and unnatural murder were committed. I will restore it to the solitude to which the better judgement of those who preceded me had consigned it; and never shall anyone, so long as I can prevent it, be exposed to a repetition of the supernatural horrors which could shake such courage as yours.'

Thus, the friends, who had met with such glee, parted in a very different mood – Lord Woodville to command the Tapestried Chamber to be unmantled and the door built up; and General Browne to seek in some less beautiful country, and with some less dignified friend, forgetfulness of the painful night which he had passed in Woodville Castle.

The Spectre of Tappington

RICHARD HARRIS BARHAM 1788–1845

'IT IS VERY ODD, though; what can have become of them?' said Charles Seaforth, as he peeped under the valance of an old-fashioned bedstead in an old-fashioned apartment of a still more old-fashioned manor-house; ' 'tis confoundedly odd and I can't make it out at all. Why, Barney, where are they! and where the devil are you?'

No answer was returned to this appeal; and the lieutenant, who was, in the main, a reasonable person – at least as reasonable a person as any young gentleman of twenty-two in 'the service' can fairly be expected to be – cooled when he reflected that his servant could scarcely reply extempore to a summons which it was impossible he should hear.

An application to the bell was the considerate result; and the footsteps of as tight a lad as ever put pipe-clay to belt sounded along the gallery.

'Come in!' said his master. An ineffectual attempt upon the door reminded Mr Seaforth that he had locked himself in. 'By heaven! this is the oddest thing of all,' said he, as he turned the key and admitted Mr Maguire into his dormitory.

'Barney, where are my pantaloons?'

'Is it the breeches?' asked the valet, casting an enquiring eye round the apartment – 'is it the breeches, sir?'

'Yes; what have you done with them?'

'Sure then your honour had them on when you went to bed, and it's hereabout they'll be, I'll be bail'; and Barney lifted a fashionable tunic from a cane-backed armchair, proceeding in his examination. But the search was vain: there was the tunic aforesaid; there was a smart-looking kerseymere waistcoat; but the most important article of all in a gentleman's wardrobe was still wanting.

'Where *can* they be?' asked the master, with a strong accent on the auxiliary verb.

'Sorrow a know I knows,' said the man.

'It *must* have been the devil, then, after all, who has been here and carried them off!' cried Seaforth, staring full into Barney's face.

Mr Maguire was not devoid of the superstition of his countrymen, still he looked as if he did not quite subscribe to the *sequitur*.

His master read incredulity in his countenance. 'Why, I tell you, Barney, I put them there, on that armchair, when I got into bed; and, by heaven! I distinctly saw the ghost of the old fellow they told me of, come in at midnight, put on my pantaloons, and walk away with them.'

'May be so,' was the cautious reply.

'I thought, of course, it was a dream; but then – where the devil are the breeches?'

The question was more easily asked than answered. Barney renewed his search, while the lieutenant folded his arms and, leaning against the toilet, sunk into a reverie.

'After all, it must be some trick of my laughter-loving cousins,' said Seaforth.

'Ah! then, the ladies!' chimed in Mr Maguire, though the observation was not addressed to him; 'and, will it be Miss Caroline, or Miss Fanny, that's stole your honour's things?'

'I hardly know what to think of it,' pursued the bereaved lieutenant, still speaking in soliloquy, with his eye resting dubiously on the chamber-door. 'I locked myself in, that's certain; and – but there must be some other entrance to the room – pooh! I remember – the private staircase; how could I be such a fool?' and he crossed the chamber to where a low oaken doorcase was dimly visible in a distant corner. He paused before it. Nothing now interfered to screen it from observation; but it bore tokens of having been at some earlier period concealed by tapestry, remains of which yet clothed the walls on either side the portal.

'This way they must have come,' said Seaforth; 'I wish with all my heart I had caught them!'

'Och! the kittens!' sighed Mr Barney Maguire.

But the mystery was yet as far from being solved as before. True there *was* the 'other door'; but then that too, on examination, was even more firmly secured than the one which opened on the gallery – two heavy bolts on the inside effectually prevented any *coup de main* on the lieutenant's bivouac from that quarter. He was more puzzled than ever; nor did the minutest inspection of the walls and door throw any light upon the subject: one thing only was clear – the breeches were gone!

'It is *very* singular,' said the lieutenant.

Tappington (generally called Tapton) Everard is an antiquated but commodious manor-house in the eastern division of the county of Kent. A former proprietor had been high-sheriff in the days of Elizabeth, and many a dark and dismal tradition was yet extant of the licentiousness of his life, and the enormity of his offences. The Glen, which the keeper's daughter was seen to enter, but never known to quit, still frowns darkly as of yore; while an ineradicable bloodstain on the oaken stair yet bids defiance to the united energies of soap and sand. But it is with one particular apartment that a deed of more especial atrocity is said to be connected.

A stranger guest – so runs the legend – arrived unexpectedly at the mansion of the 'Bad Sir Giles'. They met in apparent friendship; but the ill-concealed scowl on their master's brow told the domestics that the visit was not a welcome one; the banquet, however, was not spared; the wine-cup circulated freely – too freely, perhaps – for sounds of discord at length reached the ears of even the excluded serving-men, as they were doing their best to imitate their betters in the lower hall. Alarmed, some of them ventured to approach the parlour; one, an old and favoured retainer of the house, went so far as to break in upon his master's privacy. Sir Giles, already high in oath, fiercely enjoined his absence, and he retired; not, however, before he had distinctly heard from the stranger's lips a menace that 'there was that within his pocket which could disprove the knight's right to issue that or any other command within the walls of Tapton'.

The intrusion, though momentary, seemed to have produced a beneficial effect; the voices of the disputants fell, and the conversation was carried on thenceforth in a more subdued tone, till, as evening closed in, the domestics, when summoned to attend with lights, found not only cordiality restored, but that a still deeper carouse was meditated. Fresh stoups, and from the choicest bins, were produced; not was it till at a late, or rather early hour, that the revellers sought their chambers.

The one allotted to the stranger occupied the first floor of the eastern angle of the building, and had once been the favourite apartment of Sir Giles himself. Scandal ascribed, this preference to the facility which a private staircase, communicating with the grounds, had afforded him, in the old knight's time, of following his wicked courses unchecked by parental observation; a consideration which ceased to be of weight when the death of his father left him uncontrolled master of his estate and actions. From that period Sir Giles had established himself in what were called the 'state apartments', and the 'oaken chamber' was rarely tenanted, save on occasions of extraordinary festivity, or when the yule-log drew an unusually large accession of guests around the Christmas hearth.

On this eventful night it was prepared for the unknown visitor, who sought his couch heated and inflamed from his midnight orgies, and in the morning was found in his bed a swollen and blackened corpse. No marks of violence appeared upon the body; but the livid hue of the lips, and certain dark-coloured spots visible on the skin, aroused suspicions which those who entertained them were too timid to express. Apoplexy, induced by the excesses of the preceding night, Sir Giles's confidential leech pronounced to be the cause of his sudden dissolution. The body was buried in peace; and though some shook their heads as they witnessed the haste with which the funeral rites were hurried on, none ventured to murmur. Other events arose to distract the attention of the retainers; men's minds became occupied by the stirring politics of the day; while the near approach of that formidable armada, so vainly arrogating to itself a title which the very elements joined with human valour to disprove, soon interfered to weaken, if not obliterate, all remembrance of the nameless stranger who had died within the walls of Tapton Everard.

Years rolled on: the 'Bad Sir Giles' had himself long since gone to his account, the last, as it was believed, of his immediate line; though a few of the older tenants were sometimes heard to speak of an elder brother, who had disappeared in early life, and never inherited the estate. Rumours, too, of his having left a son in foreign lands were at one time rife; but they died away; nothing occurring to support them, the property passed unchallenged to a collateral branch of the family, and the secret, if secret there were, was buried in Denton churchyard, in the lonely grave of the mysterious stranger.

One circumstance alone occurred, after a long intervening period, to revive the memory of these transactions. Some workmen employed in grubbing an old plantation, for the purpose of raising on its site a modern shrubbery, dug up, in the execution of their task, the mildewed remnants of what seemed to have been once a garment. On more minute inspection, enough remained of silken slashes and a coarse embroidery, to identify the relics as having once formed part of a pair of trunk hose; while a few papers which fell from them, altogether illegible from damp and age, were by the unlearned rustics conveyed to the then owner of the estate.

Whether the squire was more successful in deciphering them was never known; he certainly never alluded to their contents; and little would have been thought of the matter but for the inconvenient memory of one old woman, who declared she heard her grandfather say, that when the 'stranger guest 'was poisoned, though all the rest of his clothes were there, his breeches, the supposed repository of the supposed documents, could never be found. The master of Tapton Everard smiled when he heard Dame Jones's hint of deeds which might impeach the validity of his own title in favour of some unknown descendant of some unknown heir; and the story was rarely alluded to, save by one or two miracle-mongers, who had heard that others had seen the ghost of old Sir Giles, in his nightcap, issue from the postern, enter the adjoining copse, and wring his shadowy hands in agony, as he seemed to search vainly for something hidden among the evergreens. The stranger's death-room had, of course, been occasionally haunted from the time of his decease; but the periods of visitation had latterly become very rare – even Mrs Botherby, the housekeeper, being forced to admit that, during her long sojourn at the manor, she had never 'met with anything worse than herself'; though, as the old lady afterwards added upon mature reflection, 'I must say I think I saw the devil *once*.'

Such was the legend attached to Tapton Everard and such the story which the lively Caroline Ingoldsby detailed to her equally mercurial cousin, Charles Seaforth, lieutenant in the Hon. East India Company's second regiment of Bombay Fencibles, as arm-in-arm they promenaded a gallery decked with some dozen grim-looking ancestral portraits and, among others, with that of the redoubted Sir Giles himself. The gallant commander had that very morning paid his first visit to the house of his maternal uncle, after an absence of five years passed with his regiment on the arid plains of Hindustan, whence he was now returned on a three years' furlough. He had gone out a boy – he returned a man; but the impression made upon his youthful fancy by his favourite cousin remained unimpaired, and to Tapton he directed his steps, even before he sought the home of his widowed mother – comforting himself in this breach of filial decorum by the reflection that, as the manor was so little out of his way, it would be unkind to pass, as it were, the door of his relatives, without just looking in for a few hours.

But he found his uncle as hospitable, and his cousin more charming than ever; and the looks of one, and the requests of the other, soon precluded the possibility of refusing to lengthen the 'few hours' into a few days, though the house was at the moment full of visitors.

The Peterses were there from Ramsgate; and Mr, Mrs and the two Miss Simpkinsons, from Bath, had come to pass a month with the family; and Tom Ingoldsby had brought down his college friend the Hon. Augustus Sucklethumbkin, with his groom and pointers, to take a fortnight's shooting. And then there was Mrs Ogleton, the rich young widow, with her large black eyes, who, people did say, was setting her cap at the young squire, though Mrs Botherby did not believe it; and, above all, there was Mademoiselle Pauline, her *femme de chambre*, who *mon-Dieu*'d everything and everybody, and cried '*Quel horreur!*' at Mrs Botherby's cap. In short, to use the last-named and much-respected lady's own expression, the house was 'choke-full' to the very attics – all save the 'oaken chamber', which, as the lieutenant expressed a most magnanimous disregard of ghosts, was forthwith appropriated to his particular accommodation. Mr Maguire meanwhile was fain to share the apartment of Oliver Dobbs, the squire's own man: a jocular proposal of joint occupancy having been first indignantly rejected by 'Mademoiselle', though preferred with the 'laste taste in life' of Mr Barney's most insinuating brogue.

'Come, Charles, the urn is absolutely getting cold; your breakfast will be quite spoiled: what can have made you so idle?' Such was the morning salutation of Miss Ingoldsby to the *militaire* as he entered the breakfast-room half an hour after the latest of the party.

'A pretty gentleman, truly, to make an appointment with,' chimed in Miss Frances. 'What is become of our ramble to the rocks before breakfast?'

'Oh! the young men never think of keeping a promise now,' said Mrs Peters, a little ferret-faced woman with underdone eyes.

'When I was a young man,' said Mr Peters, 'I remember I always made a point of – '

'Pray how long ago was that?' asked Mr Simpkinson from Bath.

'Why, sir, when I married Mrs Peters, I was – let me see – was – '

'Do pray hold your tongue, P., and eat your breakfast!' interrupted his better half, who had a mortal horror of chronological references; 'it's very rude to tease people with your family affairs.'

The lieutenant had by this time taken his seat in silence – a good-humoured nod, and a glance, half-smiling, half-inquisitive, being the extent of his salutation. Smitten as he was, and in the immediate presence of her who had made so large a hole in his heart, his manner was evidently *distrait*, which the fair Caroline in her secret soul attributed to his being solely occupied by her *agrémens:* how would she have bridled had she known that they only shared his meditations with a pair of breeches!

Charles drank his coffee and spiked some half-dozen eggs, darting occasionally a penetrating glance at the ladies, in hope of detecting the supposed waggery by the evidence of some furtive smile or conscious look. But in vain; not a dimple moved indicative of roguery, nor did the slightest elevation of eyebrow rise confirmative of his suspicions. Hints and insinuations passed unheeded – more particular enquiries were out of the question – the subject was unapproachable.

In the meantime, 'patent cords' were just the thing for a morning's ride; and, breakfast ended, away cantered the party over the downs, till, every faculty absorbed by the beauties, animate and inanimate, which surrounded him, Lieutenant Seaforth of the Bombay Fencibles bestowed no more thought upon his breeches than if he had been born on the top of Ben Lomond.

Another night had passed away; the sun rose brilliantly, forming with his level beams a splendid rainbow in the far-off west, whither the heavy cloud, which for the last two hours had been pouring its waters on the earth, was now flying before him.

'Ah! then, and it's little good it'll be the claning of ye,' apostrophised Mr Barney Maguire, as he deposited, in front of his master's toilet, a pair of 'bran new' jockey boots, one of Hoby's primest fits, which the lieutenant had purchased in his way through town. On that very morning had they come for the first time under the valet's depurating hand, so little soiled, indeed, from the turfy ride of the preceding day, that a less scrupulous domestic might, perhaps, have considered the application of 'Warren's Matchless', or oxalic acid, altogether superfluous. Not so Barney: with the nicest care had he removed the slightest impurity from each polished surface, and there they stood, rejoicing in their sable radiance. No wonder a pang shot across Mr Maguire's breast, as he thought on the work now cut out for them, so different from the light labours of the day before; no wonder he murmured with a sigh, as the scarce dried window-panes disclosed a road now inch deep in mud. 'Ah! then, it's little good the claning of ye!' – for well had he learned in the hall below that eight miles of stiff clay soil lay between the manor and Bolsover Abbey, whose picturesque ruins,

Like ancient Rome, majestic decay,

the party had determined to explore. The master had already commenced dressing, and the man was fitting straps upon a light pair of crane-necked spurs, when his hand was arrested by the old question – 'Barney, where are the breeches?'

They were nowhere to be found!

Mr Seaforth descended that morning, whip in hand, and equipped in a handsome green riding-frock, but no 'breeches and boots to match' were there: loose jean trousers, surmounting a pair of diminutive Wellingtons, embraced, somewhat incongruously, his nether man, *vice* the 'patent cords', returned, like yesterday's pantaloons, absent without leave. The 'top-boots' had a holiday.

'A fine morning after the rain,' said Mr Simpkinson from Bath.

'Just the thing for the 'ops,' said Mr Peters. 'I remember when I was a boy – '

'Do hold your tongue, P.,' said Mrs Peters – advice which that exemplary matron was in the constant habit of administering to 'her P.' as she called him, whenever he prepared to vent his reminiscences. Her precise reason for this it would be difficult to determine, unless, indeed, the story be true which a little bird had whispered into Mrs Botherby's ear – Mr Peters, though now a wealthy man, had received a liberal education at a charity school, and was apt to recur to the days of his muffin-cap and leathers. As usual, he took his wife's hint in good part and 'paused in his reply'.

'A glorious day for the ruins!' said young Ingoldsby. 'But, Charles, what the deuce are you about? you don't mean to ride through our lanes in such toggery as that?'

'Lassy me!' said Miss Julia Simpkinson, 'won't you be very wet?'

'You had better take Tom's cab,' quoth the squire.

But this proposition was at once overruled; Mrs Ogleton had already nailed the cab, a vehicle of all others the best adapted for a snug flirtation.

'Or drive Miss Julia in the phaeton?' No; that was the post of Mr Peters, who, indifferent as an equestrian, had acquired some fame as a whip while travelling through the midland counties for the firm of Bagshaw, Snivelby, and Ghrimes.

'Thank you, I shall ride with my cousins,' said Charles, with as much nonchalance as he could assume – and he did so: Mr Ingoldsby, Mrs Peters, Mr Simpkinson from Bath, and his eldest daughter with her album, following in the family coach. The gentleman-commoner 'voted the affair damned slow', and declined the party altogether in favour of the gamekeeper and a cigar. 'There was "no fun" in looking at old houses!' Mrs Simpkinson preferred a short *séjour* in the still-room with Mrs Botherby, who had promised to initiate her in that grand *arcanum*, the transmutation of gooseberry jam into guava jelly.

'Did you ever see an old abbey before, Mr Peters?'

'Yes, miss, a French one; we have got one at Ramsgate; he teaches the Miss Joneses to parley-voo, and is turned of sixty.'

Miss Simpkinson closed her album with an air of ineffable disdain.

Mr Simpkinson from Bath was a professed antiquary, and one of the first water; he was master of Gwillim's *Heraldry* and Mills's *History of the Crusades;* knew every plate in the *Monasticon;* had written an essay on the origin and dignity of the office of overseer, and settled the date of a Queen Anne's farthing. An influential member of the Antiquarian Society, to whose *Beauties of Bagnigge Wells* he had been a liberal subscriber, procured him a seat at the board of that learned body, since which happy epoch Sylvanus Urban had not a more indefatigable correspondent. His inaugural essay on the President's cocked hat was considered a miracle of erudition; and his account of the earliest application of gilding to gingerbread, a masterpiece of antiquarian research.

His eldest daughter was of a kindred spirit: if her father's mantle had not fallen upon her, it was only because he had not thrown it off himself; she had caught hold of its tail, however, while it yet hung upon his honoured shoulders. To souls so congenial, what a sight was the magnificent ruin of Bolsover! its broken arches, its mouldering pinnacles, and the airy tracery of its half-demolished windows. The party were in raptures; Mr Simpkinson began to meditate an essay, and his daughter an ode: even Seaforth, as he gazed on these lonely relics of the olden time, was betrayed into a momentary forgetfulness of his love and losses: the widow's eyeglass turned from her *cicisbeo's* whiskers to the mantling ivy: Mrs Peters wiped her spectacles; and 'her P' supposed the central tower 'had once been the county jail'. The squire was a philosopher, and had been there often before, so he ordered out the cold tongue and chickens.

'Bolsover Priory,' said Mr Simpkinson, with the air of a connoisseur – 'Bolsover Priory was founded in the reign of Henry the Sixth, about the beginning of the eleventh century. Hugh de Bolsover had accompanied that monarch to the Holy Land, in the expedition undertaken by way of penance for the murder of his young nephews in the Tower. Upon the dissolution of the monasteries, the veteran was enfeoffed in the lands and manor, to which he gave his own name of Bowlsover, or Bee-owls-over (by corruption Bolsover) – a Bee in chief, over three Owls, all proper, being the armorial ensigns borne by this distinguished crusader at the siege of Acre.'

'Ah! that was Sir Sidney Smith,' said Mr Peters; 'I've heard tell of him, and all about Mrs Partington, and – '

'P., be quiet, and don't expose yourself!' sharply interrupted his lady. P. was silenced, and betook himself to the bottled stout.

'These lands,' continued the antiquary, 'were held in grand serjeantry by the presentation of three white owls and a pot of honey – '

'Lassy me! how nice!' said Miss Julia. Mr Peters licked his lips.

'Pray give me leave, my dear – owls and honey, whenever the king should come a rat-catching into this part of the country.'

'Rat-catching!' ejaculated the squire, pausing abruptly in the mastication of a drumstick.

'To be sure, my dear sir: don't you remember the rats once came under the forest laws – a minor species of venison? "Rats and mice, and such small deer", eh? – Shakespeare, you know. Our ancestors ate rats ['The nasty fellows!' shuddered Miss Julia, in a parenthesis]; and owls, you know, are capital mousers – '

'I've seen a howl,' said Mr Peters: 'there's one in the Sohological Gardens – a little hook-nosed chap in a wig, only its feathers and – '

Poor P. was destined never to finish a speech.

'*Do* be quiet!' cried the authoritative voice; and the would-be naturalist shrank into his shell, like a snail in the 'Sohological Gardens'.

'You should read Blount's *Jocular Tenures*, Mr Ingoldsby,' pursued Simpkinson. 'A learned man was Blount! Why, sir, His Royal Highness the Duke of York once paid a silver horseshoe to Lord Ferrers – '

'I've heard of him,' broke in the incorrigible Peters; 'he was hanged at the Old Bailey in a silk rope for shooting Dr Johnson.'

The antiquary vouchsafed no notice of the interruption; but taking a pinch of snuff, continued his harangue.

'A silver horseshoe, sir, which is due from every scion of royalty who rides across one of his manors; and if you look into the penny county histories, now publishing by an eminent friend of mine, you will find that Langhale in County Norfolk was held by one Baldwin *per saltum, sufflatum, et pettum*; that is, he was to come every Christmas into Westminster Hall, there to take a leap, cry hem! and – '

'Mr Simpkinson, a glass of sherry?' cried Tom Ingoldsby hastily.

'Not any, thank you, sir. This Baldwin, surnamed *Le* – '

'Mrs Ogleton challenges you, sir; she insists upon it,' said Tom still more rapidly, at the same time filling a glass, and forcing it on the *sçavant*, who, thus arrested in the very crisis of his narrative, received and swallowed the potation as if it had been physic.

'What on earth has Miss Simpkinson discovered there?' continued Tom; 'something of interest. See how fast she is writing.'

The diversion was effectual; everyone looked towards Miss Simpkinson, who, far too ethereal for 'creature comforts' was seated apart on the dilapidated remains of an altar-tomb, committing eagerly to paper something that had strongly impressed her; the air – the eye in a 'fine frenzy rolling' – all betokened that the divine *afflatus* was come. Her father rose, and stole silently towards her.

'What an old boar!' muttered young Ingoldsby; alluding, perhaps, to a slice of brawn which he had just begun to operate upon, but which, from the celerity with which it disappeared, did not seem so very difficult of mastication.

But what had become of Seaforth and his fair Caroline all this while? Why, it so happened that they had been simultaneously stricken with the picturesque appearance of one of those high and pointed arches, which that eminent antiquary, Mr Horseley Curties, has described in his *Ancient Records*, as 'a *Gothic* window of the *Saxon* order'; and then the ivy clustered so thickly and so beautifully on the other side, that they went round to look at that; and then their proximity deprived it of half its effect, and so they walked across to a little knoll, a hundred yards off, and in crossing a small ravine, they came to what in Ireland they call 'a bad step' and Charles had to carry his cousin over it; and then when they had to come back, she would not give him the trouble again for the world, so they followed a better but more circuitous route, and there were hedges and ditches in the way, and stiles to get over and gates to get through, so that an hour or more had elapsed before they were able to rejoin the party.

'Lassy me!' said Miss Julia Simpkinson, 'how long you have been gone!'

And so they had. The remark was a very just as well as a very natural one. They were gone a long while, and a nice cosy chat they had; and what do you think it was all about, my dear miss?

'O, lassy me! love, no doubt, and the moon and eyes and nightingales and – '

Stay, stay, my sweet young lady; do not let the fervour of your feelings run away with you! I do not pretend to say, indeed, that one or more of these pretty subjects might not have been introduced; but the most important and leading topic of the conference was – Lieutenant Seaforth's breeches.

'Caroline,' said Charles, 'I have had some very odd dreams since I have been at Tappington.'

'Dreams, have you?' – smiled the young lady, arching her taper neck like a swan in pluming. 'Dreams, have you?'

'Ay, dreams – or dream, perhaps, I should say; for, though repeated, it was still the same. And what do you imagine was its subject?'

'It is impossible for me to divine,' said the tongue; 'I have not the least difficulty in guessing,' said the eye, as plainly as ever eye spoke.

'I dreamt – of your great-grandfather!'

There was a change in the glance – 'My great-grandfather?'

'Yes, the old Sir Giles, or Sir John, you told me about the other day: he walked into my bedroom in his short cloak of murrey-coloured velvet, his long rapier, and his Raleigh-looking hat and feather, just as the picture represents him; but with one exception.'

'And what was that?'

'Why, his lower extremities, which were visible, were those of a skeleton.'

'Well?'

'Well, after taking a turn or two about the room, and looking round him with a wistful air, he came to the bed's foot, stared at me in a manner impossible to describe – and then he – he laid hold of my pantaloons; whipped his long bony legs into them in a twinkling; and strutting up to the glass, seemed to view himself in it with great complacency. I tried to speak, but in vain. The effort, however, seemed to excite his attention; for, wheeling about, he showed me the grimmest-looking death's-head you can well imagine, and with an indescribable grin strutted out of the room.'

'Absurd, Charles! How can you talk such nonsense?'

'But, Caroline – the breeches are really gone.'

On the following morning, contrary to his usual custom, Seaforth was the first person in the breakfast-parlour. As no one else was present, he did precisely what nine young men out of ten so situated would have done; he walked up to the mantelpiece, established himself upon the rug, and subducting his coat-tails one under each arm, turned towards the fire that portion of the human frame which is considered equally indecorous to present to a friend or an enemy. A serious, not to say anxious, expression was visible upon his good-humoured countenance, and his mouth was fast buttoning itself up for an incipient whistle, when little Flo, a tiny spaniel of the Blenheim breed – the pet object of Miss Julia Simpkinson's affections – bounced out from beneath a sofa and began to bark at – his pantaloons.

They were cleverly 'built', of a light-grey mixture, a broad stripe of the most vivid scarlet traversing each seam in a perpendicular direction from hip to ankle – in short, the regimental costume of the Royal Bombay Fencibles. The animal, educated in the country, had never seen such a pair of breeches in her life – *Omne ignotum pro magnifico!* The scarlet streak, inflamed as it was by the reflection of the fire, seemed to act on Flora's nerves as the same colour does on those of bulls and turkeys; she advanced at the *pas de charge*, and her vocifera-tion, like her amazement, was unbounded. A sound kick from the disgusted officer changed its character and induced a retreat at the very moment when the mistress of the pugnacious quadruped entered to the rescue.

'Lassy me! Flo, what *is* the matter?' cried the sympathising lady, with a scrutinising glance levelled at the gentleman.

It might as well have lighted on a feather-bed. His air of imperturb-able unconsciousness defied examination; and as he would not, and Flora could not, expound, that injured individual was compelled to pocket up her wrongs. Others of the household soon dropped in and

clustered round the board dedicated to the most sociable of meals; the
urn was paraded 'hissing hot' and the cups which 'cheer, but do not
inebriate' steamed redolent of hyson and pekoe; muffins and marma-
lade, newspapers and Finnon haddies, left little room for observation
on the character of Charles's warlike 'turn-out'. At length a look from
Caroline, followed by a smile that nearly ripened to a titter, caused him
to turn abruptly and address his neighbour. It was Miss Simpkinson,
who, deeply engaged in sipping her tea and turning over her album,
seemed, like a female Chrononotonthologos, 'immersed in cogibundity
of cogitation'. An interrogatory on the subject of her studies drew from
her the confession that she was at that moment employed in putting
the finishing touches to a poem inspired by the romantic shades of
Bolsover. The entreaties of the company were of course urgent. Mr
Peters, 'who liked verses', was especially persevering, and Sappho at
length compliant. After a preparatory hem! and a glance at the mirror
to ascertain that her look was sufficiently sentimental, the poetess
began:

> 'There is a calm, a holy feeling,
>   Vulgar minds can never know,
> O'er the bosom softly stealing –
>   Chasten'd grief, delicious woe!
> Oh! how sweet at eve regaining
>   Yon lone tower's sequester'd shade –
> Sadly mute and uncomplaining – '

'You! – yeough! – yeough! – yow! – yow!' yelled a hapless sufferer
from beneath the table. It was an unlucky hour for quadrupeds; and if
'every dog will have his day', he could not have selected a more
unpropitious one than this. Mrs Ogleton, too, had a pet – a favourite
pug, whose squab figure, black muzzle, and tortuosity of tail, that
curled like a head of celery in a salad-bowl, bespoke his Dutch
extraction. 'Yow! yow yow!' continued the brute – a chorus in which
Flo instantly joined. Sooth to say, pug had more reason to express his
dissatisfaction than was given him by the muse of Simpkinson; the
other only barked for company.

Scarcely had the poetess got through her first stanza, when Tom
Ingoldsby, in the enthusiasm of the moment, became so lost in the
material world, that, in his abstraction, he unwarily laid his hand on the
cock of the urn. Quivering with emotion, he gave it such an unlucky
twist, that the full stream of its scalding contents descended on the
gingerbread hide of the unlucky Cupid. The confusion was complete;
the whole economy of the table disarranged – the company broke up in

most admired disorder – and 'vulgar minds will never know' anything more of Miss Simpkinson's ode till they peruse it in some forthcoming Annual.

Seaforth profited by the confusion to take the delinquent who had caused this 'stramash' by the arm, and to lead him to the lawn, where he had a word or two for his private ear. The conference between the young gentlemen was neither brief in its duration nor unimportant in its result. The subject was what the lawyers call tripartite, embracing the information that Charles Seaforth was over head and ears in love with Tom Ingoldsby's sister; secondly, that the lady had referred him to 'papa' for his sanction; thirdly and lastly, his nightly visitations, and consequent bereavement. At the two first items Tom smiled auspiciously – at the last he burst out into an absolute guffaw.

'Steal your breeches! Miss Bailey over again, by Jove,' shouted Ingoldsby. 'But a gentleman, you say – and Sir Giles too. I am not sure, Charles, whether I ought not to call you out for aspersing the honour of the family.'

'Laugh as you will, Tom – be as incredulous as you please. One fact is incontestable – the breeches are gone! Look here – I am reduced to my regimentals; and if these go, tomorrow I must borrow of you!'

Rochefoucault says, there is something in the misfortunes of our very best friends that does not displease us; assuredly we can, most of us, laugh at their petty inconveniences, till called upon to supply them. Tom composed his features on the instant and replied with more gravity, as well as with an expletive, which, if my Lord Mayor had been within hearing, might have cost him five shillings.

'There is something very queer in this, after all. The clothes; you say, have positively disappeared. Somebody is playing you a trick; and, ten to one, your servant has a hand in it. By the way, I heard something yesterday of his kicking up a bobbery in the kitchen and seeing a ghost, or something of that kind, himself. Depend upon it, Barney is in the plot.'

It now struck the lieutenant at once, that the usually buoyant spirits of his attendant had of late been materially sobered down, his loquacity obviously circumscribed, and that he, the said lieutenant, had actually rung his bell three separate times that very morning before he could procure his attendance. Mr Maguire was forthwith summoned and underwent a close examination. The 'bobbery' was easily explained. Mr Oliver Dobbs had hinted his disapprobation of a flirtation carrying on between the gentleman from Munster and the lady from the Rue St Honoré. Mademoiselle had boxed Mr Maguire's ears, and Mr Maguire had pulled Mademoiselle upon his knee, and the lady had *not* cried *Mon*

Dieu! And Mr Oliver Dobbs said it was very wrong; and Mrs Botherby said it was 'scandalous' and what ought not to be done in any moral kitchen; and Mr Maguire had got hold of the Honourable Augustus Sucklethumbkin's powder-flask, and had put large pinches of the best Double Dartford into Mr Dobbs's tobacco-box; and Mr Dobbs's pipe had exploded, and set fire to Mrs Botherby's Sunday cap; and Mr Maguire had put it out with the slop-basin, 'barring the wig'; and then they were all so 'cantankerous', that Barney had gone to take a walk in the garden; and then – then Mr Barney had seen a ghost.

'A what? you blockhead!' asked Tom Ingoldsby.

'Sure then, and it's meself will tell your honour the rights of it,' said the ghost-seer. 'Meself and Miss Pauline, sir – or Miss Pauline and meself, for the ladies come first, anyhow – we got tired of the hobstroppylous scrimmaging among the ould servants, that didn't know a joke when they seen one: and we went out to look at the comet, that's the roryboryalehouse, they calls him in this country – and we walked upon the lawn – and divil of any alehouse there was there at all; and Miss Pauline said it was bekase of the shrubbery maybe, and why wouldn't we see it better beyonst the trees? and so we went to the trees, but sorrow a comet did meself see there, barring a big ghost instead of it.'

'A ghost? And what sort of a ghost, Barney?'

'Och, then, devil a lie I'll tell your honour. A tall ould gentleman, he was, all in white, with a shovel on the shoulder of him, and a big torch in his fist – though what he wanted with that it's meself can't tell, for his eyes were like gig-lamps, let alone the moon and the comet, which wasn't there at all – and "Barney," says he to me – 'cause why he knew me – "Barney," says he, "what is it you're doing with the colleen there, Barney?" – Divil a word did I say. Miss Pauline screeched, and cried murther in French, and ran off with herself; and of course meself was in a mighty hurry after the lady, and had no time to stop palavering with him anyway: so I dispersed at once, and the ghost vanished in a flame of fire!'

Mr Maguire's account was received with avowed incredulity by both gentlemen; but Barney stuck to his text with unflinching pertinacity. A reference to Mademoiselle was suggested, but abandoned as neither party had a taste for delicate investigations.

'I'll tell you what, Seaforth,' said Ingoldsby, after Barney had received his dismissal, 'that there is a trick here, is evident; and Barney's vision may possibly be part of it. Whether he is most knave or fool, you best know. At all events I will sit up with you tonight, and see if I can convert my ancestor into a visiting acquaintance. Meanwhile your finger on your lip!'

'Twas now the very witching time of night,
When churchyards yawn, and graves give up their dead.

Gladly would I grace my tale with decent horror and therefore I do beseech the 'gentle reader' to believe, that if all the *succedanea* to this mysterious narrative are not in strict keeping, he will ascribe it only to the disgraceful innovations of modern degeneracy upon the sober and dignified habits of our ancestors. I can introduce him, it is true, into an old and high-roofed chamber, its walls covered on three sides with black oak wainscoting, adorned with carvings of fruit and flowers long anterior to those of Grinling Gibbons; the fourth side is clothed with a curious remnant of dingy tapestry, once elucidatory of some scriptural history, but of *which* not even Mrs Botherby could determine. Mr Simpkinson, who had examined it carefully, inclined to believe the principal figure to be either Bathsheba, or Daniel in the lions' den; while Tom Ingoldsby decided in favour of the king of Bashan. All, however, was conjecture, tradition being silent on the subject.

A lofty arched portal led into, and a little arched portal led out of, this apartment; they were opposite each other and each possessed the security of massy bolts on its interior. The bedstead, too, was not one of yesterday, but manifestly coeval with days ere Seddon was and when a good four-post 'article' was deemed worthy of being a royal bequest. The bed itself, with all appurtenances of palliasse, mattresses, etc., was of far later date, and looked most incongruously comfortable; the casements, too, with their little diamond-shaped panes and iron binding, had given way to the modern heterodoxy of the sash-window. Nor was this all that conspired to ruin the costume, and render the room a meet haunt for such 'mixed spirits' only as could condescend to don at the same time an Elizabethan doublet and Bond Street inexpressibles.

With their green morocco slippers on a modern fender, in front of a disgracefully modern grate, sat two young gentlemen, clad in 'shawl-pattern' dressing-gowns and black silk stocks, much at variance with the high cane-backed chairs which supported them. A bunch of abomination, called a cigar, reeked in the left-hand corner of the mouth of one and in the right-hand corner of the mouth of the other – an arrangement happily adapted for the escape of the noxious fumes up the chimney, without that unmerciful 'funking' each other which a less scientific disposition of the weed would have induced. A small pembroke table filled up the intervening space between them, sustaining, at each extremity, an elbow and a glass of toddy – thus in 'lonely pensive contemplation' were the two worthies occupied, when the 'iron tongue of midnight had tolled twelve'.

'Ghost-time's come!' said Ingoldsby, taking from his waistcoat pocket a watch like a gold half-crown, and consulting it as though he suspected the turret-clock over the stable of mendacity.

'Hush!' said Charles; 'did I not hear a footstep?'

There was a pause – there *was* a footstep – it sounded distinctly – it reached the door – it hesitated, stopped, and – passed on.

Tom darted across the room, threw open the door, and became aware of Mrs Botherby toddling to her chamber, at the other end of the gallery, after dosing one of the house-maids with an approved julep from the Countess of Kent's *Choice Manual*.

'Good-night, sir!' said Mrs Botherby.

'Go to the devil!' said the disappointed ghost-hunter.

An hour – two – rolled on and still no spectral visitation; nor did aught intervene to make night hideous; and when the turret-clock sounded at length the hour of three, Ingoldsby, whose patience and grog were alike exhausted, sprang from his chair, saying –

'This is all infernal nonsense, my good fellow. Deuce of any ghost shall we see tonight; it's long past the canonical hour. I'm off to bed; and as to your breeches, I'll insure them for the next twenty-four hours at least, at the price of the buckram.'

'Certainly. – Oh! thank'ee – to be sure!' stammered Charles, rousing himself from a reverie, which had degenerated into an absolute snooze.

'Good-night, my boy! Bolt the door behind me; and defy the Pope, the Devil and the Pretender!'

Seaforth followed his friend's advice and the next morning came down to breakfast dressed in the habiliments of the preceding day. The charm was broken, the demon defeated; the light greys with the red stripe down the seams were yet *in rerum natura* and adorned the person of their lawful proprietor.

Tom felicitated himself and his partner of the watch on the result of their vigilance; but there is a rustic adage which warns us against self-gratulation before we are quite 'out of the wood'. Seaforth was yet within its verge.

A rap at Tom Ingoldsby's door the following morning startled him as he was shaving – he cut his chin.

'Come in, and be damned to you!' said the martyr, pressing his thumb on the scarified epidermis. The door opened, and exhibited Mr Barney Maguire.

'Well, Barney, what is it?' quoth the sufferer, adopting the vernacular of his visitant.

'The master, sir – '

'Well, what does he want?'

'The loanst of a breeches, plase your honour.'

'Why you don't mean to tell me – By heaven, this is too good!' shouted Tom, bursting into a fit of uncontrollable laughter. 'Why, Barney, you don't mean to say the ghost has got them again?'

Mr Maguire did not respond to the young squire's risibility – the cast of his countenance was decidedly serious.

'Faith, then, it's gone they are, sure enough! Hasn't meself been looking over the bed, and under the bed, and *in* the bed, for the matter of that; and divil a ha'p'orth of breeches is there to the fore at all – I'm bothered entirely!'

'Hark'ee! Mr Barney,' said Tom, incautiously removing his thumb and letting a crimson stream 'incarnadine the multitudinous' lather that plastered his throat – 'this may be all very well with your master, but you don't humbug *me*, sir – tell me instantly, what have you done with the clothes?'

This abrupt transition from 'lively to severe' certainly took Maguire by surprise and he seemed for an instant as much disconcerted as it is possible to disconcert an Irish gentleman's gentleman.

'Me? is it meself, then, that's the ghost to your honour's thinking?' said he, after a moment's pause and with a slight shade of indignation in his tones; 'is it I would stale the master's things – and what would I do with them?'

'That you best know – what your purpose is I can't guess, for I don't think you mean to "stale" them, as you call it; but that you are concerned in their disappearance, I am satisfied. Confound this blood! – give me a towel, Barney.'

Maguire acquitted himself of the commission. 'As I've a sowl, your honour,' said he solemnly, 'little it is meself knows of the matter: and after what I've seen – '

'What you've seen! Why, what *have* you seen? – Barney, I don't want to enquire into your flirtations; but don't suppose you can palm off your saucer eyes and gig-lamps upon me!'

'Then, as sure as your honour's standing there, I saw him: and why wouldn't I, when Miss *Pauline* was to the fore as well as meself and – '

'Get along with your nonsense – leave the room, sir!'

'But the master?' said Barney, imploringly; 'and without a breeches? – sure he'll be catching cowld! – '

'Take that, rascal!' replied Ingoldsby, throwing a pair of pantaloons at, rather than to, him; 'but don't suppose, sir, you shall carry on your tricks here with impunity; recollect there is such a thing as a treadmill, and that my father is a county magistrate.'

Barney's eye flashed fire – he stood erect, and was about to speak;

but, mastering himself, not without an effort, he took up the garment and left the room as perpendicular as a Quaker.

'Ingoldsby,' said Charles Seaforth, after breakfast, 'this is now past a joke; today is the last of my stay; for, notwithstanding the ties which detain me, common decency obliges me to visit home after so long an absence. I shall come to an immediate explanation with your father on the subject nearest my heart and depart while I have a change of dress left. On his answer will my return depend! In the meantime tell me candidly – I ask it in all seriousness and as a friend – am I not a dupe to your well-known propensity to hoaxing? have you not a hand in – '

'No, by heaven, Seaforth; I see what you mean: on my honour, I am as much mystified as yourself; and if your servant – '

'Not he – if there be a trick, he at least is not privy to it.'

'If there *be* a trick? why, Charles, do you think – '

'I know not *what* to think, Tom. As surely as you are a living man, so surely did that spectral anatomy visit my room again last night, grin in my face, and walk away with my trousers; nor was I able to spring from my bed or break the chain which seemed to bind me to my pillow.'

'Seaforth!' said Ingoldsby, after a short pause, 'I will – But hush! here are the girls and my father – I will carry off the females and leave you a clear field with the governor: carry your point with him and we will talk about your breeches afterwards.'

Tom's diversion was successful; he carried off the ladies *en masse* to look at a remarkable specimen of the class *Dodecandria Monogynia* – which they could not find; while Seaforth marched boldly up to the encounter and carried 'the governor's' outworks by a *coup de main*. I shall not stop to describe the progress of the attack; suffice it that it was as successful as could have seen wished, and that Seaforth was referred back again to the lady. The happy lover was off at a tangent; the botanical party was soon overtaken; and the arm of Caroline, whom a vain endeavour to spell out the Linnaen name of a daffy-down-dilly had detained a little in the rear of the others, was soon firmly locked in his own.

> *What was the world to them,*
> *Its noise, its nonsense, and its 'breeches' all?*

Seaforth was in the seventh heaven; he retired to his room that night as happy as if no such thing as a goblin had ever been heard of and personal chattels were as well fenced in by law as real property. Not so Tom Ingoldsby: the mystery – for mystery there evidently was – had not only piqued his curiosity, but ruffled his temper. The watch of the previous night had been unsuccessful, probably because it was undisguised. Tonight he would 'ensconce himself' – not indeed 'behind the arras' – for the little that remained was, as we have seen, nailed to the wall – but in a small closet which opened from one corner of the room, and by leaving the door ajar would give to its occupant a view of all that might pass in the apartment. Here did the young ghost-hunter take up a position, with a good stout sapling under his arm, a full half-hour before Seaforth retired for the night. Not even his friend did he let into his confidence, fully determined that if his plan did not succeed, the failure should be attributed to himself alone.

At the usual hour for separation for the night, Tom saw from his concealment, the lieutenant enter his room and after taking a few turns in it, with an expression so joyous as to betoken that his thoughts were mainly occupied by his approaching happiness, proceed slowly to disrobe himself. The coat, the waistcoat, the black silk stock, were gradually discarded; the green morocco slippers were kicked off and then – ay, and then – his countenance grew grave; it seemed to occur to him all at once that this was his last state, nay, that the very breeches he had on were not his own – that tomorrow morning was his last and that if he lost *them* – A glance showed that his mind was made up; he replaced the single button he had just subducted, and threw himself upon the bed in a state of transition – half chrysalis, half grub.

Wearily did Tom Ingoldsby watch the sleeper by the flickering light of the night-lamp, till the clock striking one, induced him to increase the narrow opening which he had left for the purpose of observation. The motion, slight as it was, seemed to attract Charles's attention; for he raised himself suddenly to a sitting posture, listened for a moment, and then stood upright upon the floor. Ingoldsby was on the point of discovering himself, when, the light flashing full upon his friend's countenance, he perceived that, though his eyes were open, 'their sense was shut' – that he was yet under the influence of sleep. Seaforth advanced slowly to the toilet, lit his candle at the lamp that stood on it, then, going back to the bed's foot, appeared to search eagerly for something which he could not find. For a few moments he seemed restless and uneasy, walking round the apartment and examining the chairs, till, coming fully in front of a large swing-glass that flanked the dressing-table, he paused as if contemplating his figure in it. He now returned towards the bed, put on his slippers and, with cautious and stealthy steps, proceeded towards the little arched doorway that opened on the private staircase.

As he drew the bolt, Tom Ingoldsby emerged from his hiding-place; but the sleepwalker heard him not; he proceeded softly downstairs, followed at a due distance by his friend; opened the door which led out upon the gardens; and stood at once among the thickest of the shrubs, which there clustered round the base of a corner turret, and screened the postern from common observation. At this moment Ingoldsby had nearly spoiled all by making a false step; the sound attracted Seaforth's attention – he paused and turned; and, as the full moon shed her light directly upon his pale and troubled features, Tom marked, almost with dismay, the fixed and rayless appearance of his eyes –

> *There was no speculation in those orbs*
> *That he did glare withal.*

The perfect stillness preserved by his follower seemed to reassure him; he turned aside; and from the midst of a thickset laurustinus drew forth a gardener's spade, shouldering which he proceeded with greater rapidity into the midst of the shrubbery. Arrived at a certain point where the earth seemed to have been recently disturbed, he set himself heartily to the task of digging, till, having thrown up several shovelfuls of mould, he stopped, flung down his tools, and very composedly began to disencumber himself of his pantaloons.

Up to this moment Tom had watched him with a wary eye; he now advanced cautiously and, as his friend was busily engaged in disentangling himself from his garment, made himself master of the spade. Seaforth, meanwhile had accomplished his purpose: he stood for a moment with

> *His streamers waving in the wind,*

occupied in carefully rolling up the small-clothes into as compact a form as possible, and all heedless of the breath of heaven, which might certainly be supposed at such a moment, and in such a plight, to 'visit his frame too roughly'.

He was in the act of stooping low to deposit the pantaloons in the grave which he had been digging for them, when Tom Ingoldsby came close behind him, and with the flat side of the spade –

The shock was effectual – never again was Lieutenant Seaforth known to act the part of a somnambulist. One by one, his breeches – his trousers – his pantaloons – his silk-net tights – his patent cords – his showy greys with the broad red stripe of the Bombay Fencibles, were brought to light – rescued from the grave in which they had been buried, like the strata of a Christmas pie; and after having been well aired by Mrs Botherby, became once again effective.

The family, the ladies especially, laughed – the Peterses laughed – the Simpkinsons laughed – Barney Maguire cried 'Botheration' and Ma'mselle Pauline, '*Mon Dieu!*'

Charles Seaforth, unable to face the quizzing which awaited him on all sides, started off two hours earlier than he had proposed – he soon returned, however, and having, at his father-in-law's request, given up the occupation of Rajah-hunting and shooting Nabobs, led his blushing bride to the altar.

Mr Simpkinson from Bath did not attend the ceremony, being engaged at the Grand Junction meeting of *Sçavans*, then congregating from all parts of the known world in the city of Dublin. His essay, demonstrating that the globe is a great custard, whipped into coagulation by whirlwinds, and cooked by electricity – a little too much baked in the Isle of Portland and a thought underdone about the Bog of Allen – was highly spoken of and narrowly escaped obtaining a Bridgewater prize.

Miss Simpkinson and her sister acted as bridesmaids on the occasion; the former wrote an *epithalamium*, and the latter cried 'Lassy me!' at the clergyman's wig. Some years have since rolled on; the union has been crowned with two or three tidy little off-shoots from the family tree, of whom Master Neddy is 'grandpapa's darling' and Mary Anne mamma's particular 'Sock'. I shall only add, that Mr and Mrs Seaforth are living together quite as happily as two good-hearted, good-tempered bodies, very fond of each other, can possibly do; and that, since the day of his marriage, Charles has shown no disposition to jump out of bed or ramble out of doors o' nights – though from his entire devotion to every wish and whim of his young wife, Tom insinuates that the fair Caroline does still occasionally take advantage of it so far as to 'slip on the breeches'.

The Botathen Ghost

R. S. HAWKER 1803–1875

THERE WAS SOMETHING very painful and peculiar in the position of the clergy in the west of England throughout the seventeenth century. The Church of those days was in a transitory state and her ministers, like her formularies, embodied a strange mixture of the old belief with the new interpretation. Their wide severance also from the great metropolis of life and manners, the city of London (which in those times was civilised England, much as the Paris of our own day is France), divested the Cornish clergy in particular of all personal access to the master-minds of their age and body. Then, too, the barrier interposed by the rude rough roads of their country, and by their abode in wilds that were almost inaccessible, rendered the existence of a bishop rather a doctrine suggested to their belief than a fact revealed to the actual vision of each in his generation. Hence it came to pass that the Cornish clergyman, insulated within his own limited sphere, often without even the presence of a country squire (and unchecked by the influence of the Fourth Estate – for until the beginning of this nineteenth century, *Flindell's Weekly Miscellany*, distributed from house to house from the pannier of a mule, was the only light of the West), became developed about middle life into an original mind and man, sole and absolute within his parish boundary, eccentric when compared with his brethren in civilised regions and yet, in German phrase, 'a whole and seldom man' in his dominion of souls. He was 'the parson' in canonical phrase – that is to say, The Person, the somebody of consequence among his own people. These men were not, however, smoothed down into a monotonous aspect of life and manners by this remote and secluded existence. They imbibed, each in his own peculiar circle, the hue of surrounding objects and were tinged into a distinctive colouring and character by many a contrast of scenery and people. There was the 'light of other days', the curate by the sea-shore, who professed to check the turbulence of the 'smugglers' landing' by his presence on the sands, and who 'held the lantern' for the guidance of his flock when the nights were dark, as the only proper ecclesiastical part he could take in the proceedings. He was soothed and silenced by the gift of a keg of hollands or a chest of tea. There was the merry minister of the mines, whose cure was honeycombed by the underground men. He must needs have been artist and poet in his way, for he had to enliven his people three or four times a year, by mastering the arrangements of a 'guary' or religious mystery, which was duly performed in the topmost hollow of a green barrow or hill, of which many survive, scooped out into vast amphitheatres and surrounded by benches of turf which held two thousand spectators. Such were the historic plays, *The Creation* and *Noe's Flood*, which still exist in the original Celtic as well as the English text and suggest what critics and antiquaries these Cornish curates, masters of such revels, must have been – for the native language of Cornwall did not lapse into silence until the end of the seventeenth century. Then, moreover, here and there would be one parson more learned than his kind in the mysteries of a deep and thrilling lore of peculiar fascination. He was a man so highly humoured at college for natural gifts and knowledge of learned books which nobody else could read, that when he 'took his second orders' the bishop gave him a mantle of scarlet silk to wear upon his shoulders in church, and his lordship had put such power into it that, when the parson had it rightly on, he could 'govern any ghost or evil spirit' and even 'stop an earthquake'.

Such a powerful minister, in combat with supernatural visitations, was one Parson Rudall, of Launceston, whose existence and exploits we gather from the local tradition of his time, from surviving letters and other memoranda and indeed from his own 'diurnal' which fell by chance into the hands of the present writer. Indeed the legend of Parson Rudall and the Botathen Ghost will be recognised by many Cornish people as a local remembrance of their boyhood.

It appears, then, from the diary of this learned master of the grammar school – for such was his office as well as perpetual curate of the parish – 'that a pestilential disease did break forth in our town in the beginning of the year AD 1665; yea, and it likewise invaded my school, insomuch that therewithal certain of the chief scholars sickened and died.' 'Among others who yielded to the malign influence was Master John Eliot, the eldest son and the worshipful heir of Edward Eliot, Esquire, of Trebursey, a stripling of sixteen years of age, but of uncommon parts and hopeful ingenuity. At his own especial motion and earnest desire I did consent to preach his funeral sermon.' It should be remembered here that, howsoever strange and singular it may sound to us that a mere lad should formally solicit such a performance at the hands of his master, it was in consonance with the habitual usage of those times. The old services for the dead had been abolished by law and in the stead of sacrament and ceremony, month's mind and year's mind, the sole substitute, which survived was the general desire 'to partake', as they called it, of a posthumous discourse, replete with lofty eulogy and flattering remembrance of the living and the dead.

The diary proceeds: 'I fulfilled my undertaking, and preached over the coffin in the presence of a full assemblage of mourners and lachrymose friends. An ancient gentleman, who was then and there in the church, a Mr Bligh, of Botathen, was much affected with my discourse, and he was heard to repeat to himself certain parentheses therefrom, especially a phrase from Maro Virgilius, which I had applied to the deceased youth, "*Et puer ipse fuit cantari dignus*".

'The cause wherefore this old gentleman was moved by my applications was this: He had a first-born and only son – a child who, but a very few months before, had been not unworthy the character I drew of young Master Eliot, but who, by some strange accident, had of late quite fallen away from his parent's hopes and become moody and sullen and distraught. When the funeral obsequies were over, I had no sooner come out of church than I was accosted by this aged parent and he besought me incontinently, with a singular energy, that I would resort with him forthwith to his abode at Botathen that very night; nor could I have delivered myself from his importunity, had not Mr Eliot urged his claim to enjoy my company at his own house. Hereupon I got loose, but not until I had pledged a fast assurance that I would pay him, faithfully, an early visit the next day.'

'The Place', as it was called, of Botathen, where old Mr Bligh resided, was a low-roofed gabled manor-house of the fifteenth century, walled and mullioned and with clustered chimneys of dark-grey tone from the neighbouring quarries of Ventor-gan. The mansion was flanked by a pleasance or enclosure in one space of garden and lawn and it was surrounded by a solemn grove of stag-horned trees. It had the sombre aspect of age and of solitude and looked the very scene of strange and supernatural events. A legend might well belong to every gloomy glade around and there must surely be a haunted room somewhere within its walls. Hither, according to his appointment, on the morrow, Parson Rudall betook himself. Another clergyman, as it appeared, had been invited to meet him, who, very soon after his arrival, proposed a walk together in the pleasance, on the pretext of showing him, as a stranger, the walks and trees, until the dinner-bell should strike. There, with much prolixity and with many a solemn pause, his brother minister proceeded to 'unfold the mystery'.

A singular infelicity, he declared, had befallen young Master Bligh, once the hopeful heir of his parents and of the lands of Botathen. Whereas he had been from childhood a blithe and merry boy, 'the gladness', like Isaac of old, of his father's age, he had suddenly and of late, become morose and silent – nay, even austere and stern – dwelling apart, always solemn, often in tears. The lad had at first repulsed all questions as to the origin of this great change, but of late he had yielded to the importune researches of his parents, and had disclosed the secret cause. It appeared that he resorted every day, by a pathway across the fields, to this very clergyman's house, who had charge of his education and grounded him in the studies suitable to his age. In the course of his daily walk he had to pass a certain heath or down where the road wound along through tall blocks of granite with open spaces of grassy sward between. There in a certain spot and always in one and the same place, the lad declared that he encountered, every day, a woman with a pale and troubled face, clothed in a long loose garment of frieze, with one hand always stretched forth and the other pressed against her side. Her name, he said, was Dorothy Dinglet, for he had known her well from his childhood and she often used to come to his parents' house; but that which troubled him was that she had now been dead three years and he himself had been with the neighbours at her burial; so that, as the youth alleged, with great simplicity; since he had seen her body laid in the grave, this ghost that he saw every day must needs be her soul or ghost. 'Questioned again and again,' said the clergyman, 'he never contradicts himself; but he relates the same and the simple tale as a thing that cannot be gainsaid. Indeed, the lad's observance is keen and calm for a boy of his age. The hair of the appearance, sayeth he, is not like anything alive, but it is so soft and light that it seemeth to melt away while you look; but her eyes are set, and never blink – no, not when the sun shineth full upon her face. She maketh no steps, but seemeth to swim along the top of the grass; and her hand, which is stretched out alway, seemeth to point at something far away, out of sight. It is her continual coming, for she never faileth to meet him and to pass on, that hath quenched his spirits; and although he never seeth her by night, yet cannot he get his natural rest.'

Thus far the clergyman; whereupon the dinner-clock did sound and we went into the house. After dinner, when young Master Bligh had withdrawn with his tutor, under excuse of their books, the parents did forthwith beset me as to my thoughts about their son. Said I, warily, 'The case is strange but by no means impossible. It is one that I will study and fear not to handle, if the lad will be free with me and fulfil all that I desire.' The mother was overjoyed, but I perceived that old Mr Bligh turned pale and was downcast with some thought which, however, he did not express. Then they bade that Master Bligh should be called to meet me in the pleasance forthwith. The boy came, and he rehearsed to me his tale with an open countenance and, withal, a pretty modesty of speech. Verily he seemed *ingenui vultus puer ingenuique pudoris*. Then I signified to him my purpose. 'Tomorrow,' said I, 'we will go together to the place; and if, as I doubt not, the woman shall appear, it will be for me to proceed according to knowledge, and by rules laid down in my books.'

The unaltered scenery of the legend still survives and, like the field of the forty footsteps in another history, the place is still visited by those who take interest in the supernatural tales of old. The pathway leads along a moorland waste, where large masses of rock stand up here and there from the grassy turf and clumps of heath and gorse weave their tapestry of golden and purple garniture on every side. Amidst all these and winding along between the rocks, is a natural footway worn by the scant, rare tread of the village traveller. Just midway, a somewhat larger stretch than usual of green sod expands, which is skirted by the path and which is still identified as the legendary haunt of the phantom, by the name of Parson Rudall's Ghost.

But we must draw the record of the first interview between the minister and Dorothy from his own words. 'We met,' thus he writes, 'in the pleasance very early and before any others in the house were awake; and together the lad and myself proceeded towards the field. The youth was quite composed and carried his Bible under his arm, from whence he read to me verses, which he said he had lately picked out, to have always in his mind. These were Job 7: 14, "Thou scarest me with dreams, and terrifiest me through visions;" and Deuteronomy 28: 67, "In the morning thou shalt say, Would to God it were evening, and in the evening thou shalt say, Would to God it were morning; for the fear of thine heart wherewith thou shalt fear, and for the sight of thine eyes which thou shalt see."

'I was much pleased with the lad's ingenuity in these pious applications, but for mine own part I was somewhat anxious and out of cheer. For aught I knew that might be a *daemonium meridianum*, the most stubborn spirit to govern and guide that any man can meet and the most perilous withal. We had hardly reached the accustomed spot, when we both saw her at once gliding towards us; punctually as the ancient writers describe the motion of their "lemures, which swoon along the ground, neither marking the sand nor bending the herbage". The aspect of the woman was exactly that which had been related by the lad. There was the pale and stony face, the strange and misty hair, the eyes firm and fixed, that gazed, yet not on us, but on something that

they saw far, far away; one hand and arm stretched out, and the other
grasping the girdle of her waist. She floated along the field like a sail
upon a stream, and glided past the spot where we stood, pausingly. But
so deep was the awe that overcame me, as I stood there in the light of
day, face to face with a human soul separate from her bones and flesh,
that my heart and purpose both failed me. I had resolved to speak to
the spectre in the appointed form of words, but I did not. I stood like
one amazed and speechless, until she had passed clean out of sight. One
thing remarkable came to pass. A spaniel dog, the favourite of young
Master Bligh, had followed us, and lo! when the woman drew nigh, the
poor creature began to yell and bark piteously, and ran backward and
away, like a thing dismayed and appalled. We returned to the house
and after I had said all that I could to pacify the lad, and to soothe the
aged people, I took my leave for that time, with a promise that when I
had fulfilled certain business elsewhere, which I then alleged, I would
return and take orders to assuage these disturbances and their cause.

January 7th 1665 – At my own house, I find, by my books, what is
expedient to be done; and then Apage, Sathanas!

January 9th 1665 – This day I took leave of my wife and family, under
pretext of engagements elsewhere and made my secret journey to our
diocesan city, wherein the good and venerable bishop then abode.

January 10th – *Deo gratias*, in safe arrival in Exeter; craved and obtained
immediate audience of his lordship; pleading it was for counsel and
admonition on a weighty and pressing cause; called to the presence;
made obeisance; then and by command stated my case – the Botathen
perplexity – which I moved with strong and earnest instances and
solemn asseverations of that which I had myself seen and heard.
Demanded by his lordship, what was the succour that I had come to
entreat at his hands. Replied, licence for my exorcism, that so I might,
ministerially, allay this spiritual visitant and thus render to the living
and the dead release from this surprise. 'But,' said our bishop, 'on what
authority do you allege that I am entrusted with faculty so to do? Our
Church, as is well known, hath abjured certain branches of her ancient
power, on grounds of perversion and abuse.' 'Nay, my lord,' I humbly
answered, 'under favour, the seventy-second of the canons ratified and
enjoined on us, the clergy, anno Domini 1604, doth expressly provide,
that "no minister, *unless he hath* the licence of his diocesan bishop, shall
essay to exorcise a spirit, evil or good." Therefore it was,' I did here
mildly allege, 'that I did not presume to enter on such a work without
lawful privilege under your lordship's hand and seal.' Hereupon did

our wise and learned bishop, sitting in his chair, condescend upon the theme at some length with many gracious interpretations from ancient writers and from Holy Scriptures and I did humbly rejoin and reply, till the upshot was that he did call in his secretary and command him to draw the aforesaid faculty, forthwith and without further delay, assigning him a form, insomuch that the matter was incontinently done; and after I had disbursed into the secretary's hands certain moneys for signatory purposes, as the manner of such officers hath always been, the bishop did himself affix his signature under the *sigillum* of his see and deliver the document into my hands. When I knelt down to receive his benediction, he softly said, 'Let it be secret, Mr R. Weak brethren! weak brethren!'

This interview with the bishop and the success with which he vanquished his lordship's scruples, would seem to have confirmed Parson Rudall very strongly in his own esteem and to have invested him with that courage which he evidently lacked at his first encounter with the ghost.

The entries proceed –

January 11th 1665 – Therewithal did I hasten home and prepare my instruments and cast my figures for the onset of the next day. Took out my ring of brass and put it on the index-finger of my right hand, with the *scutum Davidis* traced thereon.

January 12th 1665 – Rode into the gateway at Botathen, armed at all points, but not with Saul's armour, and ready. There is danger from the demons, but so there is in the surrounding air every day. At early morning then and alone – for so the usage ordains – I betook me towards the field. It was void and I had thereby due time to prepare. First I paced and measured out my circle on the grass. Then I did mark my pentacle in the very midst and at the intersection of the five angles I did set up and fix my crutch of *raun* [rowan]. Lastly, I took my station south, at the true line of the meridian, and stood facing due north. I waited and watched for a long time. At last there was a kind of trouble in the air, a soft and rippling sound, and all at once the shape appeared and came on towards me gradually. I opened my parchment-scroll and read aloud the command. She paused and seemed to waver and doubt; stood still; then I rehearsed the sentence again, sounding out every syllable like a chant. She drew near my ring, but halted at first outside, on the brink. I sounded again, and now at the third time I gave the signal in Syriac – the speech which is used, they say, where such ones dwell and converse in thoughts that glide.

She was at last obedient and swam into the midst of the circle and there stood still, suddenly. I saw, moreover, that she drew back her pointing hand. All this while I do confess that my knees shook under me and the drops of sweat ran down my flesh like rain. But now, although face to face with the spirit, my heart grew calm and my mind was composed. I knew that the pentacle would govern her and the ring must bind, until I gave the word. Then I called to mind the rule laid down of old, that no angel or fiend, no spirit, good or evil, will ever speak until they have been first spoken to. N.B. This is the great law of prayer. God Himself will not yield reply until man hath made vocal entreaty, once and again. So I went on to demand, as the books advise; and the phantom made answer, willingly. Questioned wherefore not at rest. Unquiet, because of a certain sin. Asked what, and by whom. Revealed it; but it is *sub sigillo*, and therefore *nefas dictu*; more anon. Enquired, what sign she could give that she was a true spirit and not a false fiend. Stated, before next Yuletide a fearful pestilence would lay waste the land and myriads of souls would be loosened from their flesh, until, as she piteously said, 'our valleys will be full'. Asked again, why she so terrified the lad. Replied: 'It is the law: we must seek a youth or a maiden of clean life and under age, to receive messages and admonitions.' We conversed with many more words, but it is not lawful for me to set them down. Pen and ink would degrade and defile the thoughts she uttered and which my mind received that day. I broke the ring and she passed, but to return once more next day. At evensong, a long discourse with that ancient transgressor, Mr B. Great horror and remorse; entire atonement and penance; whatsoever I enjoin; full acknowledgement before pardon.

January 13th 1665 – At sunrise I was again in the field. She came in at once and, as it seemed, with freedom. Enquired if she knew my thoughts and what I was going to relate? Answered, 'Nay, we only know what we perceive and hear; we cannot see the heart.' Then I rehearsed the penitent words of the man she had come up to denounce and the satisfaction he would perform. Then said she, 'Peace in our midst.' I went through the proper forms of dismissal, and fulfilled all as it was set down and written in my memoranda; and then with certain fixed rites, I did dismiss that troubled ghost, until she peacefully withdrew, gliding towards the west. Neither did she ever afterward appear, but was allayed until she shall come in her second flesh to the valley of Armageddon on the last day.

These quaint and curious details from the 'diurnal' of a simple-hearted clergyman of the seventeenth century appear to betoken his personal persuasion of the truth of what he saw and said, although the statements are strongly tinged with what some may term the superstition, and others the excessive belief, of those times. It is a singular fact, however, that the canon which authorises exorcism under episcopal licence is still a part of the ecclesiastical law of the Anglican Church, although it might have a singular effect on the nerves of certain of our bishops if their clergy were to resort to them for the faculty which Parson Rudall obtained. The general facts stated in his diary are to this day matters of belief in that neighbourhood; and it has been always accounted a strong proof of the veracity of the Parson and the Ghost, that the plague, fatal to so many thousands, did break out in London at the close of that very year. We may well excuse a triumphant entry, on a subsequent page of the 'diurnal', with the date of July 10th 1665: 'How sorely must the infidels and heretics of this generation be dismayed when they know what this Black Death, which is now swallowing its thousands in the streets of the great city, was foretold six months agone, under the exorcisms of a country minister, by a visible and suppliant ghost! And what pleasures and improvements do such deny themselves who scorn and avoid all opportunity of intercourse with souls separate and the spirits, glad and sorrowful, which inhabit the unseen world!'

The Tell-Tale Heart

EDGAR ALLAN POE 1809–1849

TRUE! – NERVOUS – very, very dreadfully nervous I had been and am; but why will you say that I am mad? The disease had sharpened my senses – not destroyed – not dulled them. Above all was the sense of hearing acute. I heard all things in the heaven and in the earth. I heard many things in hell. How, then, am I mad? Hearken! and observe how healthily – how calmly I can tell you the whole story.

It is impossible to say how first the idea entered my brain; but once conceived, it haunted me day and night. Object there was none. Passion there was none. I loved the old man. He had never wronged me. He had never given me insult. For his gold I had no desire. I think it was his eye! yes, it was this! One of his eyes resembled that of a vulture – a pale blue eye, with a film over it. Whenever it fell upon me, my blood ran cold; and so by degrees – very gradually – I made up my mind to take the life of the old man and thus rid myself of the eye for ever.

Now this is the point. You fancy me mad. Madmen know nothing. But you should have seen me. You should have seen how wisely I proceeded – with what caution – with what foresight – with what dissimulation I went to work! I was never kinder to the old man than during the whole week before I killed him. And every night, about midnight, I turned the latch of his door and opened it – oh, so gently! And then, when I had made an opening sufficient for my head, I put in a dark lantern, all closed, closed, so that no light shone out, and then I thrust in my head. Oh, you would have laughed to see how cunningly I thrust it in! I moved it slowly – very, very slowly, so that I might not disturb the old man's sleep. It took me an hour to place my whole head within the opening so far that I could see him as he lay upon his bed. Ha! – would a madman have been so wise as this? And then, when my head was well in the room, I undid the lantern, cautiously – oh, so cautiously – cautiously (for the hinges creaked) I undid it just so much that a single thin ray fell upon the vulture eye. And this I did for seven long nights – every night just at midnight – but I found the eye always closed; and so it was impossible to do the work; for it was not the old man who vexed me, but his Evil Eye. And every morning, when the day broke, I went boldly into the chamber, and spoke courageously to him, calling him by name in a hearty tone, and enquiring how he had passed the night. So you see he would have been a very profound old man, indeed, to suspect that every night, just at twelve, I looked in upon him while he slept.

Upon the eighth night I was more than usually cautious in opening the door. A watch's minute hand moves more quickly than did mine. Never before that night had I *felt* the extent of my own powers – of my sagacity. I could scarcely contain my feelings of triumph. To think that there I was, opening the door, little by little, and he not even to dream of my secret deeds or thoughts. I fairly chuckled at the idea; and perhaps he heard me – for he moved on the bed suddenly, as if startled. Now you may think that I drew back – but no. His room was as black as pitch with the thick darkness (for the shutters were close-fastened, through fear of robbers) and so I knew that he could not see the opening of the door and I kept pushing it on steadily, steadily.

I had my head in, and was about to open the lantern, when my thumb slipped upon the tin fastening and the old man sprang up in the bed, crying out, 'Who's there?'

I kept quite still and said nothing. For a whole hour I did not move a muscle, and in the meantime I did not hear him lie down. He was still sitting up in the bed, listening – just as I have done, night after night, hearkening to the death-watches in the wall.

Presently I heard a groan and I knew it was the groan of mortal terror. It was not a groan of pain or of grief – oh, no! – it was the low stifled sound that arises from the bottom of the soul when overcharged with awe. I knew the sound well. Many a night, just at midnight, when all the world slept, it has welled up from my own bosom, deepening, with its dreadful echo, the terrors that distracted me. I say I knew it well. I knew what the old man felt, and pitied him, although I chuckled at heart. I knew that he had been lying awake ever since the first slight noise, when he had turned in the bed. His fears had been ever since growing upon him. He had been trying to fancy them causeless, but could not. He had been saying to himself, 'It is nothing but the wind in the chimney – it is only a mouse crossing the floor,' or, 'It is merely a cricket which has made a single chirp.' Yes, he had been trying to comfort himself with these suppositions; but he had found all in vain. *All in vain;* because Death, in approaching him, had stalked with his black shadow before him, and enveloped the victim. And it was the mournful influence of the unperceived shadow that caused him to feel – although he neither saw nor heard – to *feel* the presence of my head within the room.

When I had waited a long time, very patiently, without hearing him lie down, I resolved to open a little – a very, very little crevice in the lantern. So I opened it – you cannot imagine how stealthily, stealthily – until, at length, a single dim ray, like the thread of the spider, shot from out the crevice and fell upon the vulture eye.

It was open – wide, wide open – and I grew furious as I gazed upon it. I saw it with perfect distinctness – all a dull blue, with a hideous veil over it that chilled the very marrow in my bones; but I could see nothing else of the old man's face or person, for I had directed the ray, as if by instinct, precisely upon the damned spot.

And now have I not told you that what you mistake for madness is but over-acuteness of the senses? – now, I say, there came to my ears a low, dull, quick sound, such as a watch makes when enveloped in cotton. I knew *that* sound well, too. It was the beating of the old man's heart. It increased my fury, as the beating of a drum stimulates the soldier into courage.

But even yet I refrained and kept still. I scarcely breathed. I held the lantern motionless. I tried how steadily I could maintain the ray upon the eye. Meantime the hellish tattoo of the heart increased. It grew quicker and quicker, and louder and louder every instant. The old man's terror *must* have been extreme! It grew louder, I say, louder every moment! – do you mark me well? I have told you that I am nervous: so I am. And now, at the dead hour of the night, amid the dreadful silence of that old house, so strange a noise as this excited me to uncontrollable terror. Yet, for some minutes longer, I refrained and stood still. But the beating grew louder, louder! I thought the heart must burst. And now a new anxiety seized me – the sound would be heard by a neighbour! The old man's hour had come! With a loud yell I threw open the lantern and leaped into the room. He shrieked once – once only. In an instant I dragged him to the floor, and pulled the heavy bed over him. I then smiled gaily, to find the deed so far done. But, for many minutes, the heart beat on with a muffled sound. This, however, did not vex me; it would not be heard through the wall. At length it ceased. The old man was dead. I removed the bed and examined the corpse. Yes, he was stone, stone dead. I placed my hand upon the heart and held it there many minutes. There was no pulsation. He was stone dead. His eye would trouble me no more.

If still you think me mad, you will think so no longer when I describe the wise precautions I took for the concealment of the body. The night waned, and I worked hastily, but in silence. First of all I dismembered the corpse. I cut off the head and the arms and the legs.

I then took up three planks from the flooring of the chamber and deposited all between the scantlings. I then replaced the boards so cleverly, so cunningly, that no human eye – not even *his* could have detected anything wrong. There was nothing to wash out – no stain of any kind – no blood-spot whatever. I had been too wary for that. A tub had caught all – ha! ha!

When I had made an end of these labours, it was four o'clock – still dark as midnight. As the bell sounded the hour, there came a knocking at the street door. I went down to open it with a light heart – for what had I *now* to fear? There entered three men, who introduced themselves, with perfect suavity, as officers of the police. A shriek had been heard by a neighbour during the night; suspicion of foul play had been aroused; information had been lodged at the police office, and they (the officers) had been deputed to search the premises.

I smiled – for *what* had I to fear? I bade the gentlemen welcome. The shriek, I said, was my own in a dream. The old man, I mentioned, was absent in the country. I took my visitors all over the house. I bade them search – search *well*. I led them, at length, to *his* chamber. I showed them his treasures, secure, undisturbed. In the enthusiasm of my confidence, I brought chairs into the room and desired them *here* to rest from their fatigues, while I myself, in the wild audacity of my perfect triumph, placed my own seat upon the very spot beneath which reposed the corpse of the victim.

The officers were satisfied. My manner had convinced them. I was singularly at ease. They sat, and while I answered cheerily, they chatted of familiar things. But, ere long, I felt myself getting pale and wished them gone. My head ached, and I fancied a ringing in my ears; but still they sat and still chatted. The ringing became more distinct – it continued and became more distinct. I talked more freely to get rid of the feeling; but it continued and gained definitiveness – until, at length, I found that the noise was *not* within my ears.

No doubt I now grew very pale; but I talked more fluently, and with a heightened voice. Yet the sound increased – and what could I do? It was *a low, dull, quick sound – much such a sound as a watch makes when enveloped in cotton*. I gasped for breath – and yet the officers heard it not. I talked more quickly – more vehemently; but the noise steadily increased. I arose and argued about trifles, in a high key and with violent gesticulations; but the noise steadily increased. Why *would* they not be gone? I paced the floor to and fro with heavy strides, as if excited to fury by the observations of the men – but the noise steadily increased. O God! what *could* I do? I foamed – I raved – I swore! I swung the chair upon which I had been sitting, and grated it upon the boards, but the noise arose over all and continually increased. It grew louder – louder – *louder*! And still the men chatted pleasantly, and smiled. Was it possible they heard not? Almighty God! – no, no! They heard! – they suspected! – they *knew*! – they were making a mockery of my horror! – this I thought and this I think. But anything was better than this agony! Anything was more tolerable than this derision! I could bear those hypocritical smiles no longer! I felt that I must scream or die! – and now – again! hark! louder! louder! louder! *louder*! –

'Villains!' I shrieked, 'dissemble no more! I admit the deed! – tear up the planks! – here, here! – it is the beating of his hideous heart!'

The Squire's Story

ELIZABETH CLEGHORN GASKELL 1810–1865

IN THE YEAR 1769 the little town of Barford was thrown into a state of great excitement by the intelligence that a gentleman (and 'quite the gentleman,' said the landlord of the George Inn) had been looking at Mr Clavering's old house. This house was neither in the town nor in the country. It stood on the outskirts of Barford, on the roadside leading to Derby. The last occupant had been a Mr Clavering – a Northumberland gentleman of good family – who had come to live in Barford while he was but a younger son; but when some elder branches of the family died, he had returned to take possession of the family estate. The house of which I speak was called the White House, from its being covered with a greyish kind of stucco. It had a good garden to the back, and Mr Clavering had built capital stables, with what were then considered the latest improvements. The point of good stabling was expected to let the house, as it was in a hunting county; otherwise it had few recommendations. There were many bedrooms; some entered through others, even to the number of five, leading one beyond the other; several sitting-rooms of the small and poky kind, wainscoted round with wood, and then painted a heavy slate colour; one good dining-room and a drawing-room over it, both looking into the garden, with pleasant bow windows.

Such was the accommodation offered by the White House. It did not seem to be very tempting to strangers, though the good people of Barford rather piqued themselves on it, as the largest house in the town; and as a house in which 'townspeople' and 'county people' had often met at Mr Clavering's friendly dinners. To appreciate this circumstance of pleasant recollection, you should have lived some years in a little country town, surrounded by gentlemen's seats. You would then understand how a bow or a courtesy from a member of a county family elevates the individuals who receive it almost as much, in their own eyes, as the pair of blue garters fringed with silver did Mr Bickerstaff's ward. They trip lightly on air for a whole day afterwards. Now Mr Clavering was gone, where could town and county mingle?

I mention these things that you may have an idea of the desirability of the letting of the White House in the Barfordites' imagination; and to make the mixture thick and slab, you must add for yourselves the bustle, the mystery, and the importance which every little event either causes or assumes in a small town; and then, perhaps, it will be no wonder to you that twenty ragged little urchins accompanied the 'gentleman' aforesaid to the door of the White House; and that, although he was above an hour inspecting it, under the auspices of Mr Jones, the agent's clerk, thirty more had joined themselves on to the wondering crowd before his exit and awaited such crumbs of intelligence as they could gather before they were threatened or whipped out of hearing distance. Presently, out came the 'gentleman' and the lawyer's clerk. The latter was speaking as he followed the former over the threshold. The gentleman was tall, well-dressed, handsome; but there was a sinister cold look in his quick-glancing, light blue eye, which a keen observer might not have liked. There were no keen observers among the boys and ill-conditioned gaping girls. But they stood too near; inconveniently close; and the gentleman, lifting up his right hand, in which he carried a short riding-whip, dealt one or two sharp blows to the nearest, with a look of savage enjoyment on his face as they moved away whimpering and crying. An instant after, his expression of countenance had changed.

'Here!' said he, drawing out a handful of money, partly silver, partly copper, and throwing it into the midst of them. 'Scramble for it! fight it out, my lads! come this afternoon, at three, to the George, and I'll throw you out some more.' So the boys hurrahed for him as he walked off with the agent's clerk. He chuckled to himself, as over a pleasant thought. 'I'll have some fun with those lads,' he said; 'I'll teach 'em to come prowling and prying about me. I'll tell you what I'll do. I'll make the money so hot in the fire-shovel that it shall burn their fingers. You come and see the faces and the howling. I shall be very glad if you will dine with me at two; and by that time I may have made up my mind respecting the house.'

Mr Jones, the agent's clerk, agreed to come to the George at two, but, somehow, he had a distaste for his entertainer. Mr Jones would not like to have said, even to himself, that a man with a purse full of money, who kept many horses, and spoke familiarly, of noblemen – above all, who thought of taking the White House – could be anything but a gentleman; but still the uneasy wonder as to who this Mr Robinson Higgins could be, filled the clerk's mind long after Mr Higgins, Mr Higgins's servants, and Mr Higgins's stud had taken possession of the White House.

The White House was re-stuccoed (this time of a pale yellow colour) and put into thorough repair by the accommodating and delighted landlord; while his tenant seemed inclined to spend any amount of money on internal decorations, which were showy and effective in their character, enough to make the White House a nine days' wonder to the good people of Barford. The slate-coloured paints became pink and were picked out with gold; the old-fashioned banisters were replaced by newly gilt ones; but, above all, the stables were a sight to be seen. Since the days of a Roman Emperor never was there such provision made for the care, the comfort, and the health of horses. But everyone said it was no wonder, when they were led through Barford, covered up to their eyes, but curving their arched and delicate necks and prancing with short, high steps, in repressed eagerness. Only one groom came with them; yet they required the care of three men. Mr Higgins, however, preferred engaging two lads out of Barford; and Barford highly approved of his preference. Not only was it kind and thoughtful to give employment to the lounging lads themselves, but they were receiving such a training in Mr Higgins's stables as might fit them for Doncaster or Newmarket. The district of Derbyshire in which Barford was situated was too close to Leicestershire not to support a hunt and a pack of hounds. The master of the hounds was a certain Sir Harry Manley, who was *aut* a huntsman *aut nullus*. He measured a man by the 'length of his fork', not by the expression of his countenance, or the shape of his head. But as Sir Harry was wont to observe, there was such a thing as too long a fork, so his approbation was withheld until he had seen a man on horseback; and if his seat there was square and easy, his hand light, and his courage good, Sir Harry hailed him as a brother.

Mr Higgins attended the first meet of the season, not as a subscriber but as an amateur. The Barford huntsmen piqued themselves on their bold riding; and their knowledge of the country came by nature; yet this new strange man, whom nobody knew, was in at the death, sitting on his horse, both well breathed and calm, without a hair turned on the sleek skin of the latter, supremely addressing the old huntsman as he hacked off the tail of the fox; and he, the old man, who was testy even under Sir Harry's slightest rebuke and flew out on any other member of the hunt that dared to utter a word against his sixty years' experience as stable-boy, groom, poacher, and what not – he, old Isaac Wormeley, was meekly listening to the wisdom of this stranger, only now and then giving one of his quick, up-turning, cunning glances, not unlike the sharp o'er-canny looks of the poor deceased Reynard, round whom the hounds were howling, unadmonished by the short whip, which was now tucked into Wormeley's well-worn pocket. When Sir Harry rode into the copse – full of dead brushwood and wet tangled grass – and was followed by the members of the hunt, as one by one they cantered past, Mr Higgins took off his cap and bowed – half deferentially, half insolently – with a lurking smile in the corner of his eye at the discomfited looks of one or two of the laggards. 'A famous run, sir,' said Sir Harry. 'The first time you have hunted in our country; but I hope we shall see you often.'

'I hope to become a member of the hunt, sir,' said Mr Higgins.

'Most happy – proud, I am sure, to receive so daring a rider among us. You took the Cropper-gate, I fancy; while some of our friends here' – scowling at one or two cowards by way of finishing his speech. 'Allow me to introduce myself – master of the hounds.' He fumbled in his waistcoat pocket for the card on which his name was formally inscribed. 'Some of our friends here are kind enough to come home with me to dinner; might I ask for the honour?'

'My name is Higgins,' replied the stranger, bowing low. 'I am only lately come to occupy the White House at Barford, and I have not as yet presented my letters of introduction.'

'Hang it!' replied Sir Harry; 'a man with a seat like yours, and that good brush in your hand, might ride up to any door in the county (I'm a Leicestershire man!) and be a welcome guest. Mr Higgins, I shall be proud to become better acquainted with you over my dinner table.'

Mr Higgins knew pretty well how to improve the acquaintance thus begun. He could sing a good song, tell a good story, and was well up in practical jokes; with plenty of that keen worldly sense, which seems like an instinct in some men, and which in this case taught him on whom he might play off such jokes, with impunity from their resentment, and with a security of applause from the more boisterous, vehement, or prosperous. At the end of twelve months Mr Robinson Higgins was, out-and-out, the most popular member of the Barford hunt; had beaten all the others by a couple of lengths, as his first patron, Sir Harry, observed one evening, when they were just leaving the dinner table of an old hunting squire in the neighbourhood.

'Because, you know,' said Squire Hearn, holding Sir Harry by the button – 'I mean, you see, this young spark is looking sweet upon Catherine; and she's a good girl and will have ten thousand pounds down, the day she's married, by her mother's will; and – excuse me, Sir Harry – but I should not like my girl to throw herself away.'

Though Sir Harry had a long ride before him and but the early and short light of a new moon to take it in, his kind heart was so much touched by Squire Hearn's trembling, tearful anxiety, that he stopped and turned back into the dining-room to say, with more asseverations than I care to give:

'My good Squire, I may say, I know that man pretty well by this time; and a better fellow never existed. If I had twenty daughters he should have the pick of them.'

Squire Hearn never thought of asking the grounds for his old friend's opinion of Mr Higgins; it had been given with too much earnestness for any doubts to cross the old man's mind as to the possibility of its not being well founded. Mr Hearn was not a doubter or a thinker or suspicious by nature; it was simply his love for Catherine, his only daughter, that prompted his anxiety in this case; and, after what Sir Harry had said, the old man could totter with an easy mind, though not with very steady legs, into the drawing-room, where his bonny, blushing daughter Catherine and Mr Higgins stood close together on the hearth-rug – he whispering, she listening with downcast eyes. She looked so happy, so like her dead mother had looked when the Squire was a young man, that all his thought was how to please her most. His son and heir was about to be married and bring his wife to live with the Squire; Barford and the White House were not distant an hour's ride; and, even as these thoughts passed through his mind, he asked Mr Higgins if he could stay all night – the young moon was already set – the roads would be dark – and Catherine looked up with a pretty anxiety, which, however, had not much doubt in it, for the answer.

With every encouragement of this kind from the old Squire, it took everybody rather by surprise when, one morning, it was discovered that Miss Catherine Hearn was missing; and when, according to the usual fashion in such cases, a note was found, saying that she had eloped with 'the man of her heart' and gone to Gretna Green, no one could imagine why she could not quietly have stopped at home and been married in the parish church. She had always been a romantic, sentimental girl; very pretty and very affectionate and very much spoiled and very much wanting in common sense. Her indulgent father was deeply hurt at this want of confidence in his never-varying affection; but when his son came, hot with indignation from the Baronet's (his future father-in-law's house, where every form of law and of ceremony was to accompany his own impending marriage), Squire Hearn pleaded the cause of the young couple with imploring cogency, and protested that it was a piece of spirit in his daughter, which he admired and was proud of. However, it ended with Mr Nathaniel Hearn's declaring that he and his wife would have nothing to do with his sister and her husband. 'Wait till you've seen him, Nat!' said the old Squire, trembling with his distressful anticipations of family discord. 'He's an excuse for any girl. Only ask Sir Harry's opinion of him.' 'Confound Sir Harry! So that a man sits his horse well,

Sir Harry cares nothing about anything else. Who is this man – this fellow? Where does he come from? What are his means? Who are his family?'

'He comes from the south – Surrey or Somersetshire, I forget which; and he pays his way well and liberally. There's not a tradesman in Barford but says he cares no more for money than for water; he spends like a prince, Nat. I don't know who his family are, but he seals with a coat of arms, which may tell you if you want to know – and he goes regularly to collect his rents from his estates in the south. Oh, Nat! if you would but be friendly, I should be as well pleased with Kitty's marriage as any father in the county.'

Mr Nathaniel Hearn gloomed and muttered an oath or two to himself. The poor old father was reaping the consequences of his weak indulgence to his two children. Mr and Mrs Nathaniel Hearn kept apart from Catherine and her husband; and Squire Hearn durst never ask them to Levison Hall, though it was his own house. Indeed, he stole away as if he were a culprit whenever he went to visit the White House; and if he passed a night there, he was fain to equivocate when he returned home the next day; an equivocation which was well interpreted by the surly, proud Nathaniel. But the young Mr and Mrs Hearn were the only people who did not visit at the White House. Mr and Mrs Higgins were decidedly more popular than their brother and sister-in-law. She made a very pretty, sweet-tempered hostess and her education had not been such as to make her intolerant of any want of refinement in the associates who gathered round her husband. She had gentle smiles for townspeople as well as county people; and unconsciously played an admirable second in her husband's project of making himself universally popular.

But there is someone to make ill-natured remarks and draw ill-natured conclusions from very simple premises, in every place; and in Barford this bird of ill omen was a Miss Pratt. She did not hunt – so Mr Higgins's admirable riding did not call out her admiration. She did not drink – so the well-selected wines, so lavishly dispensed among his guests, could never mollify Miss Pratt. She could not bear comic songs or buffo stories – so, in that way, her approbation was impregnable. And these three secrets of popularity constituted Mr Higgins's great charm. Miss Pratt sat and watched. Her face looked immovably grave at the end of any of Mr Higgins's best stories; but there was a keen, needle-like glance of her unwinking little eyes, which Mr Higgins felt rather than saw and which made him shiver, even on a hot day, when it fell upon him. Miss Pratt was a dissenter, and, to propitiate this female Mordecai, Mr Higgins asked the dissenting minister whose services she attended to dinner; kept himself and his company in good order; gave a handsome donation to the poor of the chapel. All in vain – Miss Pratt stirred not a muscle more of her face towards graciousness; and Mr Higgins was conscious that, in spite of all his open efforts to captivate Mr Davis, there was a secret influence on the other side, throwing in doubts and suspicions and evil interpretations of all he said or did. Miss Pratt, the little, plain old maid, living on eighty pounds a year, was the thorn in the popular Mr Higgins's side, although she had never spoken one uncivil word to him; indeed, on the contrary, had treated him with a stiff and elaborate civility.

The thorn – the grief to Mrs Higgins was this. They had no children! Oh! how she would stand and envy the careless, busy motion of half a dozen children; and then, when observed, move on with a deep, deep sigh of yearning regret. But it was as well.

It was noticed that Mr Higgins was remarkably careful of his health. He ate, drank, took exercise, rested, by some secret rules of his own; occasionally bursting into an excess, it is true, but only on rare occasions – such as when he returned from visiting his estates in the south and collecting his rents. That unusual exertion and fatigue – for there were no stage-coaches within forty miles of Barford and he, like most country gentlemen of that day, would have preferred riding if there had been – seemed to require some strange excess to compensate for it; and rumours went through the town that he shut himself up and drank enormously for some days after his return. But no one was admitted to these orgies.

One day – they remembered it well afterwards – the hounds met not far from the town; and the fox was found in a part of the wild heath, which was beginning to be enclosed by a few of the more wealthy townspeople, who were desirous of building themselves houses rather more in the country than those they had hitherto lived in. Among these, the principal was a Mr Dudgeon, the attorney of Barford, and the agent for all the county families about. The firm of Dudgeon had managed the leases, the marriage settlements and the wills of the neighbourhood for generations. Mr Dudgeon's father had the responsibility of collecting the landowners' rents just as the present Mr Dudgeon had at the time of which I speak: and as his son and his son's son have done since. Their business was an hereditary estate to them; and with something of the old feudal feeling was mixed a kind of proud humility at their position towards the squires whose family secrets they had mastered and the mysteries of whose fortunes and estates were better known to the Messrs Dudgeon than to themselves.

Mr John Dudgeon had built himself a house on Wildbury Heath; a mere cottage as he called it: but though only two stories high, it spread out far and wide and workpeople from Derby had been sent for on purpose to make the inside as complete as possible. The gardens, too, were exquisite in arrangement, if not very extensive; and not a flower was grown in them but of the rarest species. It must have been somewhat of a mortification to the owner of this dainty place when, on the day of which I speak, the fox, after a long race, during which he had described a circle of many miles, took refuge in the garden; but Mr Dudgeon put a good face on the matter when a gentleman hunter, with the careless insolence of the squires of those days and that place, rode across the velvet lawn and, tapping at the window of the dining-room with his whip-handle, asked permission – no! that is not it – rather, informed Mr Dudgeon of their intention – to enter his garden in a body and have the fox unearthed. Mr Dudgeon compelled himself to smile assent with the grace of a masculine Griselda; and then he hastily gave orders to have all that the house afforded of provision set out for luncheon, guessing rightly enough that a six-hour run would give even homely fare an acceptable welcome. He bore without wincing the entrance of the dirty boots into his exquisitely clean rooms; he only felt grateful for the care with which Mr Higgins strode about, laboriously and noiselessly moving on the tips of his toes, as he reconnoitred the rooms with a curious eye.

'I'm going to build a house myself, Dudgeon; and, upon my word, I don't think I could take a better model than yours.'

'Oh! my poor cottage would be too small to afford any hints for such a house as you would wish to build, Mr Higgins,' replied Mr Dudgeon, gently rubbing his hands nevertheless at the compliment.

'Not at all! not at all! Let me see. You have dining-room, drawing-room' – he hesitated and Mr Dudgeon filled up the blank as he expected.

'Four sitting-rooms and the bedrooms. But allow me to show you over the house. I confess I took some pains in arranging it and, though far smaller than what you would require, it may, nevertheless, afford you some hints.'

So they left the eating gentlemen with their mouths and their plates quite full, and the scent of the fox overpowering that of the hasty rashers of ham; and they carefully inspected all the ground-floor rooms. Then Mr Dudgeon said: 'If you are not tired, Mr Higgins – it is rather my hobby, so you must pull me up if you are – we will go upstairs, and I will show you my sanctum.'

Mr Dudgeon's sanctum was the centre room, over the porch, which formed a balcony, and which was carefully filled with choice flowers in pots. Inside, there were all kinds of elegant contrivances for hiding the real strength of all the boxes and chests required by the particular nature of Mr Dudgeon's business: for although his office was in Barford, he kept (as he informed Mr Higgins) what was the most valuable here, as being safer than an office which was locked up and left every night. But, as Mr Higgins reminded him with a sly poke in the side, when next they met, his own house was not over-secure. A fortnight after the gentlemen of the Barford hunt lunched there, Mr Dudgeon's strong-box – in his sanctum upstairs, with the mysterious spring-bolt to the window invented by himself and the secret of which was only known to the inventor and a few of his most intimate friends, to whom he had proudly shown it – this strong-box, containing the collected Christmas rents of half a dozen landlords (there was then no bank nearer than Derby), was rifled; and the secretly rich Mr Dudgeon had to stop his agent in his purchases of paintings by Flemish artists, because the money was required to make good the missing rents.

The Dogberries and Verges of those days were quite incapable of obtaining any clue to the robber or robbers; and though one or two vagrants were taken up and brought before Mr Dunover and Mr Higgins, the magistrates who usually attended in the court-room at Barford, there was no evidence brought against them and after a couple of nights' durance in the lock-ups they were set at liberty. But it became a standing joke with Mr Higgins to ask Mr Dudgeon, from time to time, whether he could recommend him a place of safety for his valuables; or, if he had made any more inventions lately for securing houses from robbers.

About two years after this time – about seven years after Mr Higgins had been married – one Tuesday evening, Mr Davis was sitting reading the news in the coffee-room of the George Inn. He belonged to a club of gentlemen who met there occasionally to play at whist, to read what few newspapers and magazines were published in those days, to chat about the market at Derby, and prices all over the country. This Tuesday night it was a black frost; and few people were in the room. Mr Davis was anxious to finish an article in the *Gentleman's Magazine*; indeed, he was making extracts from it, intending to answer it, and yet unable with his small income to purchase a copy. So he stayed late; it was past nine, and at ten o'clock the room was closed. But while he wrote, Mr Higgins came in. He was pale and haggard with cold. Mr Davis, who had had for some time sole possession of the fire, moved politely on one side and handed to the newcomer the sole London newspaper which the room afforded. Mr Higgins accepted it, and made some remark on the intense coldness of the weather; but

Mr Davis was too full of his article, and intended reply, to fall into conversation readily. Mr Higgins hitched his chair nearer to the fire and put his feet on the fender, giving an audible shudder. He put the newspaper on one end of the table near him and sat gazing into the red embers of the fire, crouching down over them as if his very marrow were chilled. At length he said: 'There is no account of the murder at Bath in that paper?'

Mr Davis, who had finished taking his notes and was preparing to go, stopped short and asked: 'Has there been a murder at Bath? No! I have not seen anything of it – who was murdered?'

'Oh! it was a shocking, terrible murder!' said Mr Higgins, not raising his look from the fire, but gazing on with his dilated eyes till the whites were seen all round them. 'A terrible, terrible murder! I wonder what will become of the murderer? I can fancy the red glowing centre of that fire – look and see how infinitely distant it seems and how the distance magnifies it into something awful and unquenchable.'

'My dear sir, you are feverish; how you shake and shiver!' said Mr Davis, thinking privately that his companion had symptoms of fever and that he was wandering in his mind.

'Oh, no!' said Mr Higgins. 'I am not feverish. It is the night which is so cold.' And for a time he talked with Mr Davis about the article in the *Gentleman's Magazine*, for he was rather a reader himself and could take more interest in Mr Davis's pursuits than most of the people at Barford. At length it drew near to ten and Mr Davis rose up to go home to his lodgings.

'No, Davis, don't go. I want you here. We will have a bottle of port together and that will put Saunders into good humour. I want to tell you about this murder,' he continued, dropping his voice and speaking hoarse and low. 'She was an old woman and he killed her, sitting reading her Bible by her own fireside!' He looked at Mr Davis with a strange searching gaze, as if trying to find some sympathy in the horror which the idea presented to him.

'Who do you mean, my dear sir? What is this murder you are so full of? No one has been murdered here.'

'No, you fool! I tell you it was in Bath!' said Mr Higgins, with sudden passion; and then, calming himself to most velvet-smoothness of manner, he laid his hand on Mr Davis's knee, there, as they sat by the fire, and gently detaining him, began the narration of the crime he was so full of; but his voice and manner were constrained to a stony quietude; he never looked in Mr Davis's face; once or twice, as Mr Davis remembered afterwards, his grip tightened like a compressing vice.

'She lived in a small house in a quiet, old-fashioned street, she and her maid. People said she was a good old woman; but for all that, she hoarded and hoarded and never gave to the poor. Mr Davis, it is wicked not to give to the poor – wicked – wicked, is it not? I always give to the poor, for once I read in the Bible that "Charity covereth a multitude of sins." The wicked old woman never gave, but hoarded her money and saved and saved. Someone heard of it; I say she threw a temptation in his way and God will punish her for it. And this man – or it might be a woman, who knows? – and this person – heard also that she went to church in the mornings, and her maid in the afternoons; and so – while the maid was at church and the street and the house quite still and the darkness of a winter afternoon coming on – she was nodding over the Bible – and that, mark you! is a sin, and one that God will avenge sooner or later; and a step came in the dusk up the stair and that person I told you of stood in the room. At first he – no! At first, it is supposed – for, you understand, all this is mere guesswork – it is supposed that he asked her civilly enough to give him her money, or to tell him where it was; but the old miser defied him and would not ask for mercy and give up her keys, even when he threatened her, but looked him in the face as if he had been a baby – Oh, God! Mr Davis, I once dreamt when I was a little innocent boy that I should commit a crime like this and I wakened up crying; and my mother comforted me – that is the reason I tremble so now – that and the cold, for it is very, very cold!'

'But did he murder the old lady?' asked Mr Davis. 'I beg your pardon, sir, but I am interested by your story.'

'Yes! he cut her throat; and there she lies yet in her quiet little parlour, with her face upturned and all ghastly white, in the middle of a pool of blood. Mr Davis, this wine is no better than water; I must have some brandy!'

Mr Davis was horror-struck by the story, which seemed to have fascinated him as much as it had done his companion.

'Have they got any clue to the murderer?' said he. Mr Higgins drank down half a tumbler of raw brandy before he answered.

'No! no clue whatever. They will never be able to discover him; and I should not wonder, Mr Davis – I should not wonder if he repented after all, and did bitter penance for his crime; and if so – will there be mercy for him at the last day?'

'God knows!' said Mr Davis, with solemnity. 'It is an awful story,' continued he, rousing himself. 'I hardly like to leave this warm, light room and go out into the darkness after hearing it. But it must be done,' buttoning on his greatcoat. 'I can only say I hope and trust they will find out the murderer and hang him. If you'll take my advice,

Mr Higgins, you'll have your bed warmed, and drink a treacle-posset just the last thing; and, if you'll allow me, I'll send you my answer to Philologus before it goes up to old Urban.'

The next morning, Mr Davis went to call on Miss Pratt, who was not very well; and, by way of being agreeable and entertaining, he related to her all he had heard the night before about the murder at Bath; and really he made a very pretty connected story out of it and interested Miss Pratt very much in the fate of the old lady – partly because of a similarity in their situations; for she also privately hoarded money and had but one servant and stopped at home alone on Sunday afternoons to allow her servant to go to church.

'And when did all this happen?' she asked.

'I don't know if Mr Higgins named the day; and yet I think it must have been on this very last Sunday.'

'And today is Wednesday. Ill news travels fast.'

'Yes, Mr Higgins thought it might have been in the London newspaper.'

'That it could never be. Where did Mr Higgins learn all about it?'

'I don't know; I did not ask. I think he only came home yesterday: he had been south to collect his rents, somebody said.' Miss Pratt grunted. She used to vent her dislike and suspicions of Mr Higgins in a grunt whenever his name was mentioned.

'Well, I shan't see you for some days. Godfrey Merton has asked me to go and stay with him and his sister; and I think it will do me good. Besides,' added she, 'these winter evenings – and these murderers at large in the country – I don't quite like living with only Peggy to call to in case of need.'

Miss Pratt went to stay with her cousin, Mr Merton. He was an active magistrate and enjoyed his reputation as such. One day he came in, having just received his letters.

'Bad account of the morals of your little town here, Jessy!' said he, touching one of his letters. 'You've either a murderer among you or some friend of a murderer. Here's a poor old lady at Bath had her throat cut last Sunday week; and I've a letter from the Home Office, asking to lend them "my very efficient aid", as they are pleased to call it, towards finding out the culprit. It seems he must have been thirsty and of a comfortable jolly turn; for before going to his horrid work he tapped a barrel of ginger wine the old lady had set by to work; and he wrapped the spigot round with a piece of a letter taken out of his pocket, as may be supposed; and this piece of a letter was found afterwards; there are only these letters on the outside, "—ns, Esq., — arford, —egworth", which someone has ingeniously made out to mean

Barford, near Kegworth. On the other side there is some allusion to a racehorse, I conjecture, though the name is singular enough: "Church-and-King-and-down-with-the-Rump".'

Miss Pratt caught at this name immediately; it had hurt her feelings as a dissenter only a few months ago and she remembered it well.

'Mr Nat Hearn has – or had (as I am speaking in the witness-box, as it were, I must take care of my tenses), a horse with that ridiculous name.'

'Mr Nat Hearn,' repeated Mr Merton, making a note of the intelligence; then he referred to his letter from the Home Office again.

'There is also a piece of a small key, broken in the futile attempt to open a desk – well, well. Nothing more of consequence. The letter is what we must rely upon.'

'Mr Davis said that Mr Higgins told him – ' Miss Pratt began.

'Higgins!' exclaimed Mr Merton, ' —ns. Is it Higgins, the blustering fellow that ran away with Nat Hearn's sister?'

'Yes!' said Miss Pratt. 'But though he has never been a favourite of mine – '

' —ns,' repeated Mr Merton. 'It is too horrible to think of; a member of the hunt – kind old Squire Hearn's son-in-law! Who else have you in Barford with names that end in *ns?*'

'There's Jackson and Higginson and Blenkinsop and Davis and Jones. Cousin! One thing strikes me – how did Mr Higgins know all about it to tell Mr Davis on Tuesday what had happened on Sunday afternoon?'

There is no need to add much more. Those curious in lives of the highwayman may find the name of Higgins as conspicuous among those annals as that of Claude Duval. Kate Hearn's husband collected his rents on the highway, like many another 'gentleman' of the day; but, having been unlucky in one or two of his adventures and hearing exaggerated accounts of the hoarded wealth of the old lady at Bath, he was led on from robbery to murder and was hung for his crime at Derby in 1775.

He had not been an unkind husband; and his poor wife took lodgings in Derby to be near him in his last moments – his awful last moments. Her old father went with her everywhere but into her husband's cell; and wrung her heart by constantly accusing himself of having promoted her marriage with a man of whom he knew so little. He abdicated his squireship in favour of his son Nathaniel. Nat was prosperous and the helpless, silly father could be of no use to him; but to his widowed daughter the foolish, fond old man was all in all; her knight, her protector, her companion – her most faithful, loving companion. Only he ever declined assuming the office of her counsellor – shaking his head sadly and saying: 'Ah! Kate, Kate! if I had had more wisdom to have advised thee better, thou need'st not have been an exile here in Brussels, shrinking from the sight of every English person as if they knew thy story.'

I saw the White House not a month ago; it was to let, perhaps for the twentieth time since Mr Higgins occupied it; but still the tradition goes in Barford that once upon a time a highwayman lived there, and amassed untold treasures; and that the ill-gotten wealth yet remains walled up in some unknown concealed chamber; but in what part of the house no one knows.

Will any of you become tenants and try to find out this mysterious closet? I can furnish the exact address to any applicant who wishes for it.

The Story of Mary Ancel

WILLIAM MAKEPEACE THACKERAY 1811–1863

'GO MY NEPHEW,' said old Father Jacob to me, 'and complete the studies at Strasbourg: heaven surely hath ordained thee for thy ministry in these times of trouble and my excellent friend Schneider will work out the divine intention.'

Schneider was an old college friend of Uncle Jacob's, was a Benedictine monk and a man famous for his learning; as for me, I was at that time my uncle's chorister, clerk and sacristan; I swept the church, chanted the prayers with my shrill treble and swung the great copper incense-pot on Sundays and feasts; and I toiled over the Fathers for the other days of the week.

The old gentleman said that my progress was prodigious and, without vanity, I believe he was right, for I then verily considered that praying was my vocation, and not fighting, as I have found since.

You would hardly conceive [said the Captain, swearing a great oath] how devout and how learned I was in those days; I talked Latin faster than my own beautiful *patois* of Alsatian French; I could utterly overthrow in argument every Protestant (heretics, we called them) parson in the neighbourhood and there was a confounded sprinkling of these unbelievers in our part of the country. I prayed half a dozen times a day; I fasted thrice in a week and, as for penance, I used to scourge my little sides till they had no more feeling than a peg-top; such was the godly life I led at my Uncle Jacob's in the village of Steinbach.

Our family had long dwelt in this place and a large farm and a pleasant house were then in the possession of another uncle – Uncle Edward. He was the youngest of the three sons of my grandfather; but Jacob, the elder, had shown a decided vocation for the Church from, I believe, the age of three, and now was by no means tired of it at sixty. My father, who was to have inherited the paternal property, was, as I hear, a terrible scamp and scapegrace, quarrelled with his family and disappeared altogether, living and dying at Paris; so far as we knew through my mother, who came, poor woman, with me, a child of six months, on her bosom, was refused all shelter by my grandfather, but was housed and kindly cared for by my good Uncle Jacob.

Here she lived for about seven years and the old gentleman, when she died, wept over her grave a great deal more than I did, who was then too young to mind anything but toys or sweetmeats.

During this time my grandfather was likewise carried off: he left, as I said, the property to his son Edward, with a small proviso in his will that something should be done for me, his grandson.

Edward was himself a widower, with one daughter, Mary, about three years older than I, and certainly she was the dearest little treasure with which Providence ever blessed a miserly father; by the time she was fifteen, five farmers, three lawyers, twelve Protestant parsons and a lieutenant of Dragoons had made her offers: it must not be denied that she was an heiress as well as a beauty, which, perhaps, had something to do with the love of these gentlemen. However, Mary declared that she intended to live single, turned away her lovers one after another and devoted herself to the care of her father.

Uncle Jacob was as fond of her as he was of any saint or martyr. As for me, at the mature age of twelve I had made a kind of divinity of her and when we sang 'Ave Maria' on Sundays I could not refrain from turning to her, where she knelt, blushing and praying and looking like an angel, as she was. Besides her beauty, Mary had a thousand good qualities: she could play better on the harpsichord, she could dance more lightly, she could make better pickles and puddings, than any girl in Alsace; there was not a want or a fancy of the old hunk's her father or a wish of mine or my uncle's that she would not gratify if she could; as for herself, the sweet soul had neither wants nor wishes except to see us happy.

I could talk to you for a year of all the pretty kindnesses that she would do for me; how, when she found me of early mornings among my books, her presence 'would cast a light upon the day'; how she used to smooth and fold my little surplice and embroider me caps and gowns for high-feast days; how she used to bring flowers for the altar, and who could deck it so well as she? But sentiment does not come glibly from under a grizzled moustache, so I will drop it, if you please.

Amongst other favours she showed me, Mary used to be particularly fond of kissing me: it was a thing I did not so much value in those days; but I found that the more I grew alive to the extent of the benefit, the less she would condescend to confer it on me: till, at last, when I was about fourteen, she discontinued it altogether, of her own wish at least; only sometimes I used to be rude and take what she had now become so mighty unwilling to give.

I was engaged in a contest of this sort one day with Mary, when, just as I was about to carry off a kiss from her cheek, I was saluted with a staggering slap on my own, which was bestowed by Uncle Edward and sent me reeling some yards down the garden.

The old gentleman, whose tongue was generally as close as his purse, now poured forth a flood of eloquence which quite astonished me. I did not think that so much was to be said on any subject as he managed to utter on one, and that was abuse of me; he stamped, he swore, he screamed; and then, from complimenting me, he turned to Mary and saluted her in a manner equally forcible and significant: she, who was very much frightened at the commencement of the scene, grew very angry at the coarse words he used and the wicked motives he imputed to her.

'The child is but fourteen,' she said; 'he is your own nephew, and a candidate for holy orders. Father, it is a shame that you should thus speak of me, your daughter, or of one of his holy profession.'

I did not particularly admire this speech myself, but it had an effect on my uncle and was the cause of the words with which this history commences. The old gentleman persuaded his brother that I must be sent to Strasbourg and there kept until my studies for the Church were concluded. I was furnished with a letter to my uncle's old college chum, Professor Schneider, who was to instruct me in theology and Greek.

I was not sorry to see Strasbourg, of the wonders of which I had heard so much; but felt very loth as the time drew near when I must quit my pretty cousin, and my good old uncle. Mary and I managed, however, a parting walk, in which a number of tender things were said on both sides. I am told that you Englishmen consider it cowardly to cry; as for me, I wept and roared incessantly: when Mary squeezed me, for the last time, the tears came out of me as if I had been neither more nor less than a great wet sponge. My cousin's eyes were stoically dry; her ladyship had a part to play, and it would have been wrong for her to be in love with a young chit of fourteen – so she carried herself with perfect coolness, as if there was nothing the matter. I should not have known that she cared for me, had it not been for a letter which she wrote me a month afterwards – *then*, nobody was by and the consequence was that the letter was half washed away with her weeping: if she had used a watering-pot the thing could not have been better done.

Well, I arrived at Strasbourg – a dismal, old-fashioned, rickety town in those days – and straightway presented myself and letter at Schneider's door; over it was written:

COMITÉ DE SALUT PUBLIC

Would you believe it? I was so ignorant a young fellow, that I had no idea of the meaning of the words; however, I entered the citizen's room without fear and sat down in his antechamber until I could be admitted to see him.

Here I found very few indications of his reverence's profession; the walls were hung round with portraits of Robespierre, Marat and the like; a great bust of Mirabeau, mutilated, with the word *Traître* underneath; lists and Republican proclamations, tobacco-pipes and firearms. At a deal table, stained with grease and wine, sat a gentleman with a huge pigtail dangling down to that part of his person which immediately succeeds his back, and a red nightcap containing a tricolour cockade as large as a pancake. He was smoking a short pipe, reading a little book and sobbing as if his heart would break. Every now and then he would make brief remarks upon the personages or the incidents of his book, by which I could judge that he was a man of the very keenest sensibilities – 'Ah, brigand!' 'O malheureuse!' 'O Charlotte, Charlotte!' The work which this gentleman was perusing is called *The Sorrows of Werther*, it was all the rage in those days and my friend was only following the fashion. I asked him if I could see Father Schneider. He turned towards me a hideous pimpled face, which I dream of now at forty years' distance.

'Father who?' said he. 'Do you imagine that Citizen Schneider has not thrown off the absurd mummery of priesthood? If you were a little older you would go to prison for calling him Father Schneider – many a man has died for less!' And he pointed to a picture of a guillotine, which was hanging in the room.

I was in amazement.

'What is he? Is he not a teacher of Greek, an abbé, a monk until monasteries were abolished, the learned editor of the songs of Anacreon?'

'He *was* all this,' replied my grim friend; 'he is now a Member of the Committee of Public Safety and would think no more of ordering your head off than drinking this tumbler of beer.'

He swallowed, himself, the frothy liquid and then proceeded to give me the history of the man to whom my uncle had sent me for instruction.

Schneider was born in 1756: was a student at Wurzburg and afterwards entered a convent, where he remained nine years. He here became distinguished for his learning and his talents as a preacher and became chaplain to Duke Charles of Württemburg. The doctrines of the Illuminati began about this time to spread in Germany and Schneider speedily joined the sect. He had been a professor of Greek at Cologne; and being compelled, on account of his irregularity, to give up his chair, he came to Strasbourg at the commencement of the French Revolution and acted for some time a principal part as a revolutionary agent at Strasbourg.

['Heaven knows what would have happened to me had I continued long under his tuition!' said the Captain. 'I owe the preservation of my morals entirely to my entering the army. A man, sir, who is a soldier, has very little time to be wicked; except in the case of a siege and the sack of a town, when a little licence can offend nobody.']

By the time that my friend had concluded Schneider's biography, we had grown tolerably intimate and I imparted to him (with that ingenuousness so remarkable in youth) my whole history – my course of studies, my pleasant country life, the names and qualities of my dear relations and my occupations in the vestry before religion was abolished by order of the Republic. In the course of my speech I recurred so often to the name of my cousin Mary, that the gentleman could not fail to perceive what a tender place she had in my heart.

Then we reverted to *The Sorrows of Werther* and discussed the merits of that sublime performance. Although I had before felt some misgivings about my new acquaintance, my heart now quite yearned towards him. He talked about love and sentiment in a manner which made me recollect that I was in love myself; and you know that when a man is in that condition, his taste is not very refined and maudlin trash of prose or verse appearing sublime to him, provided it correspond, in some degree, with his own situation.

'Candid youth!' cried my unknown, 'I love to hear thy innocent story and look on thy guileless face. There is, alas! so much of the contrary in this world, so much terror and crime and blood, that we who mingle with it are only too glad to forget it. Would that we could shake off our cares as men and be boys, as thou art, again!'

Here my friend began to weep once more and fondly shook my hand. I blessed my stars that I had, at the very outset of my career, met with one who was so likely to aid me. What a slanderous world it is, thought I; the people in our village call these Republicans wicked and bloody-minded; a lamb could not be more tender than this sentimental bottle-nosed gentleman! The worthy man then gave me to understand that he held a place under Government. I was busy in endeavouring to discover what his situation might be, when the door of the next apartment opened and Schneider made his appearance.

At first he did not notice me, but he advanced to my new acquaintance and gave him, to my astonishment, something very like a blow.

'You drunken talking fool,' he said, 'you are always after your time. Fourteen people are cooling their heels yonder, waiting until you have finished your beer and your sentiment!'

My friend slunk muttering out of the room.

'That fellow,' said Schneider, turning to me, 'is our public executioner: a capital hand too if he would but keep decent time; but the brute is always drunk and blubbering over *The Sorrows of Werther*!'

I know not whether it was his old friendship for my uncle, or my proper merits, which won the heart of this the sternest ruffian of Robespierre's crew; but certain it is, that he became strangely attached to me and kept me constantly about his person. As for the priesthood and the Greek, they were of course very soon out of the question. The Austrians were on our frontier; every day brought us accounts of battles won; and the youth of Strasbourg and of all France, indeed, were bursting with military ardour. As for me, I shared the general mania, and speedily mounted a cockade as large as that of my friend the executioner.

The occupations of this worthy were unremitting. St Just, who had come down from Paris to preside over our town, executed the laws and the aristocrats with terrible punctuality; and Schneider used to make country excursions in search of offenders with this fellow, as a provost-marshal, at his back. In the meantime, having entered my sixteenth year, and being a proper lad of my age, I had joined a regiment of cavalry and was scampering now after the Austrians who menaced us, and now threatening the *émigrés*, who were banded at Coblentz. My love for my dear cousin increased as my whiskers grew; and when I was scarcely seventeen, I thought myself man enough to marry her and to cut the throat of anyone who should venture to say me nay.

I need not tell you that during my absence at Strasbourg, great changes had occurred in our little village and somewhat of the revolutionary rage had penetrated even to that quiet and distant place. The hideous 'Fête of the Supreme Being' had been celebrated at Paris; the practice of our ancient religion was forbidden; its professors were most of them in concealment or in exile or had expiated on the scaffold their crime of Christianity. In our poor village my uncle's church was closed and he, himself, an inmate in his brother's house, only owing his safety to his great popularity among his former flock and the influence of Edward Ancel.

The latter had taken in the Revolution a somewhat prominent part; that is, he had engaged in many contracts for the army, attended the clubs regularly, corresponded with the authorities of his department and was loud in his denunciations of the aristocrats in the neighbour-hood. But owing, perhaps, to the German origin of the peasantry and their quiet and rustic lives, the revolutionary fury which prevailed in the cities had hardly reached the country people. The occasional visit of a commissary from Paris or Strasbourg served to keep the flame alive and to remind the rural swains of the existence of a Republic in France.

Now and then, when I could gain a week's leave of absence, I returned to the village, and was received with tolerable politeness by my uncle and with a warmer feeling by his daughter.

I won't describe to you the progress of our love or the wrath of my Uncle Edward, when he discovered that it still continued. He swore and he stormed; he locked Mary into her chamber and vowed that he would withdraw the allowance he made me, if ever I ventured near her. His daughter, he said, should never marry a hopeless penniless subaltern; and Mary declared she would not marry without his consent. What had I to do? – to despair and to leave her. As for my poor Uncle Jacob, he had no counsel to give me and, indeed, no spirit left: his little church was turned into a stable, his surplice torn off his shoulders and he was only too lucky in keeping *his head* on them. A bright thought struck him: suppose you were to ask the advice of my old friend Schneider regarding this marriage? he has ever been your friend and may help you now as before.

[Here the Captain paused a little.] You may fancy [continued he] that it was droll advice of a reverend gentleman like Uncle Jacob to counsel me in this manner, and to bid me make friends with such a murderous cut-throat as Schneider; but we thought nothing of it in those days; guillotining was as common as dancing and a man was only thought the better patriot the more severe he might be. I departed forthwith to Strasbourg and requested the vote and interest of the Citizen President of the Committee of Public Safety.

He heard me with a great deal of attention. I described to him most minutely the circumstances, expatiated upon the charms of my dear Mary and painted her to him from head to foot. Her golden hair and her bright blushing cheeks, her slim waist and her tripping tiny feet; and furthermore, I added that she possessed a fortune which ought, by rights, to be mine, but for the miserly old father. 'Curse him for an aristocrat!' concluded I, in my wrath.

As I had been discoursing about Mary's charms Schneider listened with much complacency and attention: when I spoke about her fortune, his interest redoubled; and when I called her father an aristocrat, the worthy ex-Jesuit gave a grin of satisfaction, which was really quite terrible. O fool that I was to trust him so far!

The very same evening an officer waited upon me with the following note from St Just:

Strasbourg
Fifth year of the Republic one and indivisible, 11 *Ventôse.*

The citizen Pierre Ancel is to leave Strasbourg within two hours and to carry the enclosed despatches to the President of the Committee of Public Safety at Paris. The necessary leave of absence from his military duties has been provided. Instant punishment will follow the slightest delay on the road.

Salut et Fraternité.

There was no choice but obedience and off I sped on my weary way to the capital.

As I was riding out of the Paris gate I met an equipage which I knew to be that of Schneider. The ruffian smiled at me as I passed and wished me a *bon voyage*. Behind his chariot came a curious machine, or cart; a great basket, three stout poles, and several planks, all painted red, were lying in this vehicle, on the top of which was seated my friend with the big cockade. It was the *portable guillotine* which Schneider always carried with him on his travels. The *bourreau* was reading *The Sorrows of Werther* and looked as sentimental as usual.

I will not speak of my voyage in order to relate to you Schneider's. My story had awakened the wretch's curiosity and avarice and he was determined that such a prize as I had shown my cousin to be should fall into no hands but his own. No sooner, in fact, had I quitted his room than he procured the order for my absence and was on the way to Steinbach as I met him.

The journey is not a very long one; and on the next day my Uncle Jacob was surprised by receiving a message that the Citizen Schneider was in the village and was coming to greet his old friend. Old Jacob was in an ecstasy, for he longed to see his college acquaintances and he hoped also that Schneider had come into that part of the country upon the marriage-business of your humble servant. Of course Mary was summoned to give her best dinner and wear her best frock; and her father made ready to receive the new State dignitary.

Schneider's carriage speedily rolled into the courtyard and Schneider's cart followed, as a matter of course. The ex-priest only entered the house; his companion remaining with the horses to dine in private. There was a most touching meeting between him and Jacob. They talked over their old college pranks and successes; they capped Greek verses and quoted ancient epigrams upon their tutors, who had been dead since the Seven Years War. Mary declared it was quite touching to listen to the merry friendly talk of these two old gentlemen.

After the conversation had continued for a time in this strain,

Schneider drew up all of a sudden, and said, quietly, that he had come on particular and unpleasant business – hinting about troublesome times, spies, evil reports and so forth. Then he called Uncle Edward aside and had with him a long and earnest conversation: so Jacob went out and talked with Schneider's 'friend'; they speedily became very intimate, for the ruffian detailed all the circumstances of his interview with me. When he returned into the house, some time after this pleasing colloquy, he found the tone of the society strangely altered. Edward Ancel, pale as a sheet, trembling, and crying for mercy; poor Mary weeping; and Schneider pacing energetically about the apartment, raging about the rights of man, the punishment of traitors and the one and indivisible Republic.

'Jacob,' he said, as my uncle entered the room, 'I was willing, for the sake of our old friendship, to forget the crimes of your brother. He is a known and dangerous aristocrat; he holds communications with the enemy on the frontier; he is a possessor of great and ill-gotten wealth, of which he has plundered the Republic. Do you know,' said he, turning to Edward Ancel, 'where the least of these crimes, or the mere suspicion of them, would lead you?'

Poor Edward sat trembling in his chair and answered not a word. He knew full well how quickly, in this dreadful time, punishment followed suspicion; and though guiltless of all treason with the enemy, perhaps he was aware that, in certain contracts with the Government, he had taken to himself a more than patriotic share of profit.

'Do you know,' resumed Schneider, in a voice of thunder, 'for what purpose I came hither and by whom I am accompanied? I am the administrator of the justice of the Republic. The life of yourself and your family is in my hands: yonder man, who follows me, is the executer of the law; he has rid the nation of hundreds of wretches like yourself. A single word from me and your doom is sealed without hope and your last hour is come. Ho! Grégoire!' shouted he; 'is all ready?'

Grégoire replied from the court, 'I can put up the machine in half an hour. Shall I go down to the village and call the troops and the law people?'

'Do you hear him?' said Schneider. 'The guillotine is in the courtyard; your name is on my list and I have witnesses to prove your crime. Have you a word in your defence?'

Not a word came; the old gentleman was dumb; but his daughter, who did not give way to her terror, spoke for him.

'You cannot, sir,' said she, 'although you say it, *feel* that my father is guilty; you would not have entered our house thus alone if you had thought it. You threaten him in this manner because you have something to ask and to gain from us; what is it, citizen? – tell us how much you value our lives and what sum we are to pay for our ransom?'

'Sum!' said Uncle Jacob; 'he does not want money of us: my old friend, my college chum, does not come hither to drive bargains with anybody belonging to Jacob Ancel!'

'Oh, no, sir, no, you can't want money of us,' shrieked Edward; 'we are the poorest people of the village: ruined, Monsieur Schneider, ruined in the cause of the Republic.'

'Silence, father,' said my brave Mary; 'this man wants a *price:* he comes with his worthy friend yonder, to frighten us, not to kill us. If we die, he cannot touch a sou of our money; it is confiscated to the State. Tell us, sir, what is the price of our safety?'

Schneider smiled, and bowed with perfect politeness.

'Mademoiselle Marie,' he said, 'is perfectly correct in her surmise. I do not want the life of this poor drivelling old man: my intentions are much more peaceable, be assured. It rests entirely with this accomplished young lady (whose spirit I like and whose ready wit I admire), whether the business between us shall be a matter of love or death. I humbly offer myself, Citizen Ancel, as a candidate for the hand of your charming daughter. Her goodness, her beauty and the large fortune which I know you intend to give her, would render her a desirable match for the proudest man in the Republic and, I am sure, would make me the happiest.'

'This must be a jest, Monsieur Schneider,' said Mary, trembling, and turned deadly pale: 'you cannot mean this; you do not know me: you never heard of me until today.'

'Pardon me, belle dame,' replied he; 'your cousin Pierre has often talked to me of your virtues: indeed, it was by his special suggestion that I made the visit.'

'It is false! – it is a base and cowardly lie!' exclaimed she (for the young lady's courage was up). 'Pierre never could have forgotten himself and me so as to offer me to one like you. You come here with a lie on your lips – a lie against my father, to swear his life away, against my dear cousin's honour and love. It is useless now to deny it: Father, I love Pierre Ancel; I will marry no other but him – no, though our last penny were paid to this man as the price of our freedom.'

Schneider's only reply to this was a call to his friend Grégoire.

'Send down to the village for the *maire* and some gendarmes; and tell your people to make ready.'

Shall I *put the machine up?*' shouted he of the sentimental turn.

'You hear him,' said Schneider; 'Marie Ancel, you may decide the fate of your father. I shall return in two hours,' concluded he, 'and will then beg to know your decision.'

The advocate of the rights of man then left the apartment and left the family, as you may imagine, in no very pleasant mood.

Old Uncle Jacob, during the few minutes which had elapsed in the enactment of this strange scene, sat staring wildly at Schneider, and holding Mary on his knees: the poor little thing had fled to him for protection and not to her father, who was kneeling almost senseless at the window, gazing at the executioner and his hideous preparations. The instinct of the poor girl had not failed her; she knew that Jacob was her only protector, if not of her life — heaven bless him! — of her honour. 'Indeed,' the old man said, in a stout voice, 'this must never be, my dearest child – you must not marry this man. If it be the will of Providence that we fall, we shall have at least the thought to console us that we die innocent. Any man in France at a time like this would be a coward and traitor if he feared to meet the fate of the thousand brave and good who have preceded us.'

'Who speaks of dying?' said Edward. 'You, Brother Jacob? – you would not lay that poor girl's head on the scaffold, or mine, your dear brother's. You will not let us die, Mary; you will not, for a small sacrifice, bring your poor old father into danger?'

Mary made no answer. 'Perhaps,' she said, 'there is time for escape: he is to be here again in two hours; in two hours we may be safe, in concealment or on the frontier.' And she rushed to the door of the chamber, as if she would have instantly made the attempt: two gendarmes were at the door. 'We have orders, mademoiselle,' they said, 'to allow no one to leave this apartment until the return of the Citizen Schneider.'

Alas! all hope of escape was impossible. Mary became quite silent for a while; she would not speak to Uncle Jacob; and, in reply to her father's eager questions, she only replied, coldly, that she would answer Schneider when he arrived.

The two dreadful hours passed away only too quickly; and punctual to his appointment, the ex-monk appeared. Directly he entered, Mary advanced to him and said, calmly:

'Sir, I could not deceive you if I said that I freely accepted the offer which you have made me. I will be your wife; but I tell you that I love another; and that it is only to save the lives of those two old men that I yield my person up to you.'

Schneider bowed, and said: 'It is bravely spoken. I like your candour – your beauty. As for the love, excuse me for saying that is a matter of total indifference. I have no doubt, however, that it will come as soon as your feelings in favour of the young gentleman, your cousin, have lost their present fervour. That engaging young man has, at present, another mistress – Glory. He occupies, I believe, the distinguished post of corporal in a regiment which is about to march to – Perpignan, I believe.'

It was, in fact, Monsieur Schneider's polite intention to banish me as far as possible from the place of my birth; and he had, accordingly, selected the Spanish frontier as the spot where I was to display my future military talents.

Mary gave no answer to this sneer: she seemed perfectly resigned and calm. She only said:

'I must make, however, some conditions regarding our proposed marriage, which a gentleman of Monsieur Schneider's gallantry cannot refuse.'

'Pray command me,' replied the husband-elect. 'Fair lady, you know I am your slave.'

'You occupy a distinguished political rank, citizen representative,' she said; 'and we in our village are likewise known and beloved. I should be ashamed, I confess, to wed you here; for our people would wonder at the sudden marriage and imply that it was only by compulsion that I gave you my hand. Let us, then, perform this ceremony at Strasbourg, before the public authorities of the city, with the state and solemnity which befits the marriage of one of the chief men of the Republic.'

'Be it so, madam,' he answered and gallantly proceeded to embrace his bride.

Mary did not shrink from this ruffian's kiss; nor did she reply when poor old Jacob, who sat sobbing in a corner, burst out and said: 'O Mary, Mary, I did not think this of thee!'

'Silence, brother!' hastily said Edward; 'my good son-in-law will pardon your ill-humour.'

I believe Uncle Edward in his heart was pleased at the notion of the marriage; he only cared for money and rank and was little scrupulous as to the means of obtaining them.

The matter then was finally arranged; and presently, after Schneider had transacted the affairs which brought him into that part of the country, the happy bridal party set forward for Strasbourg. Uncles Jacob and Edward occupied the back seat of the old family carriage and the young bride and bridegroom (he was nearly Jacob's age) were seated majestically in front. Mary has often since talked to me of this dreadful journey. She said she wondered at the scrupulous politeness of Schneider during the route; nay, that at another period she could have listened to and admired the singular talent of this man, his great learning, his fancy, and wit; but her mind was bent upon other things and the poor girl firmly thought that her last day was come.

In the meantime, by a blessed chance, I had not ridden three leagues from Strasbourg, when the officer of a passing troop of a cavalry regiment, looking at the beast on which I was mounted, was pleased to take a fancy to it, and ordered me, in an authoritative tone, to descend and to give up my steed for the benefit of the Republic. I represented to him, in vain, that I was a soldier like himself and the bearer of despatches to Paris. 'Fool!' he said; 'do you think they would send despatches by a man who can ride at best but ten leagues a day!' And the honest soldier was so wroth at my supposed duplicity that he not only confiscated my horse, but my saddle and the little portmanteau which contained the chief part of my worldly goods and treasure. I had nothing for it but to dismount and take my way on foot back again to Strasbourg. I arrived there in the evening, determining the next morning to make my case known to the Citizen St Just, and though I made my entry without a sou, I don't know what secret exultation I felt at again being able to return.

The antechamber of such a great man as St Just was, in those days, too crowded for an unprotected boy to obtain an early audience; two days passed before I could obtain a sight of the friend of Robespierre. On the third day, as I was still waiting for the interview, I heard a great bustle in the courtyard of the house and looked out with many others at the spectacle.

A number of men and women, singing Epithalamiums and dressed in some absurd imitation of Roman costume, a troop of soldiers and gendarmerie, and an immense crowd of the *badauds* of Strasbourg, were surrounding a carriage which then entered into the court of the mayoralty. In this carriage, great God! I saw my dear Mary, and Schneider by her side. The truth instantly came upon me: the reason for Schneider's keen enquiries and my abrupt dismissal; but I could not believe that Mary was false to me. I had only to look in her face, white and rigid as marble, to see that this proposed marriage was not with her consent.

I fell back in the crowd as the procession entered the great room in which I was and hid my face in my hands: I could not look upon her as the wife of another – upon her so long loved and truly – the saint of my childhood – the pride and hope of my youth – torn from me for ever and delivered over to the unholy arms of the murderer who stood before me.

The door of St Just's private apartment opened and he took his seat at the table of mayoralty just as Schneider and his *cortège* arrived before it.

Schneider then said that he came in before the authorities of the Republic to espouse the citoyenne Marie Ancel.

'Is she a minor?' asked St Just.

'She is a minor, but her father is here to give her away.'

'I am here,' said Uncle Edward, coming eagerly forward and bowing. 'Edward Ancel, so please you, citizen representative. The worthy Citizen Schneider has done me the honour of marrying into my family.'

'But my father has not told you the terms of the marriage,' said Mary, interrupting him, in a loud, clear voice.

Here Schneider seized her hand and endeavoured to prevent her from speaking. Her father turned pale and cried, 'Stop, Mary, stop! For heaven's sake, remember your poor old father's danger.'

'Sir, may I speak?'

'Let the young woman speak,' said St Just, 'if she have a desire to talk.' He did not suspect what would be the purport of her story.

'Sir,' she said, 'two days since the Citizen Schneider entered for the first time our house; and you will fancy that it must be a love of very sudden growth which has brought either him or me before you today. He had heard from a person who is now unhappily not present of my name and of the wealth which my family was said to possess; and hence arose this mad design concerning me. He came into our village with supreme power, an executioner at his heels and the soldiery and authorities of the district entirely under his orders. He threatened my father with death if he refused to give up his daughter; and I, who knew that there was no chance of escape, except here before you, consented to become his wife. My father I know to be innocent, for all his transactions with the State have passed through my hands. Citizen representative, I demand to be freed from this marriage; and I charge Schneider as a traitor to the Republic, as a man who would have murdered an innocent citizen for the sake of private gain.'

During the delivery of this little speech, Uncle Jacob had been sobbing and panting like a broken-winded horse; and when Mary had done, he rushed up to her and kissed her and held her tight in his arms. 'Bless thee, my child!' he cried, 'for having had the courage to speak the truth and shame thy old father and me, who dared not say a word.'

'The girl amazes me,' said Schneider, with a look of astonishment. 'I never saw her, it is true, till yesterday; but I used no force: her father gave her to me with his free consent and she yielded as gladly. Speak Edward Ancel, was it not so?'

'It was, indeed, by my free consent,' said Edward, trembling.

'For shame, brother!' cried old Jacob. 'Sir, it was by Edward's free consent and my niece's; but the guillotine was in the courtyard!

Question Schneider's famulus, the man Grégoire, him who reads *The Sorrows of Werther*.'

Grégoire stepped forward and looked hesitatingly at Schneider as he said, 'I know not what took place within doors; but I was ordered to put up the scaffold without; and I was told to get soldiers and let no one leave the house.'

'Citizen St Just,' cried Schneider, 'you will not allow the testimony of a ruffian like this, of a foolish girl and a mad ex-priest, to weigh against the word of one who has done such service to the Republic: it is a base conspiracy to betray me; the whole family is known to favour the interest of the *émigrés*.'

'And therefore you would marry a member of the family and allow the others to escape: you must make a better defence, Citizen Schneider,' said St Just sternly.

Here I came forward and said that, three days since, I had received an order to quit Strasbourg for Paris immediately after a conversation with Schneider, in which I had asked him his aid in promoting my marriage with my cousin, Mary Ancel; that he had heard from me full accounts regarding her father's wealth; and that he had abruptly caused my dismissal, in order to carry on his scheme against her.

'You are in the uniform of a regiment in this town: who sent you from it?' said St Just.

I produced the order, signed by himself, and the despatches which Schneider had sent me.

'The signature is mine, but the despatches did not come from my office. Can you prove in any way your conversation with Schneider?'

'Why,' said my sentimental friend Grégoire, 'for the matter of that, I can answer that the lad was always talking about this young woman: he told me the whole story himself and many a good laugh I had with Citizen Schneider as we talked about it.'

'The charge against Edward Ancel must be examined into,' said St Just. 'The marriage cannot take place. But if I had ratified it, Mary Ancel, what would then have been your course?'

Mary felt for a moment in her bosom, and said: '*He would have died tonight – I would have stabbed him with this dagger!*'*

The rain was beating down the streets and yet they were thronged; all the world was hastening to the market-place, where the worthy Grégoire was about to perform some of the pleasant duties of his office.

* This reply, and indeed the whole of the story, is historical. An account, by Charles Nodier, in the *Revue de Paris*, suggested it to the writer.

On this occasion, it was not death that he was to inflict; he was only to expose a criminal who was to be sent on afterwards to Paris. St Just had ordered that Schneider should stand for six hours in the public *place* of Strasbourg and then be sent on to the capital, to be dealt with as the authorities might think fit.

The people followed with execrations the villain to his place of punishment; and Grégoire grinned as he fixed up to the post the man whose orders he had obeyed so often – who had delivered over to disgrace and punishment so many who merited it not.

Schneider was left for several hours exposed to the mockery and insults of the mob; he was then, according to his sentence, marched on to Paris, where it is probable that he would have escaped death, but for his own fault. He was left for some time in prison, quite unnoticed, perhaps forgotten: day by day fresh victims were carried to the scaffold and yet the Alsatian tribune remained alive; at last, by the mediation of one of his friends, a long petition was presented to Robespierre, stating his services and his innocence and demanding his freedom. The reply to this was an order for his instant execution: the wretch died in the last days of Robespierre's reign. His comrade, St Just, followed him, as you know; but Edward Ancel had been released before this, for the action of my brave Mary had created a strong feeling in his favour.

'And Mary?' said I.

Here a stout and smiling old lady entered the Captain's little room: she was leaning on the arm of a military-looking man of some forty years and followed by a number of noisy, rosy children.

'This is Mary Ancel,' said the Captain, 'and I am Captain Pierre, and yonder is the Colonel, my son; and you see us here assembled in force, for it is the fête of little Jacob yonder, whose brothers and sisters have all come from their schools to dance at his birthday.'

The Story of the Bagman's Uncle

CHARLES DICKENS 1812–1870

'MY UNCLE, gentlemen,' said the bagman, 'was one of the merriest, pleasantest, cleverest fellows that ever lived. I wish you had known him, gentlemen. On second thoughts, gentlemen, I *don't* wish you had known him, for if you had, you would have been all, by this time, in the ordinary course of nature, if not dead, at all events so near it as to have taken to stopping at home and giving up company: which would have deprived me of the inestimable pleasure of addressing you at this moment. Gentlemen, I wish your fathers and mothers had known my uncle. They would have been amazingly fond of him, especially your respectable mothers; I know they would. If any two of his numerous virtues predominated over the many that adorned his character, I should say they were his mixed punch, and his after-supper song. Excuse my dwelling on these melancholy recollections of departed worth; you won't see a man like my uncle every day in the week.

'I have always considered it a great point in my uncle's character, gentlemen, that he was the intimate friend and companion of Tom Smart, of the great house of Bilson and Slum, Cateaton Street, City. My uncle collected for Tiggin and Welps, but for a long time he went pretty near the same journey as Tom; and the very first night they met, my uncle took a fancy for Tom, and Tom took a fancy for my uncle. They made a bet of a new hat, before they had known each other half an hour, who should brew the best quart of punch and drink it the quickest. My uncle was indeed to have won the making, but Tom Smart beat him in the drinking by about half a salt-spoonful. They took another quart apiece to drink each other's health in, and were staunch friends ever afterwards. There's a destiny in these things, gentlemen; we can't help it.

'In personal appearance, my uncle was a trifle shorter than the middle size; he was a thought stouter, too, than the ordinary run of people and perhaps his face might be a shade redder. He had the jolliest face you ever saw, gentlemen: something like Punch, with a handsomer nose and chin; his eyes were always twinkling and sparkling with good humour; and a smile – not one of your unmeaning, wooden grins, but a real merry, hearty, good-tempered smile – was perpetually on his countenance. He was pitched out of his gig once, and knocked, head first, against a milestone. There he lay, stunned and so cut about the face with some gravel which had been heaped up alongside it, that, to use my uncle's own strong expression, if his mother could have revisited the earth, she wouldn't have known him. Indeed when I come to think of the matter, gentlemen, I feel pretty sure she wouldn't, for she died when my uncle was two years and seven months old and I think it's very likely that even without the gravel, his top-boots would have puzzled the good lady not a little: to say nothing of his jolly red face. However, there he lay, and I have heard my uncle say many a time, that the man said who picked him up that he was smiling as merrily as if he had tumbled out for a treat and that after they had bled him, the first faint glimmerings of returning animation were, his jumping up in bed, bursting out into a loud laugh, kissing the young woman who held the basin, and demanding a mutton chop and a pickled walnut instantly. He was very fond of pickled walnuts, gentlemen. He said he always found that, taken without vinegar, they relished the beer.

'My uncle's great journey was in the fall of the leaf, at which time he collected debts, and took orders, in the north: going from London to Edinburgh, from Edinburgh to Glasgow, from Glasgow back to Edinburgh, and thence to London by the smack. You are to understand that his second visit to Edinburgh was for his own pleasure. He used to go back for a week, just to look up his old friends; and what with breakfasting with this one, lunching with that, dining with a third and supping with another, a pretty tight week he used to make of it. I don't know whether any of you gentlemen ever partook of a real substantial hospitable Scotch breakfast and then went out to a slight lunch of a bushel of oysters, a dozen or so of bottled ale and a noggin or two of whiskey to close up with. If you ever did, you will agree with me that it requires a pretty strong head to go out to dinner and supper afterwards.

'But bless your hearts and eyebrows, all this sort of thing was nothing to my uncle! He was so well seasoned, that it was mere child's play. I have heard him say that he could see the Dundee people out any day and walk home afterwards without staggering; and yet the Dundee people have as strong heads and as strong punch, gentlemen, as you are likely to meet with between the poles. I have heard of a Glasgow man and a Dundee man drinking against each other for fifteen hours at a sitting. They were both suffocated, as nearly as could be ascertained, at the same moment, but with this trifling exception, gentlemen, they were not a bit the worse for it.

'One night, within four-and-twenty hours of the time when he had settled to take shipping for London, my uncle supped at the house of a very old friend of his, a Baillie Mac something and four syllables after it, who lived in the old town of Edinburgh. There were the baillie's wife and the baillie's three daughters and the baillie's grown-up son and three or four stout, bushy-eyebrowed, canty old Scotch fellows, that the baillie had got together to do honour to my uncle and help to make merry. It was a glorious supper. There were kippered salmon and Finnan haddocks and a lamb's head and a haggis – a celebrated Scotch dish, gentlemen, which my uncle used to say always looked to him, when it came to table, very much like a cupid's stomach – and a great many other things besides, that I forget the names of, but very good things notwithstanding. The lassies were pretty and agreeable; the baillie's wife, one of the best creatures that ever lived; and my uncle in thoroughly good cue: the consequence of which was, that the young ladies tittered and giggled and the old lady laughed out loud and the baillie and the other old fellows roared till they were red in the face, the whole mortal time. I don't quite recollect how many tumblers of whiskey toddy each man drank after supper; but this I know, that about one o'clock in the morning, the baillie's grown-up son became insensible while attempting the first verse of 'Willie brewed a peck o' maut'; and he having been, for half an hour before, the only other man visible above the mahogany, it occurred to my uncle that it was almost time to think about going: especially as drinking had set in at seven o'clock, in order that he might get home at a decent hour. But, thinking it might not be quite polite to go just then, my uncle voted himself into the chair, mixed another glass, rose to propose his own health, addressed himself in a neat and complimentary speech, and drank the toast with great enthusiasm. Still nobody woke; so my uncle took a little drop more – neat this time, to prevent the toddy disagreeing with him – and, laying violent hands on his hat, sallied forth into the street.

'It was a wild gusty night when my uncle closed the baillie's door, and setting his hat firmly on his head, to prevent the wind from taking it, thrust his hands into his pockets, and looking upwards, took a short survey of the state of the weather. The clouds were drifting over the moon at their giddiest speed: at one time wholly obscuring her: at another, suffering her to burst forth in full splendour and shed her light on all the objects around: anon, driving over her again with increased velocity and shrouding everything in darkness. "Really, this won't do," said my uncle addressing himself to the weather, as if he felt himself personally offended. "This is not at all the kind of thing for my voyage. It will not do at any price," said my uncle very impressively. Having repeated this several times, he recovered his balance with some difficulty – for he was rather giddy with looking up into the sky so long – and walked merrily on.

'The baillie's house was in the Canongate, and my uncle was going to the other end of Leith Walk, rather better than a mile's journey. On either side of him, there shot up against the dark sky, tall, gaunt, straggling houses, with time-stained fronts, and windows that seemed to have shared the lot of eyes in mortals and to have grown dim and sunken with age. Six, seven, eight stories high, were the houses; story piled above story, as children build with cards – throwing their dark shadows over the roughly paved road and making the dark night darker. A few oil lamps scattered at long distances, but they only served to mark the dirty entrance to some narrow close, or to show where a common stair communicated, by steep and intricate windings, with the various flats above. Glancing at all these things with the air of a man who had seen them too often before to think them worthy of much notice now, my uncle walked up the middle of the street, with a thumb in each waistcoat pocket, indulging, from time to time, in various snatches of song, chanted forth with such good-will and spirit, that the quiet honest folk started from their first sleep and lay trembling in bed till the sound died away in the distance; when, satisfying themselves that it was only some drunken ne'er-do-weel finding his way home, they covered themselves up warm and fell asleep again.

'I am particular in describing how my uncle walked up the middle of the street, with his thumbs in his waistcoat pockets, gentlemen, because, as he often used to say (and with great reason too), there is nothing at all extraordinary in this story, unless you distinctly understand at the beginning that he was not by any means of a marvellous or romantic turn.

'Gentlemen, my uncle walked on with his thumbs in his waistcoat pockets, taking the middle of the street to himself and singing now a verse of a love song and then a verse of a drinking one, and when he was tired of both, whistling melodiously, until he reached the North Bridge, which, at this point, connects the old and new towns of Edinburgh. Here he stopped for a minute, to look at the strange irregular clusters of lights piled one above the other, and twinkling afar off, so high in the air, that they looked like stars, gleaming from the castle walls on the one side, and the Calton Hill on the other, as if they illuminated veritable castles in the air: while the old picturesque town slept heavily on, in gloom and darkness below: its palace and chapel of

Holyrood, guarded day and night, as a friend of my uncle's used to say, by old Arthur's Seat, towering, surly and dark, like some gruff genius, over the ancient city he has watched so long. I say, gentlemen, my uncle stopped here, for a minute, to look about him; and then paying a compliment to the weather, which had a little cleared up, though the moon was sinking, walked on again, as royally as before: keeping the middle of the road with great dignity and looking as if he should very much like to meet with somebody who would dispute possession of it with him. There was nobody at all disposed to contest the point, as it happened; and so, on he went, with his thumbs in his waistcoat pockets, like a lamb.

'When my uncle reached the end of Leith Walk, he had to cross a pretty large piece of waste ground, which separated him from a short street which he had to turn down, to go direct to his lodging. Now, in this piece of waste ground, there was, at that time, an enclosure belonging to some wheelwright, who contracted with the Post Office for the purchase of old worn-out mail-coaches; and my uncle being very fond of coaches, old, young, or middle-aged, all at once took it into his head to step out of his road for no other purpose than to peep between the palings at these mails: about a dozen of which he remembered to have seen, crowded together in a very forlorn and dismantled state, inside. My uncle was a very enthusiastic, emphatic sort of person, gentlemen; so, finding that he could not obtain a good peep between the palings, he got over them and sitting himself quietly down on an old axletree, began to contemplate the mail-coaches with a deal of gravity.

'There might be a dozen of them or there might be more – my uncle was never quite certain on this point and being a man of very scrupulous veracity about numbers didn't like to say – but there they stood, all huddled together in the most desolate condition imaginable. The doors had been torn from their hinges and removed; the linings had been stripped off: only a shred hanging here and there by a rusty nail; the lamps were gone, the poles had long since vanished, the iron-work was rusty, the paint worn away; the wind whistled through the chinks in the bare woodwork; and the rain which had collected on the roofs, fell, drop by drop, into the insides with a hollow and melancholy sound. They were the decaying skeletons of departed mails, and in that lonely place, at that time of night, they looked chill and dismal.

'My uncle rested his head upon his hands and thought of the busy bustling people who had rattled about, years before, in the old coaches and were now as silent and changed: he thought of the numbers of people to whom one of those crazy, mouldering vehicles had borne, night after night, for many years, and through all weathers, the anxiously expected intelligence, the eagerly looked-for remittance, the promised assurance of health and safety, the sudden announcement of sickness and death. The merchant, the lover, the wife, the widow, the mother, the schoolboy, the very child who tottered to the door at the postman's knock – how had they all looked forward to the arrival of the old coach! And where were they all now?

'Gentlemen, my uncle used to say that he thought all this at the time, but I rather suspect he learnt it out of some book afterwards, for he distinctly stated that he fell into a kind of a doze as he sat on the old axletree looking at the decayed mail-coaches and that he was suddenly awakened by some deep church bell striking two. Now, my uncle was never a fast thinker and if he had thought all these things, I am quite certain it would have taken him till full half-past two o'clock, at the very least. I am, therefore, decidedly of opinion, gentlemen, that my uncle fell into a kind of doze, without having thought about anything at all.

'Be this as it may, a church bell struck two. My uncle woke, rubbed his eyes and jumped up in astonishment.

'In one instant after the clock struck two, the whole of this deserted and quiet spot had become a scene of most extraordinary life and animation. The mail-coach doors were on their hinges, the lining was replaced, the iron-work was as good as new, the paint was restored, the lamps were alight, cushions and great coats were on every coach-box, porters were thrusting parcels into every boot, guards were stowing away letter-bags, hostlers were dashing pails of water against the renovated wheels; numbers of men were rushing about, fixing poles into every coach; passengers arrived, portmanteaus were handed up, horses were put to; and, in short, it was perfectly clear that every mail there was to be off directly. Gentlemen, my uncle opened his eyes so wide at all this, that, to the very last moment of his life, he used to wonder how it fell out that he had ever been able to shut 'em again.

' "Now then!" said a voice, as my uncle felt a hand on his shoulder. "You're booked for one inside. You'd better get in."

' "*I* booked!" said my uncle, turning round.

' "Yes, certainly."

'My uncle, gentlemen, could say nothing; he was so very much astonished. The queerest thing of all was, that although there was such a crowd of persons, and although fresh faces were pouring in every moment, there was no telling where they came from; they seemed to start up, in some strange manner, from the ground or the air and disappear in the same way. When a porter had put his luggage in the coach, and received his fare, he turned round and was gone; and before my uncle had well begun to wonder what had become of him, half a dozen fresh ones started up, and staggered along under the weight of parcels which seemed big enough to crush them. The passengers were all dressed so oddly too – large, broad-skirted, laced coats with great cuffs, and no collars; and wigs, gentlemen – great formal wigs and a tie behind. My uncle could make nothing of it.

' "Now, *are* you going to get in?" said the person who had addressed my uncle before. He was dressed as a mail guard, with a wig on his head and most enormous cuffs to his coat, and had a lantern in one hand and a huge blunderbuss in the other, which he was going to stow away in his little armchest. "*Are* you going to get in, Jack Martin?" said the guard, holding the lantern to my uncle's face.

' "Hallo!" said my uncle, falling back a step or two. "That's familiar!"

' "It's so on the way-bill," replied the guard.

' "Isn't there a 'Mister' before it?" said my uncle – for he felt, gentlemen, that for a guard he didn't know to call him Jack Martin, was a liberty which the Post Office wouldn't have sanctioned if they had known it.

' "No; there is not," rejoined the guard coolly.

' "Is the fare paid?" enquired my uncle.

' "Of course it is," rejoined the guard.

' "It is, is it?" said my uncle. "Then here goes – which coach?"

' "This," said the guard, pointing to an old-fashioned Edinburgh and London Mail, which had the steps down and the door open. "Stop – here are the other passengers. Let them get in first."

'As the guard spoke, there all at once appeared, right in front of my uncle, a young gentleman in a powdered wig and a sky-blue coat trimmed with silver, made very full and broad in the skirts, which were lined with buckram. Tiggin and Welps were in the printed calico and waistcoat-piece line, gentlemen, so my uncle knew all the materials at once. He wore knees breeches and a kind of leggings rolled up over his silk stockings and shoes with buckles; had ruffles at his wrists, a three-cornered hat on his head and a long taper sword by his side. The flaps of his waistcoat came half-way down his thighs and the end of his cravat reached to his waist. He stalked gravely to the coach door, pulled off his hat and held it above his head at arm's length: cocking his little finger in the air at the same time, as some affected people do when they take a cup of tea. Then he drew his feet together and made a low grave bow and then put out his left hand. My uncle was just going to step forward and shake it heartily, when he perceived that these attentions were directed, not towards him, but to a young lady, who just then appeared at the foot of the steps, attired in an old-fashioned green velvet dress, with a long waist and stomacher. She had no bonnet on her head, gentlemen, which was muffed in a black silk hood, but she looked round for an instant as she prepared to get into the coach, and such a beautiful face as she discovered, my uncle had never seen – not even in a picture. She got into the coach, holding up her dress with one hand; and, as my uncle always said with a round oath, when he told the story, he wouldn't have believed it possible that legs and feet could have been brought to such a state of perfection, unless he had seen them with his own eyes.

'But, in this one glimpse of the beautiful face, my uncle saw that the young lady had cast an imploring look upon him and that she appeared terrified and distressed. He noticed, too, that the young fellow in the powdered wig, notwithstanding his show of gallantry, which was all very fine and grand, clasped her tight by the wrist when she got in and followed himself immediately afterwards. An uncommonly ill-looking fellow in a close brown wig and a plum-coloured suit, wearing a very large sword and boots up to his hips, belonged to the party; and when he sat himself down next to the young lady, who shrunk into a corner at his approach, my uncle was confirmed in his original impression that something dark and mysterious was going forward or, as he always said himself, that "there was a screw loose somewhere". It's quite surprising how quickly he made up his mind to help the lady at any peril, if she needed help.

' "Death and lightning!" exclaimed the young gentleman, laying his hand upon his sword, as my uncle entered the coach.

' "Blood and thunder!" roared the other gentleman. With this, he whipped his sword out and made a lunge at my uncle without further ceremony. My uncle had no weapon about him, but with great dexterity he snatched the ill looking gentleman's three-cornered hat from his head and receiving the point of his sword right through the crown squeezed the sides together and held it tight.

' "Pink him behind!" cried the ill-looking gentleman to his companion, as he struggled to regain his sword.

' "He had better not," cried my uncle, displaying the heel of one of his shoes in a threatening manner. "I'll kick his brains out if he has any or fracture his skull if he hasn't." Exerting all his strength at this moment, my uncle wrenched the ill-looking man's sword from his grasp and flung it clean out of the coach window; upon which the younger gentleman vociferated "Death and lightning!" again and laid his hand upon the hilt of his sword in a very fierce manner, but didn't draw it. Perhaps, gentlemen, as my uncle used to say, with a smile, perhaps he was afraid of alarming the lady.

' "Now, gentlemen," said my uncle, taking his seat deliberately, "I don't want to have any death, with or without lightning, in a lady's presence and we have had quite blood and thundering enough for one journey; so, if you please, we'll sit in our places like quiet insides. Here, guard, pick up that gentleman's carving-knife."

'As quickly as my uncle said the words, the guard appeared at the coach window, with the gentleman's sword in his hand. He held up his lantern and looked earnestly in my uncle's face as he handed it in: when, by its light, my uncle saw, to his great surprise, that an immense crowd of mail-coach guards swarmed round the window, every one of whom had his eyes earnestly fixed upon him too. He had never seen such a sea of white faces and red bodies and earnest eyes, in all his born days.

' "This is the strangest sort of thing I ever had anything to do with," thought my uncle. "Allow me to return you your hat, sir."

'The ill-looking gentleman received his three-cornered hat in silence; looked at the hole in the middle with an enquiring air; and finally stuck it on the top of his wig, with a solemnity the effect of which was a trifle impaired by his sneezing violently at the moment and jerking it off again.

' "All right!" cried the guard with the lantern, mounting into his little seat behind. Away they went. My uncle peeped out of the coach window as they emerged from the yard and observed that the other mails, with coachmen, guards, horses and passengers, complete, were driving round and round in circles, at a slow trot of about five miles an hour. My uncle burnt with indignation, gentlemen. As a commercial man, he felt that the mail-bags were not to be trifled with and he resolved to memorialise the Post Office on the subject, the very instant he reached London.

'At present, however, his thoughts were occupied with the young lady who sat in the farthest corner of the coach, with her face muffled closely in her hood: the gentleman with the sky-blue coat sitting opposite to her: and the other man in the plum-coloured suit at her side: and both watching her intently. If she so much as rustled the folds of her hood, he could hear the ill-looking man clap his hand upon his sword and could tell by the other's breathing (it was so dark he couldn't see his face) that he was looking as big as if here were going to devour her at a mouthful. This roused my uncle more and more and he resolved, come what come might, to see the end of it. He had a great admiration for bright eyes, and sweet faces, and pretty legs and feet; in short, he was fond of the whole sex. It runs in our family, gentlemen – so am I.

'Many were the devices which my uncle practised to attract the lady's attention or, at all events, to engage the mysterious gentleman in conversation. They were all in vain; the gentleman wouldn't talk and the lady didn't dare. He thrust his head out of the coach window at intervals and bawled out to know why they didn't go faster. But he called till he was hoarse – nobody paid the least attention to him. He leant back in the coach and thought of the beautiful face and the feet and legs. This answered better; it whiled away the time and kept him from wondering where he was going and how it was he found himself in such an odd situation. Not that this would have worried him much, anyway – he was a mighty free and easy, roving, devil-may-care sort of person, was my uncle, gentlemen.

'All of a sudden the coach stopped. "Hallo!" said my uncle, "what's in the wind now?"

' "Alight here," said the guard, letting down the steps.

' "Here!" cried my uncle.

' "Here," rejoined the guard.

' "I'll do nothing of the sort," said my uncle.

' "Very well, then stop where you are," said the guard.

' "I will," said my uncle.

' "Do," said the guard.

'The other passengers had regarded this colloquy with great attention; and, finding that my uncle was determined not to alight, the younger man squeezed past him, to hand the lady out. At this moment, the ill-looking man was inspecting the hole in the crown of his three-cornered hat. As the young lady brushed past, she dropped one of her gloves into my uncle's hand and softly whispered, with her lips so close to his face, that he felt her warm breath on his nose, the single word "Help!" Gentlemen, my uncle leaped out of the coach at once, with such violence that it rocked on the springs again.

' "Oh! you've thought better of it, have you?" said the guard, when he saw my uncle standing on the ground.

'My uncle looked at the guard for a few seconds, in some doubt whether it wouldn't be better to wrench his blunderbuss from him, fire it in the face of the man with the big sword, knock the rest of the company over the head with the stock, snatch up the young lady and go off in the smoke. On second thoughts, however, he abandoned this plan, as being a shade too melodramatic in the execution and followed the two mysterious men, who, keeping the lady between them, were now entering an old house, in front of which the coach had stopped. They turned into the passage and my uncle followed.

'Of all the ruinous and desolate places my uncle had ever beheld, this was the most so. It looked as if it had once been a large house of entertainment; but the roof had fallen in in many places and the stairs were steep, rugged and broken. There was a huge fireplace in the room into which they walked and the chimney was blackened with smoke; but no warm blaze lighted it up now. The white feathery dust of burnt wood was still strewed over the hearth, but the stove was cold and all was dark and gloomy.

' "Well," said my uncle, as he looked about him, "a mail travelling at the rate of six miles and a half an hour and stopping for an indefinite time at such a hole as this, is rather an irregular sort of proceeding, I fancy. This shall be made known; I'll write to the papers."

'My uncle said this in a pretty loud voice and in an open unreserved sort of manner, with the view of engaging the two strangers in conversation if he could. But, neither of them took any more notice of him than whispering to each other and scowling at him as they did so. The lady was at the farther end of the room and once she ventured to wave her hand, as if beseeching my uncle's assistance.

'At length the two strangers advanced a little and the conversation began in earnest.

' "You don't know this is a private room, I suppose, fellow?" said the gentleman in sky-blue.

' "No, I do not, fellow," rejoined my uncle. "Only if this is a private room specially ordered for the occasion, I should think the public room must be a *very* comfortable one." With this my uncle sat himself down in a high-backed chair and took such an accurate measure of the gentlemen with his eyes, that Tiggin and Welps could have supplied him with printed calico for a suit and not an inch too much or too little, from that estimate alone.

' "Quit this room," said both the men together, grasping their swords.

' "Eh?" said my uncle, not at all appearing to comprehend their meaning.

' "Quit the room, or you are a dead man," said the ill-looking fellow with the large sword, drawing it at the same time and flourishing it in the air.

' "Down with him!" cried the gentleman in sky-blue, drawing his sword also and falling back two or three yards. "Down with him!"

'The lady gave a loud scream.

'Now, my uncle was always remarkable for great boldness, and great presence of mind. All the time that he had appeared so indifferent to what was going on, he had been looking slily about for some missile or weapon of defence and at the very instant when the swords were drawn, he espied, standing in the chimney-corner, an old basket-hilted rapier in a rusty scabbard. At one bound, my uncle caught it in his hand, drew it, flourished it gallantly above his head, called aloud to the lady to keep out of the way, hurled the chair at the man in sky-blue and the scabbard at the man in plum-colour and, taking advantage of the confusion, fell upon them both, pell-mell.

'Gentlemen, there is an old story – none the worse for being true – regarding a fine young Irish gentleman, who, being asked if he could play the fiddle, replied he had no doubt he could, but he couldn't exactly say for certain, because he had never tried. This is not inapplicable to my uncle and his fencing. He had never had a sword in his hand before, except once when he played Richard the Third at a private theatre: upon which occasion it was arranged with Richmond that he was to be run through from behind, without showing fight at all; but here he was, cutting and slashing with two experienced swordsmen, thrusting and guarding and poking and slicing and acquitting himself in the most manful and dexterous manner possible, although, up to that time, he had never been aware that he had the least notion of the science. It only shows how true the old saying is, that a man never knows what he can do till he tries, gentlemen.

'The noise of the combat was terrific; each of the three combatants swearing like troopers and their swords clashing with as much noise as if all the knives and steels in Newport Market were rattling together at the same time. When it was at its very height, the lady, to encourage my uncle most probably, withdrew her hood entirely from her face and disclosed a countenance of such dazzling beauty, that he would have fought against fifty men to win one smile from it and die. He had done wonders before, but now he began to powder away like a raving mad giant.

'At this very moment, the gentleman in sky-blue turning round and seeing the young lady with her face uncovered, vented an exclamation of rage and jealousy; and turning his weapon against her beautiful bosom, pointed a thrust at her heart, which caused my uncle to utter a cry of apprehension that made the building ring. The lady stepped aside and snatching the young man's sword from his hand before he had recovered his balance, drove him to the wall and running it through him and the panelling up to the very hilt, pinned him there, hard and fast. It was a splendid example. My uncle, with a loud shout of triumph and a strength that was irresistible, made his adversary retreat in the same direction and plunging the old rapier into the very centre of a large red flower in the pattern of his waistcoat, nailed him beside his friend. There they both stood, gentlemen: jerking their arms and legs about in agony, like the toy-shop figures that are moved by a piece of pack-thread. My uncle always said, afterwards, that this was one of the surest means he knew of for disposing of an enemy; but it was liable to one objection on the ground of expense, inasmuch as it involved the loss of a sword for every man disabled.

' "The mail, the mail?" cried the lady, running up to my uncle and throwing her beautiful arms around his neck; "we may yet escape."

' "*May*!" cried my uncle; "why, my dear, there's nobody else to kill, is there?" My uncle was rather disappointed, gentlemen, for he thought a little quiet bit of love-making would be agreeable after the slaughtering, if it were only to change the subject.

' "We have not an instant to lose here," said the young lady. "He" (pointing to the young gentleman in sky-blue) "is the only son of the powerful Marquess of Filletoville."

' "Well, then, my dear, I'm afraid he'll never come to the title," said my uncle, looking coolly at the young gentleman as he stood fixed up against the wall, in the cockchafer fashion I have described. "You have cut off the entail, my love."

' "I have been torn from my home and friends by these villains," said the young lady, her features glowing with indignation. "That wretch would have married me by violence in another hour."

' "Confound his impudence!" said my uncle, bestowing a very contemptuous look on the dying heir of Filletoville.

' "As you may guess from what you have seen," said the young lady, "the party were prepared to murder me if I appealed to anyone for assistance. If their accomplices find us here, we are lost. Two minutes hence may be too late. The mail!" With these words, overpowered by her feelings and the exertion of sticking the young Marquess of Filletoville, she sank into my uncle's arms. My uncle caught her up, and bore her to the house-door. There stood the mail, with four long-tailed, flowing-maned, black horses, ready harnessed; but no coachman, no guard, no hostler even, at the horses' heads.

'Gentlemen, I hope I do no injustice to my uncle's memory, when I express my opinion, that although he was a bachelor, he *had* held some ladies in his arms before this time; I believe, indeed, that he had rather a habit of kissing barmaids; and I know that, in one or two instances, he had been seen by credible witnesses to hug a landlady in a very perceptible manner. I mention the circumstances to show what, a very uncommon sort of person this beautiful young lady must have been, to have affected my uncle in the way she did; he used to say, that as her long dark hair trailed over his arm and her beautiful dark eyes fixed themselves upon his face when she recovered, he felt so strange and nervous, that his legs trembled beneath him. But, who can look in a sweet soft pair of dark eyes without feeling queer? *I* can't; gentlemen. I am afraid to look at some eyes I know, and that's the truth of it.'

' "You will never leave me," murmured the young lady.

' "Never," said my uncle. And he meant it too.

' "My dear preserver!" exclaimed the young lady. "My dear, kind, brave preserver!"

' "Don't," said my uncle, interrupting her.

' "Why?" enquired the young lady.

' "Because your mouth looks so beautiful when you speak," rejoined my uncle, "that I am afraid I shall be rude enough to kiss it."

'The young lady put up her hand as if to caution my uncle not to do so, and said – no, she didn't say anything – she smiled. When you are looking at a pair of the most delicious lips in the world and see them gently break into a roguish smile – if you are very near them and nobody else by – you cannot better testify your admiration of their beautiful form and colour than by kissing them at once. My uncle did so and I honour him for it.

' "Hark!" cried the young lady, starting. "The noise of wheels and horses!"

' "So it is," said my uncle, listening. He had a good ear for wheels and the tramping of hoofs; but there appeared to be so many horses and carriages rattling towards them from a distance, that it was impossible to form a guess at their number. The sound was like that of fifty brakes, with six blood cattle in each.

' "We are pursued!" cried the young lady, clasping her hands. "We are pursued. I have no hope but in you!"

'There was such an expression of terror in her beautiful face, that my uncle made up his mind at once. He lifted her into the coach, told her not to be frightened, pressed his lips to hers once more and then advising her to draw up the window to keep the cold air out, mounted to the box.

' "Stay, love," cried the young lady.

' "What's the matter?" said my uncle, from the coach-box.

' "I want to speak to you," said the young lady; "only a word – only a word, dearest."

' "Must I get down?" enquired my uncle. The lady made no answer, but she smiled again. Such a smile, gentlemen! – it beat the other one all to nothing. My uncle descended from his perch in a twinkling.

' "What is it, my dear?" said my uncle, looking in at the coach window. The lady happened to bend forward at the same time and my uncle thought she looked more beautiful than she had done yet. He was very close to her just then, gentlemen, so he really ought to know.

' "What is it, my dear?" said my uncle.

' "Will you never love anyone but me – never marry anyone besides?" said the young lady.

'My uncle swore a great oath that he never would marry anybody else, and the young lady drew in her head, and pulled up the window. He jumped upon the box, squared his elbows, adjusted the ribbons, seized the whip which lay on the roof, gave one flick to the off leader and away went the four long-tailed, flowing-maned black horses, at fifteen good English miles an hour, with the mail-coach behind them. Whew! how they tore along!

'The noise behind grew louder. The faster the old mail went, the faster came the pursuers – men, horses, dogs, were leagued in the pursuit. The noise was frightful, but, above all, rose the voice of the young lady, urging my uncle on and shrieking "Faster! faster!"

'They whirled past the dark trees, as feathers would be swept before a hurricane. Houses, gates, churches, haystacks, objects of every kind they shot by, with a velocity and noise like roaring waters suddenly let loose. Still the noise of pursuit grew louder and still my uncle could hear the young lady wildly screaming "Faster! faster!"

'My uncle plied whip and rein; and the horses flew onward till they were white with foam; and yet the noise behind increased; and yet the young lady cried "Faster! faster!" My uncle gave a loud stamp on the boot in the energy of the moment and – found that it was grey morning and he was sitting in the wheelwright's yard, on the box of an old Edinburgh mail, shivering with the cold and wet and stamping his feet to warm them! He got down and looked eagerly inside for the beautiful young lady. Alas! there was neither door nor seat to the coach – it was a mere shell.

'Of course, my uncle knew very well that there was some mystery in the matter and that everything had passed exactly as he used to relate it. He remained staunch to the great oath he had sworn to the beautiful young lady: refusing several eligible landladies on her account and dying a bachelor at last. He always said, what a curious thing it was that he should have found out, by such a mere accident as his clambering over the palings, that the ghosts of mail-coaches and horses, guards, coachmen, and passengers, were in the habit of making journeys regularly every night; he used to add, that he believed he was the only living person who had ever been taken as a passenger on one of these excursions; and I think he was right, gentlemen – at least I never heard of any other.'

'I wonder what these ghosts of mail-coaches carry in their bags,' said the landlord, who had listened to the whole story with profound attention.

'The dead letters, of course,' said the bagman.

'Oh, ah – to be sure,' rejoined the landlord. 'I never thought of that.'

To Be Taken with a Grain of Salt

CHARLES DICKENS 1812–1870

I HAVE ALWAYS noticed a prevalent want of courage, even among persons of superior intelligence and culture, as to imparting their own psychological experiences when those have been of a strange sort. Almost all men are afraid that what they could relate in such wise would find no parallel or response in a listener's internal life and might be suspected or laughed at. A truthful traveller who should have seen some extraordinary creature in the likeness of a sea-serpent, would have no fear of mentioning it; but the same traveller having had some singular presentiment, impulse, vagary of thought, vision (so-called), dream or other remarkable mental impression, would hesitate considerably before he would own to it. To this reticence I attribute much of the obscurity in which such subjects are involved. We do not habitually communicate our experiences of these subjective things, as we do our experiences of objective creation. The consequence is that the general stock of experience in this regard appears exceptional, and really is so, in respect of being miserably imperfect.

In what I am going to relate I have no intention of setting up, opposing, or supporting, any theory whatever. I know the history of the Bookseller of Berlin, I have studied the case of the wife of a late Astronomer Royal as related by Sir David Brewster and I have followed the minutest details of a much more remarkable case of Spectral Illusion occurring within my private circle of friends. It may be necessary to state as to this last that the sufferer (a lady) was in no degree, however distant, related to me. A mistaken assumption on that head, might suggest an explanation of a part of my own case – but only a part – which would be wholly without foundation. It cannot be referred to my inheritance of any developed peculiarity, nor had I ever before any at all similar experience, nor have I ever had any at all similar experience since.

It does not signify how many years ago, or how few, a certain murder was committed in England, which attracted great attention. We hear more than enough of murderers as they rise in succession to their atrocious eminence and I would bury the memory of this particular brute, if I could, as his body was buried, in Newgate Jail. I purposely abstain from giving any direct clue to the criminal's individuality.

When the murder was first discovered, no suspicion fell – or I ought rather to say, for I cannot be too precise in my facts, it was nowhere publicly hinted that any suspicion fell – on the man who was afterwards brought to trial. As no reference was at that time made to him in the newspapers, it is obviously impossible that any description of him can at that time have been given in the newspapers. It is essential that this fact be remembered.

Unfolding at breakfast my morning paper, containing the account of that first discovery, I found it to be deeply interesting, I read in with close attention. I read it twice, if not three times. The discovery had been made in a bedroom and, when I laid down the paper, I was aware of a flash – rush – flow – I do not know what to call it – no word I can find is satisfactorily descriptive – in which I seemed to see that bedroom passing through my room, like a picture impossibly painted on a running river. Though almost instantaneous in its passing, it was perfectly clear; so clear that I distinctly, and with a sense of relief, observed the absence of the dead body from the bed.

It was in no romantic place that I had this curious sensation, but in chambers in Piccadilly, very near to the corner of St James's Street. It was entirely new to me. I was in my easy-chair at the moment and the sensation was accompanied with a peculiar shiver which started the chair from its position. (But it is to be noted that the chair ran easily on castors.) I went to one of the windows (there are two in the room, and the room is on the second floor) to refresh my eyes with the moving objects down in Piccadilly. It was a bright autumn morning and the street was sparkling and cheerful. The wind was high. As I looked out, it brought down from the Park a quantity of fallen leaves, which a gust took and whirled into a spiral pillar. As the pillar fell and the leaves dispersed, I saw two men on the opposite side of the way, going from west to east. They were one behind the other. The foremost man often looked back over his shoulder. The second man followed him, at a distance of some thirty paces, with his right hand menacingly raised. First, the singularity and steadiness of this threatening gesture in so public a thoroughfare, attracted my attention; and next, the more remarkable circumstance that nobody heeded it. Both men threaded their way among the other passengers, with a smoothness hardly consistent even with the action of walking on a pavement and no single creature, that I could see, gave them place, touched them or looked after them. In passing before my windows, they both stared up at me. I saw their two faces very distinctly and I knew that I could recognise them anywhere. Not that I had consciously noticed anything very remarkable in either face, except that the man who went first had an unusually lowering appearance, and that the face of the man who followed him was of the colour of impure wax.

I am a bachelor, and my valet and his wife constitute my whole establishment. My occupation is in a certain Branch Bank, and I wish that my duties as head of a Department were as light as they are popularly supposed to be. They kept me in town that autumn, when I stood in need of a change. I was not ill, but I was not well. My reader is to make the most that can be reasonably made of my feeling jaded, having a depressing sense upon me of a monotonous life and being 'slightly dyspeptic'. I am assured by my renowned doctor that my real state of health at that time justifies no stronger description, and I quote his own from his written answer to my request for it.

As the circumstances of the murder, gradually unravelling, took stronger and stronger possession of the public mind, I kept them away from mine, by knowing as little about them as was possible in the midst of the universal excitement. But I knew that a verdict of Wilful Murder had been found against the suspected murderer, and that he had been committed to Newgate for trial. I also knew that his trial had been postponed over one sessions of the Central Criminal Court, on the ground of general prejudice and want of time for the preparation of the defence. I may further have known, but I believe I did not, when, or about when, the sessions to which his trial stood postponed would come on.

My sitting-room, bedroom and dressing-room, are all on one floor. With the last, there is no communication but through the bedroom. True, there is a door in it, once communicating with the staircase; but a part of the fitting of my bath has been – and had then been for some years – fixed across it. At the same period and as a part of the same arrangement, the door had been nailed up and canvassed over.

I was standing in my bedroom late one night, giving some directions to my servant before he went to bed. My face was towards the only available door of communication with the dressing-room and it was closed. My servant's back was towards that door. While I was speaking to him I saw it open and a man look in, who very earnestly and mysteriously beckoned to me. That man was the man who had gone second of the two along Piccadilly, and whose face was of the colour of impure wax.

The figure, having beckoned, drew back and closed the door. With no longer pause than was made by my crossing the bedroom, I opened the dressing-room door and looked in. I had a lighted candle already in my hand. I felt no inward expectation of seeing the figure in the dressing-room and I did not see it there.

Conscious that my servant stood amazed, I turned round to him, and said: 'Derrick, could you believe that in my cool senses I fancied I saw a – ' As I there laid my hand upon his breast, with a sudden start he trembled violently and said, 'O Lord, yes, sir! A dead man beckoning!'

Now, I do not believe that this John Derrick, my trusty and attached servant for more than twenty years, had any impression whatever of having seen any such figure, until I touched him. The change in him was so startling when I touched him, that I fully believe he derived his impression in some occult manner from me at that instant.

I bade John Derrick bring some brandy and I gave him a dram and was glad to take one myself. Of what had proceeded that night's phenomenon, I told him not a single word. Reflecting on it, I was absolutely certain that I had never seen that face before, except on the one occasion in Piccadilly. Comparing its expression when beckoning at the door, with its expression when it had stared up at me as I stood at my window, I came to the conclusion that on the first occasion it had sought to fasten itself upon my memory and that on the second occasion it had made sure of being immediately remembered.

I was not very comfortable that night, though I felt a certainty, difficult to explain, that the figure would not return. At daylight, I fell into a heavy sleep, from which I was awakened by John Derrick's coming to my bedside with a paper in his hand.

This paper, it appeared, had been the subject of an altercation at the door between its bearer and my servant. It was a summons to me to serve upon a jury at the forthcoming sessions of the Central Criminal Court at the Old Bailey. I had never before been summoned on such a jury, as John Derrick well knew. He believed – I am not certain at this hour whether with reason or otherwise – that that class of jurors were customarily chosen on a lower qualification than mine and he had at first refused to accept the summons. The man who served it had taken the matter very coolly. He had said that my attendance or non-attendance was nothing to him; there the summons was; and I should deal with it at my own peril and not at his.

For a day or two I was undecided whether to respond to this call or take no notice of it. I was not conscious of the slightest mysterious bias, influence, or attraction, one way or other. Of that I am as strictly sure as of every other statement that I make here. Ultimately I decided, as a break in the monotony of my life, that I would go.

The appointed morning was a raw morning in the month of November. There was a dense brown fog in Piccadilly and it became positively black and in the last degree oppressive east of Temple Bar. I found the passages and staircases of the courthouse flaringly lighted with gas and the court itself similarly illuminated. I *think* that until I was conducted by officers into the Old Court and saw its crowded state, I did not know that the murderer was to be tried that day. I *think* that until I was so helped into the Old Court with considerable difficulty, I did not know into which of the two courts sitting, my summons would take me. But this must not be received as a positive assertion, for I am not completely satisfied in my mind on either point.

I took my seat in the place appropriated to jurors in waiting and I looked about the court as well as I could through the cloud of fog and breath that was heavy in it. I noticed the black vapour hanging like a murky curtain outside the great windows and I noticed the stifled sound of wheels on the straw or tan that was littered in the street; also, the hum of the people gathered there, which a shrill whistle or a louder song or hail than the rest, occasionally pierced. Soon afterwards the judges, two in number, entered and took their seats. The buzz in the court was awfully hushed. The direction was given to put the murderer to the bar. He appeared there. And in that same instant I recognised in him, the first of the two men who had gone down Piccadilly.

If my name had been called then, I doubt if I could have answered to it audibly. But it was called about sixth or eighth in the panel and I was by that time able to say 'Here!' Now, observe. As I stepped into the box, the prisoner, who had been looking on attentively but with no sign of concern, became violently agitated and beckoned to his attorney. The prisoner's wish to challenge me was so manifest, that it occasioned a pause, during which the attorney, with his hand upon the dock, whispered with his client and shook his head. I afterwards had it from that gentleman, that the prisoner's first affrighted words to him were, '*At all hazards challenge that man!*' But, that as he would give no reason for it and admitted that he had not even known my name until he heard it called and I appeared, it was not done.

Both on the ground already explained, that I wish to avoid reviving the unwholesome memory of that murderer, and also because a detailed account of his long trial is by no means indispensable to my narrative, I shall confine myself closely to such incidents in the ten days and nights during which we, the jury, were kept together, as directly bear on my own curious personal experience. It is in that and not in the murderer, that I seek to interest my reader. It is to that and not to a page of the Newgate Calendar, that I beg attention.

I was chosen foreman of the jury. On the second morning of the trial, after evidence had been taken for two hours (I heard the church clocks strike), happening to cast my eyes over my brother-jurymen, I found an inexplicable difficulty in counting them. I counted them several times, yet always with the same difficulty. In short, I made them one too many.

I touched the brother-juryman whose place was next to me and I whispered to him, 'Oblige me by counting us.' He looked surprised by the request, but turned his head and counted. 'Why,' says he, suddenly, 'We are thirt – ; but no, it's not possible. No. We are twelve.'

According to my counting that day, we were always right in detail, but in the gross we were always one too many. There was no appearance – no figure – to account for it; but I had now an inward foreshadowing of the figure that was surely coming.

The jury were housed at the London Tavern. We all slept in one large room on separate tables and we were constantly in the charge and under the eye of the officer sworn to hold us in safekeeping. I see no reason for suppressing the real name of that officer. He was intelligent, highly polite and obliging and (I was glad to hear) much respected in the City. He had an agreeable presence, good eyes, enviable black whiskers and a fine sonorous voice. His name was Mr Harker.

When we turned into our twelve beds at night, Mr Harker's bed was drawn across the door. On the night of the second day, not being disposed to lie down, and seeing Mr Harker sitting on his bed, I went and sat beside him and offered him a pinch of snuff. As Mr Harker's hand touched mine in taking it from my box, a peculiar shiver crossed him and he said: 'Who is this!'

Following Mr Harker's eyes and looking along the room, I saw again the figure I expected – the second of the two men who had gone down Piccadilly. I rose and advanced a few steps; then stopped, and looked round at Mr Harker. He was quite unconcerned, laughed and said in a pleasant way, 'I thought for a moment we had a thirteenth juryman, without a bed. But I see it is the moonlight.'

Making no revelation to Mr Harker, but inviting him to take a walk with me to the end of the room, I watched what the figure did. It stood for a few moments by the bedside of each of my eleven brother jurymen, close to the pillow. It always went to the right-hand side of the bed, and always passed out crossing the foot of the next bed. It seemed, from the action of the head, merely to look down pensively at each recumbent figure. It took no notice of me, or of my bed, which was that nearest to Mr Harker's. It seemed to go out where the moonlight came in, through a high window, as by an aerial flight of stairs.

Next morning at breakfast, it appeared that everybody present had dreamed of the murdered man last night, except myself and Mr Harker.

I now felt as convinced that the second man who had gone down Piccadilly was the murdered man (so to speak), as if it had been borne into my comprehension by his immediate testimony. But even this took place, and in a manner for which I was not at all prepared.

On the fifth day of the trial, when the case for the prosecution was drawing to a close, a miniature of the murdered man, missing from his bedroom upon the discovery of the deed, and afterwards found in a hiding-place where the murderer had been seen digging, was put in evidence. Having been identified by the witness under examination, it was handed up to the Bench, and thence handed down to be inspected by the jury. As an officer in a black gown was making his way with it across to me, the figure of the second man who had gone down Piccadilly impetuously started from the crowd, caught the miniature from the officer, and gave it to me with his own hands, at the same time saying, in a low and hollow tone – before I saw the miniature, which was in a locket – '*I was younger then, and my face was not then drained of blood.*' It also came between me and the brother juryman to whom I would have given the miniature, and between him and the brother juryman to whom he would have given it, and so passed it on through the whole of our number, and back into my possession. Not one of them, however, detected this.

At table, and generally when we were shut up together in Mr Harker's custody, we had from the first naturally discussed the day's proceedings a good deal. On that fifth day, the case for the prosecution being closed, and we having that side of the question in a completed shape before us, our discussion was more animated and serious. Among our number was a vestryman – the densest idiot I have ever seen at large – who met the plainest evidence with the most preposterous objections, and who was sided with by two flabby parochial parasites; all the three impanelled from a district so delivered over to fever that they ought to have been upon their own trial for five hundred murders. When these mischievous blockheads were at their loudest, which was towards midnight, while some of us were already preparing for bed, I again saw the murdered man. He stood grimly behind them, beckoning to me. On my going towards them, and striking into the conversation, he immediately retired. This was the beginning of a separate series of appearances, confined to that long room in which *we* were confined. Whenever a knot of my brother jurymen laid their heads together, I saw the head of the murdered man among theirs. Whenever their comparison of notes was going against him, he would solemnly and irresistibly beckon to me.

It would be borne in mind that down to the production of the miniature, on the fifth day of the trial, I had never seen the Appearance in court. Three changes occurred now that we entered on the case for the defence. Two of them I will mention together, first. The figure was now in court continually, and it never there addressed itself to me, but always to the person who was speaking at the time. For instance: the throat of the murdered man had been cut straight across. In the opening speech for the defence, it was suggested that the deceased might have cut his own throat. At that very moment, the figure, with its throat in the dreadful condition referred to (this it had concealed before), stood at the speaker's elbow, motioning across and across its windpipe, now with the right hand, now with the left, vigorously suggesting to the speaker himself the impossibility of such a wound having been self-inflicted by either hand. For another instance: a witness to character, a woman, deposed to the prisoner's being the most amiable of mankind. The figure at that instant stood on the floor before her, looking her full in the face, and pointing out the prisoner's evil countenance with an extended arm and an outstretched finger.

The third change now to be added impressed me strongly as the most marked and striking of all. I do not theorise upon it; I accurately state it, and there leave it. Although the Appearance was not itself perceived by those whom it addressed, its coming close to such persons was invariably attended by some trepidation or disturbance on their part. It seemed to me as if it were prevented, by laws to which I was not amenable, from fully revealing itself to others, and yet as if it could, invisibly, dumbly and darkly, overshadow their minds. When the leading counsel for the defence suggested that hypothesis of suicide and the figure stood at the learned gentleman's elbow, frightfully sawing at its severed throat, it is undeniable that the counsel faltered in his speech, lost for a few seconds the thread of his ingenious discourse, wiped his forehead with his handkerchief and turned extremely pale. When the witness to character was confronted by the Appearance, her eyes most certainly did follow the direction of its pointed finger and rest in great hesitation and trouble upon the prisoner's face. Two additional illustrations will suffice. On the eighth day of the trial, after the pause which was every day made early in the afternoon for a few minutes' rest and refreshment, I came back into court with the rest of the jury, some little time before the return of the judges. Standing up in the box and looking about me, I thought the figure was not there, until, chancing to raise my eyes to the gallery, I saw it bending forward and leaning over a very decent woman, as if to assure itself whether the judges had resumed their seats or not. Immediately afterwards, that woman screamed, fainted and was carried out. So with the venerable, sagacious and patient judge who conducted the trial. When the case was over, and he settled himself and his papers to sum up, the murdered man entering by the judges' door, advanced to his Lordship's desk and looked eagerly over his shoulder at the pages of his notes which he was turning. A change came over his Lordship's face; his hand stopped; the peculiar shiver that I knew so well, passed over him; he faltered, 'Excuse me gentlemen, for a few moments. I am somewhat oppressed by the vitiated air'; and did not recover until he had drunk a glass of water.

Through all the monotony of six of those interminable ten days – the same judges and others on the bench, the same murderer in the dock, the same lawyers at the table, the same tones of question and answer rising to the roof of the court, the same scratching of the judge's pen, the same ushers going in and out, the same lights kindled at the same hour when there had been any natural light of day, the same foggy curtain outside the great windows when it was foggy, the same rain pattering and dripping when it was rainy, the same footmarks of turnkeys and prisoner day after day on the same sawdust, the same keys locking and unlocking the same heavy doors – through all the wearisome monotony which made me feel as if I had been foreman of the jury for a vast period of time and Piccadilly had flourished coevally with Babylon, the murdered man never lost one trace of his distinctness in my eyes, nor was he at any moment less distinct than anybody else. I must not omit, as a matter of fact, that I never once saw the Appearance which I call by the name of the murdered man, look at the murderer. Again and again I wondered, 'Why does he not?' But he never did.

Nor did he look at me, after the production of the miniature, until the last closing minutes of the trial arrived. We retired to consider, at seven minutes before ten at night. The idiotic vestryman and his two parochial parasites gave us so much trouble, that we twice returned into court, to beg to have certain extracts from the judge's notes re-read. Nine of us had not the smallest doubt about those passages, neither, I believe, had anyone in court; the dunder-headed triumvirate, however, having no idea but obstruction, disputed them for that very reason. At length we prevailed and finally the jury returned into court at ten minutes past twelve.

The murdered man at that time stood directly opposite the jurybox, on the other side of the court. As I took my place, his eyes rested on me, with great attention; he seemed satisfied, and slowly shook a great grey veil, which he carried on his arm for the first time, over his head and whole form. As I gave in our verdict 'Guilty', the veil collapsed, all was gone, and his place was empty.

The murderer being asked by the judge, according to usage, whether he had anything to say before sentence of death should be passed upon him, indistinctly muttered something which was described in the leading newspapers of the following day as 'a few rambling, incoherent and half-audible words, in which he was understood to complain that he had not had a fair trial, because the foreman of the jury was prepossessed against him.' The remarkable declaration that he really made, was this: 'My Lord, I knew I was a doomed man when the foreman of my jury came into the box. My Lord, I knew he would never let me off, because, before I was taken, he somehow got to my bedside in the night, woke me, and put a rope round my neck.'

An Account of Some Strange
Disturbances in Aungier Street

JOSEPH SHERIDAN LE FANU 1814–1873

IT IS NOT WORTH TELLING, this story of mine – at least, not worth writing. Told, indeed, as I have sometimes been called upon to tell it, to a circle of intelligent and eager faces, lighted up by a good after-dinner fire on a winter's evening, with a cold wind rising and wailing outside, and all snug and cosy within, it has gone off – though I say it, who should not – indifferent well. But it is a venture to do as you would have me. Pen, ink and paper are cold vehicles for the marvellous and a 'reader' decidedly a more critical animal than a 'listener'. If, however, you can induce your friends to read it after nightfall and when the fireside talk has run for a while on thrilling tales of shapeless terror; in short, if you will secure me the *mollia tempora fandi*, I will go to my work, and say my say, with better heart. Well, then, these conditions presupposed, I shall waste no more words, but tell you simply how it all happened.

My cousin (Tom Ludlow) and I studied medicine together. I think he would have succeeded, had he stuck to the profession; but he preferred the Church, poor fellow, and died early, a sacrifice to contagion, contracted in the noble discharge of his duties. For my present purpose, I say enough of his character when I mention that he was of a sedate but frank and cheerful nature; very exact in his observance of truth and not by any means like myself – of an excitable or nervous temperament.

My Uncle Ludlow – Tom's father – while we were attending lectures, purchased three or four old houses in Aungier Street, one of which was unoccupied. *He* resided in the country and Tom proposed that we should take up our abode in the untenanted house, so long as it should continue unlet; a move which would accomplish the double end of settling us nearer alike to our lecture-rooms and to our amusements and of relieving us from the weekly charge of rent for our lodgings.

Our furniture was very scant – our whole equipage remarkably modest and primitive; and, in short, our arrangements pretty nearly as simple as those of a bivouac. Our new plan was, therefore, executed almost as soon as conceived. The front drawing-room was our sitting-room. I had the bedroom over it and Tom the back bedroom on the same floor, which nothing could have induced me to occupy.

The house, to begin with, was a very old one. It had been, I believe, newly fronted about fifty years before; but with this exception, it had nothing modern about it. The agent who bought it and looked into the titles for my uncle, told me that it was sold, along with much other forfeited property, at Chichester House, I think, in 1702; and had belonged to Sir Thomas Hacket, who was Lord Mayor of Dublin in James II's time. How old it was *then*, I can't say; but, at all events, it had seen years and changes enough to have contracted all that mysterious and saddened air, at once exciting and depressing, which belongs to most old mansions.

There had been very little done in the way of modernising details; and, perhaps, it was better so; for there was something queer and bygone in the very walls and ceilings – in the shape of doors and windows – in the odd diagonal site of the chimney-pieces – in the beams and ponderous cornices – not to mention the singular solidity of all the woodwork, from the banisters to the window-frames, which hopelessly defied disguise, and would have emphatically proclaimed their antiquity through any conceivable amount of modern finery and varnish.

An effort had, indeed, been made, to the extent of papering the drawing-rooms; but somehow, the paper looked raw and out of keeping; and the old woman, who kept a little dirt-pie of a shop in the lane and whose daughter – a girl of two and fifty – was our solitary handmaid, coming in at sunrise and chastely receding again as soon as she had made all ready for tea in our state apartment – this woman, I say, remembered it when old Judge Horrocks (who, having earned the reputation of a particularly 'hanging judge', ended by hanging himself, as the coroner's jury found, under an impulse of 'temporary insanity', with a child's skipping-rope, over the massive old banisters) resided there, entertaining good company, with fine venison and rare old port. In those halcyon days, the drawing-rooms were hung with gilded leather and, I dare say, cut a good figure, for they were really spacious rooms.

The bedrooms were wainscoted, but the front one was not gloomy; and in it the cosiness of antiquity quite overcame its sombre associations. But the back bedroom, with its two queerly-placed melancholy windows, staring vacantly at the foot of the bed, and with the shadowy recess to be found in most old houses in Dublin, like a large ghostly closet, which, from congeniality of temperament, had amalgamated with the bedchamber and dissolved the partition. At night-time, this 'alcove' – as our 'maid' was wont to call it – had, in my eyes, a specially sinister and suggestive character. Tom's distant and solitary candle glimmered vainly into its darkness. *There* it was always overlooking him – always itself impenetrable. But this was only part of the effect. The whole room was, I can't tell how, repulsive to me. There was, I suppose, in its proportions and features, a latent discord – a certain mysterious and indescribable relation, which jarred indistinctly upon some secret sense of the fitting and the safe and raised indefinable suspicions and apprehensions of the imagination. On the whole, as I began by saying, nothing could have induced me to pass a night alone in it.

I had never pretended to conceal from poor Tom my superstitious weakness; and he, on the other hand, most unaffectedly ridiculed my tremors. The sceptic was, however, destined to receive a lesson, as you shall hear.

We had not been very long in occupation of our respective dormitories, when I began to complain of uneasy nights and disturbed sleep. I was, I suppose, the more impatient under this annoyance, as I was usually a sound sleeper and by no means prone to nightmares. It was now, however, my destiny, instead of enjoying my customary repose, every night to 'sup full of horrors'. After a preliminary course of disagreeable and frightful dreams, my troubles took a definite form, and the same vision, without an appreciable variation in a single detail, visited me at least (on an average) every second night in the week.

Now, this dream, nightmare, or infernal illusion – which you please – of which I was the miserable sport, was on this wise: I saw, or thought I saw, with the most abominable distinctness, although at the time in profound darkness, every article of furniture and accidental arrangement of the chamber in which I lay. This, as you know, is incidental to ordinary nightmare. Well, while in this clairvoyant condition, which seemed but the lighting up of the theatre in which was to be exhibited the monotonous tableau of horror, which made my nights insupportable, my attention invariably became, I know not why, fixed upon the windows opposite the foot of my bed; and, uniformly with the same effect, a sense of dreadful anticipation always took slow but sure possession of me. I became somehow conscious of a sort of horrid but undefined preparation going forward in some unknown quarter and by some unknown agency, for my torment; and, after an interval, which always seemed to me of the same length, a picture suddenly flew up to the window, where it remained fixed, as if by an electrical attraction, and my discipline of horror then commenced, to last perhaps for hours. The picture thus mysteriously glued to the window-panes, was the portrait of an old man, in a crimson flowered silk dressing-gown, the folds of which I could now describe, with a countenance embodying a strange mixture of intellect, sensuality and power, but withal sinister and full of malignant omen. His nose was hooked, like the beak of a vulture; his eyes large, grey and prominent and lighted up with a more than mortal cruelty and coldness. These features were surmounted by a crimson velvet cap, the hair that peeped from under which was white with age, while the eyebrows retained their original blackness. Well I remember every line, hue and shadow of that stony countenance and well I may! The gaze of this hellish visage was fixed upon me, and mine returned it with the inexplicable fascination of nightmare, for what appeared to me to be hours of agony. At last –

The cock he crew; away then flew

the fiend who had enslaved me through the awful watches of the night; and, harassed and nervous, I rose to the duties of the day.

I had – I can't say exactly why, but it may have been from the exquisite anguish and profound impressions of unearthly horror, with which this strange phantasmagoria was associated – an insurmountable antipathy to describing the exact nature of my nightly troubles to my friend and comrade. Generally, however, I told him that I was haunted by abominable dreams; and, true to the imputed materialism of medicine, we put our heads together to dispel my horrors, not by exorcism, but by a tonic.

I will do this tonic justice and frankly admit that the accursed portrait began to intermit its visits under its influence. What of that? Was this singular apparition – as full of character as of terror – therefore the creature of my fancy or the invention of my poor stomach? Was it, in short, *subjective* (to borrow the technical slang of the day) and not the palpable aggression and intrusion of an external agent? That, good friend, as we will both admit, by no means follows. The evil spirit, who enthralled my senses in the shape of that portrait, may have been just as near me, just as energetic, just as malignant, though I saw him not. What means the whole moral code of revealed religion regarding the due keeping of our own bodies, soberness, temperance, etc.? here is an obvious connection between the material and the invisible; the healthy tone of the system, and its unimpaired energy, may, for aught we can tell, guard us against influences which would otherwise render life itself terrific. The mesmerist and the electro-biologist will fail upon an average with nine patients out of ten – so may the evil spirit. Special conditions of the corporeal system are indispensable to the production of certain spiritual phenomena. The operation succeeds sometimes – sometimes fails – that is all.

I found afterwards that my would-be sceptical companion had his troubles too. But of these I knew nothing yet. One night, for a wonder, I was sleeping soundly, when I was roused by a step on the lobby outside my room, followed by the loud clang of what turned out to be a large brass candlestick, flung with all his force by poor Tom Ludlow over the banisters and rattling with a rebound down the second flight of stairs; and almost concurrently with this, Tom burst open my door and bounced into my room backwards, in a state of extraordinary agitation.

I had jumped out of bed and clutched him by the arm before I had any distinct idea of my own whereabouts. There we were – in our shirts standing before the open door – staring through the great old banister opposite, at the lobby window, through which the sickly light of a clouded moon was gleaming.

'What's the matter, Tom? What's the matter with you? What the devil's the matter with you, Tom?' I demanded shaking him with nervous impatience.

He took a long breath before he answered me, and then it was not very coherently.

'It's nothing, nothing at all – did I speak? – what did I say? – where's the candle, Richard? It's dark; I – I had a candle!'

'Yes, dark enough,' I said; 'but what's the matter? – what is it? – why don't you speak, Tom? – have you lost your wits? – what is the matter?'

'The matter? – oh, it is all over. It must have been a dream – nothing at all but a dream – don't you think so? It could not be anything more than a dream.'

'Of *course*,' said I, feeling uncommonly nervous, 'it *was* a dream.'

'I thought,' he said, 'there was a man in my room and – and I jumped out of bed; and – and – where's the candle?'

'In your room, most likely,' I said, 'shall I go and bring it?'

'No; stay here – don't go; it's no matter – don't, I tell you; it was all a dream. Bolt the door, Dick; I'll stay here with you – I feel nervous. So, Dick, like a good fellow, light your candle and open the window – I am in a *shocking state*.'

I did as he asked me and, robing himself like Granuaile in one of my blankets, he seated himself close beside my bed.

Everybody knows how contagious is fear of all sorts, but more especially that particular kind of fear under which poor Tom was at that moment labouring. I would not have heard, nor I believe would he have recapitulated, just at that moment, for half the world, the details of the hideous vision which had so unmanned him.

'Don't mind telling me anything about your nonsensical dream, Tom,' said I, affecting contempt, really in a panic; 'let us talk about something else; but it is quite plain that this dirty old house disagrees with us both and hang me if I stay here any longer, to be pestered with indigestion and – and – bad nights, so we may as well look out for lodgings – don't you think so? – at once.'

Tom agreed and, after an interval, said –

'I have been thinking, Richard, that it is a long time since I saw my father and I have made up my mind to go down tomorrow and return in a day or two and you can take rooms for us in the meantime.'

I fancied that this resolution, obviously the result of the vision which had so profoundly scared him, would probably vanish next morning with the damps and shadows of night. But I was mistaken. Off went Tom at peep of day to the country, having agreed that so soon as I had secured suitable lodgings, I was to recall him by letter from his visit to my Uncle Ludlow.

Now, anxious as I was to change my quarters, it so happened, owing to a series of petty procrastinations and accidents, that nearly a week elapsed before my bargain was made and my letter of recall on the wing to Tom; and, in the meantime, a trifling adventure or two had occurred to your humble servant, which, absurd as they now appear, diminished by distance, did certainly at the time serve to whet my appetite for change considerably.

A night or two after the departure of my comrade, I was sitting by my bedroom fire, the door locked, and the ingredients of a tumbler of hot whisky-punch upon the crazy spider-table; for, as the best mode of keeping the

> Black spirits and white,
> Blue spirits and grey,

with which I was environed, at bay, I had adopted the practice recommended by the wisdom of my ancestors, and 'kept my spirits up by pouring spirits down'. I had thrown aside my volume of *Anatomy*, and was treating myself by way of a tonic, preparatory to my punch and bed, to half a dozen pages of the *Spectator*, when I heard a step on the flight of stairs descending from the attics. It was two o'clock, and the streets were as silent as a churchyard – the sounds were, therefore, perfectly distinct. There was a slow, heavy tread, characterised by the emphasis and deliberation of age, descending by the narrow staircase from above; and, what made the sound more singular, it was plain that the feet which produced it were perfectly bare, measuring the descent with something between a pound and a flop, very ugly to hear.

I knew quite well that my attendant had gone away many hours before and that nobody but myself had any business in the house. It was quite plain also that the person who was coming downstairs had no intention whatever of concealing his movements; but, on the contrary, appeared disposed to make even more noise and proceed more deliberately than was at all necessary. When the step reached the foot of the stairs outside my room, it seemed to stop; and I expected every moment to see my door open spontaneously and give admission to the original of my detested portrait. I was, however, relieved in a few seconds by hearing the descent renewed, just in the same manner, upon the staircase leading down to the drawing-rooms and thence, after another pause, down the next flight and so on to the hall, whence I heard no more.

Now, by the time the sound had ceased, I was wound up, as they say, to a very unpleasant pitch of excitement. I listened, but there was not a stir. I screwed up my courage to a decisive experiment – opened my door and in a stentorian voice bawled over the banisters, 'Who's there?' There was no answer but the ringing of my own voice through the empty old house – no renewal of the movement, nothing, in short, to give my unpleasant sensations a definite direction. There is, I think, something most disagreeably disenchanting in the sound of one's own voice under such circumstances, exerted in solitude and in vain. It redoubled my sense of isolation and my misgivings increased on perceiving that the door, which I certainly thought I had left open, was closed behind me; in a vague alarm, lest my retreat should be cut off, I got again into my room as quickly as I could, where I remained in a state of imaginary blockade, and very uncomfortable indeed, till morning.

Next night brought no return of my barefooted fellow-lodger; but the night following, being in my bed, and in the dark – somewhere, I suppose, about the same hour as before, I distinctly heard the old fellow again descending from the garrets.

This time I had had my punch and the *morale* of the garrison was consequently excellent. I jumped out of bed, clutched the poker as I passed the expiring fire, and in a moment was upon the lobby. The sound had ceased by this time – the dark and chill were discouraging; and, guess my horror, when I saw, or thought I saw, a black monster, whether in the shape of a man or a bear I could not say, standing, with its back to the wall, on the lobby, facing me, with a pair of great greenish eyes shining dimly out. Now, I must be frank and confess that the cupboard which displayed our plates and cups stood just there, though at the moment I did not recollect it. At the same time I must honestly say, that making every allowance for an excited imagination, I never could satisfy myself that I was made the dupe of my own fancy in this matter; for this apparition, after one or two shiftings of shape, as if in the act of incipient transformation, began, as it seemed on second thoughts, to advance upon me in its original form. From an instinct of terror rather than of courage, I hurled the poker, with all my force, at its head; and to the music of a horrid crash made my way into my room and double-locked the door. Then, in a minute more, I heard the horrid bare feet walk down the stairs, till the sound ceased in the hall, as on the former occasion.

If the apparition of the night before was an ocular delusion of my fancy sporting with the dark outlines of our cupboard and if its horrid eyes were nothing but a pair of inverted teacups, I had, at all events, the satisfaction of having launched the poker with admirable effect, and in true 'fancy' phrase, 'knocked its two daylights into one', as the commingled fragments of my tea-service testified. I did my best to gather comfort and courage from these evidences; but it would not do. And then what could I say of those horrid bare feet, and the regular tramp, tramp, tramp, which measured the distance of the entire staircase through the solitude of my haunted dwelling and at an hour when no good influence was stirring? Confound it! – the whole affair was abominable. I was out of spirits, and dreaded the approach of night.

It came, ushered ominously in with a thunder-storm and dull torrents of depressing rain. Earlier than usual the streets grew silent; and by twelve o'clock nothing but the comfortless pattering of the rain was to be heard.

I made myself as snug as I could. I lighted *two* candles instead of one. I forswore bed and held myself in readiness for a sally, candle in hand; for, *coute qui coute*, I was resolved to *see* the being, if visible at all, who troubled the nightly stillness of my mansion. I was fidgetty and nervous and tried in vain to interest myself with my books. I walked up and down my room, whistling in turn martial and hilarious music and listening ever and anon for the dreaded noise. I sat down and stared at the square label on the solemn and reserved-looking black bottle, until FLANAGAN & CO.'S BEST OLD MALT WHISKEY grew into a sort of subdued accompaniment to all the fantastic and horrible speculations which chased one another through my brain.

Silence, meanwhile, grew more silent, and darkness darker. I listened in vain for the rumble of a vehicle or the dull clamour of a distant row. There was nothing but the sound of a rising wind, which had succeeded the thunder-storm that had travelled over the Dublin mountains quite out of hearing. In the middle of this great city I began to feel myself alone with nature and heaven knows what beside. My courage was ebbing. Punch, however, which makes beasts of so many, made a man of me again – just in time to hear with tolerable nerve and firmness the lumpy, flabby, naked feet deliberately descending the stairs again.

I took a candle, not without a tremor. As I crossed the floor I tried to extemporise a prayer, but stopped short to listen and never finished it. The steps continued. I confess I hesitated for some seconds at the door before I took heart of grace and opened it. When I peeped out the lobby was perfectly empty – there was no monster standing on the staircase; and as the detested sound ceased, I was reassured enough to venture forward nearly to the banisters. Horror of horrors! within a stair or two beneath the spot where I stood the unearthly tread smote the floor. My eye caught something in motion; it was about the size of Goliah's foot – it was grey, heavy and flapped with a dead weight from one step to another. As I am alive, it was the most monstrous grey rat I ever beheld or imagined.

Shakespeare says – 'Some men there are cannot abide a gaping pig, and some that are mad if they behold a cat.' I went well-nigh out of my wits when I beheld this *rat*, for, laugh at me as you may, it fixed upon me, I thought, a perfectly human expression of malice; and, as it shuffled about and looked up into my face almost from between my feet, I saw, I could swear it – I felt it then and know it now, the infernal gaze and the accursed countenance of my old friend in the portrait, transfused into the visage of the bloated vermin before me.

I bounced into my room again with a feeling of loathing and horror I cannot describe and locked and bolted my door as if a lion had been at the other side. Damn him or *it*, curse the portrait and its original! I felt in my soul that the rat – yes, the *rat*, the RAT I had just seen, was that evil being in masquerade and rambling through the house upon some infernal night lark.

Next morning I was early trudging through the miry streets; and, among other transactions, posted a peremptory note recalling Tom. On my return, however, I found a note from my absent 'chum', announcing his intended return next day. I was doubly rejoiced at this, because I had succeeded in getting rooms; and because the change of scene and return of my comrade were rendered specially pleasant by the last night's half ridiculous half horrible adventure.

I slept extemporaneously in my new quarters in Digges' Street that night and next morning returned for breakfast to the haunted mansion, where I was certain Tom would call immediately on his arrival.

I was quite right – he came; and almost his first question referred to the primary object of our change of residence.

'Thank God,' he said with genuine fervour, on hearing that all was arranged. 'On *your* account I am delighted. As to myself, I assure you that no earthly consideration could have induced me ever again to pass a night in this disastrous old house.'

'Confound the house!' I ejaculated, with a genuine mixture of fear and detestation, 'we have not had a pleasant hour since we came to live here'; and so I went on and related incidentally my adventure with the plethoric old rat.

'Well, if that were *all*,' said my cousin, affecting to make light of the matter, 'I don't think I should have minded it very much.'

'Ay, but its eye – its countenance, my dear Tom,' – urged I; 'if you had seen that, you would have felt it might be *anything* but what it seemed.'

'I inclined to think the best conjurer in such a case would be an able-bodied cat,' he said, with a provoking chuckle.

'But let us hear your own adventure,' I said tartly.

At this challenge he looked uneasily round him. I had poked up a very unpleasant recollection.

'You shall hear it, Dick; I'll tell it to you,' he said. 'Begad, sir, I should feel quite queer, though, telling it *here*, though we are too strong a body for ghosts to meddle with just now.'

Though he spoke this like a joke, I think it was serious calculation. Our Hebe was in a corner of the room, packing our cracked delft tea- and dinner-services in a basket. She soon suspended operations and with mouth and eyes wide open became an absorbed listener. Tom's experiences were told nearly in these words –

'I saw it three times, Dick – three distinct times; and I am perfectly certain it meant me some infernal harm. I was, I say, in danger – in *extreme* danger; for, if nothing else had happened, my reason would most certainly have failed me, unless I had escaped so soon. Thank God. I *did* escape.

'The first night of this hateful disturbance, I was lying in the attitude of sleep, in that lumbering old bed. I hate to think of it. I was really wide awake, though I had put out my candle, and was lying as quietly as if I had been asleep; and although accidentally restless, my thoughts were running in a cheerful and agreeable channel.

'I think it must have been two o'clock at least when I thought I heard a sound in that – that odious dark recess at the far end of the bedroom. It was as if someone was drawing a piece of cord slowly along the floor, lifting it up and dropping it softly down again in coils. I sat up once or twice in my bed, but could see nothing, so I concluded it must be mice in the wainscot. I felt no emotion graver than curiosity and after a few minutes ceased to observe it.

'While lying in this state, strange to say, without at first a suspicion of anything supernatural, on a sudden I saw an old man, rather stout and square, in a sort of roan-red dressing-gown and with a black cap on his head, moving stiffly and slowly in a diagonal direction, from the recess, across the floor of the bedroom, passing my bed at the foot and entering the lumber-closet at the left. He had something under his arm; his head hung a little at one side; and, merciful God! when I saw his face . . . '

Tom stopped for a while, and then said –

'That awful countenance, which living or dying I never can forget, disclosed what he was. Without turning to the right or left, he passed beside me and entered the closet by the bed's head.

'While this fearful and indescribable type of death and guilt was passing, I felt that I had no more power to speak or stir than if I had been myself a corpse. For hours after it had disappeared, I was too terrified and weak to move. As soon as daylight came, I took courage and examined the room and especially the course which the frightful intruder had seemed to take, but there was not a vestige to indicate anybody's having passed there; no sign of any disturbing agency visible among the lumber that strewed the floor of the closet.

'I now began to recover a little. I was fagged and exhausted and, at last, overpowered by a feverish sleep. I came down late; and finding you out of spirits, on account of your dreams about the portrait, whose *original* I am now certain disclosed himself to me, I did not care to talk about the infernal vision. In fact, I was trying to persuade myself that the whole thing was an illusion and I did not like to revive in their intensity the hated impressions of the past night – or to risk the constancy of my scepticism by recounting the tale of my sufferings.

'It required some nerve, I can tell you, to go to my haunted chamber next night and lie down quietly in the same bed,' continued Tom. 'I did so with a degree of trepidation, which, I am not ashamed to say, a very little matter would have sufficed to stimulate to downright panic. This night, however, passed off quietly enough, as also the next; and so too did two or three more. I grew more confident and began to fancy that I believed in the theories of spectral illusions, with which I had at first vainly tried to impose upon my convictions.

'The apparition had been, indeed, altogether anomalous. It had crossed the room without any recognition of my presence: I had not disturbed *it* and *it* had no mission to *me*. What, then, was the imaginable use of its crossing the room in a visible shape at all? Of course it might have *been* in the closet instead of *going* there, as easily as it introduced itself into the recess without entering the chamber in a shape discernible by the senses. Besides, how the deuce had I seen it? It was a dark night; I had no candle; there was no fire; and yet I saw it as distinctly, in colouring and outline, as ever I beheld human form! A cataleptic dream would explain it all; and I was determined that a dream it should be.

'One of the most remarkable phenomena connected with the practice of mendacity is the vast number of deliberate lies we tell ourselves, whom, of all persons, we can least expect to deceive. In all this, I need hardly tell you, Dick, I was simply lying to myself and did not believe one word of the wretched humbug. Yet I went on, as men will do, like persevering charlatans and impostors, who tire people into credulity by the mere force of reiteration; so I hoped to win myself over at last to a comfortable scepticism about the ghost.

'He had not appeared a second time – that certainly was a comfort; and what, after all, did I care for him and his queer old toggery and strange looks? Not a fig! I was nothing the worse for having seen him and a good story the better. So I tumbled into bed, put out my candle and, cheered by a loud drunken quarrel in the back lane, went fast asleep.

'From this deep slumber I awoke with a start. I knew I had had a horrible dream; but what it was I could not remember. My heart was thumping furiously; I felt bewildered and feverish; I sat up in the bed and looked about the room. A broad flood of moonlight came in through the curtainless window; everything was as I had last seen it; and though the domestic squabble in the back lane was, unhappily for me, allayed, I yet could hear a pleasant fellow singing, on his way home, the then popular comic ditty called, 'Murphy Delany'. Taking advantage of this diversion I lay down again, with my face towards the fireplace, and closing my eyes, did my best to think of nothing else but the song, which was every moment growing fainter in the distance –

'Twas Murphy Delany, so funny and frisky,
    Stept into a shebeen shop to get his skin full;
He reeled out again pretty well lined with whiskey,
    As fresh as a shamrock, as blind as a bull.

'The singer, whose condition I dare say resembled that of his hero, was soon too far off to regale my ears any more; and as his music died away, I myself sank into a doze, neither sound nor refreshing. Somehow the song had got into my head and I went meandering on through the adventures of my respectable fellow-countryman, who, on emerging from the 'shebeen shop', fell into a river, from which he was fished up to be 'sat upon' by a coroner's jury, who having learned from a 'horse-doctor' that he was 'dead as a door-nail, so there was an end', returned their verdict accordingly, just as he returned to his senses, when an angry altercation and a pitched battle between the body and the coroner winds up the lay with due spirit and pleasantry.

'Through this ballad I continued with a weary monotony to plod, down to the very last line and then *da capo* and so on, in my uncomfortable half-sleep, for how long, I can't conjecture. I found myself at last, however, muttering, '*dead* as a door-nail, so there was an end'; and something like another voice within me, seemed to say, very faintly, but sharply, 'dead! dead! *dead!* and may the Lord have mercy on your soul!' and instantaneously I was wide awake and staring right before me from the pillow.

'Now – will you believe it, Dick? – I saw the same accursed figure standing full front and gazing at me with its stony and fiendish countenance not two yards from the bedside.'

Tom stopped here and wiped the perspiration from his face. I felt very queer. The girl was as pale as Tom; and, assembled as we were in the very scene of these adventures, we were all, I dare say, equally grateful for the clear daylight and the resuming bustle out of doors.

'For about three seconds only I saw it plainly; then it grew indistinct; but, for a long time, there was something like a column of dark vapour where it had been standing, between me and the wall; and I felt sure that he was still there. After a good while, this appearance went too. I took my clothes downstairs to the hall, and dressed there, with the door half open; then went out into the street and walked about the town till morning when I came back, in a miserable state of nervousness and exhaustion. I was such a fool, Dick, as to be ashamed to tell you how I came to be so upset. I thought you would laugh at me; especially as I had always talked philosophy and treated your ghosts with contempt. I concluded you would give me no quarter; and so kept my tale of horror to myself.

'Now, Dick, you will hardly believe me, when I assure you, that for many nights after this last experience, I did not go to my room at all. I used to sit up for a while in the drawing-room after you had gone up to your bed; and then steal down softly to the hall-door, let myself out, and sit in the Robin Hood tavern until the last guest went off; and then I got through the night like a sentry, pacing the streets till morning.

'For more than a week I never slept in bed. I sometimes had a snooze on a form in the Robin Hood and sometimes a nap in a chair during the day; but regular sleep I had absolutely none.

'I was quite resolved that we should get into another house; but I could not bring myself to tell you the reason and I somehow put it off from day to day, although my life was, during every hour of this procrastination, rendered as miserable as that of a felon with the constables on his track. I was growing absolutely ill from this wretched mode of life.

'One afternoon I determined to enjoy an hour's sleep upon your bed. I hated mine; so that I had never, except in a stealthy visit every day to unmake it, lest Martha should discover the secret of my nightly absence, entered the ill-omened chamber.

'As ill-luck would have it, you had locked your bedroom and taken away the key. I went into my own to unsettle the bedclothes, as usual, and give the bed the appearance of having been slept in. Now, a variety of circumstances concurred to bring about the dreadful scene through which I was that night to pass. In the first place, I was literally overpowered with fatigue and longing for sleep; in the next place, the effect of this extreme exhaustion upon my nerves resembled that of a narcotic and rendered me less susceptible than, perhaps I should in any other condition have been, of the exciting fears which had become habitual to me. Then again, a little bit of the window was open, a pleasant freshness pervaded the room and, to crown all, the cheerful sun of day was making the room quite pleasant. What was to prevent my enjoying an hour's nap *here*? The whole air was resonant with the cheerful hum of life and the broad matter-of-fact light of day filled every corner of the room.

'I yielded – stifling my qualms – to the almost overpowering temptation; and merely throwing off my coat and loosening my cravat, I lay down, limiting myself to *half* an hour's doze in the unwonted enjoyment of a feather bed, a coverlet and a bolster.

'It was horribly insidious; and the demon, no doubt, marked my infatuated preparations. Dolt that I was, I fancied, with mind and body worn out for want of sleep and an arrear of a full week's rest to my credit, that such measure as *half* an hour's sleep, in such a situation, was possible. My sleep was death-like, long, and dreamless.

'Without a start or fearful sensation of any kind, I waked gently, but completely. It was, as you have good reason to remember, long past midnight – I believe, about two o'clock. When sleep has been deep and long enough to satisfy nature thoroughly, one often wakens in this way, suddenly, tranquilly and completely.

'There was a figure seated in that lumbering, old sofa-chair, near the fireplace. Its back was rather towards me, but I could not be mistaken; it turned slowly round and, merciful heavens! there was the stony face, with its infernal lineaments of malignity and despair, gloating on me. There was now no doubt as to its consciousness of my presence and the hellish malice with which it was animated, for it arose and drew close to the bedside. There was a rope about its neck and the other end, coiled up, it held stiffly in its hand.

'My good angel nerved me for this horrible crisis. I remained for some seconds transfixed by the gaze of this tremendous phantom. He came close to the bed and appeared on the point of mounting upon it. The next instant I was upon the floor at the far side and in a moment more was, I don't know how, upon the lobby.

'But the spell was not yet broken; the valley of the shadow of death was not yet traversed. The abhorred phantom was before me there; it was standing near the banisters, stooping a little, and with one end of the rope round its own neck, was poising a noose at the other, as if to throw over mine; and while engaged in this baleful pantomime, it wore a smile so sensual, so unspeakably dreadful, that my senses were nearly overpowered. I saw and remember nothing more, until I found myself in your room.

'I had a wonderful escape, Dick – there is no disputing *that* – an escape for which, while I live, I shall bless the mercy of heaven. No one can conceive or imagine what it is for flesh and blood to stand in the presence of such a thing, but one who has had the terrific experience. Dick, Dick, a shadow has passed over me – a chill has crossed my blood and marrow and I will never be the same again – never, Dick – never!'

Our handmaid, a mature girl of two-and-fifty, as I have said, stayed her hand, as Tom's story proceeded, and by little and little drew near to us, with open mouth and her brows contracted over her little, beady black eyes, till, stealing a glance over her shoulder now and then, she established herself close behind us. During the relation, she had made various earnest comments, in an undertone; but these and her ejaculations, for the sake of brevity and simplicity, I have omitted in my narration.

'It's often I heard tell of it,' she now said, 'but I never believed it rightly till now – though, indeed, why should not I? Does not my mother, down there in the lane, know quare stories, God bless us, beyant telling about it? But you ought not to have slept in the back bedroom. She was loath to let me be going in and out of that room even in the daytime, let alone for any Christian to spend the night in it; for sure she says it was his own bedroom.'

'*Whose* own bedroom?' we asked, in a breath.

'Why, *his* – the ould Judge's – Judge Horrocks', to be sure, God rest his sowl,' and she looked fearfully round.

'Amen!' I muttered. 'But did he die there?'

'Die there! No, not quite *there*,' she said. 'Shure, was not it over the banisters he hung himself, the ould sinner, God be merciful to us all? And was not it in the alcove they found the handles of the skipping-rope cut off and the knife where he was settling the cord, God bless us, to hang himself with? It was his housekeeper's daughter owned the rope, my mother often told me, and the child never throve after and used to be starting up out of her sleep and screeching in the night time, wid dhrames and frights that cum an her; and they said how it was the speerit of the ould Judge that was tormentin' her; and she used to be roaring and yelling out to hould back the big ould fellow with the crooked neck; and then she'd screech, "Oh, the master! the master! he's stampin' at me and beckoning to me! Mother, darling, don't let me go!" And so the poor crathure died at last and the docthers said it was wather on the brain, for it was all they could say.'

'How long ago was all this?' I asked.

'Oh, then, how would I know?' she answered. 'But it must be a wondherful long time ago, for the housekeeper was an ould woman, with a pipe in her mouth and not a tooth left and better nor eighty years ould when my mother was first married; and they said she was a rale buxom, fine-dressed woman when the ould Judge come to his end; an', indeed, my mother's not far from eighty years ould herself this day; and what made it worse for the unnatural ould villain, God rest his soul, to frighten the little girl out of the world the way he did, was what was mostly thought and believed by everyone. My mother says how the poor little crathure was his own child; for he was by all accounts an ould villain every way, an' the hangin'est judge that ever was known in Ireland's ground.'

'From what you said about the danger of sleeping in that bedroom,' said I, 'I suppose there were stories about the ghost having appeared there to others.'

'Well, there *was* things said – quare things, surely,' she answered, as it seemed, with some reluctance. 'And why would not there? Sure was it not up in that same room he slept for more than twenty years? – and was it not in the *alcove* he got the rope ready that done his own business at last, the way he done many a betther man's in his lifetime? – and was not the body lying in the same bed after death and put in the coffin there, too, and carried out to his grave from it in Pether's churchyard, after the coroner was done? But there was quare stories – my mother has them all – about how one Nicholas Spaight got into trouble on the head of it.'

'And what did they say of this Nicholas Spaight?' I asked.

'Oh, for that matther, it's soon told,' she answered.

And she certainly did relate a very strange story, which so piqued my curiosity, that I took occasion to visit the ancient lady, her mother, from whom I learned many very curious particulars. Indeed, I am tempted to tell the tale, but my fingers are weary and I must defer it. But if you wish to hear it another time, I shall do my best.

When we had heard the strange tale I have *not* told you, we put one or two further questions to her about the alleged spectral visitations, to which the house had, ever since the death of the wicked old Judge, been subjected.

'No one ever had luck in it,' she told us. 'There was always cross accidents, sudden deaths and short times in it. The first that tuck it was a family – I forget their name – but at any rate there was two young ladies and their papa. He was about sixty and a stout healthy gentleman as you'd wish to see at that age. Well, he slept in that unlucky back bedroom; and, God between us an' harm! sure enough he was found dead one morning, half out of the bed, with his head as black as a sloe and swelled like a puddin', hanging down near the floor. It was a fit, they said. He was as dead as a mackerel and so *he* could not say what it was; but the ould people was all sure that it was nothing at all but the ould Judge, God bless us! that frightened him out of his senses and his life together.

'Some time after there was a rich old maiden lady took the house. I don't know which room *she* slept in, but she lived alone; and at any rate, one morning, the servants going down early to their world, found her sitting on the passage-stairs, shivering and talkin' to herself, quite mad; and never a word more could any of them or her friends get from her ever afterwards but, "Don't ask me to go, for I promised to wait for him." They never made out from her who it was she meant by *him*, but of course those that knew all about the ould house were at no loss for the meaning of all that happened to her.

'Then afterwards, when the house was let out in lodgings, there was Micky Byrne that took the same room, with his wife and three little children; and sure I heard Mrs Byrne myself telling how the children used to be lifted up in the bed at night, she could not see by what mains; and how they were starting and screeching every hour, just all as one as the housekeeper's little girl that died, till at last one night poor Micky had a dhrop in him, the way he used now and again; and what do you think in the middle of the night he thought he heard a noise on the stairs, and being in liquor, nothing less 'd do him but out he must go himself to see what was wrong. Well, after that, all she ever heard of him was himself sayin', "Oh, God!" and a tumble that shook the very house; and there, sure enough, he was lying on the lower stairs, under the lobby, with his neck smashed double undher him, where he was flung over the banisters.'

Then the handmaiden added, 'I'll go down to the lane and send up Joe Gawey to pack up the rest of the taythings and bring all the things across to your new lodgings.'

And so we all sallied out together, each of us breathing more freely, I have no doubt, as we crossed that ill-omened threshold for the last time.

Now, I may add thus much, in compliance with the immemorial usage of the realm of fiction, which sees the hero not only through his adventures, but fairly out of the world. You must have perceived that what the flesh-blood-and-bone hero of romance proper is to the regular compounder of fiction, this old house of brick-wood-and-mortar is to the humble recorder of this true tale. I, therefore, relate, as in duty bound, the catastrophe which ultimately befell it, which was simply this – that about two years subsequently to my story it was taken by a quack doctor, who called himself Baron Duhlstoerf and filled the parlour windows with bottles of indescribable horrors preserved in brandy, and the newspapers with the usual grandiloquent and mendacious advertisements. This gentleman among his virtues did not reckon sobriety and one night, being overcome with much wine, he set fire to his bed curtains, partially burned himself and totally consumed the house. It was afterwards rebuilt and for a time an undertaker established himself in the premises.

I have now told you my own and Tom's adventures, together with some valuable collateral particulars; and having acquitted myself of my engagement, I wish you a very good-night, and pleasant dreams.

Narrative of a Ghost of a Hand

Joseph Sheridan Le Fanu 1814–1873

I'm sure she believed every word she related, for old Sally was veracious. But all this was worth just so much as such talk commonly is – marvels, fabulæ, what our ancestors called winter's tales – which gathered details from every narrator and dilated in the act of narration. Still it was not quite for nothing that the house was held to be haunted. Under all this smoke there smouldered just a little spark of truth – an authenticated mystery, for the solution of which some of my readers may possibly suggest a theory, though I confess I can't.

Miss Rebecca Chattesworth, in a letter dated late in the autumn of 1753, gives a minute and curious relation of occurrences in the Tiled House, which, it is plain, although at starting she protests against all such fooleries, she has heard with a peculiar sort of interest and relates it certainly with an awful sort of particularity.

I was for printing the entire letter, which is really very singular as well as characteristic. But my publisher meets me with his *veto*; and I believe he is right. The worthy old lady's letter *is*, perhaps, too long; and I must rest content with a few hungry notes of its tenor.

That year, and somewhere about the 24th October, there broke out a strange dispute between Mr Alderman Harper, of High Street, Dublin, and my Lord Castlemallard, who, in virtue of his cousinship to the young heir's mother, had undertaken for him the management of the tiny estate on which the Tiled or Tyled House – for I find it spelt both ways – stood.

This Alderman Harper had agreed for a lease of the house for his daughter, who was married to a gentleman named Prosser. He furnished it and put up hangings and otherwise went to considerable expense. Mr and Mrs Prosser came there sometime in June, and after having parted with a good many servants in the interval, she made up her mind that she could not live in the house and her father waited on Lord Castlemallard and told him plainly that he would not take out the lease because the house was subjected to annoyances which he could not explain. In plain terms, he said it was haunted and that no servants would live there more than a few weeks and that after what his son-in-law's family had suffered there, not only should he be excused from taking a lease of it, but that the house itself ought to be pulled down as a nuisance and the habitual haunt of something worse than human malefactors.

Lord Castlemallard filed a bill in the Equity side of the Exchequer to compel Mr Alderman Harper to perform his contract, by taking out the lease. But the Alderman drew an answer, supported by no less than seven long affidavits, copies of all which were furnished to his lordship, and with the desired effect; for rather than compel him to place them upon the file of the court, his lordship struck, and consented to release him.

I am sorry the cause did not proceed at least far enough to place upon the files of the court the very authentic and unaccountable story which Miss Rebecca relates.

The annoyances described did not begin till the end of August, when, one evening, Mrs Prosser, quite alone, was sitting in the twilight at the back parlour window, which was open, looking out into the orchard, and plainly saw a hand stealthily placed upon the stone window-sill outside, as if by someone beneath the window, at her right side, intending to climb up. There was nothing but the hand, which was rather short but handsomely formed and white and plump, laid on the edge of the window-sill; and it was not a very young hand, but one aged somewhere about forty, as she conjectured. It was only a few weeks before that the horrible robbery at Clondalkin had taken place and the lady fancied that the hand was that of one of the miscreants who was now about to scale the windows of the Tiled House. She uttered a loud scream and an ejaculation of terror and at the same moment the hand was quietly withdrawn.

Search was made in the orchard, but no indications of any person's having been under the window, beneath which, ranged along the wall, stood a great column of flower-pots, which it seemed must have prevented any one's coming within reach of it.

The same night there came a hasty tapping, every now and then, at the window of the kitchen. The women grew frightened and the servant-man, taking fire-arms with him, opened the back-door, but discovered nothing. As he shut it, however, he said, 'a thump came on it', and a pressure as of somebody striving to force his way in, which frightened *him*; and though the tapping went on upon the kitchen window panes, he made no further explorations.

About six o'clock on the Saturday evening following, the cook, 'an honest, sober woman, now aged nigh sixty years', being alone in the kitchen, saw, on looking up, it is supposed, the same fat but aristo-cratic-looking hand, laid with its palm against the glass, near the side of the window and this time moving slowly up and down, pressed all the while against the glass, as if feeling carefully for some inequality in its surface. She cried out and said something like a prayer on seeing it. But it was not withdrawn for several seconds after.

After this, for a great many nights, there came at first a low and afterwards an angry rapping, as it seemed with a set of clenched knuckles, at the back-door. And the servant-man would not open it, but called to know who was there; and there came no answer, only a sound as if the palm of the hand was placed against it, and drawn slowly from side to side with a sort of soft, groping motion.

All this time, sitting in the back parlour, which, for the time, they used as a drawing-room, Mr and Mrs Prosser were disturbed by rappings at the window, sometimes very low and furtive, like a clandestine signal, and at others sudden and so loud as to threaten the breaking of the pane.

This was all at the back of the house, which looked upon the orchard as you know. But on a Tuesday night, at about half-past nine, there came precisely the same rapping at the hall-door and it went on, to the great annoyance of the master and terror of his wife, at intervals, for nearly two hours.

After this, for several days and nights, they had no annoyance whatsoever and began to think that the nuisance had expended itself. But on the night of the 13th September, Jane Easterbrook, an English maid, having gone into the pantry for the small silver bowl in which her mistress's posset was served, happening to look up at the little window of only four panes, observed through an augur-hole which was drilled through the window frame, for the admission of a bolt to secure the shutter, a white pudgy finger – first the tip and then the two first joints introduced and turned about thus way and that, crooked against the inside, as if in search of a fastening which its owner destined to push aside. When the maid got back into the kitchen, we are told 'she fell into "a swounde", and was all the next day very weak.'

Mr Prosser being, I've heard, a hard-headed and conceited sort of fellow, scouted the ghost and sneered at the fears of his family. He was privately of the opinion that the whole affair was a practical joke or a fraud and waited an opportunity of catching the rogue *in flagrante delicto*. He did not long keep this theory to himself, but let it out by degrees with no stint of oaths and threats, believing that some domestic traitor held the thread of the conspiracy.

Indeed it was time something were done; for not only his servants, but good Mrs Prosser herself, had grown to look unhappy and anxious. They kept at home from the hour of sunset and would not venture about the house after nightfall, except in couples.

The knocking had ceased for about a week; when one night, Mrs Prosser being in the nursery, her husband, who was in the parlour, heard it begin very softly at the hall-door. The air was quite still, which favoured his hearing distinctly. This was the first time there had been any disturbance at that side of the house and the character of the summons was changed.

Mr Prosser, leaving the parlour-door open, it seems, went quietly into the hall. The sound was that of beating on the outside of the stout door, softly and regularly, 'with the flat of the hand'. He was going to open it suddenly, but changed his mind; and went back very quietly, and on to the head of the kitchen stair, where was a 'strong closet' over the pantry, in which he kept his firearms, swords and canes.

Here he called his manservant, whom he believed to be honest, and, with a pair of loaded pistols in his own coat-pockets and giving another pair to him, he went as lightly as he could, followed by the man and with a stout walking-cane in his hand, forward to the door.

Everything went as Mr Prosser wished. The besieger of his house, so far from taking fright at their approach, grew more impatient; and the sort of patting which had aroused his attention at first assumed the rhythm and emphasis of a series of double-knocks.

Mr Prosser, angry, opened the door with his right arm across, cane in hand. Looking, he saw nothing; but his arm was jerked up oddly, as it might be with the hollow of a hand and something passed under it, with a kind of gentle squeeze. The servant neither saw nor felt anything, and did not know why his master looked back so hastily, cutting with his cane and shutting the door with so sudden a slam.

From that time Mr Prosser discontinued his angry talk and swearing about it and seemed nearly as averse from the subject as the rest of his family. He grew, in fact, very uncomfortable, feeling an inward persuasion that when, in answer to the summons, he had opened the hall-door, he had actually given admission to the besieger.

He said nothing to Mrs Prosser, but went up earlier to his bedroom, 'where he read a while in his Bible, and said his prayers'. I hope the particular relation of this circumstance does not indicate its singularity. He lay awake a good while, it appears; and, as he supposed, about a quarter past twelve he heard the soft palm of a hand patting on the outside of the bedroom-door and then brushed slowly along it.

Up bounced Mr Prosser, very much frightened, and locked the door, crying, 'Who's there?' but receiving no answer, but the same brushing sound of a soft hand drawn over the panels, which he knew only too well.

In the morning the housemaid was terrified by the impression of a hand in the dust of the 'little parlour' table, where they had been unpacking delft and other things the day before. The print of the naked foot in the sea-sand did not frighten Robinson Crusoe half so much. They were by this time all nervous, and some of them half-crazed, about the hand.

Mr Prosser went to examine the mark and made light of it, but, as he swore afterwards, rather to quiet his servants than from any comfortable feeling about it in his own mind; however, he had them all, one by one, into the room and made each place his or her hand, palm downward, on the same table, thus taking a similar impression from every person in the house, including himself and his wife; and his 'affidavit' deposed that the formation of the hand so impressed differed altogether from those of the living inhabitants of the house and corresponded with that of the hand seen by Mrs Prosser and by the cook.

Whoever or whatever the owner of that hand might be, they all felt this subtle demonstration to mean that it was declared he was no longer out of doors, but had established himself in the house.

And now Mrs Prosser began to be troubled with strange and horrible dreams, some of which as set out in detail, in Aunt Rebecca's long letter, are really very appalling nightmares. But one night, as Mr Prosser closed his bedchamber-door, he was struck somewhat by the utter silence of the room, there being no sound of breathing, which seemed unaccountable to him, as he knew his wife was in bed and his ears were particularly sharp.

There was a candle burning on a small table at the foot of the bed, besides the one he held in one hand, a heavy ledger, connected with his father-in-law's business being under his arm. He drew the curtain at the side of the bed and saw Mrs Prosser lying, as for a few seconds he mortally feared, dead, her face being motionless, white, and covered with a cold dew; and on the pillow, close beside her head and just within the curtains, was, as he first thought, a toad – but really the same fattish hand, the wrist resting on the pillow, and the fingers extended towards her temple.

Mr Prosser, with a horrified jerk, pitched the ledger right at the curtains, behind which the owner of the hand might be supposed to stand. The hand was instantaneously and smoothly snatched away, the curtains made a great wave and Mr Prosser got round the bed in time to see the closet-door, which was at the other side, pulled to by the same white, puffy hand, as he believed.

He drew the door open with a fling and stared in: but the closet was empty, except for the clothes hanging from the pegs on the wall and the dressing-table and looking-glass facing the windows. He shut it sharply and locked it and felt for a minute, he says, 'as if he were like to lose his wits'; then, ringing at the bell, he brought the servants and with much ado they recovered Mrs Prosser from a sort of 'trance', in which, he says, from her looks, she seemed to have suffered 'the pains of death': and Aunt Rebecca adds, 'from what she told me of her visions, with her own lips, he might have added, "and of hell also".'

But the occurrence which seems to have determined the crisis was the strange sickness of their eldest child, a little boy aged between two and three years. He lay awake, seemingly in paroxysms of terror, and the doctors who were called in, set down the symptoms to incipient water on the brain. Mrs Prosser used to sit up with the nurse, by the nursery fire, much troubled in mind about the condition of her child.

His bed was placed sideways along the wall, with its head against the door of a press or cupboard, which, however, did not shut quite close. There was a little valance, about a foot deep, round the top of the child's bed and this descended within some ten or twelve inches of the pillow on which it lay.

They observed that the little creature was quieter whenever they took it up and held it on their laps. They had just replaced him, as he seemed to have grown quite sleepy and tranquil, but he was not five minutes in his bed when he began to scream in one of his frenzies of terror; at the same moment the nurse, for the first time, detected, and Mrs Prosser equally plainly saw, following the direction of *her* eyes, the real cause of the child's sufferings.

Protruding through the aperture of the press and shrouded in the shade of the valance, they plainly saw the white fat hand, palm downwards, presented towards the head of the child. The mother uttered a scream and snatched the child from its little bed and she and the nurse ran down to the lady's sleeping-room, where Mr Prosser was in bed, shutting the door as they entered; and they had hardly done so, when a gentle tap came to it from the outside.

There is a great deal more, but this will suffice. The singularity of the narrative seems to me to be this, that it describes the ghost of a hand and no more. The person to whom that hand belonged never once appeared; nor was it a hand separated from a body, but only a hand so manifested and introduced that its owner was always, by some crafty accident, hidden from view.

In the year 1819, at a college breakfast, I met a Mr Prosser – a thin, grave, but rather chatty old gentleman, with very white hair drawn back into a pigtail – and he told us all, with a concise particularity, a story of his cousin, James Prosser, who, when an infant, had slept for some time in what his mother said was a haunted nursery in an old house near Chapelizod and who, whenever he was ill, over-fatigued, or in anywise feverish, suffered all through his life as he had done from a time he could scarce remember, from a vision of a certain gentleman, fat and pale, every curl of whose wig, every button and fold of whose laced clothes and every feature and line of whose sensual, benignant and unwholesome face, was as minutely engraven upon his memory as the dress and lineaments of his own grandfather's portrait, which hung before him every day at breakfast, dinner and supper.

Mr Prosser mentioned this as an instance of a curiously monotonous, individualised and persistent nightmare and hinted the extreme horror and anxiety with which his cousin, of whom he spoke in the past tense as 'poor Jemmie', was at any time induced to mention it.

I hope the reader will pardon me for loitering so long in the Tiled House, but this sort of lore has always had a charm for me; and people, you know, especially old people, will talk of what most interests themselves, too often forgetting that others may have had more than enough of it.

Fisher's Ghost

JOHN LANG c.1816-1864

IN THE COLONY of New South Wales, at a place called Penrith, distant from Sydney about thirty-seven miles, lived a farmer named Fisher. He had been, originally, transported, but had become free by servitude. Unceasing toil, and great steadiness of character, had acquired for him a considerable property, for a person in his station of life. His lands and stock were not worth less than four thousand pounds. He was unmarried and was about forty-five years old.

Suddenly Fisher disappeared; and one of his neighbours – a man named Smith – gave out that he had gone to England, but would return in two or three years. Smith produced a document, purporting to be executed by Fisher; and, according to this document, Fisher had appointed Smith to act as his agent during his absence. Fisher was a man of very singular habits and eccentric character and his silence about his departure, instead of creating surprise, was declared to be 'exactly like him'.

About six months after Fisher's disappearance, an old man called Ben Weir, who had a small farm near Penrith and who always drove his own cart to market, was returning from Sydney one night when he beheld, seated on a rail which bounded the road – Fisher. The night was very dark and the distance of the fence from the middle of the road was, at least, twelve yards. Weir, nevertheless, saw Fisher's figure seated on the rail. He pulled his old mare up, and called out, 'Fisher, is that you?' No answer was returned; but there, still on the rail, sat the form of the man with whom he had been on the most intimate terms. Weir – who was not drunk, though he had taken several glasses of strong liquor on the road – jumped off his cart and approached the rail. To his surprise, the form vanished.

'Well,' exclaimed old Weir, 'this is very curious, anyhow;' and, breaking several branches of a sapling so as to mark the exact spot, he remounted his cart, put his old mare into a jog-trot and soon reached his home.

Ben was not likely to keep this vision a secret from his old woman. All that he had seen he faithfully related to her.

'Hold our nonsense, Ben!' was old Betty's reply. 'You know you have been a drinking and disturbing of your imagination. Ain't Fisher agone to England? And if he had a come back, do you think we shouldn't a heard on it?'

'Ay, Betty!' said old Ben, 'but he'd a cruel gash in his forehead and the blood was all fresh like. Faith, it makes me shudder to think on't. It were his ghost.'

'How can you talk so foolish, Ben?' said the old woman. 'You must be drunk sure-ly to get on about ghostesses.'

'I tell thee I am *not* drunk,' rejoined old Ben, angrily. 'There's been foul play, Betty; I'm sure on't. There sat Fisher on the rail – not more than a matter of two mile from this. Egad, it were on his own fence that he sat. There he was, in his shirt-sleeves, with his arms a folded; just as he used to sit when he was a waiting for anybody coming up the road. Bless you, Betty, I seed 'im till I was as close as I am to thee; when, all on a sudden, he vanished, like smoke.'

'Nonsense, Ben: don't talk of it,' said old Betty, 'or the neighbours will only laugh at you. Come to bed and you'll forget all about it before tomorrow morning.'

Old Ben went to bed; but he did not next morning forget all about what he had seen on the previous night: on the contrary, he was more positive than before. However, at the earnest and often repeated request of the old woman, he promised not to mention having seen Fisher's ghost, for fear that it might expose him to ridicule.

On the following Thursday night, when old Ben was returning from market – again in his cart – he saw, seated upon the same rail, the identical apparition. He had purposely abstained from drinking that day and was in the full possession of all his senses. On this occasion old Ben was too much alarmed to stop. He urged the old mare on and got home as speedily as possible. As soon as he had unharnessed and fed the mare and taken his purchases out of the cart, he entered his cottage, lighted his pipe, sat over the fire with his better half and gave her an account of how he had disposed of his produce and what he had brought back from Sydney in return. After this he said to her, 'Well, Betty, I'm not drunk tonight, anyhow, am I?'

'No,' said Betty. 'You are quite sober, sensible like, tonight, Ben; and therefore you have come home without any ghost in your head. Ghosts! Don't believe there is such things.'

'Well, you are satisfied I am not drunk; but perfectly sober,' said the old man.

'Yes, Ben,' said Betty.

'Well, then,' said Ben, 'I tell thee what, Betty. I saw Fisher tonight agin!'

'Stuff!' cried old Betty.

'You may say *stuff*,' said the old farmer; 'but I tell you what – I saw him as plainly as I did last Thursday night. Smith is a bad 'un! Do you think Fisher would ever have left this country without coming to bid you and me goodbye?'

'It's all fancy!' said old Betty. 'Now drink your grog and smoke your pipe and think no more about the ghost. I won't hear on't.'

'I'm as fond of my grog and my pipe as most men,' said old Ben; 'but I'm not going to drink anything tonight. It may be all fancy, as you call it, but I am now going to tell Mr Grafton all I saw, and what I think;' and with these words he got up and left the house.

Mr Grafton was a gentleman who lived about a mile from old Weir's farm. He had been formerly a lieutenant in the navy, but was now on half-pay and was a settler in the new colony; he was, moreover, in the commission of the peace.

When old Ben arrived at Mr Grafton's house, Mr Grafton was about to retire to bed, but he requested old Ben might be shown in. He desired the farmer to take a seat by the fire and then enquired what was the latest news in Sydney.

'The news in Sydney, sir, is very small,' said old Ben; 'wheat is falling, but maize still keeps its price – seven and sixpence a bushel: but I want to tell you, sir, something that will astonish you.'

'What is it, Ben?' asked Mr Grafton.

'Why, sir,' resumed old Ben, 'you know I am not a weak-minded man, nor a fool, exactly; for I was born and bred in Yorkshire.'

'No, Ben, I don't believe you to be weak-minded, nor do I think you a fool,' said Mr Grafton; 'but what can you have to say that you come at this late hour and that you require such a preface?'

'That I have seen the ghost of Fisher, sir,' said the old man; and he detailed the particulars of which the reader is already in possession.

Mr Grafton was at first disposed to think with old Betty, that Ben had seen Fisher's Ghost through an extra glass or two of rum on the first night; and that on the second night, when perfectly sober, he was unable to divest himself of the idea previously entertained. But after a little consideration the words 'How very singular!' involuntarily escaped him.

'Go home, Ben,' said Mr Grafton, 'and let me see you tomorrow at sunrise. We will go together to the place where you say you saw the ghost.'

Mr Grafton used to encourage the aboriginal natives of New South Wales (that race which has been very aptly described 'the last link in the human chain') to remain about his premises. At the head of a little tribe then encamped on Mr Grafton's estate, was a sharp young man named Johnny Crook. The peculiar faculty of the aboriginal natives of New South Wales, of tracking the human foot not only over grass but over the hardest rock; and of tracking the whereabouts of runaways by signs imperceptible to civilised eyes, is well known; and this man, Johnny Crook, was famous for his skill in this particular art of tracking. He had recently been instrumental in the apprehension of several desperate bushrangers whom he had tracked over twenty-seven miles of rocky country and fields, which they had crossed bare-footed, in the hope of checking the black fellow in the progress of his keen pursuit with the horse police.

When old Ben Weir made his appearance in the morning at Mr Grafton's house, the black chief, Johnny Crook, was summoned to attend. He came and brought with him several of his subjects. The party set out, old Weir showing the way. The leaves on the branches of the saplings which he had broken on the first night of seeing the ghost were withered and sufficiently pointed out the exact rail on which the phantom was represented to have sat. There were stains upon the rail. Johnny Crook, who had then no idea of what he was required for, pronounced these stains to be 'White man's blood;' and, after searching about for some time, he pointed to a spot whereon he said a human body had been laid.

In New South Wales long droughts are not very uncommon; and not a single shower of rain had fallen for seven months previously – not sufficient even to lay the dust upon the roads.

In consequence of the time that had elapsed, Crook had no small difficulty to contend with; but in about two hours he succeeded in tracking the footsteps of one man to the unfrequented side of a pond at some distance. He gave it as his opinion that another man had been dragged thither. The savage walked round and round the pond, eagerly examining its borders and the sedges and weeds springing up around it. At first he seemed baffled. No clue had been washed ashore to show that anything unusual had been sunk in the pond; but, having finished this examination, he laid himself down on his face and looked keenly along the surface of the smooth and stagnant water. Presently he jumped up, uttered a cry peculiar to the natives when gratified by finding some long-sought object, clapped his hands and, pointing to the middle of the pond to where the decomposition of some sunken substance had produced a slimy coating streaked with prismatic colours, he exclaimed, 'White man's fat!' The pond was immediately searched; and, below the spot indicated, the remains of a body were discovered. A large stone and a rotted silk handkerchief were found near the body; these had been used to sink it.

That it was the body of Fisher there could be no question. It might have been identified by the teeth; but on the waistcoat there were some large brass buttons which were immediately recognised, both by Mr Grafton and by old Ben Weir, as Fisher's property. He had worn those buttons on his waistcoat for several years.

Leaving the body by the side of the pond and old Ben and the blacks to guard it, Mr Grafton cantered up to Fisher's house. Smith was not only in possession of all the missing man's property, but had removed to Fisher's house. It was about a mile and a half distant. He enquired for Mr Smith. Mr Smith, who was at breakfast, came out and invited Mr Grafton to alight; Mr Grafton accepted the invitation and after a few desultory observations said, 'Mr Smith, I am anxious to purchase a piece of land on the other side of the road, belonging to this estate, and I would give a fair price for it. Have you the power to sell?'

'Oh yes, sir,' replied Smith. 'The power which I hold from Fisher is a general power;' and he forthwith produced a document purporting to be signed by Fisher, but which was not witnessed.

'If you are not very busy, I should like to show you the piece of land I allude to,' said Mr Grafton.

'Oh certainly, sir. I am quite at your service,' said Smith; and he then ordered his horse to be saddled.

It was necessary to pass the pond where the remains of Fisher's body were then exposed. When they came near to the spot, Mr Grafton, looking Smith full in the face, said, 'Mr Smith, I wish to show you something. Look here!' He pointed to the decomposed body and narrowly watching Mr Smith's countenance, remarked: 'These are the remains of Fisher. How do you account for their being found in this pond?'

Smith, with the greatest coolness, got off his horse, minutely examined the remains and then admitted that there was no doubt they were Fisher's. He confessed himself at a loss to account for their discovery, unless it could be (he said) that somebody had waylaid him on the road when he left his home for Sydney; had murdered him for the gold and banknotes which he had about his person and had then thrown him into the pond. 'My hands, thank heaven!' he concluded, 'are clean. If my old friend could come to life again, he would tell you that I had no hand in his horrible murder.'

Mr Grafton knew not what to think. He was not a believer in ghosts. Could it be possible, he began to ask himself, that old Weir had committed this crime and – finding it weigh heavily on his conscience and fearing that he might be detected – had trumped up the story about the ghost – had pretended that he was led to the spot by supernatural agency – and thus by bringing the murder voluntarily to light, hoped to stifle all suspicion? But then, he considered Weir's excellent character, his kind disposition and good-nature. These at once put to flight his suspicion of Weir; but still he was by no means satisfied of Smith's guilt, much as appearances were against him.

Fisher's servants were examined and stated that their master had often talked of going to England on a visit to his friends and of leaving Mr Smith to manage his farm; and that though they were surprised when Mr Smith came and said he had 'gone at last', they did not think it at all unlikely that he had done so. An inquest was held and a verdict of wilful murder found against Thomas Smith. He was thereupon transmitted to Sydney for trial, at the ensuing sessions, in the supreme court. The case naturally excited great interest in the colony; and public opinion respecting Smith's guilt was evenly balanced.

The day of trial came; and the court was crowded almost to suffocation. The Attorney-General very truly remarked that there were circumstances connected with the case which were without any precedent in the annals of jurisprudence. The only witnesses were old Weir and Mr Grafton. Smith, who defended himself with great composure and ability, cross-examined them at considerable length and with consummate skill. The prosecution having closed, Smith addressed the jury (which consisted of military officers) in his defence. He admitted that the circumstances were strong against him; but he most ingeniously proceeded to explain them. The power of attorney, which he produced, he contended had been regularly granted by Fisher and he called several witnesses who swore that they believed the signature to be that of the deceased. He, further, produced a will, which had been drawn up by Fisher's attorney, and by that will Fisher had appointed Smith his sole executor, in the event of his death. He declined, he said, to throw any suspicion on Weir; but he would appeal to the common sense of the jury whether the ghost story was entitled to any credit; and, if it were not, to ask themselves why it had been invented? He alluded to the fact – which in cross-examination Mr Grafton swore to – that when the remains were first shown to him, he did not conduct himself as a guilty man would have been likely to do, although he was horror-stricken on beholding the hideous spectacle. He concluded by invoking the Almighty to bear witness that he was innocent of the diabolical crime for which he had been arraigned. The judge (the late Sir Francis Forbes) recapitulated the evidence. It was not an easy matter to deal with that part of it which had reference to the apparition: and if the charge of the judge had any leaning one way or the other, it was decidedly in favour of an acquittal. The jury retired; but, after deliberating for seven hours, they returned to the court, with a verdict of guilty.

The judge then sentenced the prisoner to be hanged on the following Monday. It was on a Thursday night that he was convicted. On the Sunday, Smith expressed a wish to see a clergyman. His wish was instantly attended to, when he confessed that he, and he alone, committed the murder; and that it was upon the very rail where Weir swore that he had seen Fisher's ghost sitting, that he had knocked out Fisher's brains with a tomahawk. The power of attorney he likewise confessed was a forgery, but declared that the will was genuine.

This is very extraordinary, but is, nevertheless, true in substance, if not in every particular. Most persons who have visited Sydney for any length of time will no doubt have had it narrated to them.

The Traveller's Story of a Terribly Strange Bed

WILKIE COLLINS 1824–1889

SHORTLY AFTER my education at college was finished, I happened to be staying at Paris with an English friend. We were both young men then and lived, I am afraid, rather a wild life, in the delightful city of our sojourn. One night we were idling about the neighbourhood of the Palais Royal, doubtful as to what amusement we should next betake ourselves. My friend proposed a visit to Frascati's; but his suggestion was not to my taste. I knew Frascati's, as the French saying is, by heart; had lost and won plenty of five-franc pieces there, merely for amusement's sake, until it was amusement no longer, and was thoroughly tired, in fact, of all the ghastly respectabilities of such a social anomaly as a respectable gambling-house.

'For heaven's sake,' said I to my friend, 'let us go somewhere where we can see a little genuine, blackguard, poverty-stricken gaming, with no false gingerbread glitter thrown over it all. Let us get away from fashionable Frascati's, to a house where they don't mind letting in a man with a ragged coat or a man with no coat, ragged or otherwise.'

'Very well,' said my friend, 'we needn't go out of the Palais Royal to find the sort of company you want. Here's the place just before us; as blackguard a place, by all report, as you could possibly wish to see.' In another minute we arrived at the door and entered the house.

When we got upstairs, we were admitted into the chief gambling-room. We did not find many people assembled there. But, few as the men were who looked up at us on our entrance, they were all types – lamentably true types – of their respective classes.

We had come to see blackguards; but these men were something worse. There is a comic side, more or less appreciable, in all blackguardism – here there was nothing but tragedy – mute, weird tragedy. The quiet in the room was horrible. The thin, haggard, long-haired young man, whose sunken eyes fiercely watched the turning up of the cards, never spoke; the flabby, fat-faced, pimply player, who pricked his piece of pasteboard perseveringly, to register how often black won, and how often red – never spoke; the dirty, wrinkled old man, with the vulture eyes and the darned greatcoat, who had lost his

last *sou*, and still looked on desperately, after he could play no longer –
never spoke. Even the voice of the croupier sounded as if it were
strangely dulled and thickened in the atmosphere of the room. I had
entered the place to laugh, but the spectacle before me was something
to weep over. I soon found it necessary to take refuge in excitement
from the depression of spirits which was fast stealing on me. Unfortunately I sought the nearest excitement, by going to the table and
beginning to play. Still more unfortunately, as the event will show, I
won – won prodigiously; won incredibly; won at such a rate, that the
regular players at the table crowded round me; and staring at my stakes
with hungry, superstitious eyes, whispered to one another, that the
English stranger was going to break the bank.

The game was *Rouge et Noir*. I had played at it in every city in
Europe, without, however, the care or wish to study the Theory of
Chances – that philosopher's stone of all gamblers! And a gambler in
the strict sense of the word, I had never been. I was heart-whole from
the corroding passion for play. My gaming was a mere idle amusement.
I never resorted to it by necessity, because I never knew what it was to
want money. I never practised it so incessantly as to lose more than I
could afford or to gain more than I could coolly pocket without being
thrown off my balance by my good luck. In short, I had hitherto
frequented gambling-tables – just as I frequented ballrooms and opera-
houses – because they amused me and because I had nothing better to
do with my leisure hours.

But on this occasion it was very different – now, for the first time in
my life, I felt what the passion for play really was. My success first
bewildered and then, in the most literal meaning of the word, intoxicated me. Incredible as it may appear, it is nevertheless true, that I only
lost when I attempted to estimate chances and played according to
previous calculation. If I left everything to luck and staked without any
care or consideration, I was sure to win – to win in the face of every
recognised probability in favour of the bank. At first, some of the men
present ventured their money safely enough on my colour; but I speedily
increased my stakes to sums which they dared not risk. One after
another they left off playing and breathlessly looked on at my game.

Still, time after time, I staked higher and higher and still won. The
excitement in the room rose to fever pitch. The silence was interrupted
by a deep-throated chorus of oaths and exclamations in different
languages, every time the gold was shovelled across to my side of the
table – even the imperturbable croupier dashed his rake on the floor in
a (French) fury of astonishment at my success. But one man present
preserved his self-possession; and that man was my friend. He came to

my side and, whispering in English, begged me to leave the place, satisfied with what I had already gained. I must do him the justice to say that he repeated his warnings and entreaties several times and only left me and went away after I had rejected his advice (I was to all intents and purposes gambling-drunk) in terms which rendered it impossible for him to address me again that night.

Shortly after he had gone, a hoarse voice behind me cried: 'Permit me, my dear sir! – permit me to restore to their proper place two Napoleons which you have dropped. Wonderful luck, sir! I pledge you my word of honour, as an old soldier, in the course of my long experience in this sort of thing, I never saw such luck as yours! never! Go on, sir – *Sacre mille bombes!* Go on boldly and break the bank!'

I turned round and saw, nodding and smiling at me with inveterate civility, a tall man, dressed in a frogged and braided surtout.

If I had been in my senses, I should have considered him, personally, as being rather a suspicious specimen of an old soldier. He had goggling bloodshot eyes, mangy moustachios and a broken nose. His voice betrayed a barrack-room intonation of the worst order and he had the dirtiest pair of hands I ever saw – even in France. These little personal peculiarities exercised, however, no repelling influence on me. In the mad excitement, the reckless triumph of that moment, I was ready to 'fraternise' with anybody who encouraged me in my game. I accepted the old soldier's offered pinch of snuff; clapped him on the back and swore he was the honestest fellow in the world – the most glorious relic of the Grand Army that I had ever met with. 'Go on!' cried my military friend, snapping his fingers in ecstasy – 'Go on, and win! Break the bank – *Mille tonnerres!* my gallant English comrade, break the bank!'

And I *did* go on – went on at such a rate, that in another quarter of an hour the croupier called out: 'Gentlemen! the bank has discontinued for tonight.' All the notes, and all the gold in that 'bank', now lay in a heap under my hands; the whole floating capital of the gambling-house was waiting to pour into my pockets!

'Tie up the money in your pocket-handkerchief, my worthy sir,' said the old soldier, as I wildly plunged my hands into my heap of gold. 'Tie it up, as we used to tie up a bit of dinner in the Grand Army; your winnings are too heavy for any breeches pockets that ever were sewed. There! that's it! – shovel them in, notes and all! *Credie!* what luck – Stop! another Napoleon on the floor! *Ah! Sacre petit polisson de Napoleon!* have I found thee at last? Now then, sir – two tight double knots each way with your honourable permission, and the money's safe. Feel it! feel it, fortunate sir! hard and round as a cannon-ball – *Ah, bah!* if they had only fired such cannon-balls at us at Austerlitz – *nom d'un pipe!* if they only had! And now, as an ancient grenadier, as an ex-brave of the French Army, what remains for me to do? I ask what? Simply this: to entreat my valued English friend to drink a bottle of champagne with me and toast the goddess Fortune in foaming goblets before we part!'

Excellent ex-brave! Convivial ancient grenadier! Champagne by all means! An English cheer for an old soldier! Hurrah! hurrah! Another English cheer for the goddess Fortune! Hurrah! hurrah hurrah!

'Bravo! the Englishman; the amiable, gracious Englishman, in whose veins circulates the vivacious blood of France! Another glass? *Ah, bah!* – the bottle is empty! Never mind! *Vive le vin!* I, the old soldier, order another bottle, and half a pound of *bonbons* with it!'

'No, no, ex-brave; never – ancient grenadier! *Your* bottle last time; *my* bottle this. Behold it! Toast away! The French Army! – the great Napoleon! – the present company! the croupier! the honest croupier's wife and daughters – if he has any! the ladies generally! Everybody in the world!'

By the time the second bottle of champagne was emptied, I felt as if I had been drinking liquid fire – my brain seemed all aflame. No excess in wine had ever had this effect on me before in my life. Was it the result of a stimulant acting upon my system when I was in a highly excited state? Was my stomach in a particularly disordered condition? Or was the champagne amazingly strong?

'Ex-brave of the French Army!' cried I, in a mad state of exhilaration, '*I* am on fire! how are *you*? You have set me on fire! Do you hear, my hero of Austerlitz? Let us have a third bottle of champagne to put the flame out!'

The old soldier wagged his head, rolled his goggle eyes, until I expected to see them slip out of their sockets; placed his dirty forefinger by the side of his broken nose; solemnly ejaculated, 'Coffee!' and immediately ran off into an inner room.

The word pronounced by the eccentric veteran seemed to have a magical effect on the rest of the company present. With one accord they all rose to depart. Probably they had expected to profit by my intoxication; but finding that my new friend was benevolently bent on preventing me from getting dead drunk, had now abandoned all hope of thriving pleasantly on my winnings. Whatever their motive might be, at any rate they went away in a body. When the old soldier returned and sat down again opposite to me at the table, we had the room to ourselves. I could see the croupier, in a sort of vestibule which opened out of it, eating his supper in solitude. The silence was now deeper than ever.

A sudden change, too, had come over the 'ex-brave'. He assumed a pretentiously solemn look; and when he spoke to me again his speech was ornamented by no oaths, enforced by no finger-snapping, enlivened by no apostrophes or exclamations.

'Listen, my dear sir,' said he, in mysteriously confidential tones, 'listen to an old soldier's advice. I have been to the mistress of the house (a very charming woman, with a genius for cookery!) to impress on her the necessity of making us some particularly strong and good coffee. You must drink this coffee in order to get rid of your little amiable exaltation of spirits before you think of going home – you *must*, my good and gracious friend! With all that money to take home tonight, it is a sacred duty to yourself to have your wits about you. You are known to be a winner to an enormous extent by several gentlemen present tonight, who, in a certain point of view, are very worthy and excellent fellows; but they are mortal men, my dear sir, and they have their amiable weaknesses! Need I say more? Ah, no, no! you understand me! Now, this is what you must do – send for a cabriolet when you feel quite well again – draw up all the windows when you get into it – and tell the driver to take you home only through the large and well-lighted thoroughfares. Do this; and you and your money will be safe. Do this; and tomorrow you will thank an old soldier for giving you a word of honest advice.'

Just as the ex-brave ended this oration in very lachrymose tones, the coffee came in, ready poured out in two cups. My attentive friend handed me one of the cups with a bow. I was parched with thirst, and drank it off at a draught. Almost instantly afterwards, I was seized with a fit of giddiness and felt more completely intoxicated than ever. The room whirled round and round furiously; the old soldier seemed to be regularly bobbing up and down before me like the piston of a steam-engine. I was half deafened by a violent singing in my ears; a feeling of utter bewilderment, helplessness, idiocy, overcame me. I rose from my chair, holding on by the table to keep my balance; and stammered out, that I felt dreadfully unwell – so unwell that I did not know how I was to get home.

'My dear friend,' answered the old soldier – and even his voice seemed to be bobbing up and down as he spoke – 'my dear friend, it would be madness to go home in *your* state; you would be sure to lose your money; you might be robbed and murdered with the greatest ease. *I* am going to sleep here: do *you* sleep here, too – they make up capital beds in this house – take one; sleep off the effects of the wine, and go home safely with your winnings tomorrow – tomorrow, in broad daylight.'

I had but two ideas left: one, that I must never let go hold of my handkerchief full of money; the other, that I must lie down somewhere immediately and fall off into a comfortable sleep. So I agreed to the proposal about the bed and took the offered arm of the old soldier, carrying my money with my disengaged hand. Preceded by the croupier, we passed along some passages and up a flight of stairs into the bedroom which I was to occupy. The ex-brave shook me warmly by the hand, proposed that we should breakfast together and then, followed by the croupier, left me for the night.

I ran to the wash-hand stand; drank some of the water in my jug; poured the rest out and plunged my face into it; and then sat down in a chair and tried to compose myself. I soon felt better. The change for my lungs, from the fetid atmosphere of the gambling-room to the cool air of the apartment I now occupied; the almost equally refreshing change for my eyes, from the glaring gas-lights of the 'Salon' to the dim, quiet flicker of one bedroom candle, aided wonderfully the restorative effects of cold water. The giddiness left me and I began to feel a little like a reasonable being again. My first thought was of the risk of sleeping all night in a gambling-house; my second, of the still greater risk of trying to get out after the house was closed and of going home alone at night, through the streets of Paris, with a large sum of money about me. I had slept in worse places than this on my travels; so I determined to lock, bolt and barricade my door and take my chance till the next morning.

Accordingly, I secured myself against all intrusion; looked under the bed and into the cupboard; tried the fastening of the window; and then, satisfied that I had taken every precaution, pulled off my upper clothing, put my light, which was a dim one, on the hearth among a feathery litter of wood ashes and got into bed, with the handkerchief full of money under my pillow.

I soon felt not only that I could not go to sleep, but that I could not even close my eyes. I was wide awake and in a high fever. Every nerve in my body trembled – every one of my senses seemed to be preternaturally sharpened. I tossed and rolled and tried every kind of position and perseveringly sought out the cold corners of the bed and all to no purpose. Now, I thrust my arms over the clothes; now, I poked them under the clothes, now, I violently shot my legs straight out down to the bottom of the bed; now, I convulsively coiled them up as near my chin as they would go; now, I shook out my crumpled pillow, changed it to the cool side, patted it flat, and lay down quietly on my back; now, I fiercely doubled it in two, set it up on end, thrust it against the board of the bed and tried a sitting posture. Every effort was in vain; I groaned with vexation, as I felt that I was in for a sleepless night.

What could I do? I had no book to read. And yet, unless I found out some method of diverting my mind, I felt certain that I was in the condition to imagine all sorts of horrors; to rack my brain with forebodings of every possible and impossible danger; in short, to pass the night suffering all conceivable varieties of nervous terror.

I raised myself on my elbow and looked about the room – which was brightened by a lovely moonlight pouring straight through the window – to see if it contained any pictures or ornaments that I could at all clearly distinguish. While my eyes wandered from wall to wall, a remembrance of Le Maistre's delightful little book, *Voyage autour de ma Chambre*, occurred to me. I resolved to imitate the French author and find occupation and amusement enough to relieve the tedium of my wakefulness by making a mental inventory of every article of furniture I could see and by following up to their sources the multitude of associations which even a chair, a table, or a wash-hand stand may be made to call forth.

In the nervous unsettled state of my mind at that moment, I found it much easier to make my inventory than to make my reflections and thereupon soon gave up all hope of thinking in Le Maistre's fanciful track – or, indeed, of thinking at all. I looked about the room at the different articles of furniture and did nothing more.

There was, first, the bed I was lying in; a four-post bed, of all things in the world to meet with in Paris! – yes, a thorough clumsy British four-poster, with the regular top lined with chintz – the regular fringed valance all round – the regular stifling unwholesome curtains, which I remembered having mechanically drawn back against the posts without particularly noticing the bed when I first got into the room. Then there was the marble-topped wash-hand stand, from which the water I had spilt, in my hurry to pour it out, was still dripping slowly and more slowly, on to the brick floor. Then two small chairs, with my coat, waistcoat and trousers flung on them. Then a large elbow-chair covered with dirty white dimity, with my cravat and shirt-collar thrown over the back. Then a chest of drawers with two of the brass handles off and a tawdry, broken china inkstand placed on it by way of ornament for the top. Then the dressing-table, adorned by a very small looking-glass and a very large pincushion. Then the window – an unusually large window. Then a dark old picture, which the feeble candle dimly showed me. It was the picture of a fellow in a high Spanish hat, crowned with a plume of towering feathers. A swarthy sinister ruffian, looking upwards, shading his eyes with his hand and looking intently upwards – it might be at some tall gallows at which he was going to be hanged. At any rate, he had the appearance of thoroughly deserving it.

The picture put a kind of constraint upon me to look upwards too – at the top of the bed. It was a gloomy and not interesting object and I looked back at the picture. I counted the feathers in the man's hat – they stood out in relief – three white, two green. I observed the crown of his hat, which was of a conical shape, according to the fashion supposed to have been favoured by Guido Fawkes. I wondered what he was looking up at. It couldn't be at the stars; such a desperado was neither astrologer nor astronomer. It must be at the high gallows and he was going to be hanged presently. Would the executioner come into possession of his conical crowned hat and plume of feathers; I counted the feathers again – three white, two green.

While I still lingered over this very improving and intellectual employment, my thoughts insensibly began to wander. The moonlight shining into the room reminded me of a certain moonlight night in England – the night after a picnic party in a Welsh valley. Every incident of the drive homeward, through lovely scenery, which the moonlight made lovelier than ever, came back to my remembrance, though I had never given the picnic a thought for years; though, if I had *tried* to recollect it, I could certainly have recalled little or nothing of that scene long past. Of all the wonderful faculties that help to tell us we are immortal, which speaks the sublime truth more eloquently than memory? Here was I, in a strange house of the most suspicious character, in a situation of uncertainty and even of peril, which might seem to make the cool exercise of my recollection almost out of the question; nevertheless, remembering, quite involuntarily, places, people, conversations, minute circumstances of every kind, which I had thought forgotten for ever; which I could not possibly have recalled at will, even under the most favourable auspices. And what cause had produced in a moment the whole of this strange, complicated, mysterious effect? Nothing but some rays of moonlight shining in at my bedroom window.

I was still thinking of the picnic – of our merriment on the drive home – of the sentimental young lady who *would* quote *Childe Harold* because it was moonlight. I was absorbed by these past scenes and past amusements, when, in an instant, the thread on which my memories hung snapped asunder: my attention immediately came back to present things more vividly than ever and I found myself, I neither knew why nor wherefore, looking hard at the picture again.

Looking for what?

Good God! the man had pulled his hat down on his brows! – No! the hat itself was gone! Where was the conical crown? Where the feathers – three white, two green? Not there! In place of the hat and feathers, what dusky object was it that now hid his forehead, his eyes, his shading hand?

Was the bed moving?

I turned on my back and looked up. Was I mad? drunk? dreaming? giddy again? or was the top of the bed really moving down – sinking slowly, regularly, silently, horribly, right down throughout the whole of its length and breadth – right down upon me, as I lay underneath?

My blood seemed to stand still. A deadly paralysing coldness stole all over me as I turned my head round on the pillow and determined to test whether the bed-top was really moving or not by keeping my eye on the man in the picture.

The next look in that direction was enough. The dull black, frowsy outline of the valance above me was within an inch of being parallel with his waist. I still looked breathlessly. And steadily and slowly – very slowly – I saw the figure, and the line of frame below the figure, vanish as the valance moved down before it.

I am, constitutionally, anything but timid. I have been on more than one occasion in peril of my life and have not lost my self-possession for an instant; but when the conviction first settled on my mind that the bed-top was really moving, was steadily and continuously sinking down upon me, I looked up shuddering, helpless, panic-stricken, beneath the hideous machinery for murder, which was advancing closer and closer to suffocate me where I lay.

I looked up, motionless, speechless, breathless. The candle, fully spent, went out; but the moonlight still brightened the room. Down and down, without pausing and without sounding, came the bed-top and still my panic-terror seemed to bind me faster and faster to the mattress on which I lay – down and down it sank, till the dusty odour from the lining of the canopy came stealing into my nostrils.

At that final moment the instinct of self-preservation startled me out of my trance and I moved at last. There was just room for me to roll myself sideways off the bed. As I dropped noiselessly to the floor, the edge of the murderous canopy touched me on the shoulder.

Without stopping to draw my breath, without wiping the cold sweat from my face, I rose instantly on my knees to watch the bed-top. I was literally spell-bound by it. If I had heard footsteps behind me, I could not have turned round; if a means of escape had been miraculously provided for me, I could not have moved to take advantage of it. The whole life in me was, at that moment, concentrated in my eyes.

It descended – the whole canopy, with the fringe round it, came down – down – close down; so close that there was not room now to

squeeze my finger between the bed-top and the bed. I felt at the sides
and discovered that what had appeared to me from beneath to be the
ordinary light canopy of a four-post bed, was in reality a thick, broad
mattress, the substance of which was concealed by the valance and its
fringe. I looked up and saw the four posts rising hideously bare. In the
middle of the bed-top was a huge wooden screw that had evidently
worked it down through a hole in the ceiling, just as ordinary presses
are worked down on the substance selected for compression. The
frightful apparatus moved without making the faintest noise. There
had been no creaking as it came down; there was now not the faintest
sound from the room above. Amid a dead and awful silence I beheld
before me – in the nineteenth century and in the civilised capital of
France – such a machine for secret murder by suffocation as might
have existed in the worst days of the Inquisition, in the lonely inns
among the Hartz Mountains, in the mysterious tribunals of Westphalia!
Still, as I looked on it, I could not move, I could hardly breathe, but I
began to recover the power of thinking and in a moment I discovered
the murderous conspiracy framed against me in all its horror.

My cup of coffee had been drugged and drugged too strongly. I had
been saved from being smothered by having taken an overdose of some
narcotic. How I had chafed and fretted at the fever-fit which had
preserved my life by keeping me awake! How recklessly I had confided
myself to the two wretches who had led me into this room, determined,
for the sake of my winnings, to kill me in my sleep by the surest and
most horrible contrivance for secretly accomplishing my destruction!
How many men, winners like me, had slept, as I had proposed to sleep,
in that bed and had never been seen or heard of more! I shuddered at
the bare idea of it.

But ere long, all thought was again suspended by the sight of the
murderous canopy moving once more. After it had remained on the
bed – as nearly as I could guess – about ten minutes, it began to move
up again. The villains who worked it from above evidently believed
that their purpose was now accomplished. Slowly and silently, as it had
descended, that horrible bed-top rose towards its former place. When
it reached the upper extremities of the four posts, it reached the ceiling
too. Neither hole nor screw could be seen; the bed became in
appearance an ordinary bed again – the canopy an ordinary canopy –
even to the most suspicious eyes.

Now, for the first time, I was able to move – to rise from my knees –
to dress myself in my upper clothing – and to consider of how I should
escape. If I betrayed, by the smallest noise, that the attempt to suffocate
me had failed, I was certain to be murdered. Had I made any noise

already? I listened intently, looking towards the door.

No! no footsteps in the passage outside – no sound of a tread, light or heavy, in the room above – absolute silence everywhere. Besides locking and bolting my door, I had moved an old wooden chest against it, which I had found under the bed. To remove this chest (my blood ran cold as I thought of what its contents *might* be!) without making some disturbance was impossible; and, moreover, to think of escaping through the house, now barred up for the night, was sheer insanity. Only one chance was left me – the window. I stole to it on tiptoe.

My bedroom was on the first floor, above an *entresol*, and looked into the back street. I raised my hand to open the window, knowing that on that action hung, by the merest hair's-breadth my chance of safety. They keep vigilant watch in the House of Murder. If any part of the frame cracked, if the hinge creaked, I was a lost man! It must have occupied me at least five minutes, reckoning by time – five *hours*, reckoning by suspense – to open that window. I succeeded in doing it silently – in doing it with all the dexterity of a housebreaker – and then looked down into the street. To leap the distance beneath me would be almost certain destruction! Next, I looked round at the sides of the house. Down the left side ran a thick water-pipe – it passed close by the outer edge of the window. The moment I saw the pipe, I knew I was saved. My breath came and went freely for the first time since I had seen the canopy of the bed moving down upon me!

To some men the means of escape which I had discovered might have seemed difficult and dangerous enough – to *me* the prospect of slipping down the pipe into the street did not suggest even a thought of peril. I had always been accustomed, by the practice of gymnastics, to keep up my schoolboy powers as a daring and expert climber; and knew that my head, hands and feet would serve me faithfully in any hazards of ascent or descent. I had already got one leg over the window-sill when I remembered the handkerchief filled with money under my pillow. I could well have afforded to leave it behind me, but I was revengefully determined that the miscreants of the gambling-house should miss their plunder as well as their victim. So I went back to the bed and tied the heavy handkerchief at my back by my cravat.

Just as I had made it tight and fixed it in a comfortable place, I thought I heard a sound of breathing outside the door. The chill feeling of horror ran through me again as I listened. No! dead silence still in the passage – I had only heard the night air blowing softly into the room. The next moment I was on the window-sill and the next I had a firm grip on the water-pipe with my hands and knees.

I slid down into the street easily and quietly, as I thought I should and immediately set off at the top of my speed to a branch Prefecture of Police, which I knew was situated in the immediate neighbourhood. A Sub-prefect, and several picked men among his subordinates, happened to be up, maturing, I believe, some scheme for discovering the perpetrator of a mysterious murder which all Paris was talking of just then. When I began my story, in a breathless hurry and in very bad French, I could see that the Sub-prefect suspected me of being a drunken Englishman who had robbed somebody; but he soon altered his opinion as I went on and before I had anything like concluded, he shoved all the papers before him into a drawer, put on his hat, supplied me with another (for I was bare-headed), ordered a file of soldiers, desired his expert followers to get ready all sorts of tools for breaking open doors and ripping up brick-flooring and took my arm, in the most friendly and familiar manner possible, to lead me with him out of the house. I will venture to say that when the Sub-prefect was a little boy and was taken for the first time to the play, he was not half as much pleased as he was now at the job in prospect for him at the gambling-house!

Away we went through the streets, the Sub-prefect cross-examining and congratulating me in the same breath as we marched at the head of our formidable *posse comitatus*. Sentinels were placed at the back and front of the house the moment we got to it; a tremendous battery of knocks was directed against the door; a light appeared at a window; I was told to conceal myself behind the police – then came more knocks, and a cry of 'Open in the name of the law!' At that terrible summons bolts and locks gave way before an invisible hand, and the moment after the Sub-prefect was in the passage, confronting a waiter half dressed and ghastly pale. This was the short dialogue which immediately took place:

'We want to see the Englishman who is sleeping in this house?'

'He went away hours ago.'

'He did no such thing. His friend went away; *he* remained. Show us to his bedroom!'

'I swear to you, Monsieur le Sous-préfet, he is not here! he – '

'I swear to you, Monsieur le Garçon, he is. He slept here – he didn't find your bed comfortable – he came to us to complain of it – here he is among my men – and here am I ready to look for a flea or two in his bedstead. Renaudin! [calling to one of the subordinates, and pointing to the waiter] collar that man and tie his hands behind him. Now, then, gentlemen, let us walk upstairs!'

Every man and woman in the house was secured – the 'Old Soldier' the first. Then I identified the bed in which I had slept and then we went into the room above.

No object that was at all extraordinary appeared in any part of it. The Sub-prefect looked round the place, commanded everybody to be silent, stamped twice on the floor, called for a candle, looked attentively at the spot he had stamped on and ordered the flooring there to be carefully taken up. This was done in no time. Lights were produced and we saw a deep rafted cavity between the floor of this room and the ceiling of the room beneath. Through this cavity there ran perpendicularly a sort of case of iron thickly greased; and inside the case appeared the screw, which communicated with the bed-top below. Extra lengths of screw, freshly oiled; levers covered with felt; all the complete upper works of a heavy press – constructed with infernal ingenuity so as to join the fixtures below and when taken to pieces again to go into the smallest possible compass – were next discovered and pulled out on the floor. After some little difficulty the Sub-prefect succeeded in putting the machinery together and, leaving his men to work it, descended with me to the bedroom. The smothering canopy was then lowered, but not so noiselessly as I had seen it lowered. When I mentioned this to the Sub-prefect, his answer, simple as it was, had a terrible significance. 'My men,' said he, 'are working down the bed-top for the first time – the men whose money you won were in better practice.'

We left the house in the sole possession of two police agents – every one of the inmates being removed to prison on the spot. The Sub-prefect, after taking down my '*procès-verbal*' in his office, returned with me to my hotel to get my passport. 'Do you think,' I asked, as I gave it to him, 'that any men have really been smothered in that bed, as they tried to smother *me*?'

'I have seen dozens of drowned men laid out at the morgue,' answered the Sub-prefect, 'in whose pocket-books were found letters stating that they had committed suicide in the Seine because they had lost everything at the gaming-table. Do I know how many of those men entered the same gambling-house that *you* entered? won as *you* won? took that bed as *you* took it? slept in it? were smothered in it? and were privately thrown into the river with a letter of explanation written by the murderers and placed in their pocket-books? No man can say how many or how few have suffered the fate from which you have escaped. The people of the gambling-house kept their bedstead machinery a secret from *us* – even from the police! The dead kept the rest of the secret for them. Good-night, or rather good-morning, Monsieur Faulkner! Be at my office again at nine o'clock – in the meantime, *au revoir!*'

The rest of my story is soon told. I was examined and re-examined;

the gambling-house was strictly searched all through from top to bottom; the prisoners were separately interrogated; and two of the less guilty among them made a confession. *I* discovered that the Old Soldier was the master of the gambling-house – *justice* discovered that he had been drummed out of the army as a vagabond years ago; that he had been guilty of all sorts of villainies since; that he was in possession of stolen property, which the owners identified; and that he, the croupier, another accomplice and the woman who had made my cup of coffee, were all in the secret of the bedstead. There appeared some reason to doubt whether the inferior persons attached to the house knew anything of the suffocating machinery; and they received the benefit of that doubt by being treated simply as thieves and vagabonds. As for the Old Soldier and his two head-myrmidons, they went to the galleys; the woman who had drugged my coffee was imprisoned for I forget how many years; the regular attendants at the gambling-house were considered 'suspicious' and placed under 'surveillance', and I became, for one whole week (which is a long time), the head 'lion' in Parisian society. My adventure was dramatised by three illustrious playmakers, but never saw theatrical daylight; for the censorship forbade the introduction on the stage of a correct copy of the gambling-house bedstead.

One good result was produced by my adventure, which any censorship must have approved – it cured me of ever again trying *Rouge et Noir* as an amusement. The sight of a green cloth, with packs of cards and heaps of money on it, will henceforth be for ever associated in my mind with the sight of a bed-canopy descending to suffocate me in the silence and darkness of the night.

The Phantom Coach

Amelia B. Edwards
(Amelia Ann Blandford) 1831–1892

THE CIRCUMSTANCES I am about to relate to you have truth to
recommend them. They happened to myself and my recollection of
them is as vivid as if they had taken place only yesterday. Twenty years,
however, have gone by since that night. During those twenty years I
have told the story to but one other person. I tell it now with a
reluctance which I find it difficult to overcome. All I entreat, meanwhile, is that you will abstain from forcing your own conclusions upon
me. I want nothing explained away. I desire no arguments. My mind on
this subject is quite made up and, having the testimony of my own
senses to rely upon, I prefer to abide by it.

Well! It was just twenty years ago and within a day or two of the end
of the grouse season. I had been out all day with my gun and had had
no sport to speak of. The wind was due east; the month, December; the
place, a bleak wide moor in the far north of England. And I had lost my
way. It was not a pleasant place in which to lose one's way, with the first
feathery flakes of a coming snowstorm just fluttering down upon the
heather and the leaden evening closing in all around. I shaded my eyes
with my hand and stared anxiously into the gathering darkness, where
the purple moorland melted into a range of low hills, some ten or
twelve miles distant. Not the faintest smoke-wreath, not the tiniest
cultivated patch or fence or sheep-track, met my eyes in any direction.
There was nothing for it but to walk on and take my chance of finding
what shelter I could, by the way. So I shouldered my gun again and
pushed wearily forward; for I had been on foot since an hour after
daybreak and had eaten nothing since breakfast.

Meanwhile, the snow began to come down with ominous steadiness
and the wind fell. After this, the cold became more intense and the
night came rapidly up. As for me, my prospects darkened with the
darkening sky and my heart grew heavy as I thought how my young
wife was already watching for me through the window of our little inn
parlour and thought of all the suffering in store for her throughout this
weary night. We had been married four months and, having spent our

autumn in the Highlands, were now lodging in a remote little village situated just on the verge of the great English moorlands. We were very much in love and, of course, very happy. This morning, when we parted, she had implored me to return before dusk and I had promised her that I would. What would I not have given to have kept my word!

Even now, weary as I was, I felt that with a supper, an hour's rest, and a guide, I might still get back to her before midnight, if only guide and shelter could be found.

And all this time, the snow fell and the night thickened. I stopped and shouted every now and then, but my shouts seemed only to make the silence deeper. Then a vague sense of uneasiness came upon me and I began to remember stories of travellers who had walked on and on in the falling snow until, wearied out, they were fain to lie down and sleep their lives away. Would it be possible, I asked myself, to keep on thus through all the long dark night? Would there not come a time when my limbs must fail and my resolution give way? When I, too, must sleep the sleep of death. Death! I shuddered. How hard to die just now, when life lay all so bright before me! How hard for my darling, whose whole loving heart – but that thought was not to be borne! To banish it, I shouted again, louder and longer, and then listened eagerly. Was my shout answered, or did I only fancy that I heard a far-off cry? I halloed again and again the echo followed. Then a wavering speck of light came suddenly out of the dark, shifting, disappearing, growing momentarily nearer and brighter. Running towards it at full speed, I found myself, to my great joy, face to face with an old man and a lantern.

'Thank God!' was the exclamation that burst involuntarily from my lips.

Blinking and frowning, he lifted his lantern and peered into my face.

'What for?' growled he, sulkily.

'Well – for you. I began to fear I should be lost in the snow.'

'Eh, then, folks do get cast away hereabouts fra' time to time, an' what's to hinder you from bein' cast away likewise, if the Lord's so minded?'

'If the Lord is so minded that you and I shall be lost together, friend, we must submit,' I replied; 'but I don't mean to be lost without you. How far am I now from Dwolding?'

'A gude twenty mile, more or less.'

'And the nearest village?'

'The nearest village is Wyke, an' that's twelve mile t'other side.'

'Where do you live, then?'

'Out yonder,' said he, with a vague jerk of the lantern.

'You're going home, I presume?'

'Maybe I am.'

'Then I'm going with you.'

The old man shook his head and rubbed his nose reflectively with the handle of the lantern.

'It ain't o' no use,' growled he. 'He 'ont let you in – not he.'

'We'll see about that,' I replied, briskly. 'Who is He?'

'The master.'

'Who is the master?'

'That's nowt to you,' was the unceremonious reply.

'Well, well; you lead the way and I'll engage that the master shall give me shelter and a supper tonight.'

'Eh you can try him!' muttered my reluctant guide; and, still shaking his head, he hobbled, gnome-like, away through the falling snow. A large mass loomed up presently out of the darkness, and a huge dog rushed out, barking furiously.

'Is this the house?' I asked.

'Ay, it's the house. Down, Bey!' And he fumbled in his pocket for the key.

I drew up close behind him, prepared to lose no chance of entrance and saw in the little circle of light shed by the lantern that the door was heavily studded with iron nails, like the door of a prison. In another minute he had turned the key and I had pushed past him into the house.

Once inside, I looked round with curiosity and found myself in a great raftered hall, which served, apparently, a variety of uses. One end was piled to the roof with corn, like a barn. The other was stored with flour-sacks, agricultural implements, casks and all kinds of miscellaneous lumber; while from the beams overhead hung rows of hams, flitches and bunches of dried herbs for winter use. In the centre of the floor stood some huge object gauntly dressed in a dingy wrapping-cloth, and reaching half way to the rafters. Lifting a corner of this cloth I saw, to my surprise, a telescope of very considerable size, mounted on a rude movable platform, with four small wheels. The tube was made of painted wood, bound round with bands of metal rudely fashioned; the speculum, so far as I could estimate its size in the dim light, measured at least fifteen inches in diameter. While I was yet examining the instrument and asking myself whether it was not the work of some self-taught optician, a bell rang sharply.

'That's for you,' said my guide, with a malicious grin. 'Yonder's his room.'

He pointed to a low black door at the opposite side of the hall. I crossed over, rapped somewhat loudly and went in, without waiting for an invitation. A huge, white-haired old man rose from a table covered with books and papers and confronted me sternly.

'Who are you?' said he. 'How came you here? What do you want?'

'James Murray, barrister-at-law. On foot across the moor. Meat, drink and sleep.'

He bent his bushy brows into a portentous frown.

'Mine is not a house of entertainment,' he said, haughtily. 'Jacob, how dared you admit this stranger?'

'I didn't admit him.' grumbled the old man. 'He followed me over the muir and shouldered his way in before me. I'm no match for six foot two.'

'And pray, sir, by what right have you forced an entrance into my house?'

'The same by which I should have clung to your boat, if I were drowning. The right of self-preservation.'

'Self-preservation?'

'There's an inch of snow on the ground already,' I replied, briefly; 'and it would be deep enough to cover my body before daybreak.'

He strode to the window, pulled aside a heavy black curtain and looked out.

'It is true,' he said. 'You can stay, if you choose, till morning. Jacob, serve the supper.'

With this he waved me to a seat, resumed his own and became at once absorbed in the studies from which I had disturbed him.

I placed my gun in a corner, drew a chair to the hearth and examined my quarters at leisure. Smaller and less incongruous in its arrangements than the hall, this room contained, nevertheless, much to awaken my curiosity. The floor was carpetless. The whitewashed walls were in parts scrawled over with strange diagrams and in others covered with shelves crowded with philosophical instruments, the uses of many of which were unknown to me. On one side of the fireplace, stood a bookcase filled with dingy folios; on the other, a small organ, fantastically decorated with painted carvings of medieval saints and devils. Through the half-opened door of a cupboard at the further end of the room, I saw a long array of geological specimens, surgical preparations, crucibles, retorts, and jars of chemicals; while on the mantelshelf beside me, amid a number of small objects, stood a model of the solar system, a small galvanic battery and a microscope. Every chair had its burden. Every corner was heaped high with books. The very floor was littered over with maps, casts, papers, tracings and learned lumber of all conceivable kinds.

I stared about me with an amazement increased by every fresh object upon which my eyes chanced to rest. So strange a room I had never seen; yet seemed it stranger still, to find such a room in a lone farmhouse amid those wild and solitary moors! Over and over again, I looked from my host to his surroundings and from his surroundings back to my host, asking myself who and what he could be? His head was singularly fine; but it was more the head of a poet than of a philosopher. Broad in the temples, prominent over the eyes and clothed with a rough profusion of perfectly white hair, it had all the ideality and much of the ruggedness that characterises the head of Ludwig van Beethoven. There were the same deep lines about the mouth and the same stern furrows in the brow. There was the same concentration of expression. While I was yet observing him, the door opened and Jacob brought in the supper. His master then closed his book, rose and with more courtesy of manner than he had yet shown, invited me to the table.

A dish of ham and eggs, a loaf of brown bread and a bottle of admirable sherry, were placed before me.

'I have but the homeliest farmhouse fare to offer you, sir,' said my entertainer. 'Your appetite, I trust, will make up for the deficiencies of our larder.'

I had already fallen upon the viands and now protested, with the enthusiasm of a starving sportsman, that I had never eaten anything so delicious.

He bowed stiffly and sat down to his own supper, which consisted, primitively, of a jug of milk and a basin of porridge. We ate in silence and, when we had done, Jacob removed the tray. I then drew my chair back to the fireside. My host, somewhat to my surprise, did the same and turning abruptly towards me, said: 'Sir, I have lived here in strict retirement for three-and-twenty years. During that time, I have not seen as many strange faces and I have not read a single newspaper. You are the first stranger who has crossed my threshold for more than four years. Will you favour me with a few words of information respecting that outer world from which I have parted company so long?'

'Pray interrogate me,' I replied. 'I am heartily at your service.'

He bent his head in acknowledgment; leaned forward, with his elbows resting on his knees and his chin supported in the palms of his hands; stared fixedly into the fire; and proceeded to question me.

His enquiries related chiefly to scientific matters, with the later progress of which, as applied to the practical purposes of life, he was almost wholly unacquainted. No student of science myself, I replied as well as my slight information permitted; but the task was far from easy and I was much relieved when, passing from interrogation to discussion, he began pouring forth his own conclusions upon the facts which I had been attempting to place before him. He talked and I listened spellbound. He talked till I believe he almost forgot my presence and only thought aloud. I had never heard anything like it then; I have never heard anything like it since. Familiar with all systems of all philosophies, subtle in analysis, bold in generalisation, he poured forth his thoughts in an uninterrupted stream and, still leaning forward in the same moody attitude with his eyes fixed upon the fire, wandered from topic to topic, from speculation to speculation, like an inspired dreamer. From practical science to mental philosophy; from electricity in the wire to electricity in the nerve; from Watts to Mesmer, from Mesmer to Reichenbach, from Reichenbach to Swedenborg, Spinoza, Condillac, Descartes, Berkeley, Aristotle, Plato, and the Magi and mystics of the East, were transitions which, however bewildering in their variety and scope, seemed easy and harmonious upon his lips as sequences in music. By and by – I forget now by what link of conjecture or illustration – he passed on to that field which lies beyond the boundary line of even conjectural philosophy and reaches no man knows whither. He spoke of the soul and its aspirations; of the spirit and its powers; of second sight; of prophecy; of those phenomena which, under the names of ghosts, spectres and supernatural appearances, have been denied by the sceptics and attested by the credulous, of all ages.

'The world,' he said, 'grows hourly more and more sceptical of all that lies beyond its own narrow radius; and our men of science foster the fatal tendency. They condemn as fable all that resists experiment. They reject as false all that cannot be brought to the test of the laboratory or the dissecting-room. Against what superstition have they waged so long and obstinate a war, as against the belief in apparitions? And yet what superstition has maintained its hold upon the minds of men so long and so firmly? Show me any fact in physics, in history, in archaeology, which is supported by testimony so wide and so various. Attested by all races of men, in all ages and in all climates, by the soberest sages of antiquity, by the rudest savage of today, by the Christian, the Pagan, the Pantheist, the Materialist, this phenomenon is treated as a nursery tale by the philosophers of our century. Circumstantial evidence weighs with them as a feather in the balance. The comparison of causes with effects, however valuable in physical science, is put aside as worthless and unreliable. The evidence of competent witnesses, however conclusive in a court of justice, counts for nothing. He who pauses before he pronounces, is condemned as a trifler. He who believes, is a dreamer or a fool.'

He spoke with bitterness and, having said thus, relapsed for some minutes into silence. Presently he raised his head from his hands and added, with an altered voice and manner: 'I, sir, paused, investigated, believed, and was not ashamed to state my convictions to the world. I, too, was branded as a visionary, held up to ridicule by my contemporaries, and hooted from that field of science in which I had laboured with honour during all the best years of my life. These things happened just three-and-twenty years ago. Since then, I have lived as you see me living now and the world has forgotten me, as I have forgotten the world. You have my history.'

'It is a very sad one,' I murmured, scarcely knowing what to answer.

'It is a very common one,' he replied. 'I have only suffered for the truth, as many a better and wiser man has suffered before me.'

He rose, as if desirous of ending the conversation, and went over to the window.

'It has ceased snowing,' he observed, as he dropped the curtain, and came back to the fireside.

'Ceased!' I exclaimed, starting eagerly to my feet. 'Oh, if it were only possible – but no! it is hopeless. Even if I could find my way across the moor, I could not walk twenty miles tonight.'

'Walk twenty miles tonight!' repeated my host. 'What are you thinking of?'

'Of my wife,' I replied, impatiently. 'Of my young wife, who does not know that I have lost my way and who is at this moment breaking her heart with suspense and terror.'

'Where is she?'

'At Dwolding, twenty miles away.'

'At Dwolding,' he echoed, thoughtfully. 'Yes, the distance, it is true, is twenty miles; but – are you so very anxious to save the next six or eight hours?'

'So very, very anxious, that I would give ten guineas at this moment for a guide and a horse.'

'Your wish can be gratified at a less costly rate,' said he, smiling. 'The night mail from the north, which changes horses at Dwolding, passes within five miles of this spot and will be due at a certain crossroad in about an hour and a quarter. If Jacob were to go with you across the moor and put you into the old coach-road, you could find your way, I suppose, to where it joins the new one?'

'Easily – gladly.'

He smiled again, rang the bell, gave the old servant his directions and, taking a bottle of whisky and a wineglass from the cupboard in which he kept his chemicals, said: 'The snow lies deep and it will be difficult walking tonight on the moor. A glass of usquebaugh before you start?'

I would have declined the spirit, but he pressed it on me and I drank it. It went down my throat like liquid flame and almost took my breath away.

'It is strong,' he said; 'but it will help to keep out the cold. And now you have no moments to spare. Good-night!'

I thanked him for his hospitality and would have shaken hands but that he had turned away before I could finish my sentence. In another minute I had traversed the hall, Jacob had locked the outer door behind me and we were out on the wide white moor.

Although the wind had fallen, it was still bitterly cold. Not a star glimmered in the black vault overhead. Not a sound, save the rapid crunching of the snow beneath our feet, disturbed the heavy stillness of the night. Jacob, not too well pleased with his mission, shambled on before in sullen silence, his lantern in his hand and his shadow at his feet. I followed, with my gun over my shoulder, as little inclined for conversation as himself. My thoughts were full of my late host. His voice yet rang in my ears. His eloquence yet held my imagination captive. I remember to this day, with surprise, how my over-excited brain retained whole sentences and parts of sentences, troops of brilliant images and fragments of splendid reasoning, in the very words in which he had uttered them. Musing thus over what I had heard, and striving to recall a lost link here and there, I strode on at the heels of my guide, absorbed and unobservant.

Presently – at the end, as it seemed to me, of only a few minutes – he came to a sudden halt and said: 'Yon's your road. Keep the stone fence to your right hand and you can't fail of the way.'

'This, then, is the old coach-road?'

'Ay, 'tis the old coach-road.'

'And how far do I go, before I reach the crossroads?'

'Nigh upon three mile.'

I pulled out my purse, and he became more communicative.

'The road's a fair road enough,' said he, 'for foot passengers; but 'twas over steep and narrow for the northern traffic. You'll mind where the parapet's broken away, close again the signpost. It's never been mended since the accident.'

'What accident?'

'Eh, the night mail pitched right over into the valley below – a gude fifty feet an' more – just at the worst bit o' road in the whole county.'

'Horrible! Were many lives lost?'

'All. Four were found dead and t'other two died next morning.'

'How long is it since this happened?'

'Just nine year.'

'Near the signpost, you say? I will bear it in mind. Good-night.'

'Gude night, sir, and thankee.' Jacob pocketed his half-crown, made a faint pretence of touching his hat and trudged back by the way he had come.

I watched the light of his lantern till it quite disappeared and then turned to pursue my way alone. This was no longer matter of the slightest difficulty, for, despite the dead darkness overhead, the line of stone fence showed distinctly enough against the pale gleam of the snow. How silent it seemed now, with only my footsteps to listen to; how silent and how solitary! A strange disagreeable sense of loneliness stole over me. I walked faster. I hummed a fragment of a tune. I cast up enormous sums in my head and accumulated them at compound interest. I did my best, in short, to forget the startling speculations to which I had but just been listening and, to some extent, I succeeded.

Meanwhile the night air seemed to become colder and colder and though I walked fast I found it impossible to keep myself warm. My feet were like ice. I lost sensation in my hands and grasped my gun mechanically. I even breathed with difficulty, as though, instead of traversing a quiet north country highway, I were scaling the uppermost heights of some gigantic Alp. This last symptom became presently so distressing, that I was forced to stop for a few minutes and lean against the stone fence. As I did so, I chanced to look back up the road and there, to my infinite relief, I saw a distant point of light, like the gleam of an approaching lantern. I at first concluded that Jacob had retraced his steps and followed me; but even as the conjecture presented itself, a second light flashed into sight – a light evidently parallel with the first, and approaching at the same rate of motion. It needed no second thought to show me that these must be the carriage-lamps of some private vehicle, though it seemed strange that any private vehicle should take a road professedly disused and dangerous.

There could be no doubt, however, of the fact, for the lamps grew larger and brighter every moment, and I even fancied I could already see the dark outline of the carriage between them. It was coming up very fast, and quite noiselessly, the snow being nearly a foot deep under the wheels.

And now the body of the vehicle became distinctly visible behind the lamps. It looked strangely lofty. A sudden suspicion flashed upon me. Was it possible that I had passed the crossroads in the dark without observing the signpost, and could this be the very coach which I had come to meet? No need to ask myself that question a second time, for here it came round the bend of the road, guard and driver, one outside passenger, and four steaming greys, all wrapped in a soft haze of light, through which the lamps blazed out, like a pair of fiery meteors.

I jumped forward, waved my hat and shouted. The mail came down at full speed, and passed me. For a moment I feared that I had not been seen or heard, but it was only for a moment. The coachman pulled up; the guard, muffled to the eyes in capes and comforters, and apparently sound asleep in the rumble, neither answered my hail nor made the slightest effort to dismount; the outside passenger did not even turn his head. I opened the door for myself, and looked in. There were but three travellers inside, so I stepped in, shut the door, slipped into the vacant corner, and congratulated myself on my good fortune.

The atmosphere of the coach seemed, if possible, colder than that of the outer air, and was pervaded by a singularly damp and disagreeable smell. I looked round at my fellow-passengers. They were, all three, men, and all silent. They did not seem to be asleep, but each leaned back in his corner of the vehicle, as if absorbed in his own reflections. I attempted to open a conversation.

'How intensely cold it is tonight,' I said, addressing my opposite neighbour.

He lifted his head, looked at me, but made no reply.

'The winter,' I added, 'seems to have begun in earnest.'

Although the corner in which he sat was so dim that I could distinguish none of his features very clearly, I saw that his eyes were still turned full upon me. And yet he answered never a word.

At any other time I should have felt, and perhaps expressed, some annoyance, but at the moment I felt too ill to do either. The icy coldness of the night air had struck a chill to my very marrow, and the strange smell inside the coach was affecting me with an intolerable nausea. I shivered from head to foot, and, turning to my left-hand neighbour, asked if he had any objection to an open window?

He neither spoke nor stirred.

I repeated the question somewhat more loudly, but with the same result. Then I lost patience, and let the sash down. As I did so the leather strap broke in my hand, and I observed that the glass was covered with a thick coat of mildew, the accumulation, apparently of years. My attention being thus drawn to the condition of the coach, I examined it more narrowly, and saw by the uncertain light of the outer lamps that it was in the last stage of dilapidation. Every part of it was not only out of repair, but in a condition of decay. The sashes splintered at a touch. The leather fittings were crusted over with mould, and literally rotting from the woodwork. The floor was almost breaking away beneath my feet. The whole machine, in short, was foul with damp, and had evidently been dragged from some outhouse, in which it had been mouldering away for years, to do another day or two of duty on the road.

I turned to the third passenger, whom I had not yet addressed, and hazarded one more remark.

'This coach,' I said, 'is in a deplorable condition. The regular mail, I suppose, is under repair?'

He moved his head slowly, and looked me in the face, without speaking a word. I shall never forget that look while I live. I turned cold at heart under it. I turn cold at heart even now when I recall it. His eyes glowed with a fiery unnatural lustre. His face was livid as the face of a corpse. His bloodless lips were drawn back as if in the agony of death, and showed the gleaming teeth between.

The words that I was about to utter died upon my lips, and a strange horror – a dreadful horror – came upon me. My sight had by this time become used to the gloom of the coach, and I could see with tolerable distinctness. I turned to my opposite neighbour. He, too, was looking at me, with the same startling pallor in his face and the same stony glitter in his eyes. I passed my hand across my brow. I turned to the passenger on the seat beside my own and saw – oh Heaven! how shall I describe what I saw? I saw that he was no living man – that none of them were living men, like myself! A pale phosphorescent light – the light of putrefaction – played upon their awful faces; upon their hair, dank with the dews of the grave; upon their clothes, earth-stained and dropping to pieces; upon their hands, which were as the hands of corpses long buried. Only their eyes, their terrible eyes, were living; and those eyes were all turned menacingly upon me!

A shriek of terror, a wild unintelligible cry for help and mercy, burst from my lips as I flung myself against the door and strove in vain to open it.

In that single instant, brief and vivid as a landscape beheld in the flash of summer lightning, I saw the moon shining down through a rift of stormy cloud – the ghastly signpost rearing its warning finger by the wayside – the broken parapet – the plunging horses – the black gulf below. Then, the coach reeled like a ship at sea. Then, came a mighty crash – a sense of crushing pain – and then, darkness.

It seemed as if years had gone by when I awoke one morning from a deep sleep and found my wife watching by my bedside. I will pass over the scene that ensued and give you, in half a dozen words, the tale she told me with tears of thanksgiving. I had fallen over a precipice, close against the junction of the old coach-road and the new, and had only been saved from certain death by lighting upon a deep snowdrift that had accumulated at the foot of the rock beneath. In this snowdrift I was discovered at daybreak by a couple of shepherds, who carried me to the nearest shelter and brought a surgeon to my aid. The surgeon found me in a state of raving delirium, with a broken arm and a compound fracture of the skull. The letters in my pocket-book showed my name and address; my wife was summoned to nurse me; and, thanks to youth and a fine constitution, I came out of danger at last. The place of my fall, I need scarcely say, was precisely that at which a frightful accident had happened to the north mail nine years before.

I never told my wife the fearful events which I have just related to you. I told the surgeon who attended me; but he treated the whole adventure as a mere dream born of the fever in my brain. We discussed the question over and over again, until we found that we could discuss it with temper no longer and then we dropped it. Others may form what conclusions they please – I *know* that twenty years ago I was the fourth inside passenger in that Phantom Coach.

Eveline's Visitant

Miss Braddon
(Mary Elizabeth Maxwell) 1837–1915

IT WAS AT A MASKED BALL at the Palais Royal that my fatal quarrel with my first cousin André de Brissac began. The quarrel was about a woman. The women who followed the footsteps of Philip of Orleans were the causes of many such disputes; and there was scarcely one fair head in all that glittering throng which, to a man versed in social histories and mysteries, might not have seemed bedabbled with blood.

I shall not record the name of her for love of whom André de Brissac and I crossed one of the bridges, in the dim August dawn, on our way to the waste ground beyond the church of Saint Germain des Prés.

There were many beautiful vipers in those days and she was one of them. I can feel the chill breath of that August morning blowing in my face, as I sit in my dismal chamber at my château of Puy Verdun tonight, alone in the stillness, writing the strange story of my life. I can see the white mist rising from the river, the grim outline of the Châtelet, and the square towers of Notre Dame black against the pale-grey sky. Even more vividly can I recall André's fair young face, as he stood opposite to me with his two friends – scoundrels both and alike eager for that unnatural fray. We were a strange group to be seen in a summer sunrise, all of us fresh from the heat and clamour of the Regent's saloons – André in a quaint hunting-dress copied from a family portrait at Puy Verdun, I costumed as one of Law's Mississippi Indians; the other men in like garish frippery, adorned with broideries and jewels that looked wan in the pale light of dawn.

Our quarrel had been a fierce one – a quarrel which could have but one result, and that the direst. I had struck him; and the welt raised by my open hand was crimson upon his fair womanish face as he stood opposite to me. The eastern sun shone on the face presently and dyed the cruel mark with a deeper red; but the sting of my own wrongs was fresh and I had not yet learned to despise myself for that brutal outrage.

To André de Brissac such an insult was most terrible. He was the favourite of Fortune, the favourite of women; and I was nothing – a rough soldier who had done my country good service, but in the boudoir of a Parabère was a mannerless boor.

We fought and I wounded him mortally. Life had been very sweet for him; and I think that a frenzy of despair took possession of him when he felt the life-blood ebbing away. He beckoned me to him as he lay on the ground. I went and knelt at his side.

'Forgive me, André!' I murmured.

He took no more heed of my words than if that piteous entreaty had been the idle ripple of the river near at hand.

'Listen to me, Hector de Brissac,' he said. 'I am not one who believes that a man has done with earth because his eyes glaze and his jaw stiffens. They will bury me in the old vault at Puy Verdun; and you will be master of the château. Ah, I know how lightly they take things in these days and how Dubois will laugh when he hears that Ca has been killed in a duel. They will bury me and sing masses for my soul; but you and I have not finished our affair yet, my cousin. I will be with you when you least look to see me – I, with this ugly scar upon the face that women have praised and loved. I will come to you when your life seems brightest. I will come between you and all that you hold fairest and dearest. My ghostly hand shall drop a poison in your cup of joy. My shadowy form shall shut the sunlight from your life. Men with such iron will as mine can do what they please, Hector de Brissac. It is my will to haunt you when I am dead.'

All this in short broken sentences he whispered into my ear. I had need to bend my ear close to his dying lips; but the iron will of André de Brissac was strong enough to do battle with Death and I believe he said all he wished to say before his head fell back upon the velvet cloak they had spread beneath him, never to be lifted again

As he lay there, you would have fancied him a fragile stripling, too fair and frail for the struggle called life; but there are those who remember the brief manhood of André de Brissac and who can bear witness to the terrible force of that proud nature.

I stood looking down at the young face with that foul mark upon it and God knows I was sorry for what I had done.

Of those blasphemous threats which he had whispered in my ear I took no heed. I was a soldier and a believer. There was nothing absolutely dreadful to me in the thought that I had killed this man. I had killed many men on the battlefield; and this one had done me cruel wrong.

My friends would have had me cross the frontier to escape the consequences of my act; but I was ready to face those consequences and I remained in France. I kept aloof from the court and received a hint that I had best confine myself to my own province. Many masses were chanted in the little chapel of Puy Verdun for the soul of my dead cousin, and his coffin filled a niche in the vault of our ancestors.

His death had made me a rich man; and the thought that it was so made my newly acquired wealth very hateful to me. I lived a lonely existence in the old château, where I rarely held converse with any but the servants of the household, all of whom had served my cousin and none of whom liked me.

It was a hard and bitter life. It galled me, when I rode through the village, to see the peasant-children shrink away from me. I have seen old women cross themselves stealthily as I passed them by. Strange reports had gone forth about me; and there were those who whispered that I had given my soul to the Evil One as the price of my cousin's heritage. From my boyhood I had been dark of visage and stern of manner; and hence, perhaps, no woman's love had ever been mine. I remembered my mother's face in all its changes of expression; but I can remember no look of affection that ever shone on me. That other woman, beneath whose feet I laid my heart, was pleased to accept my homage, but she never loved me; and the end was treachery.

I had grown hateful to myself and had well-nigh begun to hate my fellow-creatures, when a feverish desire seized upon me and I pined to be back in the press and throng of the busy world once again. I went back to Paris, where I kept myself aloof from the court and where an angel took compassion upon me.

She was the daughter of an old comrade, a man whose merits had been neglected, whose achievements had been ignored and who sulked in his shabby lodging like a rat in a hole, while all Paris went mad with the Scotch Financier and gentlemen and lacqueys were trampling one another to death in the Rue Quincampoix. The only child of this little cross-grained old captain of dragoons was an incarnate sunbeam, whose mortal name was Eveline Duchalet.

She loved me. The richest blessings of our lives are often those which cost us least. I wasted the best years of my youth in the worship of a wicked woman, who jilted and cheated me at last. I gave this meek angel but a few courteous words – a little fraternal tenderness – and lo, she loved me. The life which had been so dark and desolate grew bright beneath her influence; and I went back to Puy Verdun with a fair young bride for my companion.

Ah, how sweet a change there was in my life and in my home! The village children no longer shrank appalled as the dark horseman rode by, the village crones no longer crossed themselves; for a woman rode by his side – a woman whose charities had won the love of all those ignorant creatures and whose companionship had transformed the gloomy lord of the château into a loving husband and a gentle master. The old retainers forgot the untimely fate of my cousin and served me with cordial willingness, for love of their young mistress.

There are no words which can tell the pure and perfect happiness of that time. I felt like a traveller who had traversed the frozen seas of an arctic region, remote from human love or human companionship, to find himself on a sudden in the bosom of a verdant valley, in the sweet atmosphere of home. The change seemed too bright to be real; and I strove in vain to put away from my mind the vague suspicion that my new life was but some fantastic dream.

So brief were those halcyon hours, that, looking back on them now, it is scarcely strange if I am still half inclined to fancy the first days of my married life could have been no more than a dream.

Neither in my days of gloom nor in my days of happiness had I been troubled by the recollection of André's blasphemous oath. The words which with his last breath he had whispered in my ear were vain and meaningless to me. He had vented his rage in those idle threats, as he might have vented it in idle execrations. That he will haunt the footsteps of his enemy after death is the one revenge which a dying man can promise himself; and if men had power thus to avenge themselves, the earth would be peopled with phantoms.

I had lived for three years at Puy Verdun; sitting alone in the solemn midnight by the hearth where he had sat, pacing the corridors that had echoed his footfall; and in all that time my fancy had never so played me false as to shape the shadow of the dead. Is it strange, then, if I had forgotten André's horrible promise?

There was no portrait of my cousin at Puy Verdun. It was the age of boudoir art, and a miniature set in the lid of a gold bonbonnière or hidden artfully in a massive bracelet, was more fashionable than a clumsy life-size image, fit only to hang on the gloomy walls of a provincial château rarely visited by its owner. My cousin's fair face had adorned more than one bonbonnière and had been concealed in more than one bracelet; but it was not among the faces that looked down from the panelled walls of Puy Verdun.

In the library I found a picture which awoke painful associations. It was the portrait of a De Brissac, who had flourished in the time of Francis the First; and it was from this picture that my cousin André had copied the quaint hunting-dress he wore at the Regent's ball. The library was a room in which I spent a good deal of my life; and I ordered a curtain to be hung before this picture.

We had been married three months, when Eveline one day asked, 'Who is the lord of the château nearest to this?'

I looked at her in astonishment.

'My dearest,' I answered, 'do you not know that there is no other château within forty miles of Puy Verdun?'

'Indeed!' she said: 'that is strange.'

I asked her why the fact seemed strange to her; and after much entreaty I obtained from her the reason of her surprise.

In her walks about the park and woods during the last month, she had met a man who, by his dress and bearing, was obviously of noble rank. She had imagined that he occupied some château near at hand and that his estate adjoined ours. I was at a loss to imagine who this stranger could be; for my estate of Puy Verdun lay in the heart of a desolate region and unless when some traveller's coach went lumbering and jingling through the village, one had little more chance of encountering a gentleman than of meeting a demigod.

'Have you seen this man often, Eveline?' I asked.

She answered, in a tone which had a touch of sadness, 'I see him every day.'

'Where, dearest?'

'Sometimes in the park, sometimes in the wood. You know the little cascade, Hector, where there is some old neglected rock-work that forms a kind of cavern. I have taken a fancy to that spot and have spent many mornings there reading. Of late I have seen the stranger there every morning.'

'He has never dared to address you?'

'Never. I have looked up from my book and have seen him standing at a little distance, watching me silently. I have continued reading; and when I have raised my eyes again I have found him gone. He must approach and depart with a stealthy tread, for I never hear his footfall. Sometimes I have almost wished that he would speak to me. It is so terrible to see him standing silently there.'

'He is some insolent peasant who seeks to frighten you.'

My wife shook her head.

'He is no peasant,' she answered. 'It is not by his dress alone I judge, for that is strange to me. He has an air of nobility which it is impossible to mistake.'

'Is he young or old?'

'He is young and handsome.'

I was much disturbed by the idea of this stranger's intrusion on my wife's solitude; and I went straight to the village to enquire if any stranger had been seen there. I could hear of no one. I questioned the servants closely, but without result. Then I determined to accompany my wife in her walks and to judge for myself of the rank of the stranger.

For a week I devoted all my mornings to rustic rambles with Eveline in the park and woods; and in all that week we saw no one but an occasional peasant in *sabots*, or one of our own household returning from a neighbouring farm.

I was a man of studious habits and those summer rambles disturbed the even current of my life. My wife perceived this and entreated me to trouble myself no further.

'I will spend my mornings in the pleasaunce, Hector,' she said; 'the stranger cannot intrude upon me there.'

'I begin to think the stranger is only a phantasm of your own romantic brain,' I replied, smiling at the earnest face lifted to mine. 'A châtelaine who is always reading romances may well meet handsome cavaliers in the woodlands. I dare say I have Mlle Scuderi to thank for this noble stranger and that he is only the great Cyrus in modern costume.'

'Ah, that is the point which mystifies me, Hector,' she said. 'The stranger's costume is not modern. He looks as an old picture might look if it could descend from its frame.'

Her words pained me, for they reminded me of that hidden picture in the library and the quaint hunting costume of orange and purple which André de Brissac wore at the Regent's ball.

After this my wife confined her walks to the pleasaunce; and for many weeks I heard no more of the nameless stranger. I dismissed all thought of him from my mind, for a graver and heavier care had come upon me. My wife's health began to droop. The change in her was so gradual as to be almost imperceptible to those who watched her day by day. It was only when she put on a rich gala dress which she had not worn for months that I saw how wasted the form must be on which the embroidered bodice hung so loosely and how wan and dim were the eyes which had once been brilliant as the jewels she wore in her hair.

I sent a messenger to Paris to summon one of the court physicians; but I knew that many days must needs elapse before he could arrive at Puy Verdun.

In the interval I watched my wife with unutterable fear.

It was not her health only that had declined. The change was more painful to behold than any physical alteration. The bright and sunny spirit had vanished and in the place of my joyous young bride I beheld a woman weighed down by rooted melancholy. In vain I sought to fathom the cause of my darling's sadness. She assured me that she had no reason for sorrow or discontent and that if she seemed sad without a motive, I must forgive her sadness and consider it as a misfortune rather than a fault.

I told her that the court physician would speedily find some cure for her despondency, which must needs arise from physical causes, since she had no real ground for sorrow. But although she said nothing, I could see she had no hope or belief in the healing powers of medicine.

One day, when I wished to beguile her from that pensive silence in which she was wont to sit an hour at a time, I told her, laughing, that she appeared to have forgotten her mysterious cavalier of the wood and it seemed also as if he had forgotten her.

To my wonderment, her pale face became of a sudden crimson; and from crimson changed to pale again in a breath.

'You have never seen him since you deserted your woodland grotto?' I said.

She turned to me with a heart-rending look.

'Hector,' she cried, 'I see him every day; and it is that which is killing me.'

She burst into a passion of tears when she had said this. I took her in my arms as if she had been a frightened child and tried to comfort her.

'My darling, this is madness,' I said. 'You know that no stranger can come to you in the pleasaunce. The moat is ten feet wide and always full of water and the gates are kept locked day and night by old Massou. The châtelaine of a medieval fortress need fear no intruder in her antique garden.'

My wife shook her head sadly.

'I see him every day,' she said.

On this I believed that my wife was mad. I shrank from questioning her more closely concerning her mysterious visitant. It would be ill, I thought, to give a form and substance to the shadow that tormented her by too close enquiry about its look and manner, its coming and going.

I took care to assure myself that no stranger to the household could by any possibility penetrate to the pleasaunce. Having done this, I was fain to await the coming of the physician.

He came at last. I revealed to him the conviction which was my misery. I told him that I believed my wife to be mad. He saw her – spent an hour alone with her and then came to me. To my unspeakable relief he assured me of her sanity.

'It is just possible that she may be affected by one delusion,' he said; 'but she is so reasonable upon all other points, that I can scarcely bring

myself to believe her the subject of a monomania. I am rather inclined
to think that she really sees the person of whom she speaks. She
described him to me with a perfect minuteness. The descriptions of
scenes or individuals given by patients afflicted with monomania are
always more or less disjointed; but your wife spoke to me as clearly and
calmly as I am now speaking to you. Are you sure there is no one who
can approach her in that garden where she walks?'

'I am quite sure.'

'Is there any kinsman of your steward or hanger-on of your
household – a young man with a fair womanish face, very pale and
rendered remarkable by a crimson scar, which looks like the mark of a
blow?'

'My God!' I cried, as the light broke in upon me all at once. 'And the
dress – the strange old-fashioned dress?'

'The man wears a hunting costume of purple and orange,' answered
the doctor.

I knew then that André de Brissac had kept his word and that in the
hour when my life was brightest his shadow had come between me and
happiness.

I showed my wife the picture in the library, for I would fain assure
myself that there was some error in my fancy about my cousin. She
shook like a leaf when she beheld it and clung to me convulsively.

'This is witchcraft, Hector,' she said. 'The dress in that picture is the
dress of the man I see in the pleasaunce; but the face is not his.'

Then she described to me the face of the stranger; and it was my
cousin's face line for line – André de Brissac, whom she had never seen
in the flesh. Most vividly of all did she describe the cruel mark upon his
face, the trace of a fierce blow from an open hand.

After this I carried my wife away from Puy Verdun. We wandered far –
through the southern provinces and into the very heart of Switzerland.
I thought to distance the ghastly phantom and I fondly hoped that
change of scene would bring peace to my wife.

It was not so. Go where we would, the ghost of André de Brissac
followed us. To my eyes that fatal shadow never revealed itself. *That*
would have been too poor a vengeance. It was my wife's innocent heart
which André made the instrument of his revenge. The unholy presence
destroyed her life. My constant companionship could not shield her
from the horrible intruder. In vain did I watch her; in vain did I strive
to comfort her.

'He will not let me be at peace,' she said; 'he comes between us,

Hector. He is standing between us now. I can see his face with the red mark upon it plainer than I see yours.'

One fair moonlight night, when we were together in a mountain village in the Tyrol, my wife cast herself at my feet and told me she was the worst and vilest of women. 'I have confessed all to my director,' she said; 'from the first I have not hidden my sin from Heaven. But I feel that death is near me; and before I die I would fain reveal my sin to you.'

'What sin, my sweet one?'

'When first the stranger came to me in the forest, his presence bewildered and distressed me and I shrank from him as from something strange and terrible. He came again and again; by and by I found myself thinking of him and watching for his coming. His image haunted me perpetually; I strove in vain to shut his face out of my mind. Then followed an interval in which I did not see him; and, to my shame and anguish, I found that life seemed dreary and desolate without him. After that came the time in which he haunted the pleasaunce; and – O, Hector, kill me if you will, for I deserve no mercy at your hands! – I grew in those days to count the hours that must elapse before his coming, to take no pleasure save in the sight of that pale face with the red brand upon it. He plucked all old familiar joys out of my heart and left in it but one weird unholy pleasure – the delight of his presence. For a year I have lived but to see him. And now curse me, Hector; for this is my sin. Whether it comes of the baseness of my own heart or is the work of witchcraft, I know not; but I know that I have striven against this wickedness in vain.'

I took my wife to my breast and forgave her. In sooth, what had I to forgive? Was the fatality that overshadowed us any work of hers? On the next night she died, with her hand in mine; and at the very last she told me, sobbing and affrighted, that *he* was by her side.

Markheim

ROBERT LOUIS STEVENSON 1850–1894

'YES,' SAID THE DEALER, 'our windfalls are of various kinds. Some customers are ignorant and then I touch a dividend on my superior knowledge. Some are dishonest,' and here he held up the candle, so that the light fell strongly on his visitor, 'and in that case,' he continued, 'I profit by my virtue.'

Markheim had but just entered from the daylight streets and his eyes had not yet grown familiar with the mingled shine and darkness in the shop. At these pointed words and before the near presence of the flame, he blinked painfully and looked aside.

The dealer chuckled. 'You come to see me on Christmas Day,' he resumed, 'when you know that I am alone in my house, put up my shutters and make a point of refusing business. Well, you will have to pay for that; you will have to pay for my loss of time, when I should be balancing my books; you will have to pay, besides, for a kind of manner that I remark in you today very strongly. I am the essence of discretion and ask no awkward questions; but when a customer cannot look me in the eye, he has to pay for it.' The dealer once more chuckled; and then, changing to his usual business voice, though still with a note of irony, 'You can give, as usual, a clear account of how you came into the possession of the object?' he continued. 'Still your uncle's cabinet? A remarkable collector, sir!'

And the little pale, round-shouldered dealer stood almost on tip-toe, looking over the top of his gold spectacles and nodding his head with every mark of disbelief. Markheim returned his gaze with one of infinite pity and a touch of horror.

'This time,' said he, 'you are in error. I have not come to sell, but to buy. I have no curios to dispose of; my uncle's cabinet is bare to the wainscot; even were it still intact, I have done well on the Stock Exchange and should more likely add to it than otherwise and my errand today is simplicity itself. I seek a Christmas present for a lady,' he continued, waxing more fluent as he struck into the speech he had prepared; 'and certainly I owe you every excuse for thus disturbing you upon so small a matter. But the thing was neglected yesterday; I must produce my little compliment at dinner; and, as you very well know, a rich marriage is not a thing to be neglected.'

There followed a pause, during which the dealer seemed to weigh this statement incredulously. The ticking of many clocks among the curious lumber of the shop and the faint rushing of the cabs in a near thoroughfare filled up the interval of silence.

'Well, sir,' said the dealer, 'be it so. You are an old customer after all; and if, as you say, you have the chance of a good marriage, far be it from me to be an obstacle. Here is a nice thing for a lady now,' he went on, 'this hand-glass – fifteenth century, warranted; comes from a good collection, too; but I reserve the name, in the interests of my customer, who was just like yourself, my dear sir, the nephew and sole heir of a remarkable collector.'

The dealer, while he thus ran on in his dry and biting voice, had stooped to take the object from its place; and, as he had done so, a shock had passed through Markheim, a start both of hand and foot, a sudden leap of many tumultuous passions to the face. It passed as swiftly as it came and left no trace beyond a certain trembling of the hand that now received the glass.

'A glass,' he said hoarsely and then paused and repeated it more clearly. 'A glass? For Christmas? Surely not?'

'And why not?' cried the dealer. 'Why not a glass?'

Markheim was looking upon him with an indefinable expression. 'You ask me why not?' he said. 'Why, look here – look in it – look at yourself! Do you like to see it? No! nor I – nor any man.'

The little man had jumped back when Markheim had so suddenly confronted him with the mirror; but now, perceiving there was nothing worse on hand, he chuckled. 'Your future lady, sir, must be pretty hard favoured,' said he.

'I ask you,' said Markheim, 'for a Christmas present and you give me this – this damned reminder of years and sins and follies – this hand-conscience! Did you mean it? Had you a thought in your mind? Tell me. It will be better for you if you do. Come, tell me about yourself. I hazard a guess now, that you are in secret a very charitable man?'

The dealer looked closely at his companion. It was very odd, Markheim did not appear to be laughing; there was something in his face like an eager sparkle of hope, but nothing of mirth.

'What are you driving at?' the dealer asked.

'Not charitable?' returned the other gloomily. 'Not charitable; not pious; not scrupulous; unloving, unbeloved; a hand to get money, a safe to keep it. Is that all? Dear God, man, is that all?'

'I will tell you what it is,' began the dealer, with some sharpness, and then broke off again into a chuckle. 'But I see this is a love-match of yours and you have been drinking the lady's health.'

'Ah!' cried Markheim, with a strange curiosity. 'Ah, have you been in love? Tell me about that.'

'I,' cried the dealer. 'I in love! I never had the time, nor have I the time today for all this nonsense. Will you take the glass?'

'Where is the hurry?' returned Markheim. 'It is very pleasant to stand here talking; and life is so short and insecure that I would not hurry away from any pleasure – no, not even from so mild a one as this. We should rather cling, cling to what little we can get, like a man at a cliff's edge. Every second is a cliff, if you think upon it – a cliff a mile high – high enough, if we fall, to dash us out of every feature of humanity. Hence it is best to talk pleasantly. Let us talk of each other: why should we wear this mask? Let us be confidential. Who knows, we might become friends?'

'I have just one word to say to you,' said the dealer. 'Either make your purchase or walk out of my shop!'

'True, true,' said Markheim. 'Enough fooling. To business. Show me something else.'

The dealer stooped once more, this time to replace the glass upon the shelf, his thin blonde hair falling over his eyes as he did so. Markheim moved a little nearer, with one hand in the pocket of his greatcoat; he drew himself up and filled his lungs; at the same time many different emotions were depicted together on his face – terror, horror, and resolve, fascination and a physical repulsion; and through a haggard lift of his upper lip, his teeth looked out.

'This, perhaps, may suit,' observed the dealer: and then, as he began to re-arise, Markheim bounded from behind upon his victim. The long, skewerlike dagger flashed and fell. The dealer struggled like a hen, striking his temple on the shelf, and then tumbled on the floor in a heap.

Time had some score of small voices in that shop, some stately and slow as was becoming to their great age; others garrulous and hurried. All these told out the seconds in an intricate chorus of tickings. Then the passage of a lad's feet, heavily running on the pavement, broke in upon these smaller voices and startled Markheim into the conscious-ness of his surroundings. He looked about him awfully. The candle stood on the counter, its flame solemnly wagging in a draught; and by that inconsiderable movement, the whole room was filled with noise-less bustle and kept heaving like a sea; the tall shadows nodding, the gross blots of darkness swelling and dwindling as with respiration, the faces of the portraits and the china gods changing and wavering like images in water. The inner door stood ajar and peered into that leaguer of shadows with a long slit of daylight like a pointing finger.

From these fear-stricken rovings Markheim's eyes returned to the body of his victim, where it lay both humped and sprawling, incredibly small and strangely meaner than in life. In these poor, miserly clothes, in that ungainly attitude, the dealer lay like so much sawdust. Markheim had feared to see it and lo! it was nothing. And yet, as he gazed, this bundle of old clothes and pool of blood began to find eloquent voices. There it must lie; there was none to work the cunning hinges or direct the miracle of locomotion – there it must lie till it was found. Found! ay, and then? Then would his dead flesh lift up a cry that would ring over England and fill the world with the echoes of pursuit. Ay, dead or not, this was still the enemy. 'Time was that when the brains were out,' he thought; and the first word struck into his mind. Time, now that the deed was accomplished – time, which had closed for the victim, had become instant and momentous for the slayer.

The thought was yet in his mind, when, first one and then another, with every variety of pace and voice – one deep as the bell from a cathedral turret, another ringing on its treble notes the prelude of a waltz – the clocks began to strike the hour of three in the afternoon.

The sudden outbreak of so many tongues in that dumb chamber staggered him. He began to bestir himself, going to and fro with the candle, beleaguered by moving shadows and startled to the soul by chance reflections. In many rich mirrors, some of home design, some from Venice or Amsterdam, he saw his face repeated and repeated, as it were an army of spies; his own eyes met and detected him; and the sound of his own steps, lightly as they fell, vexed the surrounding quiet. And still, as he continued to fill his pockets, his mind accused him with a sickening iteration of the thousand faults of his design. He should have chosen a more quiet hour; he should have prepared an alibi; he should not have used a knife; he should have been more cautious and only bound and gagged the dealer and not killed him; he should have been more bold and killed the servant also; he should have done all things otherwise; poignant regrets, weary, incessant toiling of the mind to change what was unchangeable, to plan what was now useless, to be the architect of the irrevocable past. Meanwhile, and behind all this activity, brute terrors, like the scurrying of rats in a deserted attic, filled the more remote chambers of his brain with riot; the hand of the constable would fall heavy on his shoulder and his nerves would jerk like a hooked fish; or he beheld, in galloping defile, the dock, the prison, the gallows and the black coffin.

Terror of the people in the street sat down before his mind like a besieging army. It was impossible, he thought, but that some rumour of the struggle must have reached their ears and set on edge their curiosity; and now, in all the neighbouring houses, he divined them sitting motionless and with uplifted ear – solitary people, condemned to spend Christmas dwelling alone on memories of the past and now startingly recalled from that tender exercise; happy family parties, struck into silence round the table, the mother still with raised finger: every degree and age and humour, but all, by their own hearths, prying and hearkening and weaving the rope that was to hang him. Sometimes it seemed to him he could not move too softly; the clink of the tall Bohemian goblets rang out loudly like a bell; and alarmed by the bigness of the ticking, he was tempted to stop the clocks. And then, again, with a swift transition of his terrors, the very silence of the place appeared a source of peril and a thing to strike and freeze the passer-by; and he would step more boldly and bustle aloud among the contents of the shop and imitate, with elaborate bravado, the movements of a busy man at ease in his own house.

But he was now so pulled about by different alarms that, while one portion of his mind was still alert and cunning, another trembled on the brink of lunacy. One hallucination in particular took a strong hold on his credulity. The neighbour hearkening with white face beside his window, the passer-by arrested by a horrible surmise on the pavement – these could at worst suspect, they could not know; through the brick walls and shuttered windows only sounds could penetrate. But here, within the house, was he alone? He knew he was; he had watched the servant set forth sweethearting, in her poor best, 'out for the day' written in every ribbon and smile. Yes, he was alone, of course; and yet, in the bulk of empty house above him, he could surely hear a stir of delicate footing – he was surely conscious, inexplicably conscious of some presence. Ay, surely; to every room and corner of the house his imagination followed it; and now it was a faceless thing and yet had eyes to see with; and again it was a shadow of himself; and yet again behold the image of the dead dealer, re-inspired with cunning and hatred.

At times, with a strong effort, he would glance at the open door which still seemed to repel his eyes. The house was tall, the skylight small and dirty, the day blind with fog; and the light that filtered down to the ground storey was exceedingly faint and showed dimly on the threshold of the shop. And yet, in that strip of doubtful brightness, did there not hang wavering a shadow?

Suddenly, from the street outside, a very jovial gentleman began to beat with a staff on the shop-door, accompanying his blows with shouts and railleries in which the dealer was continually called upon by name. Markheim, smitten into ice, glanced at the dead man. But no! he lay quite still; he was fled away far beyond earshot of these blows and shoutings; he was sunk beneath seas of silence; and his name, which would once have caught his notice above the howling of a storm, had become an empty sound. And presently the jovial gentleman desisted from his knocking and departed.

Here was a broad hint to hurry what remained to be done, to get forth from this accusing neighbourhood, to plunge into a bath of London multitudes and to reach, on the other side of day, that haven of safety and apparent innocence – his bed. One visitor had come: at any moment another might follow and be more obstinate. To have done the deed and yet not to reap the profit, would be too abhorrent a failure. The money, that was now Markheim's concern; and as a means to that, the keys.

He glanced over his shoulder at the open door, where the shadow was still lingering and shivering; and with no conscious repugnance of the mind, yet with a tremor of the belly, he drew near the body of his victim. The human character had quite departed. Like a suit half-stuffed with bran, the limbs lay scattered, the trunk doubled, on the floor; and yet the thing repelled him. Although so dingy and inconsiderable to the eye, he feared it might have more significance to the touch. He took the body by the shoulders and turned it on its back. It was strangely light and supple and the limbs, as if they had been broken, fell into the oddest postures. The face was robbed of all expression; but it was as pale as wax and shockingly smeared with blood about one temple. That was, for Markheim, the one displeasing circumstance. It carried him back, upon the instant, to a certain fair-day in a fishers' village: a grey day, a piping wind, a crowd upon the street, the blare of brasses, the booming of drums, the nasal voice of a ballad singer; and a boy going to and fro, buried over head in the crowd and divided between interest and fear, until, coming out on the chief place of concourse, he beheld a booth and a great screen with pictures, dismally designed, garishly coloured: Brownrigg with her apprentice; the Mannings with their murdered guest; Weare in the death-grip of Thurtell; and a score besides of famous crimes. The thing was as dear as an illusion; he was once again that little boy; he was looking once again and with the same sense of physical revolt, at these vile pictures; he was still stunned by the thumping of the drums. A bar of that day's music returned upon his memory; and at that, for the first time, a qualm came over him, a breath of nausea, a sudden weakness of the joints, which he must instantly resist and conquer.

He judged it more prudent to confront than to flee from these considerations; looking the more hardily in the dead face, bending his mind to realise the nature and greatness of his crime. So little a while ago that face had moved with every change of sentiment, that pale mouth had spoken, that body had been all on fire with governable energies; and now, and by his act, that piece of life had been arrested, as the horologist, with interjected finger, arrests the beating of the clock. So he reasoned in vain; he could rise to no more remorseful consciousness; the same heart which had shuddered before the painted effigies of crime, looked on its reality unmoved. At best, he felt a gleam of pity for one who had been endowed in vain with all those faculties that can make the world a garden of enchantment, one who had never lived and who was now dead. But of penitence, no, not a tremor.

With that, shaking himself clear of these considerations, he found the keys and advanced towards the open door of the shop. Outside, it had begun to rain smartly; and the sound of the shower upon the roof had banished silence. Like some dripping cavern, the chambers of the house were haunted by an incessant echoing, which filled the ear and mingled with the ticking of the clocks. And, as Markheim approached the door, he seemed to hear, in answer to his own cautious tread, the steps of another foot withdrawing up the stair. The shadow still palpitated loosely on the threshold. He threw a ton's weight of resolve upon his muscles and drew back the door.

The faint, foggy daylight glimmered dimly on the bare floor and stairs; on the bright suit of armour posted, halbert in hand, upon the landing; and on the dark wood-carvings and framed pictures that hung against the yellow panels of the wainscot. So loud was the beating of the rain through all the house, that, in Markheim's ears, it began to be distinguished into many different sounds. Footsteps and sighs, the tread of regiments marching in the distance, the chink of money in the counting and the creaking of doors held stealthily ajar, appeared to mingle with the patter of the drops upon the cupola and the gushing of the water in the pipes. The sense that he was not alone grew upon him to the verge of madness. On every side he was haunted and begirt by presences. He heard them moving in the upper chambers; from the shop, he heard the dead man getting to his legs; and as he began with a great effort to mount the stairs, feet fled quietly before him and followed stealthily behind. If he were but deaf, he thought, how tranquilly he would possess his soul! And then again, and hearkening with ever fresh attention, he blessed himself for that unresting sense which held the outposts and stood a trusty sentinel upon his life. His head turned continually on his neck; his eyes, which seemed starting from their orbits, scouted on every side and on every side were half-rewarded as with the tail of something nameless vanishing. The four-and-twenty steps to the first floor were four-and-twenty agonies.

On that first storey the doors stood ajar, three of them like three ambushes, shaking his nerves like the throats of cannon. He could never again, he felt, be sufficiently immured and fortified from men's observing eyes; he longed to be home, girt in by walls, buried among bed-clothes and invisible to all but God. And at that thought he wondered a little, recollecting tales of other murderers and the fear they were said to entertain of heavenly avengers. It was not so, at least, with him. He feared the laws of nature, lest in their callous and immutable procedure they should preserve some damning evidence of his crime. He feared tenfold more, with a slavish, superstitious terror, some scission in the continuity of man's experience, some wilful illegality of nature. He played a game of skill, depending on the rules, calculating consequence from cause; and what if nature, as the defeated tyrant overthrew the chess-board, should break the mould of their succession? The like had befallen Napoleon (so writers said) when the winter changed the time of its appearance. The like might befall Markheim; the solid walls might become transparent and reveal his doings like those of bees in a glass hive; the stout planks might yield under his foot like quicksands and detain him in their clutch; ay, and there were soberer accidents that might destroy him; if, for instance, the house should fall and imprison him beside the body of his victim; or the house next door should fly on fire and the firemen invade him from all sides. These things he feared; and, in a sense, these things might be called the hands of God reached forth against sin. But about God Himself he was at ease; his act was doubtless exceptional, but so were his excuses, which God knew; it was there, and not among men, that he felt sure of justice.

When he had got safe into the drawing-room and shut the door behind him, he was aware of a respite from alarms. The room was quite dismantled, uncarpeted besides and strewn with packing-cases and incongruous furniture; several great pier-glasses, in which he beheld himself at various angles, like an actor on a stage; many pictures, framed and unframed, standing, with their faces to the wall; a fine Sheraton sideboard, a cabinet of marquetry and a great old bed, with tapestry hangings. The windows opened to the floor; but by great good fortune the lower part of the shutters had been closed and this concealed him from the neighbours. Here, then, Markheim drew in a packing-case before the cabinet and began to search among the keys. It was a long business, for there were many and it was irksome, besides; for, after all, there might be nothing in the cabinet and time was on the wing. But the closeness of the occupation sobered him. With the tail of his eye he saw the door – even glanced at it from time to time directly, like a besieged commander pleased to verify the good estate of his defences. But in truth he was at peace. The rain falling in the street sounded natural and pleasant. Presently, on the other side, the notes of a piano were wakened to the music of a hymn and the voices of many children took up the air and words. How stately, how comfortable was the melody! How fresh the youthful voices! Markheim gave ear to it smilingly, as he sorted out the keys; and his mind was thronged with answerable ideas and images; church-going children and the pealing of the high organ; children afield, bathers by the brookside, ramblers on the brambly common, kite-flyers in the windy and cloud-navigated sky; and then, at another cadence of the hymn, back again to church and the somnolence of summer Sundays and the high genteel voice of the parson (which he smiled a little to recall) and the painted Jacobean tombs and the dim lettering of the Ten Commandments in the chancel.

And as he sat thus, at once busy and absent, he was startled to his feet. A flash of ice, a flash of fire, a bursting gush of blood, went over him and then he stood transfixed and thrilling. A step mounted the stair slowly and steadily, and presently a hand was laid upon the knob and the lock clicked and the door opened.

Fear held Markheim in a vice. What to expect he knew not, whether the dead man walking or the official ministers of human justice or some chance witness blindly stumbling in to consign him to the gallows. But when a face was thrust into the aperture, glanced round the room, looked at him, nodded and smiled as if in friendly recognition and then withdrew again and the door closed behind it, his fear broke loose from his control in a hoarse cry. At the sound of this the visitant returned.

'Did you call me?' he asked pleasantly, and with that he entered the room and closed the door behind him.

Markheim stood and gazed at him with all his eyes. Perhaps there was a film upon his sight, but the outlines of the newcomer seemed to change and waver like those of the idols in the wavering candlelight of the shop; and at times he thought he knew him; and at times he thought he bore a likeness to himself; and always, like a lump of living terror, there lay in his bosom the conviction that this thing was not of the earth and not of God.

And yet the creature had a strange air of the commonplace, as he stood looking on Markheim with a smile; and when he added: 'You are looking for the money, I believe?' it was in the tones of everyday politeness.

Markheim made no answer.

'I should warn you,' resumed the other, 'that the maid has left her sweetheart earlier than usual and will soon be here. If Mr Markheim be found in this house, I need not describe to him the consequences.'

'You know me?' cried the murderer.

The visitor smiled. 'You have long been a favourite of mine,' he said; 'and I have long observed and often sought to help you.'

'What are you?' cried Markheim: 'the Devil?'

'What I may be,' returned the other, 'cannot affect the service I propose to render you.'

'It can,' cried Markheim; 'it does! Be helped by you? No, never; not by you! You do not know me yet; thank God, you do not know me!'

'I know you,' replied the visitant, with a sort of kind severity or rather firmness. 'I know you to the soul.'

'Know me!' cried Markheim. 'Who can do so? My life is but a travesty and slander on myself. I have lived to belie my nature. All men do; all men are better than this disguise that grows about and stifles them. You see each dragged away by life, like one whom bravos have seized and muffled in a cloak. If they had their own control – if you could see their faces, they would be altogether different, they would shine out for heroes and saints! I am worse than most; myself is more overlaid; my excuse is known to me and God. But, had I the time, I could disclose myself.'

'To me?' enquired the visitant.

'To you before all,' returned the murderer. 'I supposed you were intelligent. I thought – since you exist – you would prove a reader of the heart. And yet you would propose to judge me by my acts! Think of it; my acts! I was born and I have lived in a land of giants; giants have dragged me by the wrists since I was born out of my mother – the giants of circumstance. And you would judge me by my acts! But can you not look within? Can you not understand that evil is hateful to me? Can you not see within me the clear writing of conscience, never blurred by any wilful sophistry, although too often disregarded? Can you not read me for a thing that surely must be common as humanity – the unwilling sinner?'

'All this is very feelingly expressed,' was the reply, 'but it regards me not. These points of consistency are beyond my province and I care not in the least by what compulsion you may have been dragged away, so as you are but carried in the right direction. But time flies; the servant delays, looking in the faces of the crowd and at the pictures on the hoardings, but still she keeps moving nearer; and remember, it is as if the gallows itself was striding towards you through the Christmas streets! Shall I help you; I, who know all? Shall I tell you where to find the money?'

'For what price?' asked Markheim.

'I offer you the service for a Christmas gift,' returned the other.

Markheim could not refrain from smiling with a kind of bitter triumph. 'No,' said he, 'I will take nothing at your hands; if I were dying of thirst and it was your hand that put the pitcher to my lips, I should find the courage to refuse. It may be credulous, but I will do nothing to commit myself to evil.'

'I have no objection to a death-bed repentance,' observed the visitant.

'Because you disbelieve their efficacy!' Markheim cried.

'I do not say so,' returned the other; 'but I look on these things from a different side and when the life is done my interest falls. The man has lived to serve me, to spread black looks under colour of religion or to sow tares in the wheatfield, as you do, in a course of weak compliance with desire. Now that he draws so near to his deliverance, he can add but one act of service, to repent, to die smiling and thus to build up in confidence and hope the more timorous of my surviving followers. I am not so hard a master. Try me. Accept my help. Please yourself in life as you have done hitherto; please yourself more amply, spread your elbows at the board; and when the night begins to fall and the curtains to be drawn, I tell you, for your greater comfort, that you will find it even easy to compound your quarrel with your conscience and to make a truckling peace with God. I came but now from such a death-bed and the room was full of sincere mourners, listening to the man's last words: and when I looked into that face, which had been set as a flint against mercy, I found it smiling with hope.'

'And do you, then, suppose me such a creature?' asked Markheim. 'Do you think I have no more generous aspirations than to sin and sin and sin and, at the last, sneak into heaven? My heart rises at the thought. Is this, then, your experience of mankind? or is it because you find me with red hands that you presume such baseness? and is this crime of murder indeed so impious as to dry up the very springs of good?'

'Murder is to me no special category,' replied the other. 'All sins are murder, even as all life is war. I behold your race, like starving mariners on a raft, plucking crusts out of the hands of famine and feeding on each other's lives. I follow sins beyond the moment of their acting; I find in all that the last consequence is death; and to my eyes, the pretty maid who thwarts her mother with such taking graces on a question of a ball, drips no less visibly with human gore than such a murderer as yourself. Do I say that I follow sins? I follow virtues also; they differ not by the thickness of a nail, they are both scythes for the reaping angel of Death. Evil, for which I live, consists not in action but in character.

The bad man is dear to me; not the bad act, whose fruits, if we could follow them far enough down the hurtling cataract of the ages, might yet be found more blessed than those of the rarest virtues. And it is not because you have killed a dealer, but because you are Markheim, that I offer to forward your escape.'

'I will lay my heart open to you,' answered Markheim. 'This crime on which you find me is my last. On my way to it I have learned many lessons; itself is a lesson, a momentous lesson. Hitherto I have been driven with revolt to what I would not; I was a bond-slave to poverty, driven and scourged. There are robust virtues that can stand in these temptations; mine was not so: I had a thirst of pleasure. But today, and out of this deed, I pluck both warning and riches – both the power and a fresh resolve to be myself. I become in all things a free actor in the world; I begin to see myself all changed, these hands the agents of good, this heart at peace. Something comes over me out of the past; something of what I have dreamed on Sabbath evenings to the sound of the church organ, of what I forecast when I shed tears over noble books or talked, an innocent child, with my mother. There lies my life; I have wandered a few years, but now I see once more my city of destination.'

'You are to use this money on the Stock Exchange, I think?' remarked the visitor; 'and there, if I mistake not, you have already lost some thousands?'

'Ah,' said Markheim, 'but this time I have a sure thing.'

'This time, again, you will lose,' replied the visitor quietly.

'Ah, but I keep back the half!' cried Markheim.

'That also you will lose,' said the other.

The sweat started upon Markheim's brow. 'Well, then, what matter?' he exclaimed. 'Say it be lost, say I am plunged again in poverty, shall one part of me, and that the worse, continue until the end to override the better? Evil and good run strong in me, haling me both ways. I do not love the one thing, I love all. I can conceive great deeds, renunciations, martyrdoms; and though I be fallen to such a crime as murder, pity is no stranger to my thoughts. I pity the poor; who knows their trials better than myself? I pity and help them; I prize love, I love honest laughter; there is no good thing nor true thing on earth but I love it from my heart. And are my vices only to direct my life and my virtues to lie without effect, like some passive lumber of the mind? Not so; good, also, is a spring of acts.'

But the visitant raised his finger. 'For six-and-thirty years that you have been in this world,' said he, 'through many changes of fortune and varieties of humour, I have watched you steadily fall. Fifteen years ago you would have started at a theft. Three years back you would have blenched at the name of murder. Is there any crime, is there any cruelty or meanness, from which you still recoil? – five years from now I shall detect you in the fact! Downward, downward, lies your way; nor can anything but death avail to stop you.'

'It is true,' Markheim said huskily, 'I have in some degree complied with evil. But it is so with all; the very saints, in the mere exercise of living, grow less dainty and take on the tone of their surroundings.'

'I will propound to you one simple question,' said the other; 'and as you answer, I shall read to you your moral horoscope. You have grown in many things more lax; possibly you do right to be so; and at any account, it is the same with all men. But, granting that, are you in any one particular, however trifling, more difficult to please with your own conduct or do you go in all things with a looser rein?'

'In any one?' repeated Markheim, with an anguish of consideration. 'No,' he added, with despair, 'in none! I have gone down in all.'

'Then,' said the visitor, 'content yourself with what you are, for you will never change; and the words of your part on this stage are irrevocably written down.'

Markheim stood for a long while silent and indeed it was the visitor who first broke the silence. 'That being so,' he said, 'shall I show you the money?'

'And grace?' cried Markheim.

'Have you not tried it?' returned the other. 'Two or three years ago, did I not see you on the platform of revival meetings and was not your voice the loudest in the hymn?'

'It is true,' said Markheim; 'and I see clearly what remains for me by way of duty. I thank you for these lessons from my soul; my eyes are opened and I behold myself at last for what I am.'

At this moment the sharp note of the door-bell rang through the house; and the visitant, as though this were some concerted signal for which he had been waiting, changed at once in his demeanour.

'The maid!' he cried. 'She has returned, as I forewarned you, and there is now before you one more difficult passage. Her master, you must say, is ill; you must let her in, with an assured but rather serious countenance – no smiles, no overacting and I promise you success! Once the girl is within and the door closed, the same dexterity that has already rid you of the dealer will relieve you of this last danger in your path. Thenceforward you have the whole evening – the whole night, if needful – to ransack the treasures of the house and to make good your safety. This is help that comes to you with the mask of danger. Up!' he cried; 'up, friend; your life hangs trembling in the scales: up and act!'

Markheim steadily regarded his counsellor. 'If I be condemned to evil acts,' he said, 'there is still one door of freedom open – I can cease from action. If my life be an ill thing, I can lay it down. Though I be, as you say truly, at the beck of every small temptation, I can yet, by one decisive gesture, place myself beyond the reach of all. My love of good is damned to barrenness; it may, and let it be! But I have still my hatred of evil; and from that, to your galling disappointment, you shall see that I can draw both energy and courage.'

The features of the visitor began to undergo a wonderful and lovely change: they brightened and softened with a tender triumph and, even as they brightened, faded and dislimned. But Markheim did not pause to watch or understand the transformation. He opened the door and went downstairs very slowly, thinking to himself. His past went soberly before him; he beheld it as it was, ugly and strenuous like a dream, random as chance-medley – a scene of defeat. Life, as he thus reviewed it, tempted him no longer; but on the farther side he perceived a quiet haven for his bark. He paused in the passage and looked into the shop, where the candle still burned by the dead body. It was strangely silent. Thoughts of the dealer swarmed into his mind as he stood gazing. And then the bell once more broke out into impatient clamour.

He confronted the maid upon the threshold with something like a smile.

'You had better go for the police,' said he: 'I have killed your master.'

Man-Size in Marble

EDITH NESBIT 1858–1924

ALTHOUGH EVERY WORD of this story is as true as despair, I do not expect people to believe it. Nowadays a 'rational explanation' is required before belief is possible. Let me, then, at once offer the 'rational explanation' which finds most favour among those who have heard the tale of my life's tragedy. It is held that we were 'under a delusion', Laura and I, on that 31st of October; and that this supposition places the whole matter on a satisfactory and believable basis. The reader can judge, when he, too, has heard my story, how far this is an 'explanation' and in what sense it is 'rational'. There were three who took part in this: Laura and I and another man. The other man still lives and can speak to the truth of the least credible part of my story.

I never in my life knew what it was to have as much money as I required to supply the most ordinary needs – good colours, books and cab-fares – and when we were married we knew quite well that we should only be able to live at all by 'strict punctuality and attention to business'. I used to paint in those days and Laura used to write, and we felt sure we could keep the pot at least simmering. Living in town was out of the question, so we went to look for a cottage in the country, which should be at once sanitary and picturesque. So rarely do these two qualities meet in one cottage that our search was for some time quite fruitless. But when we got away from friends and house-agents, on our honeymoon, our wits grew clear again and we knew a pretty cottage when at last we saw one.

It was at Brenzett – a little village set on a hill over against the southern marshes. We had gone there, from the seaside village where we were staying, to see the church, and two fields from the church we found this cottage. It stood quite by itself, about two miles from the village. It was a long, low building, with rooms sticking out in unexpected places. There was a bit of stonework – ivy-covered and moss-grown, just two old rooms, all that was left of a big house that had once stood there – and round this stonework the house had grown up. Stripped of its roses and jasmine it would have been hideous. As it stood it was charming and after a brief examination we took it. It was absurdly cheap. There was a jolly old-fashioned garden, with grass paths and no end of hollyhocks and sunflowers and big lilies. From the window you could see the marsh-pastures and beyond them the blue, thin line of the sea.

We got a tall old peasant woman to do for us. Her face and figure were good, though her cooking was of the homeliest; but she understood all about gardening and told us all the old names of the coppices and cornfields and the stories of the smugglers and highwaymen and, better still, of the 'things that walked' and of the 'sights' which met one in lonely glens of a starlight night. We soon came to leave all the domestic business to Mrs Dorman and to use her legends in little magazine stories which brought in the jingling guinea.

We had three months of married happiness and did not have a single quarrel. One October evening I had been down to smoke a pipe with the doctor – our only neighbour – a pleasant young Irishman. Laura had stayed at home to finish a comic sketch. I left her laughing over her own jokes and came in to find her a crumpled heap of pale muslin, weeping on the window seat.

'Good heavens, my darling, what's the matter?' I cried, taking her in my arms. 'What is the matter? Do speak.'

'It's Mrs Dorman,' she sobbed.

'What has she done?' I enquired, immensely relieved.

'She says she must go before the end of the month and she says her niece is ill; she's gone down to see her now, but I don't believe that's the reason, because her niece is always ill. I believe someone has been setting her against us. Her manner was so queer – '

'Never mind, Pussy,' I said; 'whatever you do, don't cry, or I shall have to cry to keep you in countenance and then you'll never respect your man again.'

'But you see,' she went on, 'it is really serious, because these village people are so sheepy and if one won't do a thing you may be quite sure none of the others will. And I shall have to cook the dinners and wash up the hateful greasy plates; and you'll have to carry cans of water about and clean the boots and knives – and we shall never have any time for work or earn any money or anything.'

I represented to her that even if we had to perform these duties the day would still present some margin for other toils and recreations. But she refused to see the matter in any but the greyest light.

'I'll speak to Mrs Dorman when she comes back and see if I can't come to terms with her,' I said. 'Perhaps she wants a rise in her screw. It will be all right. Let's walk up to the church.'

The church was a large and lonely one and we loved to go there, especially upon bright nights. The path skirted a wood, cut through it once, and ran along the crest of the hill through two meadows and round the churchyard wall, over which the old yews loomed in black masses of shadow.

This path, which was partly paved, was called 'the bier-walk', for it had long been the way by which the corpses had been carried to burial. The churchyard was richly treed and was shaded by great elms which stood just outside and stretched their majestic arms in benediction of the happy dead. A large, low porch let one into the building by a Norman doorway and a heavy oak door studded with iron. Inside, the arches rose into darkness, and between them the reticulated windows, which stood out white in the moonlight. In the chancel, the windows were of rich glass, which showed in faint light their noble colouring and made the black oak of the choir pews hardly more solid than the shadows. But on each side of the altar lay a grey marble figure of a knight in full plate armour lying upon a low slab, with hands held up in everlasting prayer, and these figures, oddly enough, were always to be seen if there was any glimmer of light in the church. Their names were lost, but the peasants told of them that they had been fierce and wicked men, marauders by land and sea, who had been the scourge of their time and had been guilty of deeds so foul that the house they had lived in – the big house, by the way, that had stood on the site of our cottage – had been stricken by lightning and the vengeance of Heaven. But for all that, the gold of their heirs had bought them a place in the church. Looking at the bad, hard faces reproduced in the marble, this story was easily believed.

The church looked at its best and weirdest on that night, for the shadows of the yew tree fell through the windows upon the floor of the nave and touched the pillars with tattered shade. We sat down together without speaking and watched the solemn beauty of the old church with some of that awe which inspired its early builders. We walked to the chancel and looked at the sleeping warriors. Then we rested some time on the stone seat in the porch, looking out over the stretch of quiet moonlit meadows, feeling in every fibre of our being the peace of the night and of our happy love; and came away at last with a sense that even scrubbing and black-leading were but small troubles at their worst.

Mrs Dorman had come back from the village and I at once invited her to a *tête-à-tête*.

'Now, Mrs Dorman,' I said, when I had got her into my painting room, 'what's all this about your not staying with us?'

'I should be glad to get away, sir, before the end of the month,' she answered, with her usual placid dignity.

'Have you any fault to find, Mrs Dorman?'

'None at all, sir: you and your lady have always been most kind I'm sure – '

'Well, what is it? Are your wages not high enough?'

'No, sir, I gets quite enough.'

'Then why not stay?'

'I'd rather not' – with some hesitation – 'my niece is ill.'

'But your niece has been ill ever since we came. Can't you stay for another month?'

'No, sir, I'm bound to go by Thursday.'

And this was Monday!

'Well, I must say, I think you might have let us know before. There's no time now to get anyone else and your mistress is not fit to do heavy housework. Can't you stay till next week?'

'I might be able to come back next week.'

'But why must you go this week?' I persisted. 'Come, out with it.'

Mrs Dorman drew the little shawl, which she always wore, tightly across her bosom, as though she were cold. Then she said, with a sort of effort: 'They say, sir, as this was a big house in Catholic times and there was many deeds done here.'

The nature of the 'deeds' might be vaguely inferred from the inflection of Mrs Dorman's voice – which was enough to make one's blood run cold. I was glad that Laura was not in the room. She was always nervous, as highly-strung natures are, and I felt that these tales about our house, told by this old peasant woman, with her impressive manner and contagious credulity, might have made our home less dear to my wife.

'Tell me all about it, Mrs Dorman,' I said; 'you needn't mind about telling me. I'm not like the young people who make fun of such things.'

Which was partly true.

'Well, sir' – she sank her voice – 'you may have seen in the church, bedside the altar, two shapes.'

'You mean the effigies of the knights in armour,' I said cheerfully.

'I mean them two bodies, drawed out man-size in marble,' she returned, and I had to admit that her description was a thousand times more graphic than mine, to say nothing of a certain weird force and uncanniness about the phrase 'drawed out man-size in marble'.

'They do say, as on All Saints' Eve them two bodies sits up on their slabs and gets off them and then walks down the aisle, *in their marble*' – another good phrase, Mrs Dorman – 'and as the church clock strikes eleven they walks out of the church door and over the graves and along the bier-walk and if it's a wet night there's the marks of their feet in the morning.'

'And where do they go?' I asked, rather fascinated.

'They comes back here to their home, sir, and if anyone meets them – '

'Well, what then?' I asked.

But no – not another word could I get from her, save that her niece was ill and she must go.

'Whatever you do, sir, lock the door early on All Saints' Eve and make the cross-sign over the doorstep and on the windows.'

'But has anyone ever seen these things?' I persisted. 'Who was here last year?'

'No one, sir; the lady as owned the house only stayed here in summer and she always went to London a full month afore *the* night. And I'm sorry to inconvenience you and your lady, but my niece is ill and I must go on Thursday.'

I could have shaken her for her absurd reiteration of that obvious fiction, after she had told me her real reasons.

I did not tell Laura the legend of the shapes that 'walked in their marble', partly because a legend concerning our house might perhaps trouble my wife and partly, I think, from some more occult reason. This was not quite the same to me as any other story, and I did not want to talk about it till the day it was over. I had very soon ceased to think of the legend, however. I was painting a portrait of Laura, against the lattice window, and I could not think of much else. I had got a splendid background of yellow and grey sunset and was working away with enthusiasm at her face.

On Thursday Mrs Dorman went. She relented, at parting, so far as to say: 'Don't you put yourself about too much, ma'am, and if there's any little thing I can do next week I'm sure I shan't mind.'

Thursday passed off pretty well. Friday came. It is about what happened on that Friday that this is written.

I got up early, I remember, and lighted the kitchen fire and had just achieved a smoky success when my little wife came running down as sunny and sweet as the clear October morning itself. We prepared breakfast together and found it very good fun. The housework was soon done and when brushes and brooms and pails were quiet again the house was still indeed. Is it wonderful what a difference one makes in a house. We really missed Mrs Dorman, quite apart from considerations concerning pots and pans. We spent the day in dusting our books and putting them straight, and dined gaily on cold steak and coffee. Laura was, if possible, brighter and gayer and sweeter than usual and I began to think that a little domestic toil was really good for her. We had never been so merry since we were married and the walk we had that afternoon was, I think, the happiest time of all my life. When we had watched the deep scarlet clouds slowly pale into leaden grey against a pale green sky and saw the white mists curl up along the hedgerows in the distant marsh we came back to the house hand in hand.

'You are sad, my darling,' I said, half-jestingly, as we sat down together in our little parlour. I expected a disclaimer, for my own silence had been the silence of complete happiness.

To my surprise she said: 'Yes, I think I am sad, or, rather, I am uneasy. I don't think I'm very well. I have shivered three or four times since we came in; and it is not cold, is it?

'No,' I said, and hoped it was not a chill caught from the treacherous mists that roll up from the marshes in the dying night. No – she said, she did not think so.

Then, after a silence, she spoke suddenly: 'Do you ever have presentiments of evil?'

'No,' I said, smiling, 'and I shouldn't believe in them if I had.'

'I do,' she went on; 'the night my father died I knew it, though he was right away in the north of Scotland.' I did not answer in words.

She sat looking at the fire for some time in silence, gently stroking my hand. At last she sprang up, came behind me and, drawing my head back, kissed me.

'There, it's over now,' she said. 'What a baby I am! Come, light the candles and we'll have some of these new Rubenstein duets.'

And we spent a happy hour or two at the piano.

At about half-past ten I began to long for the good-night pipe, but Laura looked so white that I felt it would be brutal of me to fill our sitting-room with the fumes of strong cavendish.

'I'll take my pipe outside,' I said.

'Let me come, too.'

'No, sweetheart, not tonight; you're much too tired. I shan't be long. Go to bed or I shall have an invalid to nurse tomorrow as well as the boots to clean.'

I kissed her and was turning to go when she flung her arms round my neck and held me as if she would never let me go again. I stroked her hair.

'Come, Pussy, you're over-tired. The housework has been too much for you.'

She loosened her clasp a little and drew a deep breath.

'No. We've been very happy today, Jack, haven't we? Don't stay out too long.'

'I won't, my dearie.'

I strolled out of the front door, leaving it unlatched. What a night it was! The jagged masses of heavy dark cloud were rolling at intervals from horizon to horizon and thin white wreaths covered the stars. Through all the rush of the cloud river the moon swam, breasting the waves and disappearing again in the darkness.

I walked up and down, drinking in the beauty of the quiet earth and the changing sky. The night was absolutely silent. Nothing seemed to be abroad. There was no skurrying of rabbits or twitter of the half-asleep birds. And though the clouds went sailing across the sky, the wind that drove them never came low enough to rustle the dead leaves in the woodland paths. Across the meadows I could see the church tower standing out black and grey against the sky. I walked there thinking over our three months of happiness.

I heard a bell-beat from the church. Eleven already! I turned to go in, but the night held me. I could not go back into our little warm rooms yet. I would go up to the church.

I looked in at the low window as I went by. Laura was half-lying on her chair in front of the fire. I could not see her face, only her little head showed dark against the pale blue wall. She was quite still. Asleep, no doubt.

I walked slowly along the edge of the wood. A sound broke the stillness of the night, it was a rustling in the wood. I stopped and listened. The sound stopped too. I went on and now distinctly heard another step than mine answer mine like an echo. It was a poacher or a wood-stealer, most likely, for these were not unknown in our Arcadian neighbourhood. But whoever it was, he was a fool not to step more lightly. I turned into the wood and now the footstep seemed to come from the path I had just left. It must be an echo, I thought. The wood looked perfect in the moonlight. The large dying ferns and the brushwood showed where through thinning foliage the pale light came down. The tree trunks stood up like Gothic columns all around me. They reminded me of the church, and I turned into the bier-walk, and passed through the corpse-gate between the graves to the low porch.

I paused for a moment on the stone seat where Laura and I had watched the fading landscape. Then I noticed that the door of the church was open and I blamed myself for having left it unlatched the other night. We were the only people who ever cared to come to the church except on Sundays and I was vexed to think that through our carelessness the damp autumn airs had had a chance of getting in and injuring the old fabric. I went in. It will seem strange, perhaps, that I should have gone halfway up the aisle before I remembered – with a sudden chill, followed by as sudden a rush of self-contempt – that this was the very day and hour when, according to tradition, the 'shapes drawed out man-size in marble' began to walk.

Having thus remembered the legend and remembered it with a shiver, of which I was ashamed, I could not do otherwise than walk up towards the altar, just to look at the figures – as I said to myself; really what I wanted was to assure myself, first, that I did not believe the legend and, secondly, that it was not true. I was rather glad that I had come. I thought now I could tell Mrs Dorman how vain her fancies were and how peacefully the marble figures slept on through the ghastly hour. With my hands in my pockets I passed up the aisle. In the grey dim light the eastern end of the church looked larger than usual and the arches above the two tombs looked larger too. The moon came out and showed me the reason. I stopped short, my heart gave a leap that nearly choked me and then sank sickeningly.

The 'bodies drawed out man-size' *were gone!* and their marble slabs lay wide and bare in the vague moonlight that slanted through the east window.

Were they really gone or was I mad? Clenching my nerves, I stooped and passed my hand over the smooth slabs and felt their flat unbroken surface. Had someone taken the things away? Was it some vile practical joke? I would make sure, anyway. In an instant I had made a torch of a newspaper, which happened to be in my pocket and, lighting it, held it high above my head. Its yellow glare illumined the dark arches and those slabs. The figures *were* gone. And I was alone in the church; or was I alone?

And then a horror seized me, a horror indefinable and indescribable – an overwhelming certainty of supreme and accomplished calamity. I flung down the torch and tore along the aisle and out through the porch, biting my lips as I ran to keep myself from shrieking aloud. Oh, was I mad – or what was this that possessed me? I leaped the churchyard wall and took the straight cut across the fields, led by the light from our windows. Just as I got over the first stile a dark figure seemed to spring out of the ground. Mad still with that certainty of misfortune, I made for the thing that stood in my path, shouting, 'Get out of the way, can't you!'

But my push met with a more vigorous resistance than I had expected. My arms were caught just above the elbow and held as in a vice and the raw-boned Irish doctor actually shook me.

'Let me go, you fool,' I gasped. 'The marble figures have gone from the church; I tell you they've gone.'

He broke into a ringing laugh. 'I'll have to give ye a draught tomorrow, I see. Ye've been smoking too much and listening to old wives' tales.'

'I tell you I've seen the bare slabs.'

'Well, come back with me. I'm going up to old Palmer's – his daughter's ill; we'll look in at the church and let me see the bare slabs.'

'You go, if you like,' I said, a little less frantic for his laughter; 'I'm going home to my wife.'

'Rubbish man,' said he; 'd'ye think I'll permit that? Are ye to go saying all yer life that ye've seen solid marble endowed with vitality and me to go all me life saying ye were a coward? No, sir – ye shan't do ut.'

The night air – a human voice – and I think also the physical contact with this six feet of solid common sense, brought me back a little to my ordinary self and the word 'coward' was a mental showerbath.

'Come on, then,' I said sullenly; 'perhaps you're right.'

He still held my arm tightly. We got over the stile and back to the church. All was still as death. The place smelt very damp and earthy. We walked up the aisle. I am not ashamed to confess that I shut my eyes: I knew the figures would not be there. I heard Kelly strike a match.

'Here they are, ye see, right enough; ye've been dreaming or drinking, asking yer pardon for the imputation.'

I opened my eyes. By Kelly's expiring vesta I saw two shapes lying 'in their marble' on their slabs. I drew a deep breath.

'I'm awfully indebted to you,' I said. 'It must have been some trick of the light or I have been working rather hard, perhaps that's it. I was quite convinced they were gone.'

'I'm aware of that,' he answered rather grimly; 'ye'll have to be careful of that brain of yours, my friend, I assure ye.'

He was leaning over and looking at the right-hand figure, whose stony face was the most villainous and deadly in expression.

'By Jove,' he said, 'something has been afoot here – this hand is broken.'

And so it was. I was certain that it had been perfect the last time Laura and I had been there.

'Perhaps someone has *tried* to remove them,' said the young doctor.

'Come along,' I said, 'or my wife will be getting anxious. You'll come in and have a drop of whisky and drink confusion to ghosts and better sense to me.'

'I ought to go up to Palmer's, but it's so late now I'd best leave it till the morning,' he replied.

I think he fancied I needed him more than did Palmer's girl, so, discussing how such an illusion could have been possible and deducing from this experience large generalities concerning ghostly apparitions, we walked up to our cottage. We saw, as we walked up the garden path, that bright light streamed out of the front door and presently saw that the parlour door was open, too. Had she gone out?

'Come in,' I said, and Dr Kelly followed me into the parlour. It was all ablaze with candles, not only the wax ones, but at least a dozen guttering, glaring tallow dips, stuck in vases and ornaments in unlikely places. Light, I knew, was Laura's remedy for nervousness. Poor child! Why had I left her? Brute that I was.

We glanced round the room and at first we did not see her. The window was open and the draught set all the candles flaring one way. Her chair was empty and her handkerchief and book lay on the floor. I turned to the window. There, in the recess of the window, I saw her. Oh, my child, my love, had she gone to that window to watch for me? And what had come into the room behind her? To what had she turned with that look of frantic fear and horror? Oh, my little one, had she thought that it was I whose step she heard and turned to meet – what?

She had fallen back across a table in the window and her body lay half on it and half on the window-seat, and her head hung down over the table, the brown hair loosened and fallen to the carpet. Her lips were drawn back and her eyes wide, wide open. They saw nothing now. What had they seen last?

The doctor moved towards her, but I pushed him aside and sprang to her; caught her in my arms and cried: 'It's all right, Laura! I've got you safe, wifie.'

She fell into my arms in a heap. I clasped her and kissed her and called her by all her pet names, but I think I knew all the time that she was dead. Her hands were tightly clenched. In one of them she held something fast. When I was quite sure that she was dead and that nothing mattered at all any more, I let him open her hand to see what she held.

It was a grey marble finger.

The Canterville Ghost

Oscar Wilde 1854–1900

CHAPTER ONE

WHEN MR HIRAM B. OTIS, the American Minister, bought Canterville Chase, everyone told him he was doing a very foolish thing, as there was no doubt at all that the place was haunted. Indeed, Lord Canterville himself, who was a man of the most punctilious honour, had felt it his duty to mention the fact to Mr Otis when they came to discuss terms.

'We have not cared to live in the place ourselves,' said Lord Canterville, 'since my grand-aunt, the Dowager Duchess of Bolton, was frightened into a fit, from which she never really recovered, by two skeleton hands being placed on her shoulders as she was dressing for dinner, and I feel bound to tell you, Mr Otis, that the ghost has been seen by several living members of my family, as well as by the rector of the parish, the Revd Augustus Dampier, who is a Fellow of King's College, Cambridge. After the unfortunate accident to the Duchess, none of our younger servants would stay with us, and Lady Canterville often got very little sleep at night, in consequence of the mysterious noises that came from the corridor and the library.'

'My Lord,' answered the Minister, 'I will take the furniture and the ghost at a valuation. I come from a modern country, where we have everything that money can buy; and with all our spry young fellows painting the Old World red and carrying off your best actresses and prima-donnas, I reckon that if there were such a thing as a ghost in Europe, we'd have it at home in a very short time in one of our public museums or on the road as a show.'

'I fear that the ghost exists,' said Lord Canterville, smiling, 'though it may have resisted the overtures of your enterprising impresarios. It has been well known for three centuries, since 1584 in fact, and always makes its appearance before the death of any member of our family.'

'Well, so does the family doctor for that matter, Lord Canterville. But there is no such thing, sir, as a ghost and I guess the laws of Nature are not going to be suspended for the British aristocracy.'

'You are certainly very natural in America,' answered Lord Canterville, who did not quite understand Mr Otis's last observation, 'and if you don't mind a ghost in the house, it is all right. Only you must remember I warned you.'

A few weeks after this, the purchase was completed and at the close of the season the Minister and his family went down to Canterville Chase. Mrs Otis, who, as Miss Lucretia R. Tappan, of West 53rd Street, had been a celebrated New York belle, was now a very handsome, middle-aged woman, with fine eyes and a superb profile. Many American ladies on leaving their native land adopt an appearance of chronic ill-health, under the impression that it is a form of European refinement, but Mrs Otis had never fallen into this error. She had a magnificent constitution and a really wonderful amount of animal spirits. Indeed, in many respects, she was quite English and was an excellent example of the fact that we have really everything in common with America nowadays, except, of course, language. Her eldest son, christened Washington by his parents in a moment of patriotism, which he never ceased to regret, was a fair-haired, rather good-looking young man, who had qualified himself for American diplomacy by leading the German at the Newport Casino for three successive seasons, and even in London was well known as an excellent dancer. Gardenias and the peerage were his only weaknesses. Otherwise he was extremely sensible. Miss Virginia E. Otis was a little girl of fifteen, lithe and lovely as a fawn and with a fine freedom in her large blue eyes. She was a wonderful amazon and had once raced old Lord Bilton on her pony twice round the park, winning by a length and a half, just in front of the Achilles statue, to the huge delight of the young Duke of Cheshire, who proposed for her on the spot and was sent back to Eton that very night by his guardians, in floods of tears. After Virginia came the twins, who were usually called 'The Stars and Stripes', as they were always getting swished. They were delightful boys and with the exception of the worthy Minister the only true republicans of the family.

As Canterville Chase is seven miles from Ascot, the nearest railway station, Mr Otis had telegraphed for a waggonette to meet them, and they started on their drive in high spirits. It was a lovely July evening, and the air was delicate with the scent of the pine-woods. Now and then they heard a wood pigeon brooding over its own sweet voice or saw, deep in the rustling fern, the burnished breast of the pheasant. Little squirrels peered at them from the beech trees as they went by and the rabbits scudded away through the brushwood and over the mossy knolls, with their white tails in the air. As they entered the avenue of Canterville Chase, however, the sky became suddenly overcast with clouds, a curious stillness seemed to hold the atmosphere, a great flight of rooks passed silently over their heads and, before they reached the house, some big drops of rain had fallen.

Standing on the steps to receive them was an old woman, neatly dressed in black silk, with a white cap and apron. This was Mrs Umney, the housekeeper, whom Mrs Otis, at Lady Canterville's earnest request, had consented to keep on in her former position. She made them each a low curtsey as they alighted and said in a quaint, old-fashioned manner, 'I bid you welcome to Canterville Chase.' Following her, they passed through the fine Tudor hall into the library, a long, low room, panelled in black oak, at the end of which was a large stained-glass window. Here they found tea laid out for them and, after taking off their wraps, they sat down and began to look round, while Mrs Umney waited on them.

Suddenly Mrs Otis caught sight of a dull red stain on the floor just by the fireplace and, quite unconscious of what it really signified, said to Mrs Umney, 'I am afraid something has been spilt there.'

'Yes, madam,' replied the old housekeeper in a low voice, 'blood has been spilt on that spot.'

'How horrid,' cried Mrs Otis; 'I don't at all care for blood-stains in a sitting-room. It must be removed at once.'

The old woman smiled and answered in the same low, mysterious voice, 'It is the blood of Lady Eleanore de Canterville, who was murdered on that very spot by her own husband, Sir Simon de Canterville, in 1575. Sir Simon survived her nine years and disappeared suddenly under very mysterious circumstances. His body has never been discovered, but his guilty spirit still haunts the Chase. The blood-stain has been much admired by tourists and others and cannot be removed.'

'That is all nonsense,' cried Washington Otis; 'Pinkerton's Champion Stain Remover and Paragon Detergent will clean it up in no time,' and before the terrified housekeeper could interfere he had fallen upon his knees and was rapidly scouring the floor with a small stick of what looked like a black cosmetic. In a few moments no trace of the blood-stain could be seen.

'I knew Pinkerton would do it,' he exclaimed triumphantly, as he looked round at his admiring family; but no sooner had he said these words than a terrible flash of lightning lit up the sombre room, a fearful peal of thunder made them all start to their feet and Mrs Umney fainted.

'What a monstrous climate!' said the American Minister calmly, as he lit a long cheroot. 'I guess the old country is so over-populated that they have not enough decent weather for everybody. I have always been of opinion that emigration is the only thing for England.'

'My dear Hiram,' cried Mrs Otis, 'what can we do with a woman who faints?'

'Charge it to her like breakages,' answered the Minister; 'she won't faint after that' – and in a few moments Mrs Umney certainly came to. There was no doubt, however, that she was extremely upset and she sternly warned Mr Otis to beware of some trouble coming to the house.

'I have seen things with my own eyes, sir,' she said, 'that would make any Christian's hair stand on end and many and many a night I have not closed my eyes in sleep for the awful things that are done here.' Mr Otis, however, and his wife warmly assured the honest soul that they were not afraid of ghosts and, after invoking the blessings of Providence on her new master and mistress and making arrangements for an increase of salary, the old housekeeper tottered off to her own room.

CHAPTER TWO

The storm raged fiercely all that night, but nothing of particular note occurred. The next morning, however, when they came down to breakfast, they found the terrible stain of blood once again on the floor. 'I don't think it can be the fault of the Paragon Detergent,' said Washington, 'for I have tried it with everything. It must be the ghost.' He accordingly rubbed out the stain a second time, but the second morning it appeared again. The third morning also it was there, though the library had been locked up at night by Mr Otis himself and the key carried upstairs. The whole family were now quite interested; Mr Otis began to suspect that he had been too dogmatic in his denial of the existence of ghosts, Mrs Otis expressed her intention of joining the Psychical Society and Washington prepared a long letter to Messrs Myers and Podmore on the subject of the permanence of sanguineous stains when connected with crime. That night all doubts about the objective existence of phantasmata were removed for ever.

The day had been warm and sunny; and, in the cool of the evening, the whole family went out for a drive. They did not return home till nine o'clock, when they had a light supper. The conversation in no way turned upon ghosts, so there were not even those primary conditions of receptive expectation which so often precede the presentation of psychical phenomena. The subjects discussed, as I have since learned from Mr Otis, were merely such as form the ordinary conversation of cultured Americans of the better class, such as the immense superiority of Miss Fanny Davenport over Sarah Bernhardt as an actress; the difficulty of obtaining green corn, buckwheat cakes and hominy, even in the best English houses; the importance of Boston in the development of the world-soul; the advantages of the baggage check system in railway travelling; and the sweetness of the New York accent as compared to the London drawl. No mention at all was made of the supernatural, nor was Sir Simon de Canterville alluded to in any way. At eleven o'clock the family retired and by half-past all the lights were out. Some time after, Mr Otis was awakened by a curious noise in the corridor, outside his room. It sounded like the clank of metal and seemed to be coming nearer every moment. He got up at once, struck a match and looked at the time. It was exactly one o'clock. He was quite calm and felt his pulse, which was not at all feverish. The strange noise still continued and with it he heard distinctly the sound of footsteps. He put on his slippers, took a small oblong phial out of his dressing-case and opened the door. Right in front of him he saw, in the wan moonlight, an old man of terrible aspect. His eyes were as red burning coals; long grey hair fell over his shoulders in matted coils; his garments, which were of antique cut, were soiled and ragged, and from his wrists and ankles hung heavy manacles and rusty gyves.

'My dear sir,' said Mr Otis, 'I really must insist on your oiling those chains and have brought you for that purpose a small bottle of the Tammany Rising Sun Lubricator. It is said to be completely efficacious upon one application and there are several testimonials to that effect on the wrapper from some of our most eminent native divines. I shall leave it here for you by the bedroom candles and will be happy to supply you with more should you require it.' With these words the United States Minister laid the bottle down on a marble table and, closing his door, retired to rest.

For a moment the Canterville ghost stood quite motionless in natural indignation; then, dashing the bottle violently upon the polished floor, he fled down the corridor, uttering hollow groans and emitting a ghastly green light. Just, however, as he reached the top of the great oak staircase, a door was flung open, two little white-robed figures appeared and a large pillow whizzed past his head! There was evidently no time to be lost, so, hastily adopting the Fourth Dimension of Space as a means of escape, he vanished through the wainscoting and the house became quite quiet.

On reaching a small secret chamber in the left wing, he leaned up against a moonbeam to recover his breath and began to try and realise his position. Never, in a brilliant and uninterrupted career of three

hundred years, had he been so grossly insulted. He thought of the
Dowager Duchess, whom he had frightened into a fit as she stood
before the glass in her lace and diamonds; of the four housemaids, who
had gone off into hysterics when he merely grinned at them through the
curtains of one of the spare bedrooms; of the rector of the parish, whose
candle he had blown out as he was coming late one night from the
library and who had been under the care of Sir William Gull ever since,
a perfect martyr to nervous disorders; and of old Madame de Tremouillac,
who, having wakened up one morning early and seen a skeleton seated
in an armchair by the fire reading her diary, had been confined to her
bed for six weeks with an attack of brain fever and, on her recovery, had
become reconciled to the Church and broken off her connection with
that notorious sceptic Monsieur de Voltaire. He remembered the
terrible night when the wicked Lord Canterville was found choking in
his dressing-room, with the knave of diamonds halfway down his throat,
and confessed, just before he died, that he had cheated Charles James
Fox out of £50,000 at Crockford's by means of that very card and swore
that the ghost had made him swallow it. All his great achievements came
back to him again, from the butler who had shot himself in the pantry
because he had seen a green hand tapping at the window pane, to the
beautiful Lady Stutfield, who was always obliged to wear a black velvet
band round her throat to hide the mark of five fingers burnt upon her
white skin and who drowned herself at last in the carp-pond at the end
of the King's Walk. With the enthusiastic egotism of the true artist he
went over his most celebrated performances and smiled bitterly to
himself as he recalled to mind his last appearance as 'Red Ruben, or the
Strangled Babe', his *début* as 'Gaunt Gibeon, the Blood-sucker of Bexley
Moor', and the *furore* he had excited one lovely June evening by merely
playing ninepins with his own bones upon the lawn-tennis ground. And
after all this, some wretched modern Americans were to come and offer
him the Rising Sun Lubricator and throw pillows at his head! It was
quite unbearable. Besides, no ghosts in history had ever been treated in
this manner. Accordingly, he determined to have vengeance and
remained till daylight in an attitude of deep thought.

CHAPTER THREE

The next morning when the Otis family met at breakfast, they
discussed the ghost at some length. The United States Minister was
naturally a little annoyed to find that his present had not been accepted.
'I have no wish,' he said, 'to do the ghost any personal injury and I must

say that, considering the length of time he has been in the house, I don't think it is at all polite to throw pillows at him' – a very just remark, at which, I am sorry to say, the twins burst into shouts of laughter. 'Upon the other hand,' he continued, 'if he really declines to use the Rising Sun Lubricator, we shall have to take his chains from him. It would be quite impossible to sleep, with such a noise going on outside the bedrooms.'

For the rest of the week, however, they were undisturbed, the only thing that excited any attention being the continual renewal of the blood-stain on the library floor. This certainly was very strange, as the door was always locked at night by Mr Otis and the windows kept closely barred. The chameleon-like colour, also, of the stain excited a good deal of comment. Some mornings it was a dull (almost Indian) red, then it would be vermilion, then a rich purple, and once when they came down for family prayers, according to the simple rites of the Free American Reformed Episcopalian Church, they found it a bright emerald-green. These kaleidoscopic changes naturally amused the party very much and bets on the subject were freely made every evening. The only person who did not enter into the joke was little Virginia, who, for some unexplained reason, was always a good deal distressed at the sight of the blood-stain and very nearly cried the morning it was emerald-green.

The second appearance of the ghost was on Sunday night. Shortly after they had gone to bed they were suddenly alarmed by a fearful crash in the hall. Rushing downstairs, they found that a large suit of old armour had become detached from its stand and had fallen on the stone floor, while, seated in a high-backed chair, was the Canterville ghost, rubbing his knees with an expression of acute agony on his face. The twins, having brought their pea-shooters with them, at once discharged two pellets on him, with that accuracy of aim which can only be attained by long and careful practice on a writing-master while the United States Minister covered him with his revolver and called upon him, in accordance with Californian etiquette, to hold up his hands! The ghost started up with a wild shriek of rage and swept through them like a mist, extinguishing Washington Otis's candle as he passed and so leaving them all in total darkness. On reaching the top of the staircase he recovered himself and determined to give his celebrated peal of demoniac laughter. This he had on more than one occasion found extremely useful. It was said to have turned Lord Raker's wig grey in a single night and had certainly made three of Lady Canterville's French governesses give warning before their month was up. He accordingly laughed his most horrible laugh, till the old vaulted roof rang and rang again, but hardly had the fearful echo died away when a door opened and Mrs Otis came out in a light blue dressing-gown. 'I am afraid you are far from well,' she said, 'and have brought you a bottle of Dr Dobell's tincture. If it is indigestion, you will find it a most excellent remedy.' The ghost glared at her in fury and began at once to make preparations for turning himself into a large black dog, an accomplishment for which he was justly renowned and to which the family doctor always attributed the permanent idiocy of Lord Canterville's uncle, the Hon. Thomas Horton. The sound of approaching footsteps, however, made him hesitate in his fell purpose, so he contented himself with becoming faintly phosphorescent and vanished with a deep churchyard groan, just as the twins had come up to him.

On reaching his room he entirely broke down and became a prey to the most violent agitation. The vulgarity of the twins and the gross materialism of Mrs Otis were naturally extremely annoying, but what really distressed him most was, that he had been unable to wear the suit of mail. He had hoped that even modern Americans would be thrilled by the sight of a Spectre In Armour, if for no more sensible reason, at least out of respect for their national poet Longfellow, over whose graceful and attractive poetry he himself had whiled away many a weary hour when the Cantervilles were up in town. Besides, it was his own suit. He had worn it with great success at the Kenilworth tournament and had been highly complimented on it by no less a person than the Virgin Queen herself. Yet when he had put it on, he had been completely overpowered by the weight of the huge breastplate and steel casque and had fallen heavily on the stone pavement, barking both his knees severely and bruising the knuckles of his right hand.

For some days after this he was extremely ill and hardly stirred out of his room at all, except to keep the blood-stain in proper repair. However, by taking great care of himself, he recovered and resolved to make a third attempt to frighten the United States Minister and his family. He selected Friday, the 17th of August, for his appearance and spent most of that day in looking over his wardrobe, ultimately deciding in favour of a large slouched hat with a red feather, a winding-sheet frilled at the wrists and neck, and a rusty dagger. Towards evening a violent storm of rain came on and the wind was so high that all the windows and doors in the old house shook and rattled. In fact, it was just such weather as he loved. His plan of action was this. He was to make his way quietly to Washington Otis's room, gibber at him from the foot of the bed and stab himself three times in the throat to the sound of slow music. He bore Washington a special grudge, being quite aware that it was he who was in the habit of removing the famous

Canterville blood-stain, by means of Pinkerton's Paragon Detergent. Having reduced the reckless and foolhardy youth to a condition of abject terror, he was then to proceed to the room occupied by the United States Minister and his wife and there to place a clammy hand on Mrs Otis's forehead, while he hissed into her trembling husband's ear the awful secrets of the charnel-house. With regard to little Virginia, he had not quite made up his mind. She had never insulted him in any way, and was pretty and gentle. A few hollow groans from the wardrobe, he thought, would be more than sufficient or, if that failed to wake her, he might grabble at the counterpane with palsy-twitching fingers. As for the twins, he was quite determined to teach them a lesson. The first thing to be done was, of course, to sit upon their chests, so as to produce the stifling sensation of nightmare. Then, as their beds were quite close to each other, to stand between them in the form of a green, icy-cold corpse, till they became paralysed with fear, and finally, to throw off the winding-sheet, and crawl round the room, with white bleached bones and one rolling eye-ball, in the character of 'Dumb Daniel, or the Suicide's Skeleton', a role in which he had on more than one occasion produced a great effect and which he considered quite equal to his famous part of 'Martin the Maniac, or the Masked Mystery'.

At half-past ten he heard the family going to bed. For some time he was disturbed by wild shrieks of laughter from the twins, who, with the light-hearted gaiety of schoolboys, were evidently amusing themselves before they retired to rest, but at a quarter past eleven all was still and, as midnight sounded, he sallied forth. The owl beat against the window panes, the raven croaked from the old yew tree and the wind wandered moaning round the house like a lost soul; but the Otis family slept unconscious of their doom and high above the rain and storm he could hear the steady snoring of the Minister for the United States. He stepped stealthily out of the wainscoting, with an evil smile on his cruel, wrinkled mouth, and the moon hid her face in a cloud as he stole past the great oriel window, where his own arms and those of his murdered wife were blazoned in azure and gold. On and on he glided, like an evil shadow, the very darkness seeming to loathe him as he passed. Once he thought he heard something call and stopped; but it was only the baying of a dog from the Red Farm and he went on, muttering strange sixteenth-century curses and ever and anon brandishing the rusty dagger in the midnight air. Finally he reached the corner of the passage that led to luckless Washington's room. For a moment he paused there, the wind blowing his long grey locks about his head and twisting into grotesque and fantastic folds the nameless horror of the dead man's shroud. Then the clock struck the quarter and he felt the time was come. He chuckled to himself and turned the corner; but no sooner had he done so, than, with a piteous wail of terror, he fell back and hid his blanched face in his long, bony hands. Right in front of him was standing a horrible spectre, motionless as a carven image and monstrous as a madman's dream! Its head was bald and burnished; its face round and fat and white; and hideous laughter seemed to have writhed its features into an eternal grin. From the eyes streamed rays of scarlet light, the mouth was a wide well of fire and a hideous garment, like to his own, swathed with its silent snows the Titan form. On its breast was a placard with strange writing in antique characters, some scroll of shame it seemed, some record of wild sins, some awful calendar of crime and, with its right hand, it bore aloft a falchion of gleaming steel.

Never having seen a ghost before, he naturally was terribly frightened and, after a second hasty glance at the awful phantom, he fled back to his room, tripping up in his long winding-sheet as he sped down the corridor and finally dropping the rusty dagger into the Minister's jack-boots, where it was found in the morning by the butler. Once in the privacy of his own apartment, he flung himself down on a small pallet-bed and hid his face under the clothes. After a time, however, the brave old Canterville spirit asserted itself and he determined to go and speak to the other ghost as soon as it was daylight. Accordingly, just as the dawn was touching the hills with silver, he returned towards the spot where he had first laid eyes on the grisly phantom, feeling that, after all, two ghosts were better than one and that, by the aid of his new friend, he might safely grapple with the twins. On reaching the spot, however, a terrible sight met his gaze. Something had evidently happened to the spectre, for the light had entirely faded from its hollow eyes, the gleaming falchion had fallen from its hand and it was leaning up against the wall in a strained and uncomfortable attitude. He rushed forward and seized it in his arms, when, to his horror, the head slipped off and rolled on the floor, the body assumed a recumbent posture and he found himself clasping a white dimity bed-curtain, with a sweeping-brush, a kitchen cleaver, and a hollow turnip lying at his feet! Unable to understand this curious transformation, he clutched the placard with feverish haste and there, in the grey morning light, he read these fearful words:

Ye Otis Ghoste
Ye onlie true and originale spook
Beware of ye imitationes
All others are counterfeite

The whole thing flashed across him. He had been tricked, foiled and outwitted! The old Canterville look came into his eyes; he ground his toothless gums together; and, raising his withered hands high above his head, swore, according to the picturesque phraseology of the antique school, that when Chanticleer had sounded twice his merry horn, deeds of blood would be wrought and Murder walk abroad with silent feet.

Hardly had he finished this awful oath when, from the red-tiled roof of a distant homestead, a cock crew. He laughed a long, low, bitter laugh and waited. Hour after hour he waited, but the cock, for some strange reason, did not crow again. Finally, at half-past seven, the arrival of the housemaids made him give up his fearful vigil and he stalked back to his room, thinking of his vain hope and baffled purpose. There he consulted several books of ancient chivalry, of which he was exceedingly fond, and found that, on every occasion on which his oath had been used, Chanticleer had always crowed a second time. 'Perdition seize the naughty fowl,' he muttered, 'I have seen the day when, with my stout spear, I would have run him through the gorge and made him crow for me as 'twere in death!' He then retired to a comfortable lead coffin and stayed there till evening.

CHAPTER FOUR

The next day the ghost was very weak and tired. The terrible excitement of the last four weeks was beginning to have its effect. His nerves were completely shattered and he started at the slightest noise. For five days he kept his room and at last made up his mind to give up the point of the blood-stain on the library floor. If the Otis family did not want it, they clearly did not deserve it. They were evidently people on a low, material plane of existence and quite incapable of appreciating the symbolic value of sensuous phenomena. The question of phantasmic apparitions, and the development of astral bodies, was of course quite a different matter and really not under his control. It was his solemn duty to appear in the corridor once a week and to gibber from the large oriel window on the first and third Wednesday in every month and he did not see how he could honourably escape from his obligations. It is quite true that his life had been very evil, but, upon the other hand, he was most conscientious in all things connected with the supernatural. For the next three Saturdays, accordingly, he traversed the corridor as usual between midnight and three o'clock, taking, every possible precaution against being either heard or seen. He removed his boots, trod as lightly as possible on the old worm-eaten boards, wore a large black velvet cloak and was careful to use the Rising Sun Lubricator for oiling his chains. I am bound to acknowledge that it was with a good deal of difficulty that he brought himself to adopt this last mode of protection. However, one night, while the family were at dinner, he slipped into Mr Otis's bedroom and carried off the bottle. He felt a little humiliated at first, but afterwards was sensible enough to see that there was a great deal to be said for the invention and, to a certain degree, it served his purpose. Still, in spite of everything, he was not left unmolested. Strings were continually being stretched across the corridor, over which he tripped in the dark, and on one occasion, while dressed for the part of 'Black Isaac, or the Huntsman of Hogley Woods', he met with a severe fall, through treading on a butter-slide, which the twins had constructed from the entrance of the Tapestry Chamber to the top of the oak staircase. This last insult so enraged him, that he resolved to make one final effort to assert his dignity and social position and determined to visit the insolent young Etonians the next night in his celebrated character of 'Reckless Rupert, or the Headless Earl'.

He had not appeared in this disguise for more than seventy years; in fact, not since he had so frightened pretty Lady Barbara Modish by means of it, that she suddenly broke off her engagement with the present Lord Canterville's grandfather and ran away to Gretna Green with handsome Jack Castleton, declaring that nothing in the world would induce her to marry into a family that allowed such a horrible phantom to walk up and down the terrace at twilight. Poor Jack was afterwards shot in a duel by Lord Canterville on Wandsworth Common and Lady Barbara died of a broken heart at Tunbridge Wells before the year was out, so, in every way, it had been a great success. It was, however, an extremely difficult 'make-up', if I may use such a theatrical expression in connection with one of the greatest mysteries of the supernatural or, to employ a more scientific term, the higher-natural world, and it took him fully three hours to make his preparations. At last everything was ready and he was very pleased with his appearance. The big leather riding-boots that went with the dress were just a little too large for him and he could only find one of the two horse-pistols, but, on the whole, he was quite satisfied and at a quarter past one he glided out of the wainscoting and crept down the corridor. On reaching the room occupied by the twins, which I should mention was called the Blue Bed Chamber, on account of the colour of its hangings, he found the door just ajar. Wishing to make an effective entrance, he flung it wide open, when a heavy jug of water fell right down on him, wetting him to the skin and just missing his left shoulder by a couple of inches.

At the same moment he heard stifled shrieks of laughter proceeding from the four-post bed. The shock to his nervous system was so great that he fled back to his room as hard as he could go and the next day he was laid up with a severe cold. The only thing that at all consoled him in the whole affair was the fact that he had not brought his head with him, for, had he done so, the consequences might have been very serious.

He now gave up all hope of ever frightening this rude American family and contented himself, as a rule, with creeping about the passages in list slippers, with a thick red muffler round his throat for fear of draughts and a small arquebuse, in case he should be attacked by the twins. The final blow he received occurred on the 19th of September. He had gone downstairs to the great entrance-hall, feeling sure that there, at any rate, he would be quite unmolested, and was amusing himself by making satirical remarks on the large Saroni photographs of the United States Minister and his wife, which had now taken the place of the Canterville family pictures. He was simply but neatly clad in a long shroud, spotted with churchyard mould, had tied up his jaw with a strip of yellow linen and carried a small lantern and a sexton's spade. In fact, he was dressed for the character of 'Jonas the Graveless, or the Corpse-Snatcher of Chertsey Barn', one of his most remarkable impersonations and one which the Cantervilles had every reason to remember, as it was the real origin of their quarrel with their neighbour, Lord Rufford. It was about a quarter past two o'clock in the morning and, as far as he could ascertain, no one was stirring. As he was strolling towards the library, however, to see if there were any traces left of the blood-stain, suddenly there leaped out on him from a dark corner two figures, who waved their arms wildly above their heads and shrieked out 'BOO!' in his ear.

Seized with a panic, which, under the circumstances, was only natural, he rushed for the staircase, but found Washington Otis waiting for him there with the big garden-syringe; and being thus hemmed in by his enemies on every side and driven almost to bay, he vanished into the great iron stove which, fortunately for him, was not lit, and had to make his way home through the flues and chimneys, arriving at his own room in a terrible state of dirt, disorder and despair.

After this he was not seen again on any nocturnal expedition. The twins lay in wait for him on several occasions and strewed the passages with nutshells every night to the great annoyance of their parents and the servants, but it was of no avail. It was quite evident that his feelings were so wounded that he would not appear. Mr Otis consequently resumed his great work on the history of the Democratic Party, on which he had been engaged for some years; Mrs Otis organised a wonderful clam bake, which amazed the whole county; the boys took to lacrosse, euchre, poker and other American national games; and Virginia rode about the lanes on her pony, accompanied by the young Duke of Cheshire, who had come to spend the last week of his holidays at Canterville Chase. It was generally assumed that the ghost had gone away and, in fact, Mr Otis wrote a letter to that effect to Lord Canterville, who, in reply, expressed his great pleasure at the news and sent his best congratulations to the Minister's worthy wife.

The Otises, however, were deceived, for the ghost was still in the house and though now almost an invalid, was by no means ready to let matters rest, particularly as he heard that among the guests was the young Duke of Cheshire, whose grand-uncle, Lord Francis Stilton, had once bet a hundred guineas with Colonel Carbury that he would play dice with the Canterville ghost and was found the next morning lying on the floor of the card-room in such a helpless paralytic state, that though he lived on to a great age, he was never able to say anything again but 'Double Sixes'. The story was well known at the time, though, of course, out of respect to the feelings of the two noble families, every attempt was made to hush it up; and a full account of all the circumstances connected with it will be found in the third volume of Lord Tattle's *Recollections of the Prince Regent and his Friends.* The ghost, then, was naturally very anxious to show that he had not lost his influence over the Stiltons, with whom, indeed, he was distantly connected, his own first cousin having been married *en secondes noces* to the Sieur de Bulkeley, from whom, as everyone knows, the Dukes of Cheshire are lineally descended. Accordingly, he made arrangements for appearing to Virginia's little lover in his celebrated impersonation of 'The Vampire Monk, or the Bloodless Benedictine', a performance so horrible that when old Lady Startup saw it, which she did on one fatal New Year's Eve, in the year 1764, she went off into the most piercing shrieks, which culminated in violent apoplexy, and died in three days, after disinheriting the Cantervilles, who were her nearest relations, and leaving all her money to her London apothecary. At the last moment, however, his terror of the twins prevented his leaving his room and the little Duke slept in peace under the great feathered canopy in the Royal Bedchamber and dreamed of Virginia.

CHAPTER FIVE

A few days after this, Virginia and her curly-haired cavalier went out riding on Brockley meadows, where she tore her habit so badly in getting through a hedge, that, on her return home, she made up her mind to go up by the back staircase so as not to be seen. As she was running past the Tapestry Chamber, the door of which happened to be open, she fancied she saw someone inside and thinking it was her mother's maid, who sometimes used to bring her work there, looked in to ask her to mend her habit. To her immense surprise, however, it was the Canterville Ghost himself! He was sitting by the window, watching the ruined gold of the yellowing trees fly through the air and the red leaves dancing madly down the long avenue. His head was leaning on his hand and his whole attitude was one of extreme depression. Indeed, so forlorn and so much out of repair did he look, that little Virginia, whose first idea had been to run away and lock herself in her room, was filled with pity and determined to try and comfort him. So light was her footfall and so deep his melancholy, that he was not aware of her presence till she spoke to him.

'I am so sorry for you,' she said, 'but my brothers are going back to Eton tomorrow and then, if you behave yourself, no one will annoy you.'

'It is absurd asking me to behave myself,' he answered, looking round in astonishment at the pretty little girl who had ventured to address him, 'quite absurd. I must rattle my chains and groan through keyholes and walk about at night, if that is what you mean. It is my only reason for existing.'

'It is no reason at all for existing and you know you have been very wicked. Mrs Umney told us, the first day we arrived here, that you had killed your wife.'

'Well, I quite admit it,' said the Ghost petulantly, 'but it was a purely family matter and concerned no one else.'

'It is very wrong to kill anyone,' said Virginia, who at times had a sweet Puritan gravity, caught from some old New England ancestor.

'Oh, I hate the cheap severity of abstract ethics! My wife was very plain, never had my ruffs properly starched and knew nothing about cookery. Why, there was a buck I had shot in Hogley Woods, a magnificent pricket, and do you know how she had it sent up to table? However, it is no matter now, for it is all over and I don't think it was very nice of her brothers to starve me to death, though I did kill her.'

'Starve you to death? Oh, Mr Ghost, I mean Sir Simon, are you hungry? I have a sandwich in my case. Would you like it?'

'No, thank you, I never eat anything now; but it is very kind of you, all the same, and you are much nicer than the rest of your horrid, rude, vulgar, dishonest family.'

'Stop!' cried Virginia, stamping her foot, 'it is you who are rude and horrid and vulgar, and as for dishonesty, you know you stole the paints out of my box to try and furbish up that ridiculous blood-stain in the library. First you took all my reds, including the vermilion, and I couldn't do any more sunsets, then you took the emerald-green and the chrome-yellow and finally I had nothing left but indigo and Chinese white and could only do moonlight scenes, which are always depressing to look at and not at all easy to paint. I never told on you, though I was very much annoyed and it was most ridiculous, the whole thing; for who ever heard of emerald-green blood?'

'Well, really,' said the Ghost, rather meekly, 'what was I to do? It is a very difficult thing to get real blood nowadays and, as your brother began it all with his Paragon Detergent, I certainly saw no reason why I should not have your paints. As for colour, that is always a matter of taste: the Cantervilles have blue blood, for instance, the very bluest in England; but I know you Americans don't care for things of this kind.'

'You know nothing about it and the best thing you can do is to emigrate and improve your mind. My father will be only too happy to give you a free passage and though there is a heavy duty on spirits of every kind, there will be no difficulty about the Custom House, as the officers are all Democrats. Once in New York, you are sure to be a great success. I know lots of people there who would give a hundred thousand dollars to have a grandfather, and much more than that to have a family Ghost.'

'I don't think I should like America.'

'I suppose because we have no ruins and no curiosities,' said Virginia satirically.

'No ruins! No curiosities!' answered the Ghost; 'you have your navy and your manners.'

'Good evening; I will go and ask papa to get the twins an extra week's holiday.'

'Please don't go, Miss Virginia,' he cried; 'I am so lonely and so unhappy, and I really don't know what to do. I want to go to sleep and I cannot.'

'That's quite absurd! You have merely to go to bed and blow out the candle. It is very difficult sometimes to keep awake, especially at church, but there is no difficulty at all about sleeping. Why, even babies know how to do that and they are not very clever.'

'I have not slept for three hundred years,' he said sadly and Virginia's beautiful blue eyes opened in wonder; 'for three hundred years I have not slept and I am so tired.'

Virginia grew quite grave and her little lips trembled like rose-leaves. She came towards him and kneeling down at his side, looked up into his old withered face.

'Poor, poor Ghost,' she murmured; 'have you no place where you can sleep?'

'Far away beyond the pine-woods,' he answered, in a low dreamy voice, 'there is a little garden. There the grass grows long and deep, there are the great white stars of the hemlock flower, there the nightingale sings all night long. All night long he sings and the cold, crystal moon looks down and the yew tree spreads out its giant arms over the sleepers.'

Virginia's eyes grew dim with tears and she hid her face her hands.

'You mean the Garden of Death,' she whispered.

'Yes, Death. Death must be so beautiful. To lie in the soft brown earth, with the grasses waving above one's head, and listen to silence. To have no yesterday and no tomorrow. To forget time, to forgive life, to be at peace. You can help me. You can open for me the portals of Death's house, for Love is always with you, and Love is stronger than Death is.'

Virginia trembled, a cold shudder ran through her and for a few moments there was silence. She felt as if she was in a terrible dream.

Then the Ghost spoke again and his voice sounded like the sighing of the wind.

'Have you ever read the old prophecy on the library window?'

'Oh, often,' cried the little girl, looking up; 'I know it quite well. It is painted in curious black letters and it is difficult to read. There are only six lines:

> When a golden girl can win
> Prayer from out the lips of sin,
> When the barren almond bears,
> And a little child gives away its tears,
> Then shall all the house be still
> And peace come to Canterville.

But I don't know what they mean.'

'They mean,' he said sadly, 'that you must weep for me for my sins, because I have no tears, and pray with me for my soul, because I have no faith, and then, if you have always been sweet and good and gentle, the Angel of Death will have mercy on me. You will see fearful shapes in darkness and wicked voices will whisper in your ear, but they will not harm you, for against the purity of a little child the powers of Hell cannot prevail.'

Virginia made no answer and the Ghost wrung his hands in wild despair as he looked down at her bowed golden head. Suddenly she stood up, very pale and with a strange light in her eyes. 'I am not afraid,' she said firmly, 'and I will ask the Angel to have mercy on you.'

He rose from his seat with a faint cry of joy and taking her hand bent over it with old-fashioned grace and kissed it. His fingers were as cold as ice and his lips burned like fire, but Virginia did not falter as he led her across the dusky room. On the faded green tapestry were broidered little huntsmen. They blew their tasselled horns and with their tiny hands waved to her to go back. 'Go back! little Virginia,' they cried, 'go back!' but the Ghost clutched her hand more tightly and she shut her eyes against them. Horrible animals with lizard tails and goggle eyes, blinked at her from the carven chimney-piece and murmured, 'Beware! little Virginia, beware! we may never see you again,' but the Ghost glided on more swiftly and Virginia did not listen. When they reached the end of the room he stopped and muttered some words she could not understand. She opened her eyes and saw the wall slowly fading away like a mist and a great black cavern in front of her. A bitter cold wind swept round them and she felt something pulling at her dress. 'Quick, quick,' cried the Ghost, 'or it will be too late,' and, in a moment, the wainscoting had closed behind them and the Tapestry Chamber was empty.

CHAPTER SIX

About ten minutes later, the bell rang for tea and, as Virginia did not come down, Mrs Otis sent up one of the footmen to tell her. After a little time he returned and said that he could not find Miss Virginia anywhere. As she was in the habit of going out to the garden every evening to get flowers for the dinner-table, Mrs Otis was not at all alarmed at first, but when six o'clock struck and Virginia did not appear, she became really agitated and sent the boys out to look for her, while she herself and Mr Otis searched every room in the house. At half-past six the boys came back and said that they could find no trace of their sister anywhere. They were all now in the greatest state of excitement and did not know what to do, when Mr Otis suddenly remembered that, some few days before, he had given a band of gypsies permission to camp in the park. He accordingly at once set off for Blackfell Hollow, where he knew they were, accompanied by his eldest son and two of the farm-servants. The little Duke of Cheshire, who was perfectly frantic with anxiety, begged hard to be allowed to go too, but Mr Otis would not allow him, as he was afraid there might be a scuffle. On arriving at the spot, however, he found that the gypsies had gone and it was evident that their departure had been rather sudden, as the fire was still burning and some plates were lying on the grass. Having sent off Washington and the two men to scour the district, he ran home and despatched telegrams to all the police inspectors in the county, telling them to look out for a little girl who had been kidnapped by tramps or gypsies. He then ordered his horse to be brought round and, after insisting on his wife and the three boys sitting down to dinner, rode off down the Ascot Road with a groom. He had hardly, however, gone a couple of miles when he heard somebody galloping after him and, looking round, saw the little Duke coming up on his pony, with his face very flushed and no hat. 'I'm awfully sorry, Mr Otis,' gasped out the boy, 'but I can't eat any dinner as long as Virginia is lost. Please, don't be angry with me; if you had let us be engaged last year, there would never have been all this trouble. You won't send me back, will you? I can't go! I won't go!'

The Minister could not help smiling at the handsome young scapegrace and was a good deal touched at his devotion to Virginia, so leaning down from his horse, he patted him kindly on the shoulders and said, 'Well, Cecil, if you won't go back I suppose you must come with me, but I must get you a hat at Ascot.'

'Oh, bother my hat! I want Virginia!' cried the little Duke, laughing, and they galloped on to the railway station. There Mr Otis enquired of the station-master if anyone answering the description of Virginia had been seen on the platform, but could get no news of her. The station-master, however, wired up and down the line and assured him that a strict watch would be kept for her and, after having bought a hat for the little Duke from a linen-draper, who was just putting up his shutters, Mr Otis rode off to Bexley, a village about four miles away, which he was told was a well-known haunt of the gypsies, as there was a large common next to it. Here they roused up the rural policeman, but could get no information from him and, after riding all over the common, they turned their horses' heads homewards and reached the Chase about eleven o'clock, dead-tired and almost heart-broken. They found Washington and the twins waiting for them at the gate-house with lanterns, as the avenue was very dark. Not the slightest trace of Virginia had been discovered. The gypsies had been caught on

Brockley meadows, but she was not with them and they had explained their sudden departure by saying that they had mistaken the date of Chorton Fair and had gone off in a hurry for fear they might be late. Indeed, they had been quite distressed at hearing of Virginia's disappearance, as they were very grateful to Mr Otis for having allowed them to camp in his park, and four of their number had stayed behind to help in the search. The carp-pond had been dragged and the whole Chase thoroughly gone over, but without any result. It was evident that, for that night at any rate, Virginia was lost to them; and it was in a state of the deepest depression that Mr Otis and the boys walked up to the house, the groom following behind with the two horses and the pony. In the hall they found a group of frightened servants and lying on a sofa in the library was poor Mrs Otis, almost out of her mind with terror and anxiety and having her forehead bathed with eau-de-cologne by the old housekeeper. Mr Otis at once insisted on her having something to eat and ordered up supper for the whole party. It was a melancholy meal, as hardly anyone spoke and even the twins were awestruck and subdued, as they were very fond of their sister. When they had finished, Mr Otis, in spite of the entreaties of the little Duke, ordered them all to bed, saying that nothing more could be done that night and that he would telegraph in the morning to Scotland Yard for some detectives to be sent down immediately. Just as they were passing out of the dining-room, midnight began to boom from the clocktower and when the last stroke sounded they heard a crash and a sudden shrill cry; a dreadful peal of thunder shook the house, a strain of unearthly music floated through the air, a panel at the top of the staircase flew back with a loud noise and out on the landing, looking very pale and white, with a little casket in her hand, stepped Virginia. In a moment they had all rushed up to her. Mrs Otis clasped her passionately in her arms, the Duke smothered her with violent kisses and the twins executed a wild war-dance round the group.

'Good heavens! child, where have you been?' said Mr Otis, rather angrily, thinking that she had been playing some foolish trick on them. 'Cecil and I have been riding all over the country looking for you, and your mother has been frightened to death. You must never play these practical jokes any more.'

'Except on the Ghost! except on the Ghost!' shrieked the twins, as they capered about.

'My own darling, thank God you are found; you must never leave my side again,' murmured Mrs Otis, as she kissed the trembling child and smoothed the tangled gold of her hair.

'Papa,' said Virginia quietly, 'I have been with the Ghost. He is dead and you must come and see him. He had been very wicked, but he was really sorry for all that he had done and he gave me this box of beautiful jewels before he died.'

The whole family gazed at her in mute amazement, but she was quite grave and serious; and, turning round, she led them through the opening in the wainscoting down a narrow secret corridor, Washington following with a lighted candle, which he had caught up from the table. Finally, they came to a great oak door, studded with rusty nails. When Virginia touched it, it swung back on its heavy hinges and they found themselves in a little low room, with a vaulted ceiling and one tiny grated window. Imbedded in the wall was a huge iron ring and chained to it was a gaunt skeleton, that was stretched out at full length on the stone floor and seemed to be trying to grasp with its long fleshless fingers an old-fashioned trencher and ewer, that were placed just out of its reach. The jug had evidently been once filled with water, as it was covered inside with green mould. There was nothing on the trencher but a pile of dust. Virginia knelt down beside the skeleton and, folding her little hands together, began to pray silently, while the rest of the party looked on in wonder at the terrible tragedy whose secret was now disclosed to them.

'Hallo!' suddenly exclaimed one of the twins, who had been looking out of the window to try and discover in what wing of the house the room was situated. 'Hallo! the old withered almond tree has blossomed. I can see the flowers quite plainly in the moonlight.'

'God has forgiven him,' said Virginia gravely, as she rose to her feet, and a beautiful light seemed to illumine her face.

'What an angel you are!' cried the young Duke and he put his arm round her neck and kissed her.

CHAPTER SEVEN

Four days after these curious incidents a funeral started from Canterville Chase at about eleven o'clock at night. The hearse was drawn by eight black horses, each of which carried on its head a great tuft of nodding ostrich-plumes, and the leaden coffin was covered by a rich purple pall, on which was embroidered in gold the Canterville coat-of-arms. By the side of the hearse and the coaches walked the servants with lighted torches and the whole procession was wonderfully impressive. Lord Canterville was the chief mourner, having come up specially from Wales to attend the funeral, and sat in the first carriage along with little Virginia. Then came the United States Minister and his wife, then

Washington and the three boys and in the last carriage was Mrs Umney. It was generally felt that, as she had been frightened by the ghost for more than fifty years of her life, she had the right to see the last of him. A deep grave had been dug in the corner of the churchyard, just under the old yew tree, and the service was read in the most impressive manner by the Revd Augustus Dampier. When the ceremony was over, the servants, according to an old custom observed in the Canterville family, extinguished their torches and, as the coffin was being lowered into the grave, Virginia stepped forward and laid on it a large cross made of white and pink almond-blossoms. As she did so, the moon came out from behind a cloud and flooded with its silent silver the little churchyard and from a distant copse a nightingale began to sing. She thought of the ghost's description of the Garden of Death, her eyes became dim with tears and she hardly spoke a word during the drive home.

The next morning, before Lord Canterville went up to town, Mr Otis had an interview with him on the subject of the jewels the ghost had given to Virginia. They were perfectly magnificent, especially a certain ruby necklace with old Venetian setting, which was really a superb specimen of sixteenth-century work, and their value was so great that Mr Otis felt considerable scruples about allowing his daughter to accept them.

'My lord,' he said, 'I know that in this country mortmain is held to apply to trinkets as well as to land and it is quite clear to me that these jewels are, or should be, heirlooms in your family. I must beg you, accordingly, to take them to London with you and to regard them simply as a portion of your property which has been restored to you under certain strange conditions. As for my daughter, she is merely a child and has as yet, I am glad to say, but little interest in such appurtenances of idle luxury. I am also informed by Mrs Otis, who, I may say, is no mean authority upon Art – having had the privilege of spending several winters in Boston when she was a girl – that these gems are of great monetary worth and if offered for sale would fetch a tall price. Under these circumstances, Lord Canterville, I feel sure that you will recognise how impossible it would be for me to allow them to remain in the possession of any member of my family; and, indeed, all such vain gauds and toys, however suitable or necessary to the dignity of the British aristocracy, would be completely out of place among those who have been brought up on the severe, and I believe immortal, principles of republican simplicity. Perhaps I should mention that Virginia is very anxious that you should allow her to retain the box as a memento of your unfortunate but misguided ancestor. As it is extremely old and consequently a good deal out of repair, you may perhaps think fit to comply with her request. For my own part, I confess I am a good deal surprised to find a child of mine expressing sympathy with mediaevalism in any form and can only account for it by the fact that Virginia was born in one of your London suburbs shortly after Mrs Otis had returned from a trip to Athens.'

Lord Canterville listened very gravely to the worthy Minister's speech, pulling his grey moustache now and then to hide an involuntary smile, and when Mr Otis had ended, he shook him cordially by the hand and said, 'My dear sir, your charming little daughter rendered my unlucky ancestor, Sir Simon, a very important service and I and my family are much indebted to her for her marvellous courage and pluck. The jewels are clearly hers and, egad, I believe that if I were heartless enough to take them from her, the wicked old fellow would be out of his grave in a fortnight, leading me the devil of a life. As for their being heirlooms, nothing is an heirloom that is not so mentioned in a will or legal document and the existence of these jewels has been quite unknown. I assure you I have no more claim on them than your butler and when Miss Virginia grows up I dare say she will be pleased to have pretty things to wear. Besides, you forget, Mr Otis, that you took the furniture and the ghost at a valuation and anything that belonged to the ghost passed at once into your possession, as, whatever activity Sir Simon may have shown in the corridor at night, in point of law he was really dead and you acquired his property by purchase.'

Mr Otis was a good deal distressed at Lord Canterville's refusal and begged him to reconsider his decision, but the good-natured peer was quite firm and finally induced the Minister to allow his daughter to retain the present the ghost had given her and when, in the spring of 1890, the young Duchess of Cheshire was presented at the Queen's first drawing-room on the occasion of her marriage, her jewels were the universal theme of admiration. For Virginia received the coronet, which is the reward of all good little American girls, and was married to her boy-lover as soon as he came of age. They were both so charming and they loved each other so much that everyone was delighted at the match, except the old Marchioness of Dumbleton, who had tried to catch the Duke for one of her seven unmarried daughters and had given no less than three expensive dinner-parties for that purpose and, strange to say, Mr Otis himself. Mr Otis was extremely fond of the young Duke personally, but, theoretically, he objected to titles and, to use his own words, 'was not without apprehension lest, amid the enervating influences of a pleasure-loving aristocracy, the true principles of republican simplicity should be forgotten'. His objections, however, were completely overruled and I believe that when he walked up the aisle of St George's, Hanover Square, with his daughter leaning on his arm, there was not a prouder man in the whole length and breadth of England.

The Duke and Duchess, after the honeymoon was over, went down to Canterville Chase and on the day after their arrival they walked over in the afternoon to the lonely churchyard by the pine-woods. There had been a great deal of difficulty at first about the inscription on Sir Simon's tombstone, but finally it had been decided to engrave on it simply the initials of the old gentleman's name and the verse from the library window. The Duchess had brought with her some lovely roses, which she strewed upon the grave, and after they had stood by it for some time they strolled into the ruined chancel of the old abbey. There the Duchess sat down on a fallen pillar, while her husband lay at her feet smoking a cigarette and looking up at her beautiful eyes. Suddenly he threw his cigarette away, took hold of her hand and said to her, 'Virginia, a wife should have no secrets from her husband.'

'Dear Cecil! I have no secrets from you.'

'Yes, you have,' he answered, smiling, 'you have never told me what happened to you when you were locked up with the ghost.'

'I have never told anyone, Cecil,' said Virginia gravely.

'I know that, but you might tell me.'

'Please don't ask me, Cecil, I cannot tell you. Poor Sir Simon! I owe him a great deal. Yes, don't laugh, Cecil, I really do. He made me see what Life is and what Death signifies and why Love is stronger than both.'

The Duke rose and kissed his wife lovingly.

'You can have your secret as long as I have your heart,' he murmured.

'You have always had that, Cecil.'

'And you will tell our children someday, won't you?'

Virginia blushed.

The Haunted Doll's House

MONTAGUE RHODES JAMES 1862–1936

'I SUPPOSE YOU GET stuff of that kind through your hands pretty
often?' said Mr Dillet, as he pointed with his stick to an object which
shall be described when the time comes: and when he said it, he lied in
his throat and knew that he lied. Not once in twenty years – perhaps
not once in a lifetime – could Mr Chittenden, skilled as he was in
ferreting out the forgotten treasures of half a dozen counties, expect to
handle such a specimen. It was a collector's palaver, and Mr Chittenden
recognised it as such.

'Stuff of that kind, Mr Dillet! It's a museum piece, that is.'

'Well, I suppose there are museums that'll take anything.'

'I've seen one, not as good as that, years back,' said Mr Chittenden,
thoughtfully. 'But that's not likely to come into the market: and I'm
told they 'ave some fine ones of the period over the water. No: I'm only
telling you the truth, Mr Dillet, when I say that if you was to place an
unlimited order with me for the very best that could be got – and you
know I 'ave facilities for getting to know of such things and a
reputation to maintain – well, all I can say is, I should lead you straight
up to that one and say, "I can't do no better for you than that, sir." '

'Hear, hear!' said Mr Dillet, applauding ironically with the end of his
stick on the floor of the shop. 'How much are you sticking the innocent
American buyer for it, eh?'

'Oh, I shan't be over hard on the buyer, American or otherwise. You
see, it stands this way, Mr Dillet – if I knew just a bit more about the
pedigree – '

'Or just a bit less,' Mr Dillet put in.

'Ha, ha! you will have your joke, sir. No, but as I was saying, if I knew
just a little more than what I do about the piece – though anyone can
see for themselves it's a genuine thing, every last corner of it, and
there's not been one of my men allowed to so much as touch it since it
came into the shop – there'd be another figure in the price I'm asking.'

'And what's that: five and twenty?'

'Multiply that by three and you've got it, sir. Seventy-five's my price.'

'And fifty's mine,' said Mr Dillet.

The point of agreement was, of course, somewhere between the two, it does not matter exactly where – I think sixty guineas. But half an hour later the object was being packed and within an hour Mr Dillet had called for it in his car and driven away. Mr Chittenden, holding the cheque in his hand, saw him off from the door with smiles and returned, still smiling, into the parlour where his wife was making the tea. He stopped at the door.

'It's gone,' he said.

'Thank God for that!' said Mrs Chittenden, putting down the teapot. 'Mr Dillet, was it?'

'Yes, it was.'

'Well, I'd sooner it was him than another.'

'Oh, I don't know, he ain't a bad fellow, my dear.'

'Maybe not, but in my opinion he'd be none the worse for a bit of a shake up.'

'Well, if that's your opinion, it's my opinion he's put himself into the way of getting one. Anyhow, we shan't have no more of it and that's something to be thankful for.'

And so Mr and Mrs Chittenden sat down to tea.

And what of Mr Dillet and of his new acquisition? What it was, the title of this story will have told you. What it was like, I shall have to indicate as well as I can.

There was only just room enough for it in the car and Mr Dillet had to sit with the driver: he had also to go slow, for though the rooms of the Doll's House had all been stuffed carefully with soft cotton wool, jolting was to be avoided, in view of the immense number of small objects which thronged them; and the ten-mile drive was an anxious time for him, in spite of all the precautions he insisted upon. At last his front door was reached and Collins, the butler, came out.

'Look here, Collins, you must help me with this thing – it's a delicate job. We must get it out upright, see? It's full of little things that mustn't be displaced more than we can help. Let's see, where shall we have it? (After a pause for consideration.) Really, I think I shall have to put it in my own room, to begin with at any rate. On the big table – that's it.'

It was conveyed – with much talking – to Mr Dillet's spacious room on the first floor, looking out on the drive. The sheeting was unwound from it and the front thrown open and for the next hour or two Mr Dillet was fully occupied in extracting the padding and setting in order the contents of the rooms.

When this thoroughly congenial task was finished, I must say that it would have been difficult to find a more perfect and attractive specimen of a Doll's House in Strawberry Hill Gothic than that which now stood on Mr Dillet's large kneehole table, lighted up by the evening sun which came slanting through three tall sash-windows.

It was quite six feet long, including the Chapel or Oratory which flanked the front on the left as you faced it and the stable on the right. The main block of the house was, as I have said, in the Gothic manner; that is to say, the windows had pointed arches and were surmounted by what are called ogival hoods, with crockets and finials such as we see on the canopies of tombs built into church walls. At the angles were absurd turrets covered with arched panels. The Chapel had pinnacles and buttresses and a bell in the turret and coloured glass in the windows. When the front of the house was open you saw four large rooms, bedroom, dining room, drawing-room and kitchen, each with its appropriate furniture in a very complete state.

The stable on the right was in two storeys, with its proper complement of horses, coaches and grooms, and with its clock and Gothic cupola for the clock bell.

Pages, of course, might be written on the outfit of the mansion – how many frying pans, how many gilt chairs, what pictures, carpets, chandeliers, four-posters, table linen, glass, crockery and plate it possessed; but all this must be left to the imagination. I will only say that the base or plinth on which the house stood (for it was fitted with one of some depth which allowed of a flight of steps to the front door and a terrace, partly balustraded) contained a shallow drawer or drawers in which were neatly stored sets of embroidered curtains, changes of raiment for the inmates and, in short, all the materials for an infinite series of variations and refittings of the most absorbing and delightful kind.

'Quintessence of Horace Walpole, that's what it is: he must have had something to do with the making of it.' Such was Mr Dillet's murmured reflection as he knelt before it in a reverent ecstasy. 'Simply wonderful; this is my day and no mistake. Five hundred pound coming in this morning for that cabinet which I never cared about and now this tumbling into my hands for a tenth, at the very most, of what it would fetch in town. Well, well! It almost makes one afraid something'll happen to counter it. Let's have a look at the population, anyhow.'

Accordingly, he set them before him in a row. Again, here is an opportunity, which some would snatch at, of making an inventory of costume: I am incapable of it.

There were a gentleman and lady, in blue satin and brocade respectively. There were two children, a boy and a girl. There was a cook, a nurse, a footman and there were the stable servants, two postillions, a coachman, two grooms.

'Anyone else? Yes, possibly.'

The curtains of the four-poster in the bedroom were closely drawn round four sides of it and he put his finger in between them and felt in the bed. He drew the finger back hastily, for it almost seemed to him as if something had – not stirred, perhaps, but yielded – in an old live way as he pressed it. Then he put back the curtains, which ran on rods in the proper manner, and extracted from the bed a white-haired old gentleman in a long linen nightdress and cap, and laid him down by the rest. The tale was complete.

Dinner time was now near, so Mr Dillet spent but five minutes in putting the lady and children into the drawing-room, the gentleman into the dining-room, the servants into the kitchen and stables and the old man back into his bed. He retired into his dressing-room next door and we see or hear no more of him until something like eleven o'clock at night.

His whim was to sleep surrounded by some of the gems of his collection. The big room in which we have seen him contained his bed: bath, wardrobe, and all the appliances of dressing were in a commodious room adjoining: but his four-poster, which itself was a valued treasure, stood in the large room where he sometimes wrote and often sat and even received visitors. Tonight he repaired to it in a highly complacent frame of mind.

There was no striking clock within earshot – none on the staircase, none in the stable, none in the distant church tower. Yet it is indubitable that Mr Dillet was startled out of a very pleasant slumber by a bell tolling one.

He was so much startled that he did not merely lie breathlessly with wide-open eyes, but actually sat up in his bed.

He never asked himself, till the morning hours, how it was that, though there was no light at all in the room, the Doll's House on the kneehole table, stood out with complete clearness. But it was so. The effect was that of a bright harvest moon shining full on the front of a big white stone mansion – a quarter of a mile away it might be and yet every detail was photographically sharp. There were trees about it, too – trees rising behind the chapel and the house. He seemed to be conscious of the scent of a cool still September night. He thought he could hear an occasional stamp and clink from the stables, as of horses stirring. And with another shock he realised that, above the house, he was looking, not at the wall of his room with its pictures, but into the profound blue of a night sky.

There were lights, more than one, in the windows, and he quickly saw that this was no four-roomed house with a movable front, but one of many rooms, and staircases – a real house, but seen as if through the wrong end of a telescope. 'You mean to show me something,' he muttered to himself, and he gazed earnestly on the lighted windows. They would in real life have been shuttered or curtained, no doubt, he thought; but as it was there was nothing to intercept his view of what was being transacted inside the rooms.

Two rooms were lighted – one on the ground floor to the right of the door, one upstairs, on the left – the first brightly enough, the other rather dimly. The lower room was the dining-room: a table was laid, but the meal was over and only wine and glasses were left on the table. The man of the blue satin and the woman of the brocade were alone in the room and they were talking very earnestly, seated close together at the table, their elbows on it: every now and again stopping to listen, as it seemed. Once *he* rose, came to the window and opened it and put his head out and his hand to his ear. There was a lighted taper in a silver candlestick on a sideboard. When the man left the window he seemed to leave the room also, and the lady, taper in hand, remained standing and listening. The expression on her face was that of one striving her utmost to keep down a fear that threatened to master her – and succeeding. It was a hateful face, too; broad, flat and sly. Now the man came back and she took some small thing from him and hurried out of the room. He, too, disappeared, but only for a moment or two. The front door slowly opened and he stepped out and stood on the top of the *perron*, looking this way and that; then turned towards the upper window that was lighted and shook his fist.

It was time to look at that upper window. Through it was seen a four-post bed: a nurse or other servant in an armchair, evidently sound asleep; in the bed an old man lying: awake and, one would say, anxious, from the way in which he shifted about and moved his fingers, beating tunes on the coverlet. Beyond the bed a door opened. Light was seen on the ceiling and the lady came in: she set down her candle on a table, came to the fireside and roused the nurse. In her hand she had an old-fashioned wine bottle, ready uncorked. The nurse took it, poured some of the contents into a little silver saucepan, added some spice and sugar from casters on the table and set it to warm on the fire. Meanwhile the old man in the bed beckoned feebly to the lady, who came to him, smiling, took his wrist as if to feel his pulse and bit her lip as if in consternation. He looked at her anxiously and then pointed to the window and spoke. She nodded and did as the man below had done; opened the casement and listened – perhaps rather ostentatiously; then drew her head in and shook it, looking at the old man, who seemed to sigh.

By this time the posset on the fire was steaming and the nurse poured it into a small two-handled silver bowl and brought it to the bedside. The old man seemed disinclined for it and was waving it away, but the lady and the nurse together bent over him and evidently pressed it upon him. He must have yielded, for they supported him into a sitting position and put it to his lips. He drank most of it, in several draughts, and they laid him down. The lady left the room, smiling good-night to him, and took the bowl, the bottle and the silver saucepan with her. The nurse returned to the chair and there was an interval of complete quiet.

Suddenly the old man started up in his bed – and he must have uttered some cry, for the nurse started out of her chair and made but one step of it to the bedside. He was a sad and terrible sight – flushed in the face, almost to blackness, the eyes glaring whitely, both hands clutching at his heart, foam at his lips.

For a moment the nurse left him, ran to the door, flung it wide open, and one supposes, screamed aloud for help, then darted back to the bed and seemed to try feverishly to soothe him – to lay him down – anything. But as the lady, her husband and several servants, rushed into the room with horrified faces, the old man collapsed under the nurse's hands and lay back and the features, contorted with agony and rage, relaxed slowly into calm.

A few moments later, lights showed out to the left of the house and a coach with flambeaux drove up to the door. A white-wigged man in black got nimbly out and ran up the steps, carrying a small leather trunk-shaped box. He was met in the doorway by the man and his wife, she with her handkerchief clutched between her hands, he with a tragic face, but retaining his self-control. They led the newcomer into the dining-room, where he set his box of papers on the table and, turning to them, listened with a face of consternation at what they had to tell. He nodded his head again and again, threw out his hands slightly, declined, it seemed, offers of refreshment and lodging for the night and within a few minutes came slowly down the steps, entering the coach and driving off the way he had come. As the man in blue watched him from the top of the steps, a smile not pleasant to see stole slowly over his fat white face. Darkness fell over the whole scene as the lights of the coach disappeared.

But Mr Dillet remained sitting up in the bed: he had rightly guessed that there would be a sequel. The house front glimmered out again before long. But now there was a difference. The lights were in other windows, one at the top of the house, the other illuminating the range of coloured windows of the chapel. How he saw through these is not quite obvious, but he did. The interior was as carefully furnished as the rest of the establishment, with its minute red cushions on the desks, its Gothic stall-canopies and its western gallery and pinnacled organ with gold pipes. On the centre of the black and white pavement was a bier: four tall candles burned at the corners. On the bier was a coffin covered with a pall of black velvet.

As he looked the folds of the pall stirred. It seemed to rise at one end: it slid downwards: it fell away, exposing the black coffin with its silver handles and nameplate. One of the tall candlesticks swayed and toppled over. Ask no more, but turn, as Mr Dillet hastily did, and look in at the lighted window at the top of the house, where a boy and girl lay in two truckle-beds and a four-poster for the nurse rose above them. The nurse was not visible for the moment; but the father and mother were there, now in mourning, but with very little sign of mourning in their demeanour. Indeed, they were laughing and talking with a good deal of animation, sometimes to each other and sometimes throwing a remark to one or other of the children and again laughing at the answers. Then the father was seen to go on tiptoe out of the room, taking with him as he went a white garment that hung on a peg near the door. He shut the door after him. A minute or two later it was slowly opened again and a muffled head poked round it. A bent form of sinister shape stepped across to the truckle-beds and suddenly stopped, threw up its arms and revealed, of course, the father, laughing. The children were in agonies of terror, the boy with the bedclothes over his head, the girl throwing herself out of bed into her mother's arms. Attempts at consolation followed – the parents took the children on their laps, patted them, picked up the white gown and showed there was no harm in it and so forth; and at last putting the children back into bed, left the room with encouraging waves of the hand. As they left it, the nurse came in and soon the light died down.

Still Mr Dillet watched immovable.

A new sort of light – not of lamp or candle – a pale ugly light, began to dawn around the door-case at the back of the room. The door was opening again. The seer does not like to dwell upon what he saw entering the room: he says it might be described as a frog – the size of a man – but it had scanty white hair about its head. It was busy about the truckle-beds, but not for long. The sound of cries – faint, as if coming out of a vast distance – but, even so, infinitely appalling, reached the ear.

There were signs of a hideous commotion all over the house: lights passed along and up and doors opened and shut and running figures passed within the windows. The clock in the stable turret tolled one and darkness fell again.

It was only dispelled once more, to show the house front. At the bottom of the steps dark figures were drawn up in two lines, holding flaming torches. More dark figures came down the steps, bearing, first one, then another small coffin. And the lines of torch-bearers with the coffins between them moved silently onward to the left.

The hours of night passed on – never so slowly, Mr Dillet thought. Gradually he sank down from sitting to lying in his bed – but he did not close an eye: and early next morning he sent for the doctor.

The doctor found him in a disquieting state of nerves and recommended sea air. To a quiet place on the East Coast he accordingly repaired by easy stages in his car.

One of the first people he met on the sea front was Mr Chittenden, who, it appeared, had likewise been advised to take his wife away for a bit of a change.

Mr Chittenden looked somewhat askance upon him when they met: and not without cause.

'Well, I don't wonder at you being a bit upset, Mr Dillet. What? Yes, well, I might say 'orrible upset, to be sure, seeing what me and my poor wife went through ourselves. But I put it to you, Mr Dillet, one of two things: was I going to scrap a lovely piece like that on the one 'and, or was I going to tell customers: "I'm selling you a regular picture-palace-drama in real life of the olden time, billed to perform regular at one o'clock a.m."? Why, what would you 'ave said yourself? And next thing you know, two Justices of the Peace in the back parlour and pore Mr and Mrs Chittenden off in a spring cart to the County Asylum and everyone in the street saying, "Ah, I thought it 'ud come to that. Look at the way the man drank!" – and me next door, or next door but one, to a total abstainer, as you know. Well, there was my position. What? Me 'ave it back in the shop? Well, what do *you* think? No, but I'll tell you what I will do. You shall have your money back bar the ten pound I paid for it and you make what you can.'

Later in the day, in what is offensively called the 'smoke-room' of the hotel, a murmured conversation between the two went on for some time.

'How much do you really know about that thing and where it came from?'

'Honest, Mr Dillet, I don't know the 'ouse. Of course, it came out of the lumber room of a country 'ouse—that anyone could guess. But I'll go as far as say this, that I believe it's not a hundred miles from this place. Which direction and how far I've no notion. I'm only judging by guesswork. The man as I actually paid the cheque to ain't one of my regular men and I've lost sight of him; but I 'ave the idea that this part of the country was his beat and that's every word I can tell you. But now, Mr Dillet, there's one thing that rather physicks me – that old chap – I suppose you saw him drive up to the door – I thought so: now, would he have been the medical man, do you take it? My wife would have it so, but I stuck to it that was the lawyer, because he had papers with him and one he took out was folded up.'

'I agree,' said Mr Dillet. 'Thinking it over, I came to the conclusion that was the old man's will, ready to be signed.'

'Just what I thought,' said Mr Chittenden, 'and I took it that will would have cut out the young people, eh? Well, well! It's been a lesson to me, I know that. I shan't buy no more dolls' houses, nor waste no more money on the pictures and as to this business of poisonin' grandpa, well, if I know myself, I never 'ad much of a turn for that. Live and let live: that's bin my motto throughout life and I ain't found it a bad one.'

Filled with these elevated sentiments, Mr Chittenden retired to his lodgings. Mr Dillet next day repaired to the local institute, where he hoped to find some clue to the riddle that absorbed him. He gazed in despair at a long file of the Canterbury and York Society's publications of the Parish Registers of the district. No print resembling the house of his nightmare was among those that hung on the staircase and in the passages. Disconsolate, he found himself in a derelict room, staring at a dusty model of a church in a dusty glass case:

Model of St Stephen's Church, Coxham. Presented by
J. Merewether, Esq., of Ilbridge House, 1877. The work of
his ancestor James Merewether, d. 1786.

There was something in the fashion of it that reminded him dimly of his horror. He retraced his steps to a wall map he had noticed and made out that Ilbridge House was in Coxham Parish. Coxham was, as it happened, one of the parishes of which he had retained the name when he glanced over the file of printed registers and it was not long before he found in them the record of the burial of Roger Milford, aged 76, on the 11th September 1757, and of Roger and Elizabeth Merewether, aged 9 and 7, on the 19th of the same month. It seemed worthwhile to follow up this clue, frail as it was; and in the afternoon he drove out to Coxham. The east end of the north aisle of the church is a Milford chapel and on its north wall are tablets to the same persons; Roger, the elder, it seems, was distinguished by all the qualities which adorn 'the Father, the Magistrate, and the Man': the memorial was erected by his detached daughter Elizabeth, 'who did not long survive the loss of a parent ever solicitous for her welfare, and of two amiable children'. The last sentence was plainly an addition to the original inscription .

A yet later slab told of James Merewether, husband of Elizabeth, 'who in the dawn of life practised, not without success, those arts which, had he continued their exercise, might in the opinion of the most competent judges have earned for him the name of the British Vitruvius: but who, overwhelmed by the visitation which deprived him of an affectionate partner and a blooming offspring, passed his Prime and Age in a secluded yet elegant Retirement: his grateful Nephew and Heir indulges a pious sorrow by this too brief recital of his excellences'.

The children were more simply commemorated. Both died on the night of the 12th of September.

Mr Dillet felt sure that in Ilbridge House he had found the scene of his drama. In some old sketch book, possibly in some old print, he may yet find convincing evidence that he is right. But the Ilbridge House of today is not that which he sought; it is an Elizabethan erection of the forties, in red brick, with stone quoins and dressings.

A quarter of a mile from it, in a low part of the park, backed by ancient, stag-horned, ivy-strangled trees and thick undergrowth, are marks of a terraced platform overgrown with rough grass. A few stone balusters lie here and there and a heap or two, covered with nettles and ivy, of wrought stones with badly carved crockets. This, someone told Mr Dillet, was the site of an older house.

As he drove out of the village, the hall clock struck four and Mr Dillet started up and clapped his hands to his ears. It was not the first time he had heard that bell.

Awaiting an offer from the other side of the Atlantic, the doll's house still reposes, carefully sheeted, in a loft over Mr Dillet's stables, whither Collins conveyed it on the day when Mr Dillet started for the sea coast.

A School Story

MONTAGUE RHODES JAMES 1862–1936

TWO MEN IN A smoking-room were talking of their private-school days.

'At *our* school,' said A, 'we had a ghost's footmark on the staircase. What was it like? Oh, very unconvincing. Just the shape of a shoe, with a square toe, if I remember right. The staircase was a stone one. I never heard any story about the thing. That seems odd, when you come to think of it. Why didn't somebody invent one, I wonder?'

'You never can tell with little boys. They have a mythology of their own. There's a subject for you, by the way – The Folklore of Private Schools.'

'Yes; the crop is rather scanty, though. I imagine, if you were to investigate the cycle of ghost stories, for instance, which the boys at private schools tell each other, they would all turn out to be highly compressed versions of stories out of books.'

'Nowadays the *Strand* and *Pearson's*, and so on, would be extensively drawn upon.'

'No doubt; they weren't born or thought of in *my* time. Let's see. I wonder if I can remember the staple ones that I was told. First, there was the house with a room in which a series of people insisted on passing a night; and each of them in the morning was found kneeling in a corner and had just time to say, "I've seen it," and died.'

'Wasn't that the house in Berkeley Square?'

'I dare say it was. Then there was the man who heard a noise in the passage at night, opened his door and saw someone crawling towards him on all fours with his eye hanging out on his cheek. There was besides, let me think – Yes! the room where a man was found dead in bed with a horseshoe mark on his forehead and the floor under the bed was covered with marks of horseshoes also; I don't know why. Also there was the lady who, on locking her bedroom door in a strange house, heard a thin voice among the bed-curtains say, "Now we're shut in for the night." None of those had any explanation or sequel. I wonder if they go on still, those stories.'

'Oh, likely enough – with additions from the magazines, as I said.

You never heard, did you, of a real ghost at a private school? I thought not; nobody has that ever I came across.'

'From the way in which you said that, I gather that *you* have.'

'I really don't know, but this is what was in my mind. It happened at my private school thirty odd years ago and I haven't any explanation of it.

'The school I mean was near London. It was established in a large and fairly old house – a great white building with very fine grounds about it; there were large cedars in the garden, as there are in so many of the older gardens in the Thames valley, and ancient elms in the three or four fields which we used for our games. I think probably it was quite an attractive place, but boys seldom allow that their schools possess any tolerable features.

'I came to the school in a September, soon after the year 1870; and among the boys who arrived on the same day was one whom I took to: a Highland boy, whom I will call McLeod. I needn't spend time in describing him: the main thing is that I got to know him very well. He was not an exceptional boy in any way – not particularly good at books or games – but he suited me.

'The school was a large one: there must have been from 120 to 130 boys there as a rule and so a considerable staff of masters was required and there were rather frequent changes among them.

'One term – perhaps it was my third or fourth – a new master made his appearance. His name was Sampson. He was a tallish, stoutish, pale, black-bearded man. I think we liked him: he had travelled a good deal and had stories which amused us on our school walks, so that there was some competition among us to get within earshot of him. I remember too – dear me, I have hardly thought of it since then! – that he had a charm on his watch-chain that attracted my attention one day and he let me examine it. It was, I now suppose, a gold Byzantine coin; there was an effigy of some absurd emperor on one side; the other side had been worn practically smooth and he had had cut on it – rather barbarously – his own initials, G. W. S., and a date, July 24th 1865. Yes, I can see it now: he told me he had picked it up in Constantinople: it was about the size of a florin, perhaps rather smaller.

'Well, the first odd thing that happened was this. Sampson was doing Latin grammar with us. One of his favourite methods – perhaps it is rather a good one – was to make us construct sentences out of our own heads to illustrate the rules he was trying to make us learn. Of course that is a thing which gives a silly boy a chance of being impertinent: there are lots of school stories in which that happens – or anyhow there might be. But Sampson was too good a disciplinarian for us to think of trying that on with him. Now, on this occasion he was telling us how to express *remembering* in Latin: and he ordered us each to make a sentence bringing in the verb *memini*, "I remember". Well, most of us made up some ordinary sentence such as "I remember my father", or "He remembers his book", or something equally uninteresting: and I dare say a good many put down *Memino librum meum*, and so forth: but the boy I mentioned – McLeod – was evidently thinking of something more elaborate than that. The rest of us wanted to have our sentences passed and get on to something else, so some kicked him under the desk and I, who was next to him, poked him and whispered to him to look sharp. But he didn't seem to attend. I looked at his paper and saw he had put down nothing at all. So I jogged him again harder than before and upbraided him sharply for keeping us all waiting. That did have some effect. He started and seemed to wake up and then very quickly he scribbled about a couple of lines on his paper and showed it up with the rest. As it was the last, or nearly the last, to come in and as Sampson had a good deal to say to the boys who had written *meminiscimus patri meo* and the rest of it, it turned out that the clock struck twelve before he had got to McLeod and McLeod had to wait afterwards to have his sentence corrected. There was nothing much going on outside when I got out, so I waited for him to come. He came very slowly when he did arrive and I guessed there had been some sort of trouble.

' "Well," I said, "what did you get?"

' "Oh, I don't know,' said McLeod, "nothing much: but I think Sampson's rather sick with me."

' "Why, did you show him up some rot?"

' "No fear," he said. "It was all right as far as I could see: it was like this: *Memento* – that's right enough for remember, and it takes a genitive – *memento putei inter quatuor taxos.*"

' "What silly rot!" I said. "What made you shove that down? What does it mean?"

' "That's the funny part," said McLeod. "I'm not quite sure what it does mean. All I know is, it just came into my head and I corked it down. I know what *I think* it means, because just before I wrote it down I had a sort of picture of it in my head: I believe it means 'Remember the well among the four' – what are those dark sort of trees that have red berries on them?"

' "Mountain ashes, I s'pose you mean."

' "I never heard of them," said McLeod; "no, *I'll* tell you – yews."

' "Well, and what did Sampson say?"

' "Why, he was jolly odd about it. When he read it he got up and went to the mantelpiece and stopped quite a long time without saying anything, with his back to me. And then he said, without turning round and rather quiet, 'What do you suppose that means?' I told him what I thought; only I couldn't remember the name of the silly tree; and then he wanted to know why I put it down and I had to say something or other. And after that he left off talking about it and asked me how long I'd been here and where my people lived and things like that; and then I came away; but he wasn't looking a bit well."

'I don't remember any more that was said by either of us about this. Next day McLeod took to his bed with a chill or something of the kind and it was a week or more before he was in school again. And as much as a month went by without anything happening that was noticeable. Whether or nor Mr Sampson was really startled, as McLeod had thought, he didn't show it. I am pretty sure, of course, now, that there was something very curious in his past history, but I'm not going to pretend that we boys were sharp enough to guess any such thing.

'There was one other incident of the same kind as the last which I told you. Several times since that day we had had to make up examples in school to illustrate different rules, but there had never been any row except when we did them wrong. At last there came a day when we were going through those dismal things which people call conditional sentences, and we were told to make a conditional sentence, expressing a future consequence. We did it, right or wrong, and showed up our bits of paper and Sampson began looking through them. All at once he got up, made some odd sort of noise in his throat and rushed out by a door that was just by his desk. We sat there for a minute or two and then – I suppose it was incorrect – but we went up, I and one or two others, to look at the papers on his desk. Of course I thought someone must have put down some nonsense or other and Sampson had gone off to report him. All the same, I noticed that he hadn't taken any of the papers with him when he ran out. Well, the top paper on the desk was written in red ink – which no one used – and it wasn't in anyone's hand who was in the class. They all looked at it – McLeod and all – and took their dying oaths that it wasn't theirs. Then I thought of counting the bits of paper. And of this I made quite certain: that there were seventeen bits of paper on the desk and sixteen boys in the form. Well, I bagged the extra paper and kept it and I believe I have it now. And now you will want to know what was written on it. It was simple enough and harmless enough, I should have said:

Si tu non veneris ad me, ego veniam ad te,

which means, I suppose, "If you don't come to me, I'll come to you." '

'Could you show me the paper?' interrupted the listener.

'Yes, I could: but there's another odd thing about it. That same afternoon I took it out of my locker – I know for certain it was the same bit, for I made a finger-mark on it – and no single trace of writing of any kind was there on it. I kept it, as I said, and since that time I have tried various experiments to see whether sympathetic ink had been used, but absolutely without result.

'So much for that. After about half an hour Sampson looked in again: said he had felt very unwell and told us we might go. He came rather gingerly to his desk and gave just one look at the uppermost paper: and I suppose he thought he must have been dreaming: anyhow, he asked no questions.

'That day was a half-holiday and next day Sampson was in school again, much as usual. That night the third and last incident in my story happened.

'We – McLeod and I – slept in a dormitory at right angles to the main building. Sampson slept in the main building on the first floor. There was a very bright full moon. At an hour which I can't tell exactly, but some time between one and two, I was woken up by somebody shaking me. It was McLeod; and a nice state of mind he seemed to be in. "Come," he said – "come! there's a burglar getting in through Sampson's window."

' As soon as I could speak, I said, "Well, why not call out and wake everybody up "

' "No, no," he said, "I'm not sure who it is: don't make a row: come and look."

' Naturally I came and looked and naturally there was no one there. I was cross enough and should have called McLeod plenty of names; only – I couldn't tell why – it seemed to me that there *was* something wrong – something that made me very glad I wasn't alone to face it. We were still at the window looking out, and as soon as I could, I asked him what he had heard or seen.

' "I didn't *hear* anything at all," he said, "but about five minutes before I woke you, I found myself looking out of this window here and there was a man sitting or kneeling on Sampson's window-sill and looking in and I thought he was beckoning."

' "What sort of man?"

' McLeod wriggled. "I don't know," he said, "but I can tell you one thing – he was beastly thin: and he looked as if he was wet all over: and," he said, looking round and whispering as if he hardly liked to hear himself, "I'm not at all sure that he was alive."

'We went on talking in whispers some time longer, and eventually crept back to bed. No one else in the room woke or stirred the whole time. I believe we did sleep a bit afterwards, but we were very cheap next day.

'And next day Mr Sampson was gone: not to be found: and I believe no trace of him has ever come to light since. In thinking it over, one of the oddest things about it all has seemed to me to be the fact that neither McLeod nor I ever mentioned what we had seen to any third person whatever. Of course no questions were asked on the subject, and if they had been, I am inclined to believe that we could not have made any answer: we seemed unable to speak about it.

'That is my story,' said the narrator. 'The only approach to a ghost story connected with a school that I know, but still, I think, an approach to such a thing.'

The sequel to this may perhaps be reckoned highly conventional; but a sequel there is and so it must be produced. There had been more than one listener to the story and, in the latter part of that same year or of the next, one such listener was staying at a country house in Ireland.

One evening his host was turning over a drawer full of odds and ends in the smoking-room. Suddenly he put his hand upon a little box. 'Now,' he said, 'you know about old things; tell me what that is.' My friend opened the little box and found in it a thin gold chain with an object attached to it. He glanced at the object and then took off his spectacles to examine it more narrowly. 'What's the history of this?' he asked. 'Odd enough,' was the answer. 'You know the yew thicket in the shrubbery: well, a year or two back we were cleaning out the old well that used to be in the clearing here and what do you suppose we found?'

'Is it possible that you found a body?' said the visitor, with an odd feeling of nervousness.

'We did that: but what's more, in every sense of the word, we found two.'

'Good heavens! Two? Was there anything to show how they got there? Was this thing found with them?'

'It was. Amongst the rags of the clothes that were on one of the bodies. A bad business, whatever the story of it may have been. One body had the arms tight round the other. They must have been there thirty years or more – long enough before we came to this place. You may judge we filled the well up fast enough. Do you make anything of what's cut on that gold coin you have there?'

'I think I can,' said my friend, holding it to the light (but he read it without much difficulty); 'it seems to be G. W. S., July 24th 1865.'

Thurnley Abbey

PERCEVAL LANDON

THREE YEARS AGO I was on my way out to the East and as an extra day in London was of some importance, I took the Friday evening mail-train to Brindisi instead of the usual Thursday morning Marseilles express. Many people shrink from the long forty-eight-hour train journey through Europe and the subsequent rush across the Mediterranean on the nineteen-knot *Isis* or *Osiris*; but there is really very little discomfort on either the train or the mailboat and unless there is actually nothing for me to do, I always like to save the extra day and a half in London before I say goodbye to her for one of my longer tramps. This time – it was early, I remember, in the shipping season, probably about the beginning of September – there were few passengers and I had a compartment in the P & O Indian express to myself all the way from Calais. All Sunday I watched the blue waves dimpling the Adriatic and the pale rosemary along the cuttings; the plain white towns, with their flat roofs and their bold 'duomos', and the grey-green gnarled olive orchards of Apulia. The journey was just like any other. We ate in the dining-car as often and as long as we decently could. We slept after luncheon; we dawdled the afternoon away with yellow-backed novels; sometimes we exchanged platitudes in the smoking-room and it was there that I met Alastair Colvin.

Colvin was a man of middle height, with a resolute, well-cut jaw; his hair was turning grey; his moustache was sun-whitened, otherwise he was clean-shaven – obviously a gentleman and obviously also a pre-occupied man. He had no great wit. When spoken to, he made the usual remarks in the right way and I dare say he refrained from banalities only because he spoke less than the rest of us; most of the time he buried himself in the Wagon-lit Company's timetable, but seemed unable to concentrate his attention on any one page of it. He found that I had been over the Siberian railway and for a quarter of an hour he discussed it with me. Then he lost interest in it and rose to go to his compartment. But he came back again very soon and seemed glad to pick up the conversation again.

Of course this did not seem to me to be of any importance. Most travellers by train become a trifle infirm of purpose after thirty-six hours' rattling. But Colvin's restless way I noticed in somewhat marked contrast with the man's personal importance and dignity; especially ill suited was it to his finely made large hand with strong, broad, regular nails and its few lines. As I looked at his hand I noticed a long, deep and recent scar of ragged shape. However, it is absurd to pretend that I thought anything was unusual. I went off at five o'clock on Sunday afternoon to sleep away the hour or two that had still to be got through before we arrived at Brindisi.

Once there, we few passengers transhipped our hand baggage, verified our berths – there were only a score of us in all – and then, after an aimless ramble of half an hour in Brindisi, we returned to dinner at the Hôtel International, not wholly surprised that the town had been the death of Virgil. If I remember rightly, there is a gaily painted hall at the International – I do not wish to advertise anything, but there is no other place in Brindisi at which to await the coming of the mails – and after dinner I was looking with awe at a trellis overgrown with blue vines, when Colvin moved across the room to my table. He picked up *Il Secolo*, but almost immediately gave up the pretence of reading it. He turned squarely to me and said: 'Would you do me a favour?'

One doesn't do favours to stray acquaintances on continental expresses without knowing something more of them than I knew of Colvin. But I smiled in a noncommittal way and asked him what he wanted.

I wasn't wrong in part of my estimate of him; he said bluntly: 'Will you let me sleep in your cabin on the *Osiris*?' And he coloured a little as he said it.

Now, there is nothing more tiresome than having to put up with a stable-companion at sea and I asked him rather pointedly: 'Surely there is room for all of us?' I thought that perhaps he had been partnered off with some mangy Levantine and wanted to escape from him at all hazards.

Colvin, still somewhat confused, said: 'Yes; I am in a cabin by myself. But you would do me the greatest favour if you would allow me to share yours.'

This was all very well, but, besides the fact that I always sleep better when alone, there had been some recent thefts on board English liners, and I hesitated, frank and honest and self-conscious as Colvin was. Just then the mail-train came in with a clatter and a rush of escaping steam and I asked him to see me again about it on the boat when we started. He answered me curtly – I suppose he saw the mistrust in my manner – 'I am a member of White's.' I smiled to myself as he said it, but I remembered in a moment that the man – if he were really what he claimed to be and I make no doubt that he was – must have been sorely put to it before he urged the fact as a guarantee of his respectability to a total stranger at a Brindisi hotel.

That evening, as we cleared the red and green harbour-lights of Brindisi, Colvin explained. This is his story in his own words.

'When I was travelling in India some years ago, I made the acquaintance of a youngish man in the woods and forests. We camped out together for a week and I found him a pleasant companion. John Broughton was a light-hearted soul when off duty, but a steady and capable man in any of the small emergencies that continually arise in that department. He was liked and trusted by the natives, and though a trifle over-pleased with himself when he escaped to civilisation at Simla or Calcutta, Broughton's future was well assured in Government service, when a fair-sized estate was unexpectedly left to him and he joyfully shook the dust of the Indian plains from his feet and returned to England. For five years he drifted about London. I saw him now and then. We dined together about every eighteen months and I could trace pretty exactly the gradual sickening of Broughton with a merely idle life. He then set out on a couple of long voyages, returned as restless as before, and at last told me that he had decided to marry and settle down at his place, Thurnley Abbey, which had long been empty. He spoke about looking after the property and standing for his constituency in the usual way. Vivien Wilde, his *fiancée*, had, I suppose, begun to take him in hand. She was a pretty girl with a deal of fair hair and rather an exclusive manner; deeply religious in a narrow school, she was still kindly and high-spirited and I thought that Broughton was in luck. He was quite happy and full of information about his future.

'Among other things, I asked him about Thurnley Abbey. He confessed that he hardly knew the place. The last tenant, a man called Clarke, had lived in one wing for fifteen years and seen no one. He had been a miser and a hermit. It was the rarest thing for a light to be seen at the Abbey after dark. Only the barest necessities of life were ordered and the tenant himself received them at the side-door. His one half-caste manservant, after a month's stay in the house, had abruptly left without warning and had returned to the Southern States. One thing Broughton complained bitterly about: Clarke had wilfully spread the rumour among the villagers that the Abbey was haunted and had even condescended to play childish tricks with spirit-lamps and salt in order to scare trespassers away at night. He had been detected in the act of this tomfoolery, but the story spread and no one, said Broughton, would venture near the house except in broad daylight. The hauntedness of Thurnley Abbey was now, he said with a grin, part of the gospel of the countryside, but he and his young wife were going to change all that. Would I propose myself any time I liked? I, of course, said I would and equally, of course, intended to do nothing of the sort without a definite invitation.

'The house was put in thorough repair, though not a stick of the old furniture and tapestry were removed. Floors and ceilings were relaid: the roof was made watertight again and the dust of half a century was scoured out. He showed me some photographs of the place. It was called an Abbey, though as a matter of fact it had been only the infirmary of the long-vanished Abbey of Closter some five miles away. The larger part of this building remained as it had been in pre-Reformation days, but a wing had been added in Jacobean times and that part of the house had been kept in something like repair by Mr Clarke. He had in both the ground and first floors set a heavy timber door, strongly barred with iron, in the passage between the earlier and the Jacobean parts of the house and had entirely neglected the former. So there had been a good deal of work to be done.

'Broughton, whom I saw in London two or three times about this period, made a deal of fun over the positive refusal of the workmen to remain after sundown. Even after the electric light had been put into every room, nothing would induce them to remain, though, as Broughton observed, electric light was death on ghosts. The legend of the Abbey's ghosts had gone far and wide and the men would take no risks. They went home in batches of five and six and even during the daylight hours there was an inordinate amount of talking between one and another, if either happened to be out of sight of his companion. On the whole, though nothing of any sort or kind had been conjured up even by their heated imaginations during their five months' work upon the Abbey, the belief in the ghosts was rather strengthened than otherwise in Thurnley because of the men's confessed nervousness, and local tradition declared itself in favour of the ghost of an immured nun.

' "Good old nun!" said Broughton.

'I asked him whether in general he believed in the possibility of ghosts and, rather to my surprise, he said that he couldn't say he entirely disbelieved in them. A man in India had told him one morning in camp that he believed that his mother was dead in England, as her vision had come to his tent the night before. He had not been alarmed, but had said nothing and the figure vanished again. As a matter of fact, the next possible *dak-walla* brought on a telegram announcing the mother's death. "There the thing was," said Broughton. But at

Thurnley he was practical enough. He roundly cursed the idiotic selfishness of Clarke, whose silly antics had caused all the inconvenience. At the same time, he couldn't refuse to sympathise to some extent with the ignorant workmen. "My own idea," said he, "is that if a ghost ever does come in one's way, one ought to speak to it."

'I agreed. Little as I knew of the ghost world and its conventions, I had always remembered that a spook was in honour bound to wait to be spoken to. It didn't seem much to do and I felt that the sound of one's own voice would at any rate reassure oneself as to one's wakefulness. But there are few ghosts outside Europe – few, that is, that a white man can see – and I had never been troubled with any. However, as I have said, I told Broughton that I agreed.

'So the wedding took place and I went to it in a tall hat which I bought for the occasion and the new Mrs Broughton smiled very nicely at me afterwards. As it had to happen, I took the Orient Express that evening and was not in England again for nearly six months. Just before I came back I got a letter from Broughton. He asked if I could see him in London or come to Thurnley, as he thought I should be better able to help him than anyone else he knew. His wife sent a nice message to me at the end, so I was reassured about at least one thing. I wrote from Budapest that I would come and see him at Thurnley two days after my arrival in London and as I sauntered out of the Pannonia into the Kerepesi Utcza to post my letters, I wondered of what earthly service I could be to Broughton. I had been out with him after tiger on foot and I could imagine few men better able at a pinch to manage their own business. However, I had nothing to do, so after dealing with some small accumulations of business during my absence, I packed a kit-bag and departed to Euston.

'I was met by Broughton's great limousine at Thurnley Road station and after a drive of nearly seven miles we echoed through the sleepy streets of Thurnley village, into which the main gates of the park thrust themselves, splendid with pillars and spread-eagles and tom-cats rampant atop of them. I never was a herald, but I know that the Broughtons have the right to supporters – heaven knows why! From the gates a quadruple avenue of beech trees led inwards for a quarter of a mile. Beneath them a neat strip of fine turf edged the road and ran back until the poison of the dead beech-leaves killed it under the trees. There were many wheel-tracks on the road and a comfortable little pony trap-jogged past me laden with a country parson and his wife and daughter. Evidently there was some garden party going on at the Abbey. The road dropped away to the right at the end of the avenue and I could see the Abbey across a wide pasturage and a broad lawn thickly dotted with guests.

'The end of the building was plain. It must have been almost mercilessly austere when it was first built, but time had crumbled the edges and toned the stone down to an orange-lichened grey wherever it showed behind its curtain of magnolia, jasmine, and ivy. Farther on was the three-storeyed Jacobean house, tall and handsome. There had not been the slightest attempt to adapt the one to the other, but the kindly ivy had glossed over the touching-point. There was a tall flèche in the middle of the building, surmounting a small bell tower. Behind the house there rose the mountainous verdure of Spanish chestnuts all the way up the hill.

'Broughton had seen me coming from afar and walked across from his other guests to welcome me before turning me over to the butler's care. This man was sandy-haired and rather inclined to be talkative. He could, however, answer hardly any questions about the house; he had, he said, only been there three weeks. Mindful of what Broughton had told me, I made no enquiries about ghosts, though the room into which I was shown might have justified anything. It was a very large low room with oak beams projecting from the white ceiling. Every inch of the walls, including the doors, was covered with tapestry, and a remarkably fine Italian fourpost bedstead, heavily draped, added to the darkness and dignity of the place. All the furniture was old, well made and dark. Underfoot there was a plain green pile carpet, the only new thing about the room except the electric light fittings and the jugs and basins. Even the looking-glass on the dressing-table was an old pyramidal Venetian glass set in heavy repoussé frame of tarnished silver.

'After a few minutes' cleaning up, I went downstairs and out upon the lawn, where I greeted my hostess. The people gathered there were of the usual country type, all anxious to be pleased and roundly curious as to the new master of the Abbey. Rather to my surprise and quite to my pleasure, I rediscovered Glenham, whom I had known well in old days in Barotseland: he lived quite close, as, he remarked with a grin, I ought to have known. "But," he added, "I don't live in a place like this." He swept his hand to the long, low lines of the Abbey in obvious admiration and then, to my intense interest, muttered beneath his breath, "Thank God!" He saw that I had overheard him and turning to me said decidedly, "Yes, 'thank God' I said, and I meant it. I wouldn't live at the Abbey for all Broughton's money."

' "But surely," I demurred, "you know that old Clarke was discovered in the very act of setting light to his bug-a-boos?"

'Glenham shrugged his shoulders. "Yes, I know about that. But there is something wrong with the place still. All I can say is that Broughton is a different man since he has lived here. I don't believe that he will remain much longer. But – you're staying here? – well, you'll hear all about it tonight. There's a big dinner, I understand." The conversation turned off to old reminiscences and Glenham soon after had to go.

'Before I went to dress that evening I had twenty minutes' talk with Broughton in his library. There was no doubt that the man was altered, gravely altered. He was nervous and fidgety and I found him looking at me only when my eye was off him. I naturally asked him what he wanted of me. I told him I would do anything I could, but that I couldn't conceive what he lacked that I could provide. He said with a lustreless smile that there was, however, something and that he would tell me the following morning. It struck me that he was somehow ashamed of himself and perhaps ashamed of the part he was asking me to play. However, I dismissed the subject from my mind and went up to dress in my palatial room. As I shut the door a draught blew out the Queen of Sheba from the wall and I noticed that the tapestries were not fastened to the wall at the bottom. I have always held very practical views about spooks and it has often seemed to me that the slow waving in firelight of loose tapestry upon a wall would account for ninety-nine per cent of the stories one hears. Certainly the dignified undulation of this lady with her attendants and huntsmen – one of whom was untidily cutting the throat of a fallow deer upon the very steps on which King Solomon, a grey-faced Flemish nobleman with the order of the Golden Fleece, awaited his fair visitor – gave colour to my hypothesis.

'Nothing much happened at dinner. The people were very much like those of the garden party. A young woman next me seemed anxious to know what was being read in London. As she was far more familiar than I with the most recent magazines and literary supplements, I found salvation in being myself instructed in the tendencies of modern fiction. All true art, she said, was shot through and through with melancholy. How vulgar were the attempts at wit that marked so many modern books! From the beginning of literature it had always been tragedy that embodied the highest attainment of every age. To call such works morbid merely begged the question. No thoughtful man – she looked sternly at me through the steel rim of her glasses – could fail to agree with me. Of course, as one would, I immediately and properly said that I slept with Pett Ridge and Jacobs under my pillow at night and that if *Jorrocks* weren't quite so large and cornery, I would add him to the company. She hadn't read any of them, so I was saved – for a time. But I remember grimly that she said that the dearest wish of her life was to be in some awful and soul-freezing situation of horror and I remember that

she dealt hardly with the hero of Nat Paynter's vampire story, between
nibbles at her brown-bread ice. She was a cheerless soul and I couldn't
help thinking that if there were many such in the neighbourhood, it was
not surprising that old Glenham had been stuffed with some nonsense
or other about the Abbey. Yet nothing could well have been less creepy
than the glitter of silver and glass and the subdued lights and cackle of
conversation all round the dinner-table.

'After the ladies had gone I found myself talking to the rural dean. He
was a thin, earnest man, who at once turned the conversation to old
Clarke's buffooneries. But, he said, Mr Broughton had introduced such
a new and cheerful spirit, not only into the Abbey, but, he might say,
into the whole neighbourhood, that he had great hopes that the
ignorant superstitions of the past were from henceforth destined to
oblivion. Thereupon his other neighbour, a portly gentleman of
independent means and position, audibly remarked "Amen", which
damped the rural dean and we talked of partridges past, partridges
present and pheasants to come. At the other end of the table Broughton
sat with a couple of his friends, red-faced hunting men. Once I noticed
that they were discussing me, but I paid no attention to it at the time. I
remembered it a few hours later.

'By eleven all the guests were gone and Broughton, his wife and I
were alone together under the fine plaster ceiling of the Jacobean
drawing-room. Mrs Broughton talked about one or two of the
neighbours and then, with a smile, said that she knew I would excuse
her, shook hands with me and went off to bed. I am not very good at
analysing things, but I felt that she talked a little uncomfortably and
with a suspicion of effort, smiled rather conventionally and was
obviously glad to go. These things seem trifling enough to repeat, but I
had throughout the faint feeling that everything was not square. Under
the circumstances, this was enough to set me wondering what on earth
the service could be that I was to render – wondering also whether the
whole business were not some ill-advised jest in order to make me
come down from London for a mere shooting-party.

'Broughton said little after she had gone. But he was evidently
labouring to bring the conversation round to the so-called haunting of
the Abbey. As soon as I saw this, of course I asked him directly about it.
He then seemed at once to lose interest in the matter. There was no
doubt about it: Broughton was somehow a changed man, and to my
mind he had changed in no way for the better. Mrs Broughton seemed
no sufficient cause. He was clearly very fond of her and she of him. I
reminded him that he was going to tell me what I could do for him in
the morning, pleaded my journey, lighted a candle and went upstairs

with him. At the end of the passage leading into the old house he grinned weakly and said, "Mind, if you see a ghost, do talk to it; you said you would." He stood irresolutely a moment and then turned away. At the door of his dressing-room he paused once more: "I'm here," he called out, "if you should want anything. Good-night," and he shut his door.

'I went along the passage to my room, undressed, switched on a lamp beside my bed, read a few pages of *The Jungle Book* and then, more than ready for sleep, turned the light off and went fast asleep.

'Three hours later I woke up. There was not a breath of wind outside. There was not even a flicker of light from the fireplace. As I lay there, an ash tinkled slightly as it cooled, but there was hardly a gleam of the dullest red in the grate. An owl cried among the silent Spanish chestnuts on the slope outside. I idly reviewed the events of the day, hoping that I should fall off to sleep again before I reached dinner. But at the end I seemed as wakeful as ever. There was no help for it. I must read my *Jungle Book* again till I felt ready to go off, so I fumbled for the pear at the end of the cord that hung down inside the bed and I switched on the bedside lamp. The sudden glory dazzled me for a moment. I felt under my pillow for my book with half-shut eyes. Then, growing used to the light, I happened to look down to the foot of my bed.

'I can never tell you really what happened then. Nothing I could ever confess in the most abject words could even faintly picture to you what I felt. I know that my heart stopped dead and my throat shut automatically. In one instinctive movement I crouched back up against the head-board of the bed, staring at the horror. The movement set my heart going again and the sweat dripped from every pore. I am not a particularly religious man, but I had always believed that God would never allow any supernatural appearance to present itself to man in such a guise and in such circumstances that harm, either bodily or mental, could result to him. I can only tell you that at that moment both my life and my reason rocked unsteadily on their seats.'

The other *Osiris* passengers had gone to bed. Only he and I remained leaning over the starboard railing, which rattled uneasily now and then under the fierce vibration of the over-engined mailboat. Far over, there were the lights of a few fishing-smacks riding out the night, and a great rush of white combing and seething water fell out and away from us overside.

At last Colvin went on:

'Leaning over the foot of my bed, looking at me, was a figure swathed in a rotten and tattered veiling. This shroud passed over the head, but left both eyes and the right side of the face bare. It then followed the line of the arm down to where the hand grasped the bed-end. The face was not entirely that of a skull, though the eyes and the flesh of the face were totally gone. There was a thin, dry skin drawn tightly over the features and there was some skin left on the hand. One wisp of hair crossed the forehead. It was perfectly still. I looked at it and it looked at me and my brains turned dry and hot in my head. I had still got the pear of the electric lamp in my hand and I played idly with it; only I dared not turn the light out again. I shut my eyes, only to open them in a hideous terror the same second. The thing had not moved. My heart was thumping and the sweat cooled me as it evaporated. Another cinder tinkled in the grate and a panel creaked in the wall.

'My reason failed me. For twenty minutes, or twenty seconds, I was able to think of nothing else but this awful figure, till there came, hurtling through the empty channels of my senses, the remembrance that Broughton and his friends had discussed me furtively at dinner. The dim possibility of its being a hoax stole gratefully into my unhappy mind and once there, one's pluck came creeping back along a thousand tiny veins. My first sensation was one of blind unreasoning thankfulness that my brain was going to stand the trial. I am not a timid man, but the best of us needs some human handle to steady him in time of extremity and in this faint but growing hope that after all it might be only a brutal hoax, I found the fulcrum that I needed. At last I moved.

'How I managed to do it I cannot tell you, but with one spring towards the foot of the bed I got within arm's-length and struck out one fearful blow with my fist at the thing. It crumbled under it and my hand was cut to the bone. With a sickening revulsion after my terror, I dropped half-fainting across the end of the bed. So it was merely a foul trick after all. No doubt the trick had been played many a time before: no doubt Broughton and his friends had had some large bet among themselves as to what I should do when I discovered the gruesome thing. From my state of abject terror I found myself transported into an insensate anger. I shouted curses upon Broughton. I dived rather than climbed over the bed-end on to the sofa. I tore at the robed skeleton – how well the whole thing had been carried out, I thought – I broke the skull against the floor and stamped upon its dry bones. I flung the head away under the bed and rent the brittle bones of the trunk in pieces. I snapped the thin thigh-bones across my knee and flung them in different directions. The shin-bones I set up against a stool and broke with my heel. I raged like a Berserker against the loathly thing and stripped the ribs from the backbone and slung the breastbone against the cupboard. My fury increased as the work of destruction went on. I tore the frail rotten veil into twenty pieces and the dust went up over everything, over the clean blotting-paper and the silver inkstand. At last my work was done. There was but a raffle of broken bones and strips of parchment and crumbling wool. Then, picking up a piece of the skull – it was the cheek and temple bone of the right side, I remember – I opened the door and went down the passage to Broughton's dressing-room. I remember still how my sweat-dripping pyjamas clung to me as I walked. At the door I kicked and entered.

'Broughton was in bed. He had already turned the light on and seemed shrunken and horrified. For a moment he could hardly pull himself together. Then I spoke. I don't know what I said. Only I know that from a heart full and over-full with hatred and contempt, spurred on by shame of my own recent cowardice, I let my tongue run on. He answered nothing. I was amazed at my own fluency. My hair still clung lankily to my wet temples, my hand was bleeding profusely and I must have looked a strange sight. Broughton huddled himself up at the head of the bed just as I had. Still he made no answer, no defence. He seemed preoccupied with something besides my reproaches and once or twice moistened his lips with his tongue. But he could say nothing though he moved his hands now and then, just as a baby who cannot speak moves its hands.

'At last the door into Mrs Broughton's room opened and she came in, white and terrified. "What is it? What is it? Oh, in God's name! what is it?" she cried again and again and then she went up to her husband and sat on the bed in her nightdress and the two faced me. I told her what the matter was. I spared her husband not a word for her presence there. Yet he seemed hardly to understand. I told the pair that I had spoiled their cowardly joke for them. Broughton looked up.

' "I have smashed the foul thing into a hundred pieces," I said. Broughton licked his lips again and his mouth worked. "By God!" I shouted, "it would serve you right if I thrashed you within an inch of your life. I will take care that not a decent man or woman of my acquaintance ever speaks to you again. And there," I added, throwing the broken piece of the skull upon the floor beside his bed, "there is a souvenir for you, of your damned work tonight!"

'Broughton saw the bone and in a moment it was his turn to frighten me. He squealed like a hare caught in a trap. He screamed and screamed till Mrs Broughton, almost as bewildered as myself, held on to him and coaxed him like a child to be quiet. But Broughton – and as he moved I thought that ten minutes ago I perhaps looked as terribly ill as he did – thrust her from him and scrambled out of the bed on to the floor and still screaming put out his hand to the bone. It had blood on it from my hand. He paid no attention to me whatever. In truth I said nothing. This was a new turn indeed to the horrors of the evening. He rose from the floor with the bone in his hand and stood silent. He seemed to be listening. "Time, time, perhaps," he muttered, and almost at the same moment fell at full length on the carpet, cutting his head against the fender. The bone flew from his hand and came to rest near the door. I picked Broughton up, haggard and broken, with blood over his face. He whispered hoarsely and quickly, "Listen, listen!" We listened.

'After ten seconds' utter quiet, I seemed to hear something. I could not be sure, but at last there was no doubt. There was a quiet sound as of one moving along the passage. Little regular steps came towards us over the hard oak flooring. Broughton moved to where his wife sat, white and speechless, on the bed, and pressed her face into his shoulder.

'Then, the last thing that I could see as he turned the light out, he fell forward with his own head pressed into the pillow of the bed. Something in their company, something in their cowardice, helped me and I faced the open doorway of the room, which was outlined fairly clearly against the dimly lighted passage. I put out one hand and touched Mrs Broughton's shoulder in the darkness. But at the last moment I too failed. I sank on my knees and put my face in the bed. Only we all heard. The footsteps came to the door and there they stopped. The piece of bone was lying a yard inside the door. There was a rustle of moving stuff and the thing was in the room. Mrs Broughton was silent: I could hear Broughton's voice praying, muffled in the pillow: I was cursing my own cowardice. Then the steps moved out again on the oak boards of the passage and I heard the sounds dying away. In a flash of remorse I went to the door and looked out. At the end of the corridor I thought I saw something that moved away. A moment later the passage was empty. I stood with my forehead against the jamb of the door almost physically sick.

' "You can turn the light on," I said, and there was an answering flare. There was no bone at my feet. Mrs Broughton had fainted. Broughton was almost useless and it took me ten minutes to bring her to. Broughton only said one thing worth remembering. For the most part he went on muttering prayers. But I was glad afterwards to recollect that he had said that thing. He said in a colourless voice, half as a question, half as a reproach, "You didn't speak to her."

'We spent the remainder of the night together. Mrs Broughton

actually fell off into a kind of sleep before dawn, but she suffered so
horribly in her dreams that I shook her into consciousness again. Never
was dawn so long in coming. Three or four times Broughton spoke to
himself. Mrs Broughton would then just tighten her hold on his arm,
but she could say nothing. As for me, I can honestly say that I grew
worse as the hours passed and the light strengthened. The two violent
reactions had battered down my steadiness of view and I felt that the
foundations of my life had been built upon the sand. I said nothing and
after binding up my hand with a towel, I did not move. It was better so.
They helped me and I helped them and we all three knew that our
reason had gone very near to ruin that night. At last, when the light
came in pretty strongly and the birds outside were chattering and
singing, we felt that we must do something. Yet we never moved. You
might have thought that we should particularly dislike being found as
we were by the servants: yet nothing of that kind mattered a straw and
an overpowering listlessness bound us as we sat, until Chapman,
Broughton's man, actually knocked and opened the door. None of us
moved. Broughton, speaking hardly and stiffly, said, "Chapman you
can come back in five minutes." Chapman, was a discreet man, but it
would have made no difference to us if he had carried his news to the
"room" at once.

'We looked at each other and I said I must go back. I meant to wait
outside till Chapman returned. I simply dared not re-enter my
bedroom alone. Broughton roused himself and said that he would
come with me. Mrs Broughton agreed to remain in her own room for
five minutes if the blinds were drawn up and all the doors left open.

'So Broughton and I, leaning stiffly one against the other, went down
to my room. By the morning light that filtered past the blinds we could
see our way and I released the blinds. There was nothing wrong in the
room from end to end, except smears of my own blood on the end of
the bed, on the sofa and on the carpet where I had torn the thing to
pieces.'

Colvin had finished his story. There was nothing to say. Seven bells
stuttered out from the fo'c'sle and the answering cry wailed through
the darkness. I took him downstairs.

'Of course I am much better now, but it is a kindness of you to let me
sleep in your cabin.'

In the Cliff Land of the Dane

HOWARD PEASE

A letter to the Reverend Laurence Sterne at Coxwold from John Hall Stevenson at Skelton Castle, as set down by his nephew Freddy Hall.

THE TRUTH IS, reverend sir, that being eventually designed for the Bar, I had taken up this quest with an additional vigour, for here was a mystery wherein my Lord Chief-Justice himself would have had a difficulty in seeing the proper clue on't.

For some months previous to my sojourn at Skelton Castle there had been mysterious midnight thefts of sheep, heifers and suchlike cattle on the hills about here, Redcar, and Danby-way, and even on occasion a murder added, as in the case of poor Jack Moscrop, the shepherd, who was found in the early morning with his head cut in twain, as though by some mighty cleaver, stark dead and cold on the low-lying ground beyond Kirkleatham.

Much disquietude had been caused thereby amongst the farmer folk, and the whole countryside was agape with excitement and conjecture, but nothing had been discovered as to the malefactor, though many tales were told, more especially by the womenfolk, who put down all mishaps to the same unknown agent.

Some said 'twas a black man who had escaped off a foreign ship that had been stranded by Teesmouth, but in that case one would imagine that such an one would have eaten his victim raw, whereas the sheep and heifers that were killed had always been 'gralloched', as the Scotch term it, that is, had been cut open with a knife and disembowelled and the carcases removed.

Some again avowed 'twas an agent of the Prince of Darkness, for there were hoofmarks of an unshod horse discovered on one or two occasions leading up and away from the scene of the slaughter and blood drops alongside, as though the booty had been slung from the horse's quarters and there dripped down as he sped along.

Now as you may imagine, I too had battered my brain with various conjectures, but without practical result till one night after hunting all day and having lamed my mare badly with an overreach, I was returning slowly homeward by a short cut across Eston Nab, so as to strike the Guisboro' Road and thence straight to Skelton.

'Twas a stormy November night, time about nine o'clock, for I had stayed supper with a friendly yeoman, one Petch, of a noted family hereabout, and was trudging a-foot, so as to ease the mare, along the desolate hill-top, where in a kind of basin there lies a lonely pool of water, set round in the further side by a few draggled, wind-torn firs.

There was a swamped moon overhead, shining now and again as wreckage shows amongst billows, the gleam but momentary, so that when I caught sight of a kneeling figure across t'other side of the mere I could scarce distinguish anything at all, whether 'twere a boggart, as they say here, or some solitary shepherd seeking his sheep

However, at that moment there was a break overhead and the moon, rheumy-eyed, shook her head clear of cloud, whereby I saw plain enough 'twas a tall, burly man kneeling beside some object or other and a mighty big horse standing a bit to the rearward of him.

I drew nigher without being perceived, and the light still holding, saw that 'twas a young stirk or heifer the man was disembowelling.

'Ha, ha!' shouts I, without a further thought than that here was the midnight miscreant and cattle-stealer and that I had caught him red-handed.

With that he lifts his head and gazes across the pool at me fixedly for an instant of time, then with a whistle to his horse, leaps to his feet, vaults to the saddle and swings away at a hand gallop round the mere's edge, the moonlight flashing back from some big axe he was carrying in his right hand.

'Tally ho!' shouted I, commencing to run after him, bethinking me he was for escaping, but no sooner had he rounded the edge some hundred and fifty yards away than I saw 'twas he who was chasing me.

Another look at him tearing towards me was sufficient to change my resolution and hot foot I tore round to t'other end, trusting to win to the wood's edge before he could catch me up.

I heard the hard breathing of the horse close behind me, the crunch of his hoofs coming quicker and quicker; one fleeting glimpse I threw backward and saw a bright axe gleam above me, then my foot catching in a tussock, I sank headlong, the horse's hoofs striking me as I fell.

I must suppose – for at that moment the moon was swallowed again by a swirl of cloud – that in the changing light he had missed his blow, and finding myself unhurt, I was able to gain my feet, make a double and gain the wall's edge by the plantation before he had caught me up once more. Just as I vaulted over a crash of stones sounded, some loose ones at top grazing my foot as I touched the ground on the far side.

The wood, however, was pitch black, thick with unpruned trees; I bent double and dived deeper into its gloomy belly.

'Safe now,' thinks I, as utterly outdone I sank on a noiseless bed of pine-needles; and by the Lord Harry 'twas none too soon, for if it hadn't been for the kindly moon dipping I'd have been in two pieces by now. 'To Jupiter Optimus Maximus I owe an altar,' says I, in my first recovered breath, and, 'curse that infernal reiver,' says I in my second, 'but I'll be up ends with him yet.'

No sound came from without; all was still, save for the soughing in the pines overhead.

A quarter of an hour passed perhaps and I determined to creep to the wall and see if my assailant were anywhere visible.

The wind had freshened; the clouds were unravelling to its touch, and I could see clearly enough now across the desolate hill-top. Nothing living showed save my mare, who was cropping the coarse grass tufts just where I had left her.

Surmounting the wall, I approached the spot where I had seen the reiver first. There lay red remnants that clearly told a tale. The carcase, however, had been 'lifted' and I could trace the direction in which my raider had gone by the drops of blood that lay here and there by the side of the horse's track.

As the ground in places was soft with peat or bog, by a careful examination of the hoof marks of his horse, I was able to ascertain the direction in which he had gone, which seemed to be nearly due north-east or at least east by north. The marks proved another thing, moreover, and that is, that here was the same miscreant who had killed the shepherd and carried off the cattle elsewhere, for 'twas an unshod horse that had galloped over Eston Nab top that night.

'Twas sore-footed that I gained home at last, but all the way I discussed a many plans for the discovery and punishment of my moss-trooper.

'Tis an unpleasant remembrance to have fled; next time we met I swore to be in a better preparation for the encounter.

Next morning I started to explore, for I knew something of the direction. I knew also that my man was a tall, well-built, burly fellow with a big ruddy beard and the horse a fine seventeen-hands roan that would be known far and wide in the district.

Determining to stay out till I had discovered somewhat, I rode down to the low-lying ground between Boulby and Redcar, as being the

likeliest region to get news of horse or man and, sure enough, at the
second time of enquiry, I was informed at a farmhouse that some six
months ago Farmer Allison, away over by Stokesly, had lost a fine, big,
upstanding roan stallion, of which he had been inordinately proud.

Of the man, though, I could glean nothing, till finally, a good
housewife, overhearing her man and myself conversing, cried out, 'Eh!
but by my surely, there's that Red Tom o' the 'Fisherman's Rest', nigh
to Saltburn, that's new come there, who features him you speak of; but
he's nowt but a 'fondy', oaf-rocked, they say he is; why, Moll who
hawks t' fish about says his wife beats him an' maks him wash up t'
dishes – the man being a soart o' cholterhead by all accounts.'

However, 'fondy' or no, I was sworn to go and see for myself, though
the thought that 'twas perhaps a disguise the reiver had worn gave me
discomfort and made my quest seem foolish enough.

As I drew close to the little tavern above the cliff, I could hear a
dispute going on inside; then a crash as of some crockery falling and
shortly a big, burly man with an auburn beard came tumbling forth in
an awkward haste, pursued by the high tone of a woman's voice within.

Shaking his sleeve free of some water-drops, he sat down on a low
rock near hand and fell knitting at a stocking he proceeded to draw
from his jacket.

' 'Tis surely the man,' says I to myself, for in height, build, and
colour of hair, he seemed the fellow of the midnight raider, but yet it
seemed impossible; there might be a brother, however.

I rode up to him and asked if I could bait my horse and seek
refreshment within.

'Ay, sir, surely ye can; if ye'll dismount I'll tak your horse, sir, an' give
him a feed o' corn,' and shambling away he touched a greasy lock at me
as he led my horse to the stable behind.

I turned to the inn and encountered mine hostess, fuming within
the bar.

'Please draw me a pot of ale, ma'am,' says I, 'while my horse gets a
feed. Your good man, I suppose 'tis, who took him away outside?'

'Ay, he's mine, so says t' Church an' t' law, Aah b'lieve, but 'od rabbit
him, Aah says, who knaws the clumsiness o' the creature. Just fit for
nowt else but cuttin' up t' bait for t' harrin' fishin'.'

'Been here long?' says I further, carelessly.

'Six months mair or less,' says she with a snap, eyeing me suspiciously.

'Well, here's for luck and a smarter man at the next time of asking,'
and with that I tossed down the ale, paid the reckoning and strode out
to the stable, for nothing further was to be got out of the vinegar lips of
Mrs Boniface.

I looked narrowly round the low-roofed and ill-lit stable, but no sign of a big roan horse anywhere did I see, only a jack-spavined cob, such as a fishwife might hawk her fish about with.

'Ever seen or heard tell of that big roan of Farmer Allison's, strayed, stolen, or lost, about six months since?' so I accosted Boniface anew, on finding him rubbing down my horse's hocks with a bit of straw.

'Noah, sir, not Aah; Aah nevver seen 'im, sir. What soart o' a mak o' horse was 'e, sir?'

I looked him full in the face as question and answer passed and not a shred of intelligence could I detect in his opaque, fish-like eyes.

'Oaf-rocked', truly enough; he seemed as incapable of dissimulation as a stalled ox and with a heavy feeling of disappointment I enquired what was to pay and rode away down the slope.

'Curious,' I mused, 'how imagination plays one tricks at times! Once get the idea of a red beard into your mind and Barbarossa is as often met with as the robin redbreast.'

Then all in a moment my eye caught in the spongy bottom a thin mark cut clearly crescentwise upon the turf. There was something strangely familiar about the horseshoe curve. Then I remembered the unshod roan of the night before.

'Twas the same impress, for in neither case was there any trace of the iron rim. 'Where the horse is the rider will not be far away,' thinks I, and hope kindled afresh in my heart, as I rode slowly on, resolving various conjectures.

I determined finally to go call upon the farmer at Kirkleatham, whose heifer it was, as I had learnt, that had been killed and carried off the night before.

He was said to be tightfisted, so probably would be in a mood for revenge and ready enough to join in any scheme for discovery of the reiver.

As luck had it, Farmer Johnson was within doors and in a fine taking about the loss of his beast: he was ready to swear an oath that he wouldn't rest till he had caught the malefactor and agreed upon the instant to watch out every night in the week with me round about the Fisherman's Rest on chance of coming across the suspect either going or returning.

'Ay, Aah'll gan mahself, an' Aah'll tak feyther's owd gun wi' me there, for Ah'll stan' none o' his reiver tricks, an' Tom and Jack, they 'll come along too, an' 'od burn him, but we'll nab him betwixt us, the impudent scoundrel, if it's a leevin' man he is.'

By eight o'clock we four had ensconced ourselves in hiding-places on all sides of the little inn, having tethered our horses within a small but thick-grown covert above the rise that led to the inn door. Here I stationed myself and for better vision climbed a tree wherefrom I commanded the whole situation. The others hid themselves as they found shelter convenient, one below the cliff's edge some two hundred yards to the east, another amongst broken boulders to the southward, while Farmer Johnson crouched behind the wall that girt the road leading past the ale-house from the north.

'Twas weary work watching, more by token that that night nothing appeared save a thirsty fisherman or two and a stray, shuffle-footed vagrant or the like.

Next night the same and I for one was growing somewhat cold, but Farmer Johnson, bull-like in his obstinacy, swore he wouldn't shave his chin till he had 'caught summat', so off we started on the third night to our rendezvous.

'The third time brings luck,' thought I, as I squatted down in the fork of the same old twisted elm; 'and 'tis something stormy this evening, which might suit our reiver's tastes.'

It would then be about eight of the clock, as I may suppose, the wind from the seaward, the clouds lowering, fringed with a moonlight border like broidery on a cloak, and that raw, cold touch in the air that chills worse than the hardest winter's frost.

The night grew stormier; vapour lifted upward and assumed strange and threatening shape. The cloud forms might be the giants rising up out of Jotunheim and advancing to attack Odin and the Aesir – the evil wolf Fenrir in the van – his bristles silvered by the moon.

An hour passed and I began to wish I had never undertaken the quest or mentioned the matter to Farmer Johnson, when I heard, as if some way off, not exactly a neigh, but a sort of defiant snorting, such as a stallion breathes forth when he wishes to be free. Then a sound as of a heavy stone falling succeeded, mingled with a scraping and a trampling noise.

Craning my neck forward, I saw under a broadened fringe of moonlight the roan horse with the ruddy-bearded reiver beside him. They had evidently crept through some secret passage that issued into the bottom below me.

I was just upon the point of raising the hue and cry on him when an action of his took me by surprise.

Holding up his battle-axe – for such was his weapon – he raised it aloft, then thrust its handle deep into the soft moss of the hollow. Next, he threw the horse's reins over the head of it and sinking down upon his knees, appeared to be pouring forth a prayer to heaven, expressed in old Danish, which I have set down in English as nearly as I can:

Vafoder, the swiftness of Sleipnir
Breathe Thou into my roan.
Let him fly like Thy ravens,
Black Munin and Hugi.
May my axe be as Thor's,
When he wieldeth Miolnir,
Winged Thor's mighty weapon,
The pride of Valhalla.
This grant me, O Odin,
Grim, Ygg and All Father.

He then drew forth from his breast a small phial and having set up a square stone beside him poured forth into the cup or hollow at the top liquid of a dark colour, which I imagined must be either blood or wine. This done, he seemed to fall to prayer afresh, but in so low a tone that I could not catch the words of his utterance with any distinctness.

Then he leapt to his feet, lifted the axe, tossed it into the air, caught it as it fell and had vaulted upon the stallion's back before I had even recovered from my first astonishment.

'Tally-ho!' shouts I, 'yonder he goes; forward Mr Johnson! forrard Tom and Jack!' and, scrambling down my tree, I made for my horse.

The next thing I heard was a 'pang', evidently the discharge of Farmer Johnson's musket, and thereat a weird, smothered, savage note of pain and rage broke out upon the night.

Seizing my horse I mounted and rode out of the covert across a gap in the wall. Dimly I could see a centaur-like figure plunging and snorting upon the short turf by the cliff's edge, then three figures running from the north, south and east towards it.

The roan horse plunged and reared like one demented; the rider sitting the while firm and supple as an Indian; then, seizing on a sudden the bit 'twixt his teeth, off set the stallion at a tearing gallop southward.

Away I followed hotly, the others giving chase and halloaing in the background.

Dyke after dyke we flew headlong in the grey-white mist – the space still even betwixt us – then, at a sudden high dry-stone wall, which loomed up as a wave of darkness seaward, my horse jumped short and down we fell together on the turf beyond.

As I lay there for a moment or two, I was certain I heard a heavy rumbling of rock or stone by the cliff edge hard by, followed by a deep plunge far below into the sea.

I rose to my feet and looked around me. There was no sign of horse or rider; both had disappeared.

The cliff here made a sudden bend inland, so that I could even catch the come and go of the waves in the far void below and I felt 'twas lucky for me that I had been riding the nethermost line of the twain of us.

Cautiously approaching the edge, I noticed it had been just broken away under the tramplings of a horse and as I peeped over I caught sight of an indistinct figure lying on a broad slab of rock below that jutted out some way from the cliff.

Feeling carefully around for support of root or stone, I made my way down and discovered, as I had already conjectured, 'twas the reiver that lay there.

He was lying motionless, spread on his back, and was murmuring to himself as I drew close.

I knelt beside him to lift him up and could catch, as I tried to raise him, what he was saying.

'Whisht ye, then, whisht, Effie, Aah never meant to break t' dish, Aah tell thee. Leave us aloan, then, lass, doan't plague t' life out of a man. Ay, Aah'll fetch t' coo in i' guid time, there's no call t' bang us that gait.'

Then he babbled indistinctly; his lips grew whiter and ceased from moving; and when the others had come up I think he was already dead.

As I rode off for the physician in Redcar, I minded me I had once read in a book, reverend sir, that this same Cleveland was once 'the Cliff-Land of the Danes', and that the older name of Roseberry Topping – the famous hill of these parts – was Othenesberg, or Odin's Hill, together with much else of an antiquarian interest and varied conjecture, which I must even leave to wiser heads than mine to determine the true issues of, as well as their bearing upon the events just narrated, but this I may say, that here is the same 'crazy tale' my cousin mentioned to you, set down in all true verisimilitude by, reverend sir, your very faithful and humble servant to command,

FREDDY HALL

Laura

SAKI (H. H. MUNRO) 1870–1916

'You aren't really dying, are you?' asked Amanda.

'I have the doctor's permission to live till Tuesday,' said Laura.

'But today is Saturday; this is serious!' gasped Amanda.

'I don't know about it being serious; it is certainly Saturday,' said Laura.

'Death is always serious,' said Amanda.

'I never said I was going to die. I am presumably going to leave off being Laura, but I shall go on being something. An animal of some kind, I suppose. You see, when one hasn't been very good in the life one has just lived, one reincarnates in some lower organism. And I haven't been very good, when one comes to think of it. I've been petty and mean and vindictive and all that sort of thing when circumstances have seemed to warrant it.'

'Circumstances never warrant that sort of thing,' said Amanda hastily.

'If you don't mind my saying so,' observed Laura, 'Egbert is a circumstance that would warrant any amount of that sort of thing. You're married to him – that's different; you've sworn to love, honour, and endure him: I haven't.'

'I don't see what's wrong with Egbert,' protested Amanda.

'Oh, I dare say the wrongness has been on my part,' admitted Laura dispassionately; 'he has merely been the extenuating circumstance. He made a thin, peevish kind of fuss, for instance, when I took the collie puppies from the farm out for a run the other day.'

'They chased his young broods of speckled Sussex and drove two sitting hens off their nests, besides running all over the flower beds. You know how devoted he is to his poultry and garden.'

'Anyhow, he needn't have gone on about it for the entire evening and then have said, "Let's say no more about it," just when I was beginning to enjoy the discussion. That's where one of my petty vindictive revenges came in,' added Laura with an unrepentant chuckle; 'I turned the entire family of speckled Sussex into his seedling shed the day after the puppy episode.'

'How could you?' exclaimed Amanda.

'It came quite easy,' said Laura; 'two of the hens pretended to be laying at the time, but I was firm.'

'And we thought it was an accident!'

'You see,' resumed Laura, 'I really have some grounds for supposing that my next incarnation will be in a lower organism. I shall be an animal of some kind. On the other hand, I haven't been a bad sort in my way, so I think I may count on being a nice animal, something elegant and lively, with a love of fun. An otter, perhaps.'

'I can't imagine you as an otter,' said Amanda.

'Well, I don't suppose you can imagine me as an angel, if it comes to that,' said Laura.

Amanda was silent. She couldn't.

'Personally I think an otter life would be rather enjoyable,' continued Laura; 'salmon to eat all the year around and the satisfaction of being able to fetch the trout in their own homes without having to wait for hours till they condescend to rise to the fly you've been dangling before them; and an elegant svelte figure – '

'Think of the otter hounds,' interposed Amanda, 'how dreadful to be hunted and harried and finally worried to death!'

'Rather fun with half the neighbourhood looking on, and anyhow not worse than this Saturday-to-Tuesday business of dying by inches; and then I should go on into something else. If I had been a moderately good otter I suppose I should get back into human shape of some sort; probably something rather primitive – a little brown, unclothed Nubian boy, I should think.'

'I wish you would be serious,' sighed Amanda; 'you really ought to be if you're only going to live till Tuesday.'

As a matter of fact Laura died on Monday.

'So dreadfully upsetting,' Amanda complained to her uncle-in-law, Sir Lulworth Quayne. 'I've asked quite a lot of people down for golf and fishing and the rhododendrons are just looking their best.'

'Laura always was inconsiderate,' said Sir Lulworth; 'she was born during Goodwood week, with an Ambassador staying in the house who hated babies.'

'She had the maddest kind of ideas,' said Amanda; 'do you know if there was any insanity in her family?'

'Insanity? No, I never heard of any. Her father lives in West Kensington, but I believe he's sane on all other subjects.'

'She had an idea that she was going to be reincarnated as an otter,' said Amanda.

'One meets with those ideas of reincarnation so frequently, even in the West,' said Sir Lulworth, 'that one can hardly set them down as being mad. And Laura was such an unaccountable person in this life that I should not like to lay down definite rules as to what she might be doing in an after state.'

'You think she really might have passed into some animal form?' asked Amanda. She was one of those who shape their opinions rather readily from the standpoint of those around them.

Just then Egbert entered the breakfast-room, wearing an air of bereavement that Laura's demise would have been insufficient, in itself, to account for.

'Four of my speckled Sussex have been killed,' he exclaimed; 'the very four that were to go to the show on Friday. One of them was dragged away and eaten right in the middle of that new carnation bed that I've been to such trouble and expense over. My best flower bed and my best fowls singled out for destruction; it almost seems as if the brute that did the deed had special knowledge how to be as devastating as possible in a short space of time.'

'Was it a fox, do you think?' asked Amanda.

'Sounds more like a polecat,' said Sir Lulworth.

'No,' said Egbert, 'there were marks of webbed feet all over the place, and we followed the tracks down to the stream at the bottom of the garden; evidently an otter.'

Amanda looked quickly and furtively across at Sir Lulworth.

Egbert was too agitated to eat any breakfast and went out to superintend the strengthening of the poultry yard defences.

'I think she might at least have waited till the funeral was over,' said Amanda in a scandalised voice.

'It's her own funeral, you know,' said Sir Lulworth; 'it's a nice point in etiquette how far one ought to show respect to one's own mortal remains.'

Disregard for mortuary convention was carried to further lengths next day; during the absence of the family at the funeral ceremony the remaining survivors of the speckled Sussex were massacred. The marauder's line of retreat seemed to have embraced most of the flower beds on the lawn, but the strawberry beds in the lower garden had also suffered.

'I shall get the otter hounds to come here at the earliest possible moment,' said Egbert savagely.

'On no account! You can't dream of such a thing!' exclaimed Amanda. 'I mean, it wouldn't do, so soon after a funeral in the house.'

'It's a case of necessity,' said Egbert; 'once an otter takes to that sort of thing it won't stop.'

'Perhaps it will go elsewhere now that there are no more fowls left,' suggested Amanda.

'One would think you wanted to shield the beast,' said Egbert.

'There's been so little water in the stream lately,' objected Amanda; 'it seems hardly sporting to hunt an animal when it has so little chance of taking refuge anywhere.'

'Good gracious!' fumed Egbert, 'I'm not thinking about sport. I want to have the animal killed as soon as possible.'

Even Amanda's opposition weakened when, during church time on the following Sunday, the otter made its way into the house, raided half a salmon from the larder and worried it into scaly fragments on the Persian rug in Egbert's studio.

'We shall have it hiding under our beds and biting pieces out of our feet before long,' said Egbert, and from what Amanda knew of this particular otter she felt that the possibility was not a remote one.

On the evening preceding the day fixed for the hunt Amanda spent a solitary hour walking by the banks of the stream, making what she imagined to be hound noises. It was charitably supposed by those who overheard her performance, that she was practising for farmyard imitations at the forthcoming village entertainment.

It was her friend and neighbour, Aurora Burret, who brought her news of the day's sport.

'Pity you weren't out; we had quite a good day. We found it at once, in the pool just below your garden.'

'Did you – kill?' asked Amanda.

'Rather. A fine she-otter. Your husband got rather badly bitten in trying to "tail it". Poor beast, I felt quite sorry for it, it had such a human look in its eyes when it was killed. You'll call me silly, but do you know who the look reminded me of? My dear woman, what is the matter?'

When Amanda had recovered to a certain extent from her attack of nervous prostration Egbert took her to the Nile Valley to recuperate. Change of scene speedily brought about the desired recovery of health and mental balance. The escapades of an adventurous otter in search of a variation of diet were viewed in their proper light. Amanda's normally placid temperament reasserted itself. Even a hurricane of shouted curses, coming from her husband's dressing-room, in her husband's voice, but hardly in his usual vocabulary, failed to disturb her serenity as she made a leisurely toilet one evening in a Cairo hotel.

'What is the matter? What has happened?' she asked in amused curiosity.

'The little beast has thrown all my clean shirts into the bath! Wait till

I catch you, you little – '

'What little beast?' asked Amanda, suppressing a desire to laugh; Egbert's language was so hopelessly inadequate to express his outraged feelings.

'A little beast of a naked brown Nubian boy,' spluttered Egbert.

And now Amanda is seriously ill.

APPENDIX

Three True Ghost Stories

The Story of Euphemia Hewit

JAMES HOGG, the Ettrick Shepherd, 1770–1835

This comes from 'Anecdotes of Ghosts and Apparitions'
published in the January 1835 issue of *Fraser's Magazine*.

MR DAVID HUNTER, only son to the farmer of Clun-keigh, once told
me one of the strangest stories I ever heard, though many I have
dragged together. He said that he went to court a very dear and lovely
girl, Phemie Hewit, and spent about three hours with her in the
fondest endearment; kissed her, shook hands and left her about two
o'clock on a winter morning. He said he was sometimes whistling a
tune to himself – for, like me, he sawed a good deal on the fiddle; but
he was all the way thinking and thinking of Phemie and whether he
would take her home to his father's house or get a cottage of his own
built on the farm; when, behold! after he was almost close to his
father's house and had walked about three miles and a half, he met with
Phemie coming leisurely to meet him, with her gown-skirt drawn over
her lovely chestnut locks, as she always had when she went out to the
courting.

'Mercy on us, Phemie!' exclaimed he, 'but ye surely are keen o' the
courting the night, when ye're come a' the gate here for another brash
at it.'

'I forgot two things,' said she; 'and as I kenned we were never to
meet again, I coudna part wi' you without telling you: in the first place,
you are never to gang back to Auchenvew again to the courting; for
things are no a' right there.'

'What's wrang about Auchenvew, Phemie?'

'O your Margaret's no just as she should be, poor woman; an' I'm
very sorry for her; but ye maunna gang back again, else ye're sure to get
o'er the fingers' ends.'

'Now, Phemie, that's sheer jealousy, for which I am sure you have
little reason.'

'O, I dare say you gaed for her for an hour or twa's diversion; but you
did gang; and mind you're no to do it again.'

'Weel, my dear woman, I gie you my word o' honour that I never shall gang back to the courting again. But, Phemie, what was it you said about us never meeting again?'

'O, yes, we'll meet again; but I'll be dead before then! and my principal errand here this morning was to get your blessing; for when you kissed me and parted with me, you did not say "God bless you, Phemie!" which you never neglected before since ever we met. Now, I could not part with you without your blessing.'

'I dinna understand you this morning, Phemie. We are never to meet again. And you are to be dead before we meet again. What is the meaning of all this? Remember you are engaged to meet me on the 7th of next month at the easternmost tree of the Grennan Wood.'

'Well, I'll meet you there.'

'Well, God bless you, my dear girl; and I'm sure I give that blessing with all my heart and soul.'

David stretched out his hand to seize hers, to draw her to him and kiss her. There was no hand and no Phemie there! He wheeled round and round and called her name. 'Phemie! Phemie Hewit! My dear woman, what's come o' you or where are ye?' But he ran with all his speed and called in vain; there was no Phemie to be seen nor heard. He stood in breathless astonishment, recommending himself to all the blessed trinity and then saying audibly, 'The mercy and grace of heaven be around me! Is it possible that I have seen my dear Phemie's wraith? No, it is impossible; for it looked and spoke so like her sweet self – it could not be a sprit. But there was something very mysterious about her this morning, in following me so far; nay, in outwalking me, meeting me and uttering the words she did. But it was herself, there is no doubt of it; and she has given me the slip in a most unaccountable manner.'

David went home, and awakened his youngest sister, Mary, who gave him something to drink; but he could not speak an intelligible sentence to her and she thought he was either drunk or very ill and sat up with him till day. He slept none, but sighed, moaned and turned himself in the bed; and he continued thoughtful and ill for several days; but at length he arose and went about his father's business. This visionary courting night was on the 28th of January or February. I have forgot which; and the lovers were engaged to meet on the 7th of the next month at their trysting tree.

Now the families of the two lovers were not on very good terms; they were, I believe, rather adverse to one another. They were of different tenets in religion and never met either at church or in society. But the only son of the one family fell in love with the youngest daughter of the other at a Thornhill fair, trysted her to meet him, courted her and won her affections and they engaged themselves to one another. They were a very amiable pair and I knew them both very well, David was a handsome, stout fellow, upwards of six feet high, and Phemie a gentle, mild-looking creature, with a face something what one would suppose an angel's to be, but rather pale-looking and apparently not long for this world. She was, nevertheless, lively, witty and good-humoured and had a most affectionate and benevolent heart.

Well, the 7th of the month came and David attended punctually at the hour. He had not sat a minute and a half until Phemie came, with the skirt of her frock round her head, as usual.

'Come away, Phemie! you are true to your word as ever,' said he.

'Yes, you see I have come as I promised; for I would not break my tryste with you; but I have very short time to stay.'

'Well, come and sit under my plaid, for the time that you have to stay, my dear lassie, and let me caress you; for I have had heavy thoughts and sad misgivings about you since I last saw you.'

'No, I cannot come under your plaid, nor court tonight, for reasons that you will soon come to know. But I came principally to inform you that you are not to come back to court me till I send you word or come and tell you myself: yes, I think I'll come and tell you myself and then you are safe to come.'

'You cannot come under my plaid? I must not come to court you again until you come and tell me to do so? Will you really come and tell me that I must come and woo you, Phemie? Phemie, my dear! there is a mystery about you of late which I cannot comprehend.'

David was looking down to the ground at this moment, pondering on the words of his beloved; and when he looked up again he saw Phemie gliding away from him. He sprang to his feet and pursued her, calling her name in a sort of loud whisper; but she continued to fly on; and, though very near, he could not overtake her till she entered the minister's house by the back gate that led through the kirkyard. David's eyes were opened; he saw at once that the elegant and genteel minister had seduced his sweetheart's affections; and he now conceived that he understood all her demeanour and everything she had said to him. So he rushed into the kitchen: there were two servant-girls in it and he asked them, with a voice of fury, where Phemie was.

Now, I must tell, that this parson had got a bad word with some young ladies, both married and unmarried; and though for my part I never believed a word of it, yet the report spread, which weaned the parson's congregation from him, all save a few gentlemen who came to dine at the manse every Sunday. David was perfectly enraged; for he perceived his road straight before him.

'Where is Phemie?' cried he.

'What Phemie?' said the one girl; 'What Phemie?' said the other.

'Why Phemie Hewit,' cried he fiercely. 'I know how matters are going on; so you need not make any of your confounded pretences of ignorance to me! I followed her in here this minute; so tell me instantly where she is or bring your master to answer to me.'

'Phemie Hewit!' said the one girl; 'Phemie Hewit!' said the other. And with that one of them (Sarah Robson) ran ben to the minister and said, 'For God's sake, sir, come butt an' speak to Mr David Hunter; he is come in raving mad and asking for Phemie Hewit and seems to think that you have her concealed in the house.'

Mr Nevison, with all his usual suavity of manners, came into the kitchen, asked Mr Hunter how he was and how his father and sisters were.

'I'm no that ill, sir; I hae nae grit reason to complain o' onything or onybody excepting you. Where is my sweetheart, sir? I followed her in here this minute and if ye dinna gie her up to me I'll burn the house aboon your head!'

'Your sweetheart, Mr David? Whom do you mean. Is it one of my servant-girls; for there is no other woman in the house, to my knowledge?'

'No, sir, it is Phemie Hewit that I want – my own Phemie Hewit – my betrothed! I followed her in here at your back gate this instant and I insist on seeing her.'

'Phemie Hewit!' exclaimed the two servant-girls; 'Phemie Hewit!' exclaimed the minister. 'My dear sir, you are raving and out of your senses; there was but one Phemie Hewit whom I knew in all this country, the merchant's daughter of Thornhill, and she is dead and was buried here, within six paces of the back of my house, the day before yesterday.'

'Come now, sir, that is a hoax to get me off,' cried David, in a loud tone, betwixt laughing and crying. 'That winna do; tell me the truth at aince. That is ower serious a matter to joke on; therefore, for the sake of heaven and this poor heart, tell me the real truth.'

'I tell you the real truth, Mr Hunter. I was at her funeral myself and laid her left shoulder into the grave and saw engraved in gold letters on the coffin-lid, "Euphemia Hewit, aged 22".'

David's whole frame grew rigid, his hands and his eyes turned up convulsively; and, after uttering a few internal groans, or rather shrieks, he fell backward in a swoon. They carried him to bed and he soon came again to his senses; but the distress of his mind was deplorable.

He lay at the manse for nearly three weeks; and though the minister administered every anodyne to him that he possessed or could procure, his patient remained in a very precarious and unsettled state and continued to exclaim, every day, 'O, had I been but warned of it! to have watched by her dying bed and received her parting blessing and her parting breath between my lips and to have laid her head in an honoured grave, I would have been satisfied! But to be parted thus! O, my beloved Phemie, would to God I had died for thee! O my Phemie, my Phemie!'

We had some fine curling on the ice after this, therefore I think it must have been about the end of February; and we were all astonished to find that our friend David, one of the best and strongest curlers of us all, never appeared on the ice. So one evening I went that way to take my tea with the family and see what was the matter; for he and I were great cronies and talked much about religion and the Scriptures and sometimes about the lasses, but not often. But he had a strong attachment to me and said one day, before all the club, that there was nothing in the world he would court independence so much for as to keep me independent.

I found him pale and emaciated, sitting in the kitchen, with his plaid about him. He took no tea; he ate not a bite of bread; he spoke not a word. My blood ran chill to my heart; for he was a good lad and I loved him.

As we were going into the parlour for our tea, his sister Margaret took me aside and said, 'I am very glad that you have come tonight; for we are perplexed about Davie. Something extraordinary seems to have happened to him; but we know nothing and he is continually speaking about you. See if you can find out what it is that distresses him.'

'He is sadly changed, indeed, for the worse,' said I; 'and I am very much alarmed about him. He is too retired and too thoughtful. Could you not persuade Jane Wilson or Nancy M'Turk or Jane Armstrong, to come over and stay with you for awhile? I have seen each of these put him into high glee and good humour.'

'He would not once look or speak to any of them,' said she. 'His spirits are broken and I am afraid he is not long for this world.'

'For God's sake, do not say so, Miss Margaret,' said I. 'But I am sure he will open his mind to me.'

He set me on my way as far as the limits of his father's farm that night and related the above narrative, adding, 'She has, you see, promised to call on me again and inform me when I am to meet her; and do you not think that when that happens it will be a warning for me to prepare for leaving this world?'

'Yes I do, David,' said I. 'After what has already happened, in such a mysterious way, between you and your beloved, I believe that when your Phemie comes and gives you this intimation, even in a dream, it will be a death-warning to you and that you must prepare to meet her in another and a better world.'

'O no, no, not in a dream,' said he; 'she is with me in every dream, evening, midnight and morning. I see her, I caress her, kiss her and bless her, without ever once recollecting that the grave separates us. O no, not in a dream! I shall see her face to face and speak to her as a man speaketh to his friend; and when that happens, if it should ever happen, I shall send you word.'

This was at the laight gate. So we shook hands and parted; for I durst not let him stand longer in the cold. But he continued to grow worse and worse, until one morning, about the beginning of May, a servant came posting me on horseback and requested me to go and see Mr David Hunter, who was very poorly and wished particularly to see me. I obeyed the summons with alacrity and found him in bed, very low indeed.

He desired his two sisters to go out and then, taking my hand, he said, 'Now, my dear friend, my time is come – the time which I have long desired. I have seen my Phemie again today.'

'But only in a dream, David, I am sure. Consider yourself; only in a dream.'

'No, I was wide awake and sensible as at this moment while speaking to you. The door was standing open, to give me air. I was all alone, which you know I choose mostly to be, for prayer and meditation, when in glided my Phemie, with the train of her grey frock drawn over her lovely locks. I had no thought, no remembrance that she was dead. It was impossible to think so; for her smile was so sweet, so heavenly, even more beatific than I had ever seen it and her complexion was that of the pale rose. She threw her locks back from each cheek with her left hand and said, "You see I have come to invite you as I promised, David. Are you ready to meet me tonight at our trysting tree and at the usual hour."

' "I am afraid, my beloved Phemie, that I shall scarcely be able to attend," said I.

' "Yes, but you will," said she, "and you must not disappoint me, for I will await your arrival." And with a graceful curtsy and a smile she retired, saying, as she left the room, "God be with you till then, David." '

This narrative quite confounded me. It was a long time before I could either act or think. At length I sat down on his bedside and took his hand in mine; it was worn to the hand of a skeleton. I felt his pulse; that strong and manly pulse had dwindled into a mere shiver, with an interval every seven or eight strokes. I easily perceived that it was all over with him.

'How do you think my pulse is?' said he.

'The pulse is not amiss,' said I; 'but you may depend on Phemie's word. You will meet her tonight at the trysting-hour, I have no doubt of it. When is your trysting-hour, for I think you may rely on Phemie's word?'

'O yes, O yes!' said he. 'Phemie never told a lie in her life and it would be absurd to think she would do it now. Let me have your prayers, my dear friend, let me have your prayers to take with me and I will trust my Redeemer for the rest!'

These were the last words he uttered in this life and he uttered them with a creaking voice perfectly sepulchral. I called in his father and his two sisters and told them that David was dying, and that I wished, by his own desire, to pray with him before parting with him for ever. His sisters were like to burst their hearts with crying; but the old father seemed perfectly resigned. I sung the fifth verse of the thirty-first psalm – I remember it well; and read about the latter half of the fifteenth chapter of the 1st of Corinthians; and if I did not pray eloquently, I am sure I did fervently. When I had done, he seized my hand feebly and held it, until death loosed his grasp; for the trysting-hour was fast approaching; and whether he longed for it or wished to remain a little longer in this to him miserable state of existence, I cannot tell; but he turned his eye frequently to the clock that stood right opposite to his bed and exactly at the trysting-hour he expired. The two young lovers were virtuous and lovely in their lives and in their deaths they were but shortly divided.

A Ghostly Manifestation

A Clergyman

This story by an anonymous clergyman appeared in the
July 1884 issue of *Murray's Magazine*. Included also is a
comment from a later issue by the Honorary Secretary
of the Society for Psychical Research.

BEFORE I TELL MY STORY it will be well for me to make it perfectly
clear that it is a perfectly true one. As a lad and as a young man, neither
ghosts nor the idea of ghosts ever troubled me. I heard strange stories
of them, told with all the vivid description which would tend to
frighten sleep away – told too when the wind was howling outside, the
rain pattering against the windows and the only light visible that which
found its way through the chinks in the shutters to the 'pitch-dark'
outside – told when everybody was ready for bed. But they never
disturbed my slumbers. I could listen to any number of them at any
time and they never had any effect on me. In fact I disbelieved them
thoroughly and though I could not doubt the veracity of the narrator, I
always regarded them as the outcome of a strong imagination or the
result of too heavy and too late dinners. A white tombstone in a
churchyard did not frighten me on a very dark night, nor did the
mysterious movements of a donkey which had broken into it, cause me
to start, as he moved in the darkness in and out amongst the graves. So
that I was thoroughly unprepared for anything like a personal experience and considered myself one of the last persons likely to be affected
by anything like a ghostly manifestation.

But now to my story, which I shall tell simply, as the affair took place,
leaving it to the reader to draw his or her own conclusion.

And to make it quite intelligible I must explain the accompanying
ground-plan of the house where it happened. The house itself was a
large one, built of brick, and was what is called a 'flat'; that is, it had no
regular upstairs rooms, though over the ceiling there was a great deal of
room under the roof; and the lower inside walls had been carried up to
the roof to support it, a doorway being made to get from one part to
the other. The walls were thick and the doors and windows were made

of heavy hard wood. There was not a pane of glass in the house and both doors and windows – except two doors, of which more presently – were fastened by unusually strong iron bolts. My wife and I – for my wife was with me and shared all my experiences – always entered the house by the big doorway leading into the large semicircular porch, where our palanquins were kept. Passing on, we came to the passage. Going along this, we came first of all to the door on our left hand, opening into the dining-room. On our right, directly opposite this dining-room door, was another door at the foot of a circular staircase, in the thick wall leading up to the empty spaces under the roof. Straight in front of us was the door leading into the great central reception-room, which contained no furniture except an armoire, a table and a few chairs. There was a large front door to this room, but it was seldom open and we rarely used it, our visitors coming mostly through the porch and passage. Going further on, we came to our bedroom, which contained only our bed, a travelling chest of drawers, which served as a dressing-table, a wash-stand and one or two chairs. Leading out from this was another room which we did not use, simply because we did not need it.

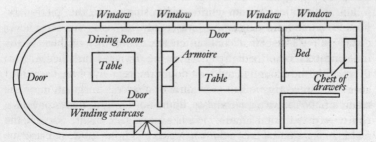

Ground Plan of House

And now I must call your attention to our bedroom door. It was made of wood, the lower half being panelled, but the upper half was fitted with framework to receive panes of glass which had not yet been inserted. The door had neither lock nor bolt. There was only an iron ring, hanging loosely, by which the door could be pulled to. But it could not be closed, for at the bottom, close to the side on which the hinges worked, it caught against the sill, which had not been suffi-ciently planed away to allow the door to shut properly, and so it was always ajar and could very easily be shaken backwards and forwards, as it stuck on the place where it caught; and in shaking, the iron ring, to which I have referred, clattered against the door, making a great noise in a more or less empty large house. The door was like this:

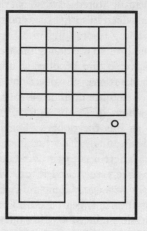

The only remark I have to make about the other door, leading up into the spiral staircase, is, that it opened outwards, and was simply fastened by an ordinary door-latch.

The affair of which I am writing took place on a large island in the East, far away from England – in a country full of ghost stories and equally full of a belief in all kinds of ghostly manifestations. I had heard, but had taken no notice of them. The native town to which we had gone in search of health contained very few foreigners and fewer acquaintances; consequently we had to 'shift for ourselves', and with the small amount of luggage we took with us, found our home in this large house, which we rented from a native. We liked it; the air was fresh, very pure and bracing; medical help was at hand and with our cook and servants and my pupils we settled in; the house was surrounded by its own grounds and the kitchen, as usual, stood away by itself.

We were simply on a visit: we did not burden ourselves with unnecessary furniture, but were content with buying what few things we needed and servants and pupils did not add much to our burden, for during the day they were all engaged in one way or another and, provided they had a fairly comfortable mat or mattress on which to lie, did not care very much *where* they slept. Cook, a swarthy son of Madras, guarded his kitchen and cooking utensils at night; my pupils curled up on their mattresses upstairs, in the 'room' at the top of the spiral staircase under the roof; and my wife's maid slept under the dining-room table on her mattress, which was removed every morning the first thing and brought in the last thing at night. I always saw them all safely in the house, and go each to his or her own apartment, before retiring myself, and made it my nightly practice to see that all the doors and windows were securely bolted – for we did not care to lose the few things we had with us, which in such a far distant place could not easily be replaced.

The few days we had been in the house had passed pleasantly and the nights undisturbed, save by the howling of dogs outside, when one night our pupils were later than usual in coming in to retire for the night. I went to look after them and found them and the maid all gathered round the bright fire in the kitchen, busy in amusing and interesting conversation. Their eyes were glistening in the firelight and their laugh was very hearty.

'Come boys,' I said, 'it is time for you to be going to rest now. And you,' to the maid, 'bring in your mattress, for it is night.'

Immediately there was a dead silence. The laughter was hushed: gloomy countenances at once appeared and a kind of furtive enquiring glance was cast from one to the other. Not one of them attempted to move, except the maid. I may here say that the boys' ages ranged from about ten years to fourteen.

'Come, boys!' I repeated, 'come along; it's time for going to rest now: why do you wait?'

Still there was no answer.

'Are you not tired?' I enquired.

Then one vouchsafed an answer.

'Please, sir, we are afraid to go!' he said in a trembling voice.

'Afraid, my boy!' I exclaimed in surprise, 'afraid of what? There is nothing and nobody here to harm you: what are you afraid of?'

'They are afraid, sir!' chimed in the maid.

'Afraid of what?' I again demanded. 'Have you seen any thieves about?'

'No, sir,' she replied; 'but they are afraid to go;' and that was all I could get out of her.

'Come along, boys! and don't be mere children,' I said to encourage them; 'the light is ready for you and the house will be safely fastened up as usual.'

'True, sir,' said one of them, John by name; 'but we are afraid. Last night – '

'What?' I enquired in wonder.

'Last night, sir,' he went on to say, 'there were fearful noises upstairs where we sleep. We heard men fighting and we trembled – '

'Nonsense!' I cried. 'Cook, what did you give the boys for their supper last night?'

'Only beef and rice, sahib,' he replied; 'the same as they always have.'

'And no more? nothing else?'

'No, sahib.'

'Then you boys were dreaming or heard the rats. *I* heard nothing and saw nothing. So come along!'

I went into the house and they followed me. On reaching the door at the foot of the spiral staircase I gave them their lantern (not an open candle, for fear of fire) and one of them again exclaimed –

'We are afraid, sir! we cannot sleep up there.'

'Nonsense, boys!' I replied firmly; 'there is nothing there worse than yourselves! I am down below and the maid sleeps in the dining-room right under you; there is nothing to cause fear, so go along.'

Without another word they took the lantern and filed off upstairs. When the last had gone I carefully latched the door, saw the maid into her sleeping quarters under the dining-room table, examined all the bolts as usual and went off to bed.

I told my wife what had happened and she put it down to nightmare on the boys' part. However it passed out of our heads. We always kept a light burning in our room at night – a small hand paraffin lamp. This was kept on the chest of drawers against the wall opposite the foot of the bed. In course of time I turned it down very low and got into bed, with my head as usual quite close to the door. It was a small room, rather, and the bed came almost up to the frame of the door. Meantime, I had, of course, pulled the door to, as far as it would go, but could not actually close it, so it hung ajar at the place where it caught the sill. The framework for the glass we had covered with a curtain.

I was tired and glad to get some rest and sleep, more particularly as I was just recovering from a very sharp attack of a weakening illness. My wife very soon went off to sleep, soundly, and I quickly followed her. The house was perfectly quiet and I was fast asleep, when – '*Scratch, scratch, scratch, scratch, rattle, rattle, bang, bang, rattle, rattle, bang, scratch!*' and up I jumped, upright in bed, my wife jumping up at the same moment. In an instant all the blood in my body seemed to curdle, my face grew pale and cold and we instantly asked each of the other in a whisper, 'What's that?'

Scratch, scratch, scratch, scratch, rattle, rattle, bang, bang, bang, rattle, scratch, scratch, scratch, at the door close to my head, as if a thousand or ten thousand cats were scratching and tearing away furiously at one of the lower panels and the vibration of the door caused the loosely hanging iron ring to make a fearful din as it was brought in contact with the wood.

We listened – breathless! A pause! only for two seconds, however, and then it set off again, *Scratch, scratch, rattle, rattle, bang, bang*!

'What is it?' I enquired of my wife.

'I don't know,' she replied – she was all of a tremor; but 'This won't do!' thought I, and out I sprang from bed, the noises meanwhile continuing with unabated fury, and I rushed to the lamp and turned it up. Instantly the noise ceased! I scarcely seemed to *think* what to be about – if burglars were in the house I was powerless against them – if the noises were of supernatural origin, what then? – if the result of some cleverly designed plan to frighten us, it must be exposed. These thoughts seemed to flash through my mind and, quick as thought, I slipped on my dressing-gown, seized the lamp and made for the door. It was as I had left it exactly! I pushed it open and went out into the big central reception-room, which the small lamp scarcely lit up. I looked behind the door where the sounds came from and there was nothing! Next, I went carefully to every door and window, looked into every corner, examined the armoire, everything was fastened, the house was perfectly silent – there was nothing!

I went back to my room.

'Have you seen anything?' my wife asked me.

'No,' I replied; 'everything is fastened and just as we left it. It is strange.'

I turned down the lamp again and got into bed, wondering all the time what it was and what it meant and little inclined for sleep.

No sooner was my head on the pillow than – *Scratch, scratch, scratch, bang, bang, clatter, clatter, bang*! – it began again.

I flew out of bed, hurried into my dressing-gown, turned up the lamp, again sallied forth and with the same result. Instantly the noise stopped! All was quiet; every door and window was safely bolted – all as I had left it! But thinking that, perhaps, the natives might be playing tricks on us, I examined the neighbourhood of the door whence the sounds came, very, very carefully. There was no string, no wire, either at top or bottom, or nail to which it could be attached. The wall, every inch of which I examined, was solid as bricks could make it. The floor? I examined that too. It was a beautiful floor, inlaid with different kinds of wood forming an artistic pattern. Every bit of wood was in its place – there was no trap-door, no sign of interference of any kind. Hence there was no trickery or cunningly devised means of frightening me out of my wits as well as out of bed. I was puzzled and beaten! Again I went off to bed, after turning down the lamp, and again, no sooner was my head on the pillow than, *Scratch, scratch, scratch, bang, bang, clatter, clatter, bang*! it went again.

'That's it!' I cried, as I again sprang out of bed. 'It's getting tiresome now,' I said to my wife; 'I can't make it out! But if I can only get hold of the evildoer, he shall feel *this*,' for I felt angry at the continued disturbance and seizing a huge stick with one hand and the lamp with the other, out I went again. But the noise had stopped as quickly as before and again all was quiet. Again I examined every window and door – all were safely fastened!

It then struck me that perhaps, as the noise was so terrific and peculiar, possibly my wife's maid had heard it, or could account for it. I must confess I felt hopelessly puzzled and, without being alarmed, was certainly very uncomfortable. What was the noise? Who or what made it? The iron ring made that awful banging, but what caused the clattering sound and the furious scratching? So going into the dining-room I called to the maid by name and said –

'Are you awake?'

'Yes, sir,' was her reply; and she raised herself on her mattress and threw back the cloth in which she had enveloped her head.

'Why are you awake?' I enquired; 'I too can't sleep. Have you heard the rats racing about?'

I shall not forget the look she gave me as I held the small lamp near her and its light lit up her dark face. The eyes seemed to light up of themselves and a look of disgusted weariness crept over her features.

'Rats!' she exclaimed. '*That's* not rats and I am afraid. *I* heard them!'

'Heard what?' I asked. 'If the sound did not come from frolicsome rats, what made it? There are no people in the house except ourselves and the boys are upstairs asleep.'

'They are spirits!' she exclaimed. 'I heard them and a row they have been making. I have been listening to them – but I kept my head covered for fear. I heard them rushing with a kind of noiseless step to your door; then scratching and rattling it; then I heard them rush back to the door at the foot of the stairs and rattle, rattle away at the latch; then back to your room again, backwards and forwards, backwards and forwards. They *have* been making a row. They are spirits and I wish they would rest, for I want to sleep!'

'So do I,' I replied. Her words rather staggered me, yet account for these noises on any other hypothesis I could not. But spirits! and in my own house and close to the head of my bed! Strange; but what was it? I was as wide awake as possible. Every faculty was in good working order and now the utter disbelief of years gone by was to be rudely – and I thought it very rude of them so to intrude on my rest and peace of mind – shattered.

The maid threw her cloth over her head again and retired under the table; but her room, too, was innocent of anything capable of being turned to account for causing the noise.

Again I retired to my room, but would not tell my wife what the maid said. Quite enough for me to have my own thoughts on the matter without disturbing *her* peace of mind.

'However,' I thought to myself, 'if I can put a stop to this, I will. If I can only get this door over the bad place at the bottom, whoever or whatever they may be won't be able to make it shake again and we shall be saved all the clatter.' So with a great effort I lifted the door so as to bring it over the uneven place and then with a strong pull I closed it tight at last.

'Now shake it if you can!' I thought, and turning down the lamp once more went off to bed.

Vain hope of peace! The enemy, whoever or whatever the enemy was, seemed to be simply infuriated with my attempt to baulk him, for no sooner was my head on my pillow again than the scratching was renewed with tenfold vigour as if the very door would be torn to pieces. It was simply awful and I seemed to expect to hear shrieks of anger added to the frightful scratching. I sat up in bed and looked at the door. It could not and did not move and the iron ring hung motionless; but down in that far corner, that poor panel seemed to be the point of attack of a thousand fiends.

Suddenly I cried out in the native tongue, 'Be quiet, and listen, O ye, whoever and whatever ye are,' and strange to say, no sooner did I begin to speak than perfect silence – dead silence reigned. 'Listen, O ye, whoever and whatever ye are,' I continued, 'for *I* don't know; only yourselves know. Ye are free to come to my house and visit me during the daytime, but now it is night. I am tired and want to sleep, so get ye to your houses! If ye be friends, speak! if ye be not, depart; or if ye will not depart, be quiet and enjoy yourselves in peace, for I am tired and want to sleep. So good-night!'

Alas! my little address had no effect. Quite the contrary! At it they went again and I pitied the poor door. If they scratched furiously before, now they seemed to tear away at it mercilessly. How they did peg away at it! and the noise was almost deafening. However there seemed to be nothing more to be done. I had been out and examined everything. All was safe. I had used plain words and words of persuasion and they had had no effect. So I gave up in simple despair and left the 'spirits' to their own sweet pleasure.

It was not long past midnight and quite tired and worn out I dropped off to sleep to the music of the scratching and tearing close to my head, and in the very early morning I woke to the sweet music of the scratching which still continued!

'I must find out what it is, if I can!' I thought. Just then I heard the door in the porch at the other end of the house open, so I knew someone was going out. Is the mystery about to be solved? No, for the scratching still continued with unabated fury! There was the attack on the panel still going on as hard as ever. But the open door allowed a certain amount of light to get through to our door and I thought I would avail myself of it.

'I'll catch you this time!' I thought. 'If there be springs or trap-door, wires or string I'll see what they are.'

So whilst the noise will still progressing I very quietly and noiselessly drew myself up in bed, ready for a spring. I stretched out my left hand and pushed aside the curtain over the frame for the glass in the door very quietly and cautiously, sprang out of bed, and in less than half a second my head was through the opening for one of the panes and I was gazing at the place whence the sounds came and narrowly searching for something, though *what* I did not know. But quick as I had been, it or they had been as quick! for no sooner was my head through the opening than the noise ceased! there was no wire or string to be seen, no trap door of any kind, a mouse could not have got away, all was silent!

'I cannot understand it,' I said to my wife. 'But I shall get up now and go for your early coffee.'

I partially dressed, put on my dressing-gown, threw open the windows and was going out to the kitchen to get the usual morning coffee for my wife, when, just as I got opposite the door leading to the spiral staircase, I met the boys coming down. I saw at once there was something wrong. The poor boys' faces were gloomy and of a pallid hue; there was not the usual cheery 'Good-morning, sir', and depression and even anxiety seemed to be written on their countenances.

'How have you slept, my boys?' I enquired of them – and they knew absolutely nothing of my night's experience.

'Slept, sir?' they enquired in return, in astonishment; 'we have not slept. How could we?'

'Why?' I enquired.

'Tell him, John,' said one of them; whilst another broke in, 'Although you command us to sleep up there again, we cannot. We are killed with fright!'

'What is it?' I again enquired.

Then John spoke.

'It was awful, sir, and we cannot bear it. It was this. What we heard the night before last we also heard last night, but it was far worse. There were, as it seemed to us, two men upstairs engaged in a fierce struggle.

They seemed to be in the middle of the house, under the roof, and they fought desperately. We heard a kind of whispering, quarrelling, as it were, but we heard no words. It seemed as if one was wearing boots and the other was not. Then the one wearing boots ran and the other ran after him, backwards and forwards, backwards and forwards, all in the dark; down they ran, down the stairs and we heard them rattling the latch as if they wanted to get out. Back then they would come and rush past us and as they passed the air was icy cold! Then they would fight and struggle again and we heard the whispering sound; then again they would run, the one wearing boots ran first, then the other after him. Down they would run, down the stairs again, and rattle the latch – and I was terribly frightened,' the poor boy added, almost crying, 'for once as they were going down, one of them seized my leg and dragged me half-way down. His hands were like ice,' he said, drawing his shoulders together and shivering at the remembrance, 'but he let go and I crawled back to my place again trembling. This went on for a long time. Then they fought again and at last the one without boots threw down the one with boots; he then danced about, then fell himself. Then all was quiet.'

It was strange and I was silent. What to think I knew not, nor do I to this day. The other boys confirmed John's statement and stood looking frightened and sorely puzzled. I am perfectly certain that *I* was not mistaken; the maid had heard the extraordinary sounds, the movements of 'spirits' *down*stairs, and the rattling of the latch; and now confirmation came from the boys of something terribly uncanny. In the full-flood light of day I examined every inch of wall and floor near that door, but there was neither mark on it, nor place for string, wire or trap-door near it. All was perfect.

I mentioned this extraordinary affair to a doctor living near and he and his wife arranged to sleep in the house with us the next night. We spent the evening at his house and we all went to our own about 9 p.m. Sitting outside, round the door of the porch, I found my servants, together with the son of the landlord, to whom I had sent word of the affair.

'Well, lads,' I said, as we approached them, 'have you seen or heard anything?'

The landlord's son answered, 'We have not seen anything, but whilst we have been sitting here we heard a sound, as of someone hurling a big stone against your bedroom door.'

'Was anyone in the house?'

'No, sir,' they all answered.

We went in and examined everything, but found neither stone nor mark.

The doctor and I bedded down on a couple of mattresses in the reception-room on the floor, opposite the front door. His wife slept with mine; and the boys went upstairs with the menservants and the landlord's son, feeling safe in their company. The doctor soon fell asleep, but I kept awake. At about 11 p.m. I heard a steady march over me of one – only one – marching backwards and forwards. This was kept on at a steady pace till 12. Then there was a furious bang at the front door as of a huge stone having been hurled against it. There was then a howling of dogs and then all was quiet. I heard nothing more, neither did those upstairs, but that was the last night I slept in that house. Others tried to live there afterwards, but had to leave. What was it?

Now for a bit of history by way of explanation, *if it can be explained*. The king of the country had a few years before been assassinated – strangled. He was surprised in his palace and, in full dress as he was, chased from room to room by the assassin, until at length he tried to find safety in hiding amongst the rafters, just under the roof. From his hiding-place he was dragged and slain.

The actual regicide died in the house where I lived, on a bedstead close to the door whence all the noises proceeded – he died there about three months before I took the house, within three yards of where my pillow was! Of this fact I was not then aware.

I can only ask, how is it to be explained? and add, that this story is absolutely true in every respect.

A CLERGYMAN*

* I may be permitted to add (if anyone should feel disposed to doubt the truth of this story) that I have fully explained to the editor of this magazine, whilst supplying him privately with facts, the reasons which have led me to withhold my name. I can only repeat that it is absolutely true and that if suitable means could be found I shall be happy to give anyone, privately, the details of where and when the affair occurred which I have described.

Correspondence on 'A Ghostly Manifestation'

To the Editor of Murray's Magazine

Sir – In *Murray's Magazine* for July appeared a remarkable narrative, entitled 'A Ghostly Manifestation'. It was signed 'A Clergyman': and contained a promise that names and further information would be given to a serious enquirer. The clergyman, whom I will call Mr X, has kindly replied to my questions on the matter and has sent me the corroborative statement of his wife, the only other white witness of the phenomena. There is little doubt, I think, that the events occurred substantially as narrated and the question, therefore, is as to their explanation.

In scrutinising such records one has first to consider – not what natural explanation will fit the phenomena as *recorded*, for this would usually be to seek in vain – but what natural explanation will fit the record with *least allowance* for exaggeration and for defects of observation and memory. In this case a hoax on the part of the boys seemed to me, though a strained, yet a possible explanation. But Mr X explains to me that the boys as well as the servant formed part of his own party; were strangers in the capital and dependent on himself for protection. 'No other native,' he adds, 'had access to the house after we were once in.' Nor were any rats seen in the house.

There are many well-attested cases, some of which have been set forth by Mrs Sidgwick in Part VIII of the *Proceedings of the Society for Psychical Research* (Trübner & Co.), where various persons, simultaneously or successively, have experienced hallucinatory sights or sounds in the same house to an extent which places the coincidence of their hallucinations beyond the range of chance. In some (but not in all) of these cases there are, as in the present instances, circumstances in the history of the house which, while previously unknown to the observers, do nevertheless *fit in* to some extent with the phenomena observed. For reasons too long to give here, I personally think it not impossible that some vague series of reminiscences on the part of a deceased person, some dream of a dead man's, may occasionally affect survivors in the form of a hallucination.

Assuming, for discussion's sake, that this was here the case, I may add that I do not suppose that the door actually moved. Mr X, naturally enough, assumes that it did shake; although he tells me that he did not *see* it shake. But even had he *seen* it shake, I should have doubted whether it actually did so. The subjoined case, if you care to print it, will illustrate my meaning.

39 Strand, Calcutta, May 1884

The experience I and my wife have had in Calcutta is curious, inasmuch as the manifestation was prolonged and I have been able to form no theory about it of any sort. We occupied the upper flat of a large house for several years. Three or four months before we left for England, we were one night roused from sleep by the violent rattling of a door-handle as if a man were trying to force an entry. The noise ceased as I went to the door, which I opened, but there was nobody in the next room. I must here premise, as important, that this door had a defective latch; the catch did not act. It had a brass door-handle and it was my custom every night to put a piece of plank under this handle, one end of the plank resting on the floor, so that by kicking the plank at the bottom the handle was tightly jammed and the door, therefore, securely fastened. This disturbance constantly occurred. We were awakened again and again by the noise. I tried everything I could think of to find out the cause. I kept a light burning in the next room and when the noise occurred, ran into the verandah and looked through the venetians. There was the light burning all right, but nothing else. This went on for several months. At length, as usual, we were wakened by the noise and as I got up I saw it was nearly daylight and I said to my wife, 'Now I may find out something.' I advanced to the door, the handle rattling violently, and I *saw* it shaking, as I thought; but when I put my hand on the knob I found it immovable – it was so tightly wedged by the plank I spoke of, that I could not move it in the least, though stronger than the average. I kicked away the plank and, as usual, found nothing on the other side of the door. Shortly after this we left for England. I may add that we are now living in the same flat, that we found the door-handle had been taken off this particular door only, which is now fastened by a padlock and that I tried to find out from the landlord something about this door, but without success. We have been in the flat since April 4th, but so far have not been disturbed. I am, of course, convinced that when I *saw* the handle shaken it was an optical delusion; it could not have been shaken, it was so securely wedged.

PAUL BIRD

Calcutta, 25th July 1884

I am happy to add what I can in corroboration of my husband's statements. The visitation to the door-handle in our bedroom, here in Calcutta, can never be forgotten, because it was such a very strange affair and so utterly inexplicable. The door-handle was wedged so very firmly by the plank, as described by my husband, yet the noise, produced so mysteriously, was so very loud and sustained. It was a quicker and more vibratory noise than I could ever produce myself by taking hold of the handle, when liberated, and rattling it and I have never succeeded in producing an exactly similar sound, though I have sometimes tried to illustrate it when telling the story to friends.

GERTRUDE BIRD

Mr X. mentions to me another point of interest. There were two small dogs in the room; and these dogs slept undisturbed through all the noises which woke and kept awake their master and mistress. This fact, while certainly tending to show that the noises were *hallucinatory* and not real waves of sound – and so far supporting the theory of their ghostly origin – may surprise those who believe that if anything 'ghostly' is to be seen or heard, a dog will certainly see or hear it. Generally dogs seem to do so; but Mr X's case confirms a supposition which we had already made, viz. that when the animals are present and do *not* observe the phantasmal sights or sounds, their owners are likely to forget to mention them.

The narrative as it stands – or say, rather, the existence in our collection of dozens of *bona fide* narratives of similar type – points a moral which I must conclude by urging on every reader. The hallucinations of sane persons form a subject of enquiry full of the most interesting problems, which much wider information – but nothing short of this – may enable us to solve to the profit of science. In order to get this information, a 'census of hallucinations' is being conducted in England and in France. The object is to get from 50,000 persons an answer – and particulars, if the answer is 'yes' – to the following question: 'Have you ever, when believing yourself to be completely awake, had a vivid impression of seeing or being touched by a living being or inanimate object or of hearing a voice; which impression, so far as you could discover, was not due to any external physical cause?'

Professor Sidgwick (Hillside, Cambridge) will supply census-forms and instructions on application. From whatever point of view we regard these matters, there can be no doubt that *more facts* are the first thing needed; and this census seems a likely way to procure them.

I am, sir, faithfully yours,

FREDERIC W. H. MYERS
Honorary Secretary, Society for Psychical Research,
Leckhampton House, Cambridge

Ghost in the Tower

Edmund Lenthal Swifte

Edmund Swifte wrote this account of the Tower of London ghost in *Notes and Queries*, 8 September 1860, in answer to a reader's question. Included also are some of the letters arising out of his recollection.

THE QUESTION

Is there not a ghost story connected with the Tower of London? and what is it? Has not the ghost or appearance, been seen once at least during this century and with fatal results?

K. B.

THE REPLY

I have often purposed to leave behind me a faithful record of all that I personally know of this strange story; and K.B.'s enquiry now puts me upon consigning it to the general repertory of *Notes and Queries*. Forty-three years have passed and its impression is as vividly before me as on the moment of its occurrence. Anecdotage, said Wilkes, is an old man's dotage, and at eighty-three I may be suspected of lapsing into omissions or exaggerations: but there are yet survivors who can testify that I have not at any time either amplified or abridged my ghostly experiences.

In 1814 I was appointed Keeper of the Crown Jewels in the Tower, where I resided with my family till my retirement in 1852. One Saturday night in October 1817, about 'the witching hour', I was at supper with my then wife, our little boy and her sister, in the sitting-room of the Jewel House, which – then comparatively modernised – is said to have been the 'doleful prison' of Anna Boleyn and of the ten bishops whom Oliver Cromwell piously accommodated therein. For an accurate picture of the *locus in quo* my scene is laid, I refer to George Cruikshank's woodcut on page 384 of Ainsworth's *Tower of London*; and I am persuaded that my gallant successor in office, Colonel Wyndham, will not refuse its collation with my statement.

The room was – as it still is – irregularly shaped, having three doors and two windows, which last are cut nearly nine feet deep into the outer wall; between these is a chimney-piece projecting far into the room and (then) surmounted with a large oil picture. On the night in question, the doors were all closed, heavy and dark cloth curtains were let down over the windows and the only light in the room was that of two candles on the table. I sat at the foot of the table, my son on my right hand, his mother fronting the chimney-piece and her sister on the opposite side. I had offered a glass of wine and water to my wife, when, on putting it to her lips, she paused and exclaimed, 'Good God! what is that?' I looked up and saw a cylindrical figure, like a glass tube, seemingly about the thickness of my arm and hovering between the ceiling and the table: its contents appeared to be a dense fluid, white and pale azure, like to the gathering of a summer cloud and incessantly rolling and mingling within the cylinder. This lasted about two minutes, when it began slowly to move *before* my sister in law; then, following the oblong shape of the table, *before* my son and myself; passing *behind* my wife, it paused for a moment over her right shoulder (observe, there was no mirror opposite to her in which she could then behold it). Instantly she crouched down and with both hands covering her shoulder, she shrieked out, 'Oh, Christ! it has seized me!' Even now, while writing, I feel the fresh horror of that moment. I caught up my chair, struck at the wainscot behind her, rushed upstairs to the other children's room and told the terrified nurse what I had seen. Meanwhile, the other domestics had hurried into the parlour, where their mistress recounted to them the scene, even as I was detailing it above stairs.

The marvel – some will say the absurdity – of all this is enhanced by the fact that *neither my sister-in-law nor my son beheld this 'appearance'* – as K. B. rightly terms it – though to their mortal vision it was as 'apparent' as to my wife's and mine. When I the next morning related the night's horrors to our chaplain, after the service in the Tower church, he asked me might not *one* person have his natural senses deceived? And if *one*, why might not *two*? My answer was, if *two*, why not two thousand? an argument which would reduce history, secular or sacred, to a fable. But why should I here discuss things not dreamed of in our philosophy?

I am bound to add, that, shortly before this strange event, some young lady residents in the Tower had been, I know not wherefore, suspected of making phantasmagorial experiments at their windows, which, be it observed, had *no* command whatever on any windows in my dwelling. An additional sentry was accordingly posted, so as to overlook any such attempt.

Happen, however, as it might, following hard at heel the visitation of my household, one of the night sentries at the Jewel Office was, as he said, alarmed by a figure like a huge bear issuing from underneath the door; he thrust at it with his bayonet, which stuck in the door, even as my chair dinted the wainscot; he dropped in a fit and was carried senseless to the guard-room. His fellow-sentry declared that the man was neither asleep nor drunk, he himself having seen him the moment before awake and sober. Of all this, I avouch nothing more than that I saw the poor man in the guard-house prostrated with terror and that in two or three days the 'fatal result', be it of fact or of fancy, was – *that he died.*

My story may claim more space than *N. & Q.* can afford: desiring to be circumstantial, I have been diffuse. This I leave to the editor's discretion: let it only be understood, that to *all* which I have herein set forth *as seen by myself,* I absolutely pledge my faith and my honour.

EDMUND LENTHAL SWIFTE

REPLY

This unfortunate affair took place in January 1816 and shows the extreme folly of attempting to frighten with the shade of a supernatural appearance the bravest of men. Before the burning of the armouries there was a paved yard in front of the Jewel House, from which a gloomy and ghost-like doorway led down a flight of steps to the Mint. Some strange noises were heard in this gloomy corner; and on a dark night at twelve the sentry saw a figure like a bear cross the pavement and disappear down the steps. This so terrified him that he fell and in a few hours, after having recovered sufficiently to tell the tale, he died. It was fully believed to have arisen from phantasmagoria and the governor, with the colonel of the regiment, doubled the sentry and used such energetic precautions that no more ghosts haunted the Tower from that time. The soldier bore a high character for bravery and good conduct. I was then in my thirtieth year and was present when his body was buried with military honours in the Flemish burial ground, St Catherine's.   GEORGE OFFOR

REPLY

Is Colonel Swifte aware of the publication made by Dr Wm Gregory in his *Letters . . . on Animal Magnestism,* London, 1851, page 494, &c.? There are circumstances mentioned in this account, certainly not obtained *directly* from Colonel S. (as he is called), on which I think it very desirable, after his full account, that his comment should be made. Such are – the court-martial held on the soldier – his acquittal by means of Colonel Swifte's evidence that he was not asleep, but had been singing a minute or two before the occurrence – the declaration of the sergeant that such appearances were not uncommon, &c. I should suppose that all this is the additional snow which the ball has got by rolling.   A. De Morgan

REPLY

Until now I have been very sceptical in matters of this kind, but I must confess this strange account by Mr Swifte has impressed me with considerable interest. It was too circumstantial to attribute the appearance to optical delusion, and the depth of the window recesses and the closed dark cloth curtains forbid the possibility of the action of a magic lantern or phantasmagoria. Will Mr Swifte oblige me and through me several interested friends, with further information.

1 Was Mr Swifte's son old enough to understand the vision or to be impressed by the circumstance?

2 What was the impression of the sister-in-law respecting the affair, as evidenced by the horror and expressions of Mr and Mrs Swifte?

3 How did the phantom disappear and did it assume any other form?

It must truly have made a profound impression upon the family and haunted the imagination continually. Very few would have had the courage to continue the residence. The warders tell of a spectre said to flit about Sir Walter Raleigh's apartments.

George Lloyd

REPLY

When the catholic page of *N. & Q.* was opened to my story, I became bound to satisfy its correspondents upon every personal and local circumstance. I, therefore, readily answer Mr Lloyd's reasonable and seasonable questions:

1 My son had nearly closed his seventh year; and was endowed with more than the ordinary intelligence of childhood. Assuredly, he was not terrified with what he did not see; but he was exceedingly scared at his mother's outcry and my agitation.

2 His aunt, to whom likewise the phantom had been invisible and who knew nothing of its presence till she heard it described by her sister, treated it as our joint hallucination; contenting herself with the chaplain's logic – that the illusion which possessed one person's mind could as readily possess another's.

3 It did not assume any other form; but, in the moment of my wife's exclamation and my striking at it with my chair, it crossed the upper end of the table and disappeared in the recess of the opposite window.

4 That unforgettable night was continually discussed among us (my boy alone excepted, to protect his young mind from its impression), until he and they had quitted this world of realities wherein it is still my surviving mystery.

The preternatural transcends my philosophy; and the doctrine of chances does not, I suppose, deal with impossibilities. *Nequeo monstrare, sentio tantum;* I forbear, therefore, comment or inference, hardly expecting that my most absolute pledge of veracity shall ensure what I might claim in sublunary matters.

Sir Walter Raleigh and the other eidola of the Tower may be left to its officials' traditional snowball.

Professor De Morgan has made me, for the first time, aware of Dr Gregory's publication. His account of this strange incident was not obtained 'directly' from me, seeing that I never had the pleasure of his acquaintance; and his indirect details, as alluded to by Professor De Morgan, present a curious assemblage of errors. I have already stated that I heard the ill-fated soldier described in the Tower guard-room by his follow-sentinel, not as 'singing a minute or two before the occurrence', but as, *immediately* before it, awake and alert at his post, exchanging with him some casual remark. Of the sergeant's comment, that 'such appearances were not uncommon', I am as unaware as of the summary '&c.' wherein Professor De Morgan includes Dr Gregory's other reminiscences; or of the 'court-martial', whereat I did *not* attend, and of course bore no testimony to his wakefulness. Let Professor De Morgan be assured that the forty-three winters which have since that date blanched my head have not added one single flake to his traditional snowball: the gatherings of which, whatever may be their increment under Dr Gregory's manipulation, are to me an unknown quantity.

Of the military title attributed to me, I have hitherto been equally unconscious; my only martial experience having been during 1796–1803, when I bore arms in Ireland as a member of the Lawyers'

Corps – a service which I would right gladly resume in 1861, with whatever spirit and strength might then be abiding in me.

EDMUND LENTHAL SWIFTE

REPLY

Enclosed is the story of an apparition in York Castle, alluded to by Mr Swifte. The appearance, it will be seen, was not dissimilar to that which caused the death of the soldier in the Tower. The preceding story about a witch is not worth quoting.

One of my soldiers being on guard about eleven in the night at the gate of Clifford Tower, the very night after the witch was arraigned, he heard a great noise at the castle; and going to the porch, he there saw a scroll of paper creep from under the door, which, as he imagined by moonshine, turned first into the shape of a monkey and thence assumed the form of a turkey cock, which passed to and fro by him. Surprised at this, he went to the prison and called the under-keeper, who came and saw the scroll dance up and down and creep under the door, where there was scarce an opening of the thickness of half-a-crown. This extraordinary story I had from the mouth of both one and the other.

Memoirs of Sir John Reresby, page 238

H.

WORDSWORTH CLASSICS

REQUESTS FOR INSPECTION COPIES Lecturers wishing to obtain copies of Wordsworth Classics, Wordsworth Poetry Library or Wordsworth Classics of World Literature titles on inspection are invited to contact: Dennis Hart, Wordsworth Editions Ltd, Crib Street, Ware, Herts SG12 9ET; E-mail: dennis.hart@wordsworth-editions.com. Please quote the author, title and ISBN of the titles in which you are interested; together with your name, academic address, E-mail address, the course on which the books will be used and the expected enrolment.

Teachers wishing to inspect specific core titles for GCSE or A level courses are also invited to contact Wordsworth Editions at the above address.

Inspection copies are sent solely at the discretion of Wordsworth Editions Ltd.

JANE AUSTEN
Emma
Mansfield Park
Northanger Abbey
Persuasion
Pride and Prejudice
Sense and Sensibility

ARNOLD BENNETT
Anna of the Five Towns
The Old Wives' Tale

R. D. BLACKMORE
Lorna Doone

M. E. BRADDON
Lady Audley's Secret

ANNE BRONTË
Agnes Grey
The Tenant of Wildfell Hall

CHARLOTTE BRONTË
Jane Eyre
The Professor
Shirley
Villette

EMILY BRONTË
Wuthering Heights

JOHN BUCHAN
Greenmantle
The Island of Sheep
John Macnab
Mr Standfast
The Thirty-Nine Steps
The Three Hostages

SAMUEL BUTLER
Erewhon
The Way of All Flesh

LEWIS CARROLL
Alice in Wonderland

M. CERVANTES
Don Quixote

ANTON CHEKHOV
Selected Stories

G. K. CHESTERTON
The Club of Queer Trades
Father Brown: Selected Stories
The Man Who Was Thursday
The Napoleon of Notting Hill

ERSKINE CHILDERS
The Riddle of the Sands

JOHN CLELAND
Fanny Hill – Memoirs of a Woman of Pleasure

WILKIE COLLINS
The Moonstone
The Woman in White

JOSEPH CONRAD
Almayer's Folly
Heart of Darkness
Lord Jim
Nostromo
Sea Stories
The Secret Agent
Selected Short Stories
Victory

J. FENIMORE COOPER
The Last of the Mohicans

STEPHEN CRANE
The Red Badge of Courage

THOMAS DE QUINCEY
Confessions of an English Opium Eater

DANIEL DEFOE
Moll Flanders
Robinson Crusoe

CHARLES DICKENS
Barnaby Rudge
Bleak House
Christmas Books
David Copperfield
Dombey and Son
Ghost Stories
Great Expectations
Hard Times
Little Dorrit
Martin Chuzzlewit
The Mystery of Edwin Drood
Nicholas Nickleby
The Old Curiosity Shop
Oliver Twist
Our Mutual Friend
Pickwick Papers
Sketches by Boz
A Tale of Two Cities

BENJAMIN DISRAELI
Sybil

FYODOR DOSTOEVSKY
Crime and Punishment
The Idiot

ARTHUR CONAN DOYLE
The Adventures of Sherlock Holmes
The Case-Book of Sherlock Holmes
The Return of Sherlock Holmes
The Best of Sherlock Holmes
The Hound of the Baskervilles
The Lost World & Other Stories
Sir Nigel
A Study in Scarlet & The Sign of Four
The Valley of Fear
The White Company

GEORGE DU MAURIER
Trilby

ALEXANDRE DUMAS
The Count of
Monte Cristo
The Three Musketeers

MARIA EDGEWORTH
Castle Rackrent

GEORGE ELIOT
Adam Bede
Daniel Deronda
Felix Holt the Radical
Middlemarch
The Mill on the Floss
Silas Marner

HENRY FIELDING
Tom Jones

RONALD FIRBANK
Valmouth &
Other Stories

F. SCOTT FITZGERALD
The Diamond as Big as
the Ritz & Other Stories
The Great Gatsby
Tender is the Night

GUSTAVE FLAUBERT
Madame Bovary

JOHN GALSWORTHY
In Chancery
The Man of Property
To Let

ELIZABETH GASKELL
Cranford
North and South
Wives and Daughters

GEORGE GISSING
New Grub Street

OLIVER GOLDSMITH
The Vicar of Wakefield

KENNETH GRAHAME
The Wind in the Willows

G. & W. GROSSMITH
Diary of a Nobody

H. RIDER HAGGARD
She

THOMAS HARDY
Far from the Madding
Crowd
Jude the Obscure
The Mayor of
Casterbridge

A Pair of Blue Eyes
The Return of the Native
Selected Short Stories
Tess of the D'Urbervilles
The Trumpet Major
Under the Greenwood
Tree
The Well-Beloved
Wessex Tales
The Woodlanders

NATHANIEL
HAWTHORNE
The Scarlet Letter

O. HENRY
Selected Stories

JAMES HOGG
The Private Memoirs and
Confessions of a Justified
Sinner

HOMER
The Iliad
The Odyssey

E. W. HORNUNG
Raffles: The Amateur
Cracksman

VICTOR HUGO
The Hunchback of
Notre Dame
Les Misérables
IN TWO VOLUMES

HENRY JAMES
The Ambassadors
Daisy Miller &
Other Stories
The Europeans
The Golden Bowl
The Portrait of a Lady
The Turn of the Screw &
The Aspern Papers
What Maisie Knew

M. R. JAMES
Ghost Stories
Ghosts and Marvels

JEROME K. JEROME
Three Men in a Boat

JAMES JOYCE
Dubliners
A Portrait of the Artist
as a Young Man

OMAR KHAYYAM
The Rubaiyat
TRANSLATED BY E. FITZGERALD

RUDYARD KIPLING
The Best Short Stories
Captains Courageous
Kim
The Man Who
Would Be King
& Other Stories
Plain Tales from
the Hills

D. H. LAWRENCE
The Plumed Serpent
The Rainbow
Sons and Lovers
Women in Love

SHERIDAN LE FANU
In a Glass Darkly
Madam Crowl's Ghost &
Other Stories

GASTON LEROUX
The Phantom of the Opera

JACK LONDON
Call of the Wild &
White Fang

KATHERINE MANSFIELD
Bliss & Other Stories

GUY DE MAUPASSANT
The Best Short Stories

HERMAN MELVILLE
Billy Budd & Other
Stories
Moby Dick
Typee

GEORGE MEREDITH
The Egoist

H. H. MUNRO
The Collected Stories
of Saki

SHIKH NEFZAOUI
The Perfumed Garden
TRANSLATED BY
SIR RICHARD BURTON

THOMAS LOVE
PEACOCK
Headlong Hall &
Nightmare Abbey

EDGAR ALLAN POE
Tales of Mystery and
Imagination

FREDERICK ROLFE
Hadrian VII

SIR WALTER SCOTT
Ivanhoe
Rob Roy

DISTRIBUTION

AUSTRALIA & PAPUA NEW GUINEA
Peribo Pty Ltd
58 Beaumont Road, Mount Kuring-Gai
NSW 2080, Australia
Tel: (02) 457 0011 Fax: (02) 457 0022

CZECH REPUBLIC
Bohemian Ventures s r. o.,
Delnicka 13, 170 00 Prague 7
Tel: 042 2 877837 Fax: 042 2 801498

FRANCE
Copernicus Diffusion
81 Rue des Entrepreneurs, Paris 75015
Tel: 01 53 95 38 00 Fax: 01 53 95 38 01

GERMANY & AUSTRIA
Taschenbuch-Vertrieb
Ingeborg Blank GmbH
Lager und Buro Rohrmooser Str 1
85256 Vierkirchen/Pasenbach
Tel: 08139-8130/8184 Fax: 08139-8140

Tradis Verlag und Vertrieb GmbH (Bookshops)
Postfach 90 03 69, D-51113 Köln
Tel: 022 03 31059 Fax: 022 03 39340

GHANA, THE GAMBIA, LIBERIA,
CAMEROON & SIERRA LEONE
Readwide Bookshop Ltd
1st Floor, Kingsway Business
Kingsway Building, Adabraka
P O Box 0600, Osu – Accra, Ghana
Tel: 00233 21663347 Fax: 00233 21663725

GREAT BRITAIN
Wordsworth Editions Ltd
Cumberland House, Crib Street
Ware, Hertfordshire SG12 9ET
Tel: 01920 465167 Fax: 01920 462267

INDIA
Om Books International
4379/4B, Prakash House, Ansari Road
Darya Ganj, New Delhi – 110002
Tel: 3263363/3265303 Fax: 3278091
E-mail: sales@ombooks.com

ISRAEL
Sole Agent – **Timmy Marketing Limited**
55 Rehov HaDekel, Lapid, Hevel Modi'in
Tel: 972-8-9765874 Fax: 972-8-9766552
e-mail: timmy@bezeqint.net

ITALY
Tarab Edizioni S R L
Via S. Zanobi No 37
50129 Firenze, Italy
Tel: 0039 055 490209
Fax: 0039 055 473515
NEW ZEALAND & FIJI
Allphy Book Distributors Ltd
4-6 Charles Street, Eden Terrace, Auckland,
Tel: (09) 3773096 Fax: (09) 3022770

MALAYSIA & BRUNEI
Vintrade SDN BHD
5 & 7 Lorong
Datuk Sulaiman 7
Taman Tun Dr Ismail
60000 Kuala Lumpur,
Malaysia
Tel: (603) 717 3333 Fax: (603) 719 2942

MALTA & GOZO
Agius & Agius Ltd
42A South Street, Valletta VLT 11
Tel: 234038 - 220347 Fax: 241175

PHILIPPINES
I J Sagun Enterprises
P O Box 4322 CPO Manila, 2 Topaz Road,
Greenheights Village, Taytay, Rizal
Tel: 631 80 61 TO 66

POLAND
Top Mark Centre
Urbanistow 1 M 51
02397 Warszawa, Poland
Tel: 004822 319439 Fax: 004822 6582676

SOUTH AFRICA
Chapter Book Agencies
Postnet Private bag X10016
Edenvale, 1610 Gauteng, South Africa
Tel: (++27) 11 425 5990
Fax: (++27) 11 425 5997

SLOVAK REPUBLIC
Slovak Ventures s r. o.,
Stefanikova 128, 949 01 Nitra
Tel/Fax: 042 87 525105/6/7

SPAIN
Ribera Libros, S.L.
Poligono Martiartu, Calle 1 - no 6
48480 Arrigorriaga, Vizcaya
Tel: 34 4 6713607 (Almacen)
34 4 4418787 (Libreria)
Fax: 34 4 6713608 (Almacen)
34 4 4418029 (Libreria)

UNITED STATES OF AMERICA
(Education only)
NTC/Contemporary
Publishing Company
4225 West Touhy Avenue
Lincolnwood (Chicago)
Illinois 60646-4622
USA
Tel: (847) 679 5500 Fax: (847) 679 2494

DIRECT MAIL
Bibliophile Books
5 Thomas Road, London E14 7BN,
Tel: 0171-515 9222 Fax: 0171-538 4115
Order hotline 24 hours Tel: 0171-515 9555
Cash with order + £2.50 p&p (UK)